WHEN THE SWALLOWS COME AGAIN

By Victor Pemberton and available from Headline

Our Family
Our Street
Our Rose
The Silent War
Nellie's War
My Sister Sarah
Goodnight Amy
Leo's Girl
A Perfect Stranger
Flying With The Angels
The Chandler's Daughter
We'll Sing At Dawn
The Other Side Of The Track
A Long Way Home
When The Swallows Come Again

WHEN THE SWALLOWS COME AGAIN

Victor Pemberton

headline

First published in 2008 by
HEADLINE PUBLISHING GROUP

1

Cataloguing in Publication Data is available from the British Library

ISBN 978 0 7553 3457 5

Typeset in Bembo by Palimpsest Book Production Limited,
Grangemouth, Stirlingshire

Printed and bound in the UK by CPI Mackays, Chatham ME5 8TD

Headline's policy is to use papers that are natural, renewable and recyclable products and
made from wood grown in sustainable forests. The logging and manufacturing processes are
expected to conform to the environmental regulations of the country of origin.

HEADLINE PUBLISHING GROUP
An Hachette Livre UK Company
338 Euston Road
London NW1 3BH

www.headline.co.uk
www.hachettelivre.co.uk

For David,
for everything.

'True Hope is swift,
And flyes with swallowes wing . . .'

William Shakespeare, *Richard III*

Prologue

Soon it would be dawn. Soon, the rooftops of dear old London town would be bathed in the majestic gold of a June sunrise, the flat, grey roof tiles brought to life by the start of another day. Despite the rumble of the occasional night bus in the East End of London's Bow Road, the air was still and quiet. Even the local moggies had given up hissing and growling at each other, retreating into the cool of their favourite backstreet alleys, where there was still the hope of rescuing some discarded morsels of fish and chips in greasy old newspapers, all of which carried dramatic headlines about the D-Day landings by Allied forces in northern France just a week or so before.

There was no doubt in anyone's mind that the war was nearly over. Those who had survived the worst of the London Blitz were at last able to breathe the fresh air of freedom, freedom from nightly visits down the air-raid shelters, freedom from the constant threat of danger and menace in the skies above. The people of London were beginning to dry the tears in their eyes, to leave behind the ugly memories of war in their own backyards. However, those moments of high optimism came to an abrupt end at precisely 4.50 that morning, when a strange, unidentified sound gradually spluttered across the sky from the East, like the exhaust of an ancient motorcycle. The only person who noticed it was old Ron Keller, a local milkman who was just turning into Grove Road from one of the backstreets in the distance. But as the alien sound grew closer and closer, more early risers peered out of their windows and looked up towards the sky. What they saw was a sinister-shaped black-painted plane with clipped wings and a huge gush of flame bursting from its tail. As the shocked onlookers stared, just as the menacing machine was almost overhead, the earsplitting sound cut out, and with a rush of air the dark black shape nose-dived towards the ground. The explosion that followed was immense, and immediately sent a plume of black smoke spiralling up into the gradually brightening sky, whilst from every house and street, the shattering of windows and crumbling of masonry brought shrieks of alarm from the entire district. When the smoke finally cleared, all that was left of the railway bridge high across Bow Road was a huge gap, a mass of dangling railway lines, and a scattering of rubble which had in turn blasted all the nearby terraced houses.

Once the air had calmed down again, the local residents emerged from their hiding places beneath kitchen tables and beds, something which they had hoped never to have to do again. When the frenzied sound of the horns and bells of the emergency services approached from every direction, the East End knew only too well that, for them, the war was about to start all over again.

Chapter 1

Mary Trimble and her neighbours rushed out from their houses in a panic. Although Roden Street in North London was a couple of bus rides away from the East End, the sound of the massive explosion in Grove Road had been heard for miles around, creating utter pandemonium up and down the entire length of the long back-street. It had been quite a time since anyone had been startled by the sound of a bomb.

'Wot the bleedin' 'ell's goin' on now?' screeched old Nora, Mary's upstairs tenant, as she leaned out of her window on the top floor, hairnet pulled down tightly over her curlers. 'I didn't 'ear no siren!'

'Nor did I!' yelled another irate female neighbour further down the street. 'What do they think they're playin' at?'

'What's going on?' yawned Mary's young sister, Doris, as she came out from the house rubbing her eyes wearily. 'What was that bang?'

'We don't know, Dodo,' replied Mary, putting a comforting arm around the child's shoulders, her large blue eyes reflecting the early morning light as she and everyone else scanned the sky anxiously. 'But I'm sure there's nothing to worry about.'

'Don't you believe it!' moaned Fred Parfitt, from next door, as usual butting in where he wasn't wanted. 'I told yer a few weeks back, we ain't seen the last of 'Itler yet. Got a few tricks left up 'is sleeve, I tell yer!'

Mary could have hit him. Fred always knew *everything*, or at least he thought he did, which was why she called him Mr Know-It-All. In fact, she had nicknames for all her neighbours, including her upstairs tenant, Nora Kelly, when she was out of sight, Mary always referred her to as 'Nutty Nora'.

'Well if they fink *I'm* goin' ter start sleepin' down that Anderson again,' growled Nutty Nora, 'they've got annuver fink comin'! As far as *I'm* concerned, this war's over!' Without another word, she went back inside and slammed down the window.

By now the residents had moved into their usual separate groups; the women, arms crossed, sticking together to castigate whoever was responsible for not sounding that air-raid siren at nearby Hornsey Road police station, and the men, some of them still in their long johns and lighting up dog-ends, exchanging their own expert ideas about what Hitler was to getting up to now. This get-together had not taken place for quite some time, not since the days during the big Blitz a few years before, when, night and day, German bombs were quite literally raining down from the sky every few minutes.

'It's true,' said a quiet woman just beside Mary. 'I did think that now our boys've landed in France, it'd be all over bar the shouting.'

Mary, still holding on to her sister Dodo, tried to comfort the woman. She had always had a great respect for Letty Hobbs, who lived with her husband and family down the road at number thirteen. The poor woman had gone through a great deal during her lifetime, struggling to give support to her husband who had lost a leg in the First World War. 'I really don't think it's anything too much to worry about, Mrs Hobbs,' Mary replied. 'Probably just a one-off somewhere.'

'A one-off can kill a lot of people, dear,' replied Letty, shaking her head sombrely.

The air was suddenly echoing to the familiar distant clanging of ambulance, police car, and fire-engine bells. The emergency services were back in action again.

It was some time before the neighbours returned to their homes. The lively street chatter was soon replaced by an eerie silence. By now, the sun was beginning to rise over the rooftops, and a long shaft of early morning light transformed one side of the long Victorian terrace of lower middle-class houses into a dazzling array of pure gold. It was the dawn of another day, a day when many questions were going to be asked, a day of uncertainty.

Granddad Trimble was in no mood to be pacified. It was bad enough that he'd been woken up by all that fuss in the street outside early in the morning, but to be kept waiting for his porridge showed a great lack of care and consideration for a man of his advancing years. It was so unlike his granddaughter Mary. She was always so good about making sure that his porridge was on the table the moment he came down to breakfast. The only thing that stopped him from complaining was that he knew what a handful she had to cope with, looking after not only him but also two young sisters and a brother. After all, Mary was only twenty years old, and, because of the tragic death of her parents in the Bethnal Green tube disaster the year before, she had had to take on all the responsibility of looking after the family, and that included Granddad, who was a difficult enough old cuss at the best of times. 'I'ope yer've put enough sugar in terday,' said the old boy, the moment Mary put the bowl of steaming hot porridge down in front of him. 'It tasted bleedin' awful yesterday.'

'It's not my fault, Granddad,' replied Mary, wiping the sweat from her forehead with the back of her hand. 'You've had your sugar ration for the week. You'll have to make do with saccharin tablets till I get your next lot of coupons.'

Granddad grunted and pulled a face as he took his first spoonful of porridge.

Before Mary had a chance to get back into the scullery, her young brother Billy burst into the tiny back parlour where the family ate their meals. Plonking himself down at the table opposite Granddad, he barked, 'Give us the jam!' without mentioning the magic word, '*please*'.

'Have you washed yet?' asked Mary, passing the half-filled jar of strawberry jam.

'Don't need ter wash twice a day,' the boy replied, his dark, unruly hair uncombed and flopping all over the top of his head. 'I washed last night.'

'Dirty little sod!' mumbled Granddad, porridge all over his chin. 'Yer wouldn't get away wiv that if yer dad was alive.'

Billy pulled a rude face at the old man, making quite sure he hadn't been seen doing so.

'Just make sure you wash before you go to school,' said Mary strictly, cutting the boy a thick slice of bread. 'I don't want any more notes from your schoolteacher like the one I had the other day. Miss Hatton says you always look scruffy. And she's very annoyed at the way you behave in class.'

'Stupid ol' cow!' retorted Billy, spreading a thick load of jam on to his slice of bread.

'Billy Trimble!' snapped Mary, turning on him. 'Don't you dare use that kind of language about your teacher! Everyone knows Miss Hatton's a wonderful person.'

'I don't wanna be a ballet dancer!' growled Billy oblivious of the fact that his mouth was full of bread and jam.

'Miss Hatton doesn't only teach ballet,' insisted Mary. 'She teaches the most beautiful English. I should know, because I was in her class.'

Billy, who was just coming up to ten, pulled a face and ignored his big sister.

'Mind you,' said Mary, pouring Granddad a cup of tea from the large china teapot, 'it must be an uphill task trying to teach *you* anything!'

Mary's two sisters came into the room. Thelma was almost sixteen years old, and always behaved as though she was superior to the rest of her family. Without saying a word to anyone, she eased herself down on to a chair on one side of the table and immediately started using two fingers to rearrange her carefully combed short light brown hair. Her young sister Dodo, which had been her mother's nickname for her, plonked herself down next to Billy, immediately grabbing the jar of jam from him. 'After that bomb went off,' grumbled Dodo, who was nearly eleven, 'I went straight back ter bed. But I didn't get a wink er beauty sleep.'

'That's 'cos you're so ugly!' spluttered Billy, his mouth still full of bread and jam.

Dodo gave him a sharp nudge with her shoulder. He did the same to her.

'Cut it out, you two!' snapped Mary. 'Hurry up and have your breakfast and get to school.' Ever since she had been in Miss Hatton's class at school, Mary had practised hard not to speak like a guttersnipe, which is more than she could say for her youngest sister and her brother. 'And as a matter of fact, Dodo,' she continued, 'nobody knows if it *was* a bomb. It might have been a gas explosion or something.'

'Well, I don't care *what* it was,' replied Dodo, whose unruly long dark brown hair looked as though it hadn't been combed for a week, 'it woke me up!'

'Oh do shut up, Do,' sneered Thelma, bored as usual with her younger sister. 'Everyone knows the war's over.'

'Ha!' snorted Granddad, who was lighting up his pipe. 'Some 'opes!'

Mary sighed despondently. Ever since her mum and dad had died she had done her best to keep the family together, but there were times when their constant bickering got her down. She was always relieved when she had to go to work, for, once her sisters and brother had gone to school, she had a few hours to herself. With this in mind, she left them all to have their breakfast, and went out into the scullery and collected a basket of clothes which she had washed in the old stone boiler the night before.

In the small backyard outside, the Anderson shelter was barely visible beneath the pile of earth which had covered it since the start of the war nearly five years before. It had been used by the family for protection night after weary night during the height of the 1940 London Blitz. Every time she went out into the yard, Mary always wondered what would have happened if there had been a direct hit on the house, especially if it had collapsed on top of the tiny, fragile shelter. It took her several minutes to hang out the washing, for, despite having to do all the chores and go off to her job at the British Restaurant each day, her sisters and brother were never exactly eager to help. The sun was now up, and beginning to radiate some heat, but it was muggy, with low-hanging grey clouds, a sure sign of rain, especially after the thunderstorms which had delayed the start of the Allied forces' D-Day landings in France a week or so before. When she had finished hanging out the washing, she wiped the sweat from her forehead with the back of her hand and stood with her face raised up towards the sky, hoping to embrace what little breeze there was.

Although she had a thin, wiry frame, there was strength in her arms, and she had more energy than the entire family put together. Just like her mum; same strength, same determination to get on with life, same long flaxen-coloured hair which some compared to the current wartime screen goddesses Betty Grable and Alice Faye. At the end of the backyard were the backyards of Mayton Street, which had taken the full blast of an aerial torpedo that had come down on a row of shops in nearby Seven Sisters Road. Most of the windows at the back of those houses were wide open, everyone trying to get some fresh air in the early morning humidity. Mary tried not to stare too hard, just in case she was accused of peering into her neighbours' rooms, which is what young Billy was always up to when he used his dad's old binoculars. There was no sign of the neighbours this morning, although she could hear intense activity coming from nearby Mayton Street fire station. It was at times like this when Mary missed her mum the most. They used to do so much together, the washing, the ironing, the daily chores that helped to keep the house so spick and span. Above all, she missed the little chats she and her mum had had, the way she could share all her intimate problems, unlike some of the daughters she knew who kept their secrets to themselves. Yes, she had loved her mum so much. They had had so much in common. She had loved her dad, too. He had been such a quiet, unassuming man, who wanted nothing more in life than to be with his family, and to go to his job at the Gas, Light and Coke Company each day. But Don Trimble was a man's man, and his real favourite had been the only boy in the family. Billy Trimble was the spitting image of his dad, same dark hair and blue-grey eyes – oh yes, the spitting

8

image. But Billy had a perpetual cheeky, mischievous grin. He was a little ruffian, which was *not* like his dad.

'Ain't you goin' ter be late fer work?'

Mary turned with a start to find her granddad standing right behind her, the smell of his strong pipe tobacco drifting towards her face. 'I'm not due in until half past today,' she replied. 'They're trying to repair one of the gas stoves in the kitchen. Have the kids finished their breakfast yet?'

'They've all gone ter school, fank Gord!' grunted the old man, sourly. 'Needless ter say, they've left all the washin'. up. That's the trouble, yer spoil 'em too much. They should buckle down an' give yer a bit er 'elp.'

'They're only kids, Granddad,' replied Mary, perching herself on one of the sandbags piled up in front of the Anderson shelter. 'They've got no mum or dad to tell them what's right or wrong. The least I can do is to look after them.'

Granddad took a deep, agitated puff of his pipe. 'That's bunkum, an' you know it!' he said, spitting out a bit of tobacco which had stuck to his tongue. 'That Thelma's nearly sixteen. She's old enuff ter stand on 'er own two feet an' give you a break once in a while.'

'Thelma's a good girl, Granddad,' replied Mary. 'I know she's a bit difficult at times, but I was just as awkward at her age.'

'Ha!' snorted Granddad. 'Yer only twenty years old yerself. You're takin' on too much fer a gel your age.'

Mary smiled back at him. Although she knew what a cantankerous old cuss her granddad could be at times, she was very fond of him. He meant well, and did his best not to be a trouble around the house. Time had not been kind to the old man. Losing his wife Winnie, who died of consumption a few years before, had been a terrible blow for him, and it had taken a lot of persuasion from Mary's mum and dad to get the poor old boy to move in with the family. 'Things will be different when the war's over,' Mary dreamed out loud. 'One day we'll all go on a nice holiday, and wash the war right out of our minds.'

''Oliday?' Granddad nearly choked on his pipe. 'Best *we* can 'ope for is the beano next Sunday.'

Mary did a double-take. 'The beano!' she exclaimed. 'Oh yes, I'd forgotten all about that. Are you sure Mr Barrington meant what he said? I mean, you're not usually allowed to take families on pub outings. Beanos are only for men.'

'Well, yer can fank yer dad fer that,' said Granddad, his pipe sending a thin plume of baccy smoke up into the air. 'You know full well 'e was one 'er the favourites in the Saloon Bar round the Eaglet. It shocked the daylights out of the customers when 'e an' yer mum copped it down that tube in Befnal Green last year. Takin' you an' the family on the beano is their way of tryin' ter say 'ow much they fawt of yer dad.'

Mary listened to what the old man said with a sinking feeling that had not left her since they first received the news that their mum and dad were amongst the hoard of victims who had been trampled to death in that nightmare tube disaster. 'I must say, it's very thoughtful of them,' she replied with a sigh. 'But aren't these outings just an excuse for a good booze-up?'

Granddad snorted indignantly. 'Nuffin' wrong wiv that, young lady,' he said. 'I've no doubt there'll be plenty er lemonades an' fings fer you and the kids.'

'Oh, I'm not being ungrateful,' Mary said quickly. 'As a matter of fact, I'm looking forward to a day down by the sea. Southend has got such wonderful bracing air. When I was young, Dad used to take us for a walk along the pier. The wind was so strong at times, it nearly blew us off our feet. But I loved the way the seagulls swept down low over us as we walked. They always seemed so cross that we hadn't brought anything for them to eat. All I hope is that there are no incidents whilst we're there.'

'Incidents?'

'Well, the war isn't over yet,' said Mary. 'And after that explosion this morning—'

Even as she spoke, the backyard shook when another explosion in the distance echoed throughout the neighbourhood.

'Oh God!' she gasped. 'Another one!'

Above them, a top-floor window in the house was flung open, and old Nutty Nora was hanging out over the window ledge yelling out at the top of her voice. 'Did yer 'ear that!' she shrieked, causing two of her hair curlers to fall down into the yard below. 'They're at it again!'

Mary called up to her. 'Can you see anything?'

Nora squinted in the weak sunlight to scan the rooftops in the distance. 'No, nuffin! Can't see a bl— No – wait a minute! Smoke! There's smoke coming from the uvver side er the river . . . Must be down south somewhere. Blimey, just look at it!'

Fred Parfitt's head suddenly appeared over the garden wall. 'Some sorta new bombs!' he called. 'They're comin' over in planes wiv no pilots.

'What!' cried Mary, whose heart was beating so fast she was quite breathless.

'I just 'eard it on the wireless,' spluttered Fred. 'They've told people not ter go too far from the shelters.'

'Oh!' gasped Mary, rushing back into the house. 'I must get to the school. I hope to God the kids are safe!'

Highgate Hill was looking just as majestic as ever. Despite the Blitz during the early part of the war, most of the elegant Edwardian houses up there had escaped relatively unscathed, which was unlike the carnage caused by high explosive and incendiary bombs of every description in nearby Archway and neighbouring Holloway. Further down the Hill, a humble stone statue of a cat still marked the spot where the legendary Dick Whittington and his furry friend had allegedly long ago heard the distant Bow bells proclaiming, '*Turn again Whittington, thrice Lord Mayor of London.*' Highgate was a leafy, prosperous part of the capital city, much loved by locals and out-of-town visitors alike, who flocked to nearby Hampstead Heath for the fresh air and fairgrounds on every Bank Holiday of the year. However, the people who ate in the British Restaurant down the hill at the Archway Junction were hardly prosperous. Set up in a church hall by the Islington Borough Council, most of the patrons came from average working-class homes in nearby Holloway and Kentish Town, where for the princely sum of one shilling and sixpence, they could sit down to a three-course meal of spam, corned beef or fish pie, powdered potato, and any vegetables provided by local growers from their allotments. If you had run out of food ration coupons, then the British Restaurant was the place to go, for no coupons were required there, which was why there were always queues outside.

Once Mary had checked that Dodo and Billy were safe in the school air-raid shelters, she made her way to work. By the time she reached the restaurant to start her regular day's job as a washer-up, the place was buzzing with animated chit-chat about the three explosions that had been heard during the course of the morning. As usual, the place was packed, and the smell of fag smoke drifted across the makeshift dining tables containing their set menu of cottage pie and cabbage. The word had got around that flying bombs without pilots were dropping in various parts of London, and thanks to the BBC news on the wireless, everyone was on a high state of alert.

'Grove Road?' asked a barrow-boy from Kentish Town, who was sitting with one of his mates smoking like a chimney whilst Mary cleared the empty plates from their table. 'Where the bleedin' 'ell's that?'

'East End,' replied his mate, in flat cap and red-spotted choker. 'Somewhere 'round the Mile End Road, I 'eard. Come down on a train bridge, so they say.'

Mary felt her inside churn over. She knew that part of London only too well because her Aunt Gladys and Uncle Cyril lived over that way. 'Anyone killed?' she asked, joining in the conversation.

'Don't know, gel,' replied the bloke with the cap. 'Bit early ter say just yet. But apparently a train down the line had ter break pretty quick. If it 'ad gone over the bridge when that fing come down . . . phew! It don't bear finkin' about.'

Mary rushed off with the plates to the makeshift kitchen, and started washing them up immediately in a large enamel bowl filled with hot water from a kettle on the gas stove. Everyone was talking doom, about the mysterious explosions, and the fear that this was the start of another, new kind of Blitz.

'Ol' Lord Haw-Haw said it was was goin' ter 'appen,' said Maisie Stringer, who shared the washing-up duties with Mary. 'Me an' Mum 'eard 'im on the wireless last night. My kid bruvver managed to tune in ter short-wave.'

'Maisie,' chided Mary, her long flaxen hair tied in a bow beneath a headscarf, 'the Government has asked us not to listen to that man. Lord Haw-Haw's a Nazi, a traitor. All he wants to do is to lower our morale so that we just give in to his pals in Berlin.'

'Even so,' insisted Maisie, ''e *did* warn us. We can't afford to ignore 'im.'

Mary wasn't impressed by what Maisie was saying. 'Lord' Haw-Haw, as he had been nicknamed during the early years of the war, was nothing less than a menace, and she just hoped that one day he would be caught and strung up.

The restaurant was now bursting with the sound of chit-chat and heated arguments about what Churchill and his government should do about the new threat. The chaos was so bad that the supervisor Sheila Nestor, a grey-haired woman in her sixties, had to ask some of the customers who had eaten their food to leave the place in order to make room for the people queuing outside. 'See if you can get rid of *her*,' she said to Mary, indicating a neatly dressed middle-aged woman who had been sitting for quite a long time at a crowded table scribbling something down on a large notepad. 'She's in here every day, first one in, always sits at that same table.'

Mary didn't like the order to ask someone to leave, but as she had been asked to do so by her supervisor, she had no choice. Going straight to the table to collect the empty dishes there, she spoke discreetly and politely to the woman, who was wearing a smart one-piece black dress and headscarf, and surely looked as though she could afford a better meal than that provided by the British Restaurant. 'Sorry, madam,' said Mary, as softly as she could above the din all around, 'but if you've finished your meal, would you mind vacating the table? There are people waiting outside.'

When the woman looked up from her notepad, Mary saw a beautiful face, with a pure white complexion, dark painted eyebrows, cherry-shaped red lips, and lovely almond-shaped eyes. 'I'm sorry,' she said with a soft Chinese accent. 'I was just finishing off my sponge and custard.' With a twinkle in her eyes, she grinned. 'It's not what I'm used to eating, but since I've paid for it, I'd better get my money's worth.'

The three middle-aged flat-capped workmen sitting at the same table pretended not to even notice the woman's presence.

Mary looked flustered, and didn't know what to do. She had seen the woman several times during the past week, sitting at the same table for longer than anyone else there.

'Don't worry,' the woman said with an understanding smile, closing the notepad. 'It's time I was going, anyway.' She got up, collected her purse, and tucked the notepad under her arm. 'You know, you're a very pretty child.'

The woman's remark took Mary completely by surprise, and she quickly started to collect the remainder of the plates from the table.

'Oh, please don't be embarrassed,' continued the woman. 'When I see an interesting face, I like to admire it. I suppose you could call me an observer – a recorder of life.'

Mary tried to smile, as though she knew exactly what the woman was saying, which she didn't.

The woman turned to go. But as she went, she stopped and turned. 'I'll be in tomorrow at the same time. I hope I'll see you again?'

Still holding the pile of empty dishes, Mary paused just long enough to see the woman slowly wind her way through the crowd of customers and disappear through the front doors of the hall.

The main thoroughfare of Holloway Road was unusually quiet. By the time Mary had got off the number 609 trolleybus at the Nag's Head that evening, most people, unnerved by reports that during the morning five of the Germans' new pilotless planes had come down in residential areas in and around London, had left work early and were going home to their air-raid shelters as fast as their legs could carry them. Despite the golden serenity of the evening sun, the sky

14

did indeed look ominous. As she hurried home down Seven Sisters Road, Mary constantly looked up anxiously at the small puffs of dense white clouds as she tried to imagine what these new monster machines looked like, and the immense danger they now threatened everyone with.

'Don't look good, do it, gel?' said Charlie, the news-vendor on the corner of Hertslet Road, as Mary collected Granddad's copy of the *Evening News*. Charlie had sold newspapers to the Trimble family for years, and had known Mary since she was a little kid. 'Once our blokes did that landing in France the uvver day, I fawt we was past all this. But it only goes ter show – that slimey bugger 'Itler ain't goin' ter give up till 'e's rottin' in 'is grave!'

'I know, Charlie,' replied Mary disconsolately. She had always had a soft spot for the old chap who, despite once having spent a short spell in Pentonville Prison for taking underhand gambling bets from the locals, was the salt of the earth. 'I must say, I'm getting nervous. They can send those planes anywhere they want, and there's not a thing we can do about it.'

'Oh, don't you worry about that,' replied Charlie, with his familiar cheery smile, and a whistling sound as he spoke through a gap in the front of his top teeth. 'Just remember wot our boys in blue did in their Spitfires during the Blitz. And we've still got the Ack-Ack. This is Jerry's last fling. They're tryin' ter get their own back 'cos we've been bombin' them just as much as they've bombed us.'

'But d'you think this is the start of a new kind of Blitz?' Mary asked anxiously. 'Will it go on?'

'Nah!' insisted Charlie confidently. 'They can't 'ave many of those fings – not when our blokes are closin' in on 'em over there.' Despite Charlie's traditional optimism, his words sounded hollow; during the day, one of his mates, who was in an Army Defence team, had told him about the reports coming through that Jerry was massing hundreds, maybe even thousands, of the pilotless flying bombs in Holland. But Charlie was keeping that bit of information to himself. He didn't want to scare the daylights out of anyone.

15

When she reached the top of Roden Street, Mary was relieved to see that things were no different to usual. The neighbourhood kids, now out of school, were running about laughing and yelling, rolling hoops, skipping up and down along the pavement, and playing their favourite street games such as Hopscotch, Cowboys and Indians, Cops and Robbers, and brandishing home-made guns and rifles, emulating the war now being played out so ferociously in France. Mary was too engrossed in her newspaper to take much notice of them all, but she did occasionally acknowledge their calls before finally disappearing into the house, where she was not at all pleased to be met by old Nutty Nora calling down to her from the landing upstairs.

'Yer better start gettin' that shelter dried out,' said the old girl. 'They say on the wireless we're goin' ter get more of these bleedin' flyin' bombs.'

'As far as I know there's no water down there, Mrs Kelly,' replied Mary, wearily. 'At least there wasn't the last time I looked. If you and your brother want to start sleeping down there again it'll be all right with me. I can always take Granddad and the kids to the public shelter in Jackson Road.'

Mary remembered only too well the terrible nights during the Blitz when the family were forced to share the tiny Anderson shelter with their lodger, old Nutty Nora.

Fortunately, Nutty Nora's brother, Les, who shared the two upstairs rooms with her, had always solidly refused to go down into the shelter at night, opting instead to take his chances in his own bed. He was practically a recluse, who never spoke to anyone, even when he saw them. But his sister never missed a night down the shelter, pinching the top bunk so that Mary and the kids had to rough it on the lower bunk and two rickety deckchairs.

'I'm sorry, Mrs Kelly,' continued Mary, moving off towards the back parlour, 'but I've got to get the kids' tea.'

'Ha!' scoffed the old girl as she struggled back up the stairs. 'Sounds as though they ain't in no 'urry fer that!'

Mary didn't quite take in what Nutty Nora had said, and went straight into the back parlour, where Granddad was waiting for his evening newspaper. There was no sign of the kids, who at this time were usually spread around the parlour table waiting impatiently for their teatime meal. 'Where are Thelma and Dodo?' she asked.

'Gorn out,' snorted Granddad, immediately snatching the newspaper from Mary. 'All free of 'em — fank Gord!'

'Gone out?' asked Mary, a bit het up. 'Where to?'

'I presume they've gorn off wiv your mate,' mumbled the old man from behind his newspaper. 'Fawt yer knew all about it. *She* said yer did.'

Mary immediately pulled the newspaper away from him. '*What* mate?' she demanded impatiently. 'What are you talking about?'

'The woman who come ter the door,' snapped Granddad irritably. 'She said she knows yer, saw you up at the Rest'raunt terday. She took the three kids out fer some water ice from Tony's barrer . . .'

'Christ Almighty, Granddad!' exploded Mary. 'I don't know who you're talking about. Who is this woman? Where has she taken them?'

Granddad suddenly felt a bit guilty, and slumped back into his armchair. 'I haven't the foggiest *who* she is,' he grunted irritably. 'All I know is she was waitin' fer the kids when they come out of school. Billy come in ter tell me that she knew their big sister, and that she was takin' them off fer a water ice up at Finsbury Park.'

'Oh God!' gasped Mary. Before her startled granddad could say another word, she had rushed out into the street.

Mary's feet couldn't run fast enough. She had never moved along Seven Sisters Road so fast in all her life, and by the time she had reached Italian Tony's water ice barrow outside the gates of Finsbury Park, she was so breathless she could hardly breathe. 'Have you seen my brother and two sisters, Tony?' she panted. 'Did they come here with someone?'

'I saw your eldest sister,' replied a rather baffled Tony. The jovial, middle-aged Italian who had lived with his English wife for many years, and had thereby managed to escape a wartime detention order, knew Mary and her family well, having served them plenty of ice-cream cornets before rationing made milk so hard to get. 'She bought

17

three cornets, but I didn't see the others. I couldn't tell you if they were with anyone.'

Mary rushed off in a real fluster, disappearing through the gates into the park before Tony had a chance to ask her what was wrong. So much was going through her head. Who was this woman who had taken her sisters and brother off without asking anyone's permission? What if she had molested them, or harmed them in any way? It didn't bear thinking about! In her mind she was already churning over hurrying down to the Hornsey Road Police Station which had been so badly bombed during the Blitz. She looked around frantically for any sign of the three kids, searching every area that she knew so well, including the children's playground, the football ground, the railway bridge, and every path within striking distance that she could think of. However, just as she was hurrying along the path that led to the boating lake, she caught her first sight of the three of them, Thelma, Dodo and Billy, strolling along aimlessly towards her, as though they hadn't a care in the world. But when they caught sight of Mary, their expressions soon changed, and they came to a dead halt.

'Where the hell have you been!' Mary roared, her face like thunder. 'What do you mean by leaving the house without letting me know?'

'What's all the fuss about?' replied Thelma, haughtily. 'We were perfectly safe.'

Mary went straight to her and, eyeball to eyeball, growled, 'You're only children, Thelma! You are *never* safe if I don't know what's happened to you. Now who was this woman you went with?'

Thelma glared back at her, thoroughly indignant at being described in such a way.

'It was a nice lady,' replied Dodo, who looked as though she might burst into tears at any moment. 'She says she knows you. She says she was with you at the restaurant only today.'

Mary's heart missed a beat.

'She's a Chinese lady,' said Billy, defiantly. 'She give us this.' He unrolled a large piece of paper which he was holding in his right hand.

Mary took the paper and looked at it. It was a beautiful pencil-drawn group portrait of Thelma, Dodo and Billy, set against the backdrop of the boating lake.

'She's a lovely lady,' said Thelma. 'Such beautiful, slanting eyes, and white smooth skin.'

'She's ever so nice,' added Dodo.

'She bought us all water ices,' said Billy enthusiastically.

Mary continued to stare in awe at the drawing. In the moments of silence whilst she did so, her mind was consumed with her memory of the Chinese woman who had spent so much time at the table in the British Restaurant that lunchtime. Who was she? How did she know about the three kids, and where Mary and they lived? What did she want? What was this woman up to? Her flesh went cold at the thought of the danger her sisters and brother could have been in. 'Where is she now?' she asked, looking all around.

'Haven't the faintest idea,' replied Thelma dismissively.

'She just said "Cheerio" and went off,' said Dodo.

Mary quickly rolled up the drawing and tucked it under her arm. 'Home!' she snapped at them all. Grabbing hold of Dodo's hand, she turned and practically frogmarched them all briskly back towards the park gates. They were soon lost in the crowds of people who were just coming in to the park for their evening strolls. Mary didn't notice any of them. All she could think about were all the angry questions that woman was going to have to answer the moment she set eyes on her again.

Chapter 2

The Orange Luxury coach parked in Hornsey Road just outside the Eaglet pub, may not have quite been as luxurious as its name suggested, but it was certainly about to give a great deal of pleasure and excitement to the Eaglet's patrons, who had assembled to embark on their annual 'beano' one day pub outing to Southend-on-Sea on the Essex coast. Needless to say, most of the passengers would be male, of middle to old age, and the baggage compartment was crammed full of crates of beer. But as Mary and her young sisters and brother were going along as the guests of the organisers, there were several bottles of Tizer, lemonade, and ginger beer to keep them satisfied, and before the coach had even set off, Billy Trimble was already tucking into several bags of Smith's crisps, recklessly discarding the small blue bags of salt on to the floor as he did so.

'Come along now, boys an' gels!' called Ken Barrington, the principal organiser of the annual event. He was a large rotund figure with a balding head of grey hair and a heart of gold. 'Sun's been up for over an hour. If yer wanna a dip in the briny yer'd better get a move on!'

There were a few light-hearted guffaws from the men as they boarded the coach, but not from Granddad Trimble, who always found these early starts bad for his rheumatism; they made him very grumpy indeed. Like all the others, he couldn't wait to drown his sorrows in a quart bottle of brown ale.

Mary had a bit of a job getting the family settled on the coach, for although they had the long back seat to themselves, Dodo and Billy scrapped like cat and dog for the best window seat, and only calmed down when Mary separated them by putting them both in opposite window seats.

The coach finally left to cheers and whistles from the pub customers, all of whom had paid two shillings each for their seat and one and sixpence more for the huge quantities of booze, half of which would be consumed long before they got to their final destination. Apart from Ken Barrington, Mary knew only one or two of her fellow passengers, such as Fred Know-It-All from next door, Sid Battersby, who lived in Annette Road, and who had only recently retired as a plumber up at the Arsenal Football Stadium. However, Granddad knew most of them, for he was a regular at the Eaglet, especially at the weekends, where he played darts and drank brown ale until he could hardly stand up.

The coach had hardly reached the outskirts of north-east London when the inevitable sing-song suddenly brought out the deafening, unmusical roars of 'Run, Rabbit, Run', and by the time they had got through 'She'll Be Comin' Round the Mountains', and 'The Lambeth Walk', they had hardly cleared the main road alongside Epping Forest. Billy Trimble loved it all, and much to the irritation of Thelma and Dodo, he sang louder than anyone else. Mary, who had at least hoped for a bit of sleep on the outward journey, soon realised that that was never going to be possible, for even when she did manage to close her eyes her mind was still preoccupied with the one burning question that had plagued her for the past few days, ever since she found her two sisters and brother in Finsbury Park. Who *was* that Chinese woman who came to the house, and why had she, from that moment on, kept away from the restaurant? Her first thought was to go to the police and tell them what had happened, but when she thought about it carefully, nothing *had* happened, only that the three kids had clearly thoroughly enjoyed being in the woman's company. And then she thought about that beautiful sketched portrait of the kids the woman had drawn. It was all so strange, so baffling.

'Enjoyin' yerself, Mary?'

Mary's eyes sprang open to find Ken Barrington turning round from the seat just in front of her. 'Oh yes, Mr Barrington,' she said with great appreciation. 'It was so good of you to invite us along.'

Ken beamed. 'Think nuffin' of it, gel,' he replied. 'Your dad meant a lot to us. When *you* lost him, it was a big blow to all of us, too, back at the boozer. Salt of the earth – him *and* your ma. This is the least we could do for 'em.'

Mary smiled gratefully.

'Yer know,' said Ken, shaking his head mournfully, 'it should never've happened. Them dyin' like that was so – so unnecessary. I mean, all them people gettin' trampled ter death down the escalator just 'cos some of 'em panicked when they 'eard the ack-ack guns firing outside the station. A bleedin' waste of good people's lives.'

Although Mary agreed with what Ken had said, she tried not to think about it too much. She had spent so much time grieving for her mum and dad, and she was now doing her best to put that terrible period of time behind her. In any case, she had other things to worry her, for the coach skidded to a halt when someone up front suddenly shouted out, 'Buzz bomb!'

The kids were first at the nearside window, where they immediately caught their first glimpse of the sinister black flying bomb that was streaking across the sky, a red light flashing on its tail and a trail of thick black vapour following on behind.

'Up there!' yelled Billy, excitedly.

'I can see it!' shrieked Dodo, pointing up through the top half of the open window.

'Everyone down!' yelled Ken Barrington.

Mary immediately grabbed Billy and Dodo and pushed them face down on to the floor of the coach. 'Down, Thelma!' she barked.

Thelma, totally unflustered, did as she was told.

It seemed a lifetime whilst everyone flattened themselves on the floor of the coach and waited for the inevitable cut-out of the flying bomb's engines. In fact, it took no more than fifteen seconds before the explosion came, rattling the windows and rocking the coach from side to side. When calm returned, the first thing everyone wanted to do was to get off the coach, and there was a mad scramble to do so.

Mary breathed a sigh of relief when she had got her sisters and brother and granddad out into the fresh air. Although shaken, all of them remained calm. Behind them, the male passengers yelled obscenities at the blank sky, and shook their heads in despair as they saw a plume of thick black smoke spiralling up into the air from London in the distance behind them. Whilst they were standing there, however, another flying bomb approached from the East, followed quickly behind by another, and then another. It was an incredible sight, with flames pouring from the rear engines of the deadly pilotless aircraft, and the peaceful rural air pierced by the sound of chugging engines. Everyone held their breath until the buzz bombs had passed over, then waited for the three separate explosions which followed in quick succession.

'D'yer fink it's safe ter go on, Ken?' called one of the male passengers.

'If anyone's shook up by all this,' returned Ken, 'we can turn back. Wot d'yer say?'

There was a loud chorus of 'No!' from the passengers, together with more yelled obscenities by one or two of the gang, including Fred Know-It-All.

'Wot about *you*, little lady?' Ken asked Mary. 'Are you goin' ter be all right if we go on?'

'Off course we are!' Thelma answered defiantly on behalf of her sisters and brother.

'We'll do whatever you decide, Mr Barrington,' replied Mary, calmly.

'Is there any Tizer?' was Billy Trimble's only contribution.

By the time the coach drew to a halt on the seafront at Southend-on-Sea, most of the beano passengers were already in high spirits, mainly due to the amount of brown ale, Guinness and bitter they had consumed during what had turned out to be a hazardous journey out from Holloway. Granddad Trimble was decidedly shaky on his legs, and Mary was relieved to know that he was going off on the inevitable pub crawl with the other patrons of the Eaglet, leaving her and the kids free to make their way to the hot sausage and mash café. Southend was looking glorious in the hot sunshine, but like all the other seaside resorts, holidaymakers and day trippers were mainly confined to deck-chairs and public benches on the seafront, as many of the beach areas were still restricted and sealed off with barbed wire in the event of a possible enemy invasion.

None of the Trimble family had ever been on a day trip to Southend without having a Rossi's ice-cream, which had somehow become a symbol of this much-loved family resort. So many people had declared it the finest ice-cream in the world, with its creamy twirl created in front of your very eyes by the assistant with a large metal spoon. Today was no exception, and the three Trimble kids were there, drooling, and waiting anxiously in the long queue within minutes of getting off the coach. The one exception was Mary, for although she loved Rossi's too, she had more practical matters to think of, one of which was the fear of not having enough money to pay for ice-cream *and* sausage and mash for her brother and sisters. Sitting on the sea wall on the opposite side of the road, watching the three kids move up closer and closer in the queue, her mind turned inevitably towards the family's finances, and how she was going to keep up with the weekly rent payments back home. Although Granddad meant well, financially he was no help at all, for what little money he had managed to save over the years had obviously been squandered on booze and betting. The trouble was that the job up at the British Restaurant paid Mary only a pittance, and with three siblings, her granddad and herself to support, there was only just enough money to go around. No. The only solution was to find a better-paid job, but she had no idea how to go about finding one. Losing her mum and dad was not only a tragedy in itself, but it had placed a huge responsibility on her head that she had not been prepared for.

'Nothin' like a bit of sea breeze ter brush the cobwebs away, eh, Mary?'

Mary turned with a start to find Frank Corbett looking down at her.

Frank was a tall, lean man, who always seemed to wear the same flat cap, white shirt, grey flannels and braces every time she saw him. 'Hello, Mr Corbett,' she replied pleasantly. 'Aren't you going with the others?'

'Nah,' replied Frank, resting one foot on the wall and staring out at the sea. 'Don't really want ter spend the 'ole day in a pub. We can do that any time back 'ome.' He perched alongside her. 'I love Southend. Always cheers me up when I look out at that sea. When me an' my missus were courtin' we 'ad a lot of good times down here. Cockles and whelks, eels an' mash, an' a nice cup er tea – can't beat it.'

Mary agreed with a smile. Her dad always had a lot of time for Frank Corbett, mainly because, when they were kids, they had both gone to Shelbourne Road School. Her dad used to say that Frank was the one man he knew he could always trust, especially during the times when he shared any concerns he had about the family. 'I miss the pier, though,' replied Mary wistfully, looking out at the famous pier which jutted out from the cobbled seashore for over a mile, but which, since the start of the war, had remained sadly deserted.

'Oh, they'll open it up again,' Frank assured her, 'once they get rid of Jerry. Be good to see the old Kursaal open up again. This place ain't the same wivout the Amusement Park.' He turned his gaze back from the pier to Mary. 'Yer mum an' dad thought the world of you, yer know.'

'I know they loved all their kids dearly,' replied Mary.

'Oh, don't get me wrong,' said Frank awkwardly. 'They treasured *all* their kids. But – well – they was always on their toes about Thelma.'

Mary swung him a curious look. 'Thelma?'

'Yer dad din't like some of the fings she got up to,' replied Frank sheepishly. 'She used ter scare the pants off 'im. 'Speshully since that day one of the blokes in the pub saw her up West.' He suddenly realised Mary was staring anxiously at him. 'Oh, I know I shouldn't really be talkin' to yer like this, Mary, but yer dad – well, 'e often used ter talk fings over wiv me.'

'What do you mean, Mr Corbett?' Mary asked falteringly. 'Somebody saw Thelma up the West End?'

Frank nodded awkwardly. 'Yer didn't know?'

Mary shook her head.

Frank took off his cap and wiped his forehead with it. He had a short, military-style haircut which was just beginning to turn grey. 'It was just before what 'appened over at Bethnal Green, just a week or so before yer mum an' dad—' He stopped in mid-sentence. 'Apparently Thelma was up near the Dilly, made up ter the nines. She was just comin' out of a pub wiv a yank – a GI.'

Mary gasped. She was completely taken aback. 'But – she's nearly sixteen now,' she said. 'When did she do all this? How?'

Frank flicked a quick glance across at Thelma, Dodo and Billy, who were gradually edging their way towards the front of the long ice-cream queue. 'From what yer dad told me, it was one Saturday, when she said she was goin' ter spend the day wiv her mates up 'Ornsey Road.'

'But she always spends Saturdays with them,' replied Mary, with incomprehension.

'Accordin' to yer dad,' said Frank with a sigh, 'it wasn't the first time.'

Mary stared across the road at Thelma. She was absolutely devastated.

'Look,' continued Frank, keeping his voice low. 'I know this ain't none of my business, but there's somefin' more you should know about, Mary. I 'aven't discussed this wiv anyone, but the fact is, Thelma's under age. If anyone finds out about wot she's doin', if they tell the welfare people up the Town 'All or anyfin' . . .'

Mary's eyes were like saucers. 'The Welfare?'

'Remember, Mary,' warned Frank, ominously. '*You're* the one that's lookin' after the family. *You're* the one that's responsible for 'em. There're people 'round our way who reckon that you're too young ter be bringin' up a family on yer own.'

'But that's ridiculous!' Mary protested, springing to her feet. 'I'll be twenty-one next year.'

'I'm just tellin' yer, Mary,' said Frank, with great difficulty. 'I just want yer ter know . . . well . . . the dangers if somefin' ain't done about Thelma.'

26

'Three cheers! Hip, hip, hooray!'

The roar of Billy and Dodo's voices as they rushed across the road with Thelma, all tucking into their ice-cream cornets, brought the conversation between Mary and Frank to a halt.

'I'd better be gettin' back ter the lads,' said Frank, quickly moving off. 'Be'ave yerselves, you lot!' he yelled to the three kids, carefully avoiding an exchange of looks with Thelma. However, he had only gone a few paces when he stopped, and came back to Mary. 'Almost fergot,' he said, digging into his trousers pockets.

'The lads asked me ter give yer this,' he said quietly, handing over two one-pound notes to Mary. 'They had a bit of a whip-round.'

Mary took the pound notes, and stared at them with a mixture of distress and relief. 'Mr Corbett!' she uttered falteringly. 'I – don't – know what to say.'

Frank smiled back reassuringly at her. 'Might come in 'andy fer yer sausage an' mash.'

Before Mary could say another word, he was gone, marching off briskly back to the pub like a soldier on the parade ground.

'What we goin' to do now?' asked Billy, who had almost finished his ice-cream cornet.

Mary looked at him, then at Dodo. She was close to tears. Once again her father's pals had saved the day. Yes, there would be sausage and mash after all, and maybe enough left over for the kids to spend the odd penny or two in one of the seafront amusement arcades. Finally, she looked at Thelma, who was quite obviously bored with the thought of having to spend the day with her sisters and brother. 'Let's go for a walk,' Mary said determinedly, her eyes fixed on Thelma. 'We could do with some fresh air.'

Despite the fact that the sausages were filled with more bread than meat, they were delicious, and it took very little time for the Trimbles to tuck into them. During the family's annual day's outing to Southend, the sausage and mash shop on the seafront had always been the favourite place for a good old-fashioned 'blow-out', and now that the worry of how she was going to pay the bill had been lifted by the generous

27

'whip-round' of the Eaglet patrons, Mary was able to sit back and enjoy her lunch. Nonetheless, she still had plenty of things on her mind, and whilst Dodo and Billy were noisily using up all the remaining pennies in one of the amusement arcades, she pondered how best she was going to deal with what Frank Corbett had told her about Thelma, and what would happen if the Welfare up at the Town Hall were to find out about what her reckless young sister was getting up to. Something had to be done, and done quickly. But how? Unless she could find a job with more pay, not only would the kids be taken away from her, but there also would be no way she could afford to pay the weekly rent payments which were already several weeks overdue.

The return journey back to Holloway turned out, as expected, to be high spirited and boozy, with endless drunken sing-songs on the Orange Luxury coach piercing the humid summer air of the quiet Essex countryside. By the time the beano revellers had reached the outskirts of north-east London, the amount of booze consumed necessitated a 'relief' stop, which meant that a secluded, leafy area had to be found pretty quickly if accidents were to be avoided. The spot chosen was the edge of some woods just outside a small village, which was set back from the main road.

Whilst bladders were being emptied with great relief by a scattering of men in the bushes, Mary, Thelma, Dodo and Billy got off the coach to stretch their legs, and breathe in some fresh air in contrast to the stifling beer fumes and fag smoke on the coach. As the driver had allowed a fifteen-minute stopover, Dodo and Billy rushed off into the woods to do a bit of exploring, leaving Mary and Thelma to amble along a grassy path bordered each side by wild buttercups and mead-owsweet. However, it wasn't too long before Thelma was complaining about being stung on her legs by nettles, which was her way of saying that she didn't want to do much walking. Nonetheless, this was Mary's chance to tackle her about some of the things Frank Corbett had been saying about her.

'What do you do with yourself on Saturday afternoons, Thelma?'

Mary's sudden question took Thelma completely off-guard; so much so, that she came to a halt and swung back a glare at her. 'What're you talking about?' she snapped.

'You're never at home on Saturday afternoons,' replied Mary, trying to sound as casual as she possibly could. 'I just wondered where you went?'

Thelma shot back a look of thunder at her. For once she had stopped fingering her short, light brown hair, and her normally clear, white complexion was flushed with anger. 'You know very well where I go!' she growled, haughtily. 'I go up to Amy Jenkin's. I *always* go up to Amy's place on Saturdays!'

'What do you and Amy do when you go up to see her?' persisted Mary.

Thelma was now spluttering, fighting for words. 'Amy's my friend!' she said, turning to go. 'We like spending time together. And in any case, it's none of your business *what* we do!' She broke away, and started to hurry back to the road.

'I was just wondering where you – *and* Amy – managed to find the bus fare to go up to the West End?'

This was like a thunderbolt for Thelma, so much so that it stopped her dead in her tracks. She turned back slowly and glared scathingly at her elder sister. 'You're not my mother!' she snapped. 'I'm almost sixteen years old. I don't have to tell my *sister* everything I do.'

'You're under my care and protection, Thelma,' replied Mary, calmly. 'You, Dodo and Billy – I'm responsible for everything any of you do. If anything goes wrong, *I'm* the one who has to carry the can – not you.'

'I'm old enough to take care of myself, Mary,' retorted Thelma. 'I'm old enough now to make my own decisions. That's what *she* said.'

Mary did a double take. '*She?*'

There was a suggestion of a smirk on Thelma's face. 'That Chinese woman – Mrs Ling. She told me straight out – at my age I have the right to make my own decisions.'

Mary was taken aback, but before she had time to react, they were distracted by an hysterical scream from Dodo somewhere in the woods. 'Mary!'

'Oh my God!' gasped Mary, rushing off.

Thelma was only too glad to see her go, and quickly made her way back to the coach, but most of the men went hurrying after Mary.

Dodo's screams echoed around the tall oak and chestnut trees. Mary eventually found her, perched on the banks of a fast-flowing river where a young bloke, fully clothed, was swimming heavily towards Billy who was struggling to keep his head above the water.

'Mary!' yelled Dodo, over and over again, whilst Billy was coughing and spluttering, and yelling his head off in a panic.

'Hold on, Billy!' shouted Mary, desperately. 'Hold on!'

The men from the coach finally caught up with Mary, but as most of them were none too steady on their feet, they merely watched frantically as the young bloke managed to reach Billy, hold the boy with a vice-like grip under his armpits, and gradually support him back towards the riverbank. The moment they reached safety, there was a loud burst of applause and shouts of 'Well done, mate!' from all the relieved onlookers.

Mary grabbed Billy out of the young man's arms, and yanked him out of the water. 'You stupid fool!' she yelled at him, more out of relief than anger. 'Just look at you! You could have drowned! For God's sake, Billy – what's the matter with you?'

Billy, drenched to the skin and shivering with the cold, had a huge grin on his face. 'All I did was climb up the branch on that tree,' he explained, with an unconcerned shrug. 'It broke, an' I fell in!'

'What sort of a mother d'you think you are?' growled the young bloke, who was only in his early twenties, shirt and trousers absolutely dripping with water. 'Don't you realise that river's got a really dangerous undercurrent? Three people were drowned there last year!' He was so angry he totally ignored what Mary was trying to say. 'That's the trouble with you town people,' he ranted in a rural Essex burr. 'You think you know so much, but you know *nothin'* – nothin' at all!'

'Look, Mr . . .' Mary tried to explain, attempting to thank the young bloke for saving Billy's life. But he was far too worked up to listen to her.

'Get those clothes off him!' barked the young bloke, rushing off to a farmhouse just visible in the woods nearby. 'Just look at him – he's frozen stiff! If he doesn't dry off, he'll land up in the hospital. Wait here!'

Mary and the others watched in absolute astonishment, as the young bloke hurried back to what looked like an old woodland farmhouse buried nearby in the heart of the woods.

'Got a chip on 'is shoulder, that one!' called one of the men as they gathered around to see if there was anything they could do to help.

'Best get you back on the coach,' said Ken Barrington, still a bit shaky on his feet. 'That young feller's right. Billy'll catch 'is death standin' out 'ere. There's a bit of a nip in the air out of the sun.'

Before they all had a chance to move, and whilst Mary was peeling off Billy's shirt, the young man rushed back from the house with a large towel. 'Here!' he called. 'Put this round him.' He quickly wrapped the towel around Billy's shoulders, and left Mary to dry the boy. 'And the next time, keep an eye on your kids!'

Mary was too astonished to answer the young man. All she could do was watch him rush off and disappear into the house.

Chapter 3

Tanya Ling made her way along Junction Road heading for the British Restaurant in the old church hall. Her movements were graceful and effortless, taking perfectly spaced steps, all of which seemed to match her lithe body, spotless white complexion, and short, jet-black hair. The first time Mary had set eyes on her she thought she was quite tall for a Chinese woman, and that she should be wearing some kind of a patterned silk dress. But Tanya Ling was not all she appeared to be.

Maisie Stringer was shocked when she saw the Chinese woman coming into the restaurant and sitting down at her usual table in the corner over by the window. After she had delivered the plate of spam fritters, boiled potatoes and tinned peas to one of her customers, she rushed back into the kitchen to see the supervisor, Sheila Nestor. 'She's back!' gasped Maisie, excitedly. 'She's at the same table!'

'Who's back?' barked Sheila, who was hot and flustered, helping the two elderly lady cooks by mixing up a bowl of batter for the spam fritters. 'Who's back? What are you talking about, girl?'

'That woman!' persisted Maisie, whose squeaky voice competed with a whistling kettle on the stove. 'The one who comes in nearly every day. That Chinese woman Mary told us about.'

Sheila swung round with a start. 'She's here — *now*?'

'The same table,' replied Maisie, jumping up and down with agitation. 'This is the first time she's been in since Mary told us about her takin' the kids up to Finsbury Park.'

Sheila waited not a minute longer. Grabbing a tea cloth she dried her hands and strode straight out into the restaurant, zigzagging her way around the tables to where Tanya Ling was sitting, sketching on a large blank pad.

'Excuse me!'

Sheila's gruff North London voice startled Tanya, who looked up to face a terse look from the woman in charge.

'I don't know who you are, or what you are,' growled Sheila, 'but this is a place where people come to eat, not to draw pictures.'

Tanya smiled back sweetly. 'I'm waiting to give my order,' she replied softly, her cherry-red lips hardly moving as she spoke. 'Spam and potatoes?'

'I'm sorry,' retorted Sheila formally, a curl of grey hair falling across her forehead, 'but I must ask you to leave. We have no time for your sort here.'

Tanya's expression remained impassive. She tried hard not to react. 'Forgive me,' she replied. 'I don't understand.'

'You're using this place under false pretences,' said Sheila, stiffening, keeping her voice down to avoid drawing the attention of the other customers. 'We reserve the right to decline service to anyone.'

This really stung Tanya, and for one brief moment, her passive smile faded. 'Is Mary Trimble here, please?' she replied. 'I'd like to speak to her.'

'*Miss* Trimble is not here today,' said Sheila forcefully, determined to show that she meant business. 'We know all about you, and we don't want you in this restaurant. Now please don't make a fuss, or I shall have to call the police.'

Tanya was really shocked. 'The police?' she spluttered. 'What on earth do you mean?'

'I've asked you politely,' persisted Sheila. 'Please don't make me call for assistance.'

Tanya looked around, where a sea of faces was looking at her; flat caps, overalls, large burly men with unlit fags behind their ears and mouths slowly chewing spam fritters, and indignant middle-aged women in hats and young girls wearing headscarves, trying to imagine that their lunch at the Ritz was being interrupted by a foreign intruder. With disbelief, Tanya closed her sketch pad, and slowly stood up.

Maisie and the two elderly cooks peered around the kitchen door watching in awed fascination. The restaurant went so quiet you could have heard a pin drop.

'I really don't understand,' said Tanya, with incomprehension. 'I've done nothing wrong.'

'Please go!' replied Sheila, calmly, standing aside to let Tanya pass.

Tanya paused awkwardly for a moment, then reluctantly made her way to the door. Once she was outside on the pavement, she paused only long enough to listen to the noise of knives and forks and the buzz of lively chatter returning to the restaurant dining hall behind her.

Mary joined the queue at Dorners the butcher's shop in Hornsey Road. Fortunately, as it was midweek, the queue wasn't very long; it was also raining and there wasn't much cover on the pavement in front of the shop window. But, as far as Mary was concerned, the wait was worthwhile. The family loved hot saveloys and pease pudding. Not only were they cheap at twopence a portion, and were exempt from ration coupons, but they also would re-heat well in the oven when the kids got back from school that evening. Mary was enjoying her day off from the restaurant. Apart from Sundays, it was her only time off. When she was finally served, however, the smell of the saveloys and pease pudding being wrapped up in newspaper and greaseproof bags soon played havoc with Mary's empty stomach; she was so tempted to taste a steaming hot saveloy that it was a real effort for her to place the parcel unopened into her string bag.

Within the last hour or so, the weather had become overcast, with light rain and low, dark grey clouds, which made the pavements quite slippery, and by the time Mary had got back home her headscarf and light summer dress were wet and clammy. Feeling quite uncomfortable, the last thing she wanted was to find Granddad coming out into the passage to meet her.

'Where've yer been?' asked the old man irritably, wearing only his vest, trousers and braces. 'Yer've bin gone fer ages.'

'I had to queue,' replied Mary calmly, closing the door behind her, refusing to respond to his irritation. 'Anyway, what's the rush? It *is* my day off, you know.'

'Yer've got a visitor.'

Mary came to an abrupt halt. 'Visitor?'

Granddad quickly disappeared back into the back parlour.

Mary followed him, and, to her astonishment, she found a young bloke getting up to greet her from a chair at the table. ''Allo, Miss,' he said awkwardly, with his Essex burr. It was the same boy who had rescued young Billy from the river during the Eaglet pub's beano.

'What are *you* doing here?' asked Mary, taken aback.

'I hope you don't mind,' replied the young man, clutching a trilby hat in one hand, and looking ill at ease in his grey baggy flannel trousers, white shirt and v-necked pullover. 'I knew you were on the Eaglet beano, so I asked Mr Barrington where you lived. I know this part of Holloway pretty well. My dad works round 'ere.' He paused only briefly before adding self-consciously, 'I came to apologise.'

'Apologise?' asked Mary, still clutching her string bag with the saveloys and pease pudding. 'What for?'

'Fer the way I talked to you that day,' replied the boy. 'I mean, I didn't know at the time that you – I mean, that you wasn't . . . I was just stupid, that's all.'

'And you came all this way to tell us?'

'Bleedin' bonkers!' grunted Granddad, before leaving the room.

'We're the ones who should be apologising to *you*,' said Mary, putting the string bag on to the table. 'My brother Billy was the stupid one, not you.'

The young man began to relax a little. 'Well, I just wanted you to know, that's all.' He started to move towards the door.

'Look,' Mary said quickly, pulling off her wet headscarf. 'Just give me a minute to get changed, then I'll make us a cup of tea.'

The boy looked ill at ease again. 'I – I don't know . . .'

'It's raining outside,' said Mary. 'Just have a cuppa until it stops. It's the least I can do to say thank you.'

'I – I don't know,' said the boy awkwardly.

'*Please,*' pleaded Mary. 'I'd like it.'

When she came back to the parlour after changing her dress, Mary brought the towel the young man had given to her to wrap around Billy. 'This is yours,' she said, holding out the towel. 'Thank you so much for lending it.'

The boy shook his head. 'Why don't you keep it,' he replied. 'I've got plenty more back home. Anyway, I'm back an' forth down 'ere all the time ter see my dad. I'm sure we'll bump into each other.'

This comment somewhat surprised Mary. She smiled gently and put the towel down on to the table. 'What's your name?'

'Mr Backer,' replied the boy formally.

Again Mary smiled. But this time it was more of a grin.

'Len,' added the boy quickly. 'Most people back 'ome call me Lennie.'

Mary held out her hand. 'My name's Mary,' she said. 'Mary Trimble.'

'Yes, I know,' replied Lennie, shaking her hand and adding quickly, 'Mr Barrington told me.'

'Just give me a moment to put the kettle on.' Mary briefly disappeared into the kitchen. Whilst she was doing so, she watched the boy carefully through the scullery window, puzzled that he had come all the way from Essex to apologise for the way he had talked to her. The local boys Mary knew were just not like that; they were only interested in one thing, and *they* certainly wouldn't apologise for *anything.* 'Milk and sugar?' she called, once she had made the pot of tea.

'No sugar, thanks,' returned Lennie.

Mary was relieved, as it was the end of the month, and the family's meagre sugar ration was almost exhausted. 'So how long did it take you to come in from where you live?' she asked as she brought in two cups of tea.

'Not so long,' Lennie replied, taking the cup and saucer from her. 'There's a Green Line bus just five minutes' walk from the house. It takes less than an hour from there to Holloway Road.'

Mary sat down at the table opposite him. 'Don't you ever get lonely living out there in the middle of those woods?' she asked.

Lennie almost seemed to take exception to that question. 'Why should I get lonely?' he retorted. 'I much prefer my own company to other people's.' He suddenly seemed to realize that his reply had been a bit sharp. 'I'm not on me own,' he continued. 'I live with my mum. Well – that's not quite true. I look after my mum. She's not very well.'

'Oh, I'm sorry to hear that,' said Mary. 'What's wrong with her?'

Lennie lowered his eyes briefly, and said nothing. Mary watched him carefully, as he sipped his tea. It was her first real chance to get a closer look at him, and she felt attracted to his ruddy complexion, sandy-coloured hair, and what looked like a day's growth of stubble on his face and chin.

'She gets confused,' said Lennie, his blue eyes looking up at her. 'It's mainly because she can't remember things. Just before the war started she had a kind of breakdown. She can't do things for herself any more, so I look after her.'

Mary was puzzled. 'But what about your dad?' she asked. 'Didn't you say he worked round here somewhere?'

'He and my mum split up years ago,' replied Lennie, lowering his eyes and returning to his tea again. 'They hadn't been getting on well for quite a time, so he – well – he walked out on her. I was s'pposed to be called up for the Army, but because there was no one else to look after mum, I got exempt.'

'That wasn't very nice of your dad, was it?'

Lennie's eyes flicked up in anger at her. 'What do *you* know about it? What does *anyone* know? That's the trouble with people. They always have to interfere in things they know nothing about.'

Mary was quite taken aback by his sudden outburst. 'I'm sorry,' she said, embarrassed. 'I didn't mean to interfere. I just thought—'

Lennie put down his cup, and stood with his back towards her at the oven grate. 'I'm sorry. I didn't mean *you*,' he said forlornly, his voice barely audible. He remained silent for a brief moment, then started to mumble. 'They just didn't get on, that's all. I didn't blame Dad.' He turned around to face her. 'I didn't blame Mum neither. Trouble is, she'd been spoilt all her life. Everyone spoiled her – my gran and granddad, my Uncle Ron – everyone spoilt her. It just – pushed her over the edge.' Aware that he had shared perhaps too much with a complete stranger, he went back to sit opposite Mary at the table and changed the subject. 'Mr Barrington says you work in a restaurant.'

Lennie's change of mood helped Mary to relax. 'Well, I wouldn't exactly call it a restaurant,' she replied lightly. 'It's more like a glorified café. But it serves a cause. The food's cheap, and you can sometimes get food there that you can't always get on the ration.'

'But you like working there?'

Mary shrugged. 'I wouldn't exactly say that,' she replied. 'It's not easy to look after my brother and sisters and Granddad on the wages they pay me. And there are rumours that as soon as the war's over, they'll be shutting the place down.'

'Why don't you get a better-paid job?' asked Lennie, who seemed genuinely concerned.

'There's a war on,' she replied, after a sip of tea. 'I wouldn't know where to start looking.'

Lennie paused for a moment before speaking again. 'Maybe I could help you,' he said.

The Marlborough Theatre, or the Marlborough Picture Theatre as it had once been known, nestled comfortably between two nondescript buildings in the Holloway Road, directly opposite the Nag's Head pub. Designed by the great theatre architect Frank Matcham, whose master-pieces included the Hippodrome and Palladium theatres in London, together with the magnificent London Coliseum, and the majestic Grand Theatre in Blackpool, the Marlborough had once been home to opera, ballet, music hall, and the 'new age' of both silent and sound films. True, its exterior had seen better days, but not even the great London Blitz of 1940 had deterred its regular crowd of cinemagoers from queuing up for their much-needed ration of fantasy and escapism. Mary had been to the Marlborough many times. When her mum and dad were alive, the Trimble family had often sat together side by side in the plush red stalls, munching their mum's spam and pickle sandwiches, drinking hot tea from a vacuum flask or cups of lemonade and Tizer. 'Picture Night' at the Marlborough was like an indoor picnic at the picture house they all loved best. That's why the idea of getting a job in the place filled Mary with excitement – and trepidation.

'Dad's been a projectionist here now for over twenty years,' said Lennie, as he and Mary made their way up the well-worn stone staircase at the rear of the theatre which led to the projection room in the gallery area of the auditorium. 'I don't know how he manages. He lost a foot in the trenches in the last war. The artifical one they gave him has never fitted properly.'

Mary followed Lennie up the steps, hardly able to see anything in the dim flickering light from the gas lamps on the wall of each landing.

The first continuous double-bill programme of the day was in full swing. The 'B' feature detective thriller, *The Falcon Strikes Back*, had just given way to the colourful main feature musical, *Greenwich Village*, and as Lennie led Mary into the projection room, the soundtrack of the effervescent 'Brazilian bombshell', Carmen Miranda, competed with her dazzling Technicolor image on the flickering cinema screen down below.

'Dad,' said Lennie, with Mary at his side. 'This is Mary Trimble.'

'Oh yes,' replied Ernie Backer, whose attention was very much focused on the film running through the film gate of the projector. 'And who's Mary Trimble?'

Lennie's reply was a bit faltering. 'She's – a friend of mine.'

Ernie turned round to look. Mary was standing quite nervously near the door, the flickering light from the projector dancing across her face. 'Please ter meet you, little lady,' he said, with a smile.

Relieved, Mary smiled back.

'Is that job still goin'?' asked Lennie. 'The one downstairs?'

'The part-time?' asked Ernie, after taking a quick check of the screen through the projection hole. He shrugged. 'Far as I know. Unless old Bickley's got someone else in mind.'

'Could you put in a word for Mary?' Lennie asked. 'She could do with the cash. She's got a family to keep.'

'Brother and sisters,' Mary added quickly. 'And my granddad.'

Ernie came back to them. He was now having to compete with a song from Carmen Miranda's leading man, Don Ameche. 'Where'd yer come from, little lady?' he asked. In the dim, flickering light he looked a bit like his son.

'Just round the corner,' replied Mary. 'Roden Street. It's just behind the Nag's Head.'

Ernie nodded, wiped his hands on a greasy rag. 'Don't worry,' he replied, with a grin. 'I know Roden Street all right. Used ter 'ave a lady friend lived round there – till she ditched me. 'Ave yer ever worked in a pitture house before?'

Mary flicked an anxious glance at Lennie. 'No, I haven't,' she replied.

'But she's been here lots of times,' added Lennie. 'She saw *Sweeney Todd* here. Isn't that right, Mary?'

Mary nodded vigorously.

Ernie shook his head. 'Pretty nasty bit of work fer a young gel like you, I would have thought,' he replied. 'Todd Slaughter cuttin' people's throats ain't everyone's cup of tea.'

'I love going to the pictures, Mr Backer,' said Mary, almost pleading. 'All my family do.'

'It's one fing sittin' down watchin' a pitture, little lady,' said Ernie. 'It's diff'rent when you 'ave ter show people ter their seats. If anyone trips over in the dark, the poor ol' usherette's the one who takes the blame.'

'Come on, Dad,' pleaded Lennie. 'Do me a favour. Have a word with old Bickley.'

Ernie looked from his son to Mary. He liked the girl, there was no doubt about that – well, what he could see of her in the dim light of the projection room. 'All I can do is ter ask,' he said, going to the internal telephone on the wall. 'The ol' man's got a mind of 'is own.' He took the receiver and dialled.

Mary bit her lip anxiously.

40

''Ello,' Ernie called down the telephone. 'Is that you, Mavis? 'As the ol' man got anyone fer the part-time yet?' He listened, then, without giving anything away, turned to look across at Mary and Lennie. 'Right. Is he in 'is office now? OK. Just tell 'im I'm sendin' someone down to apply fer the job. 'Er name's Mary Trimble. I'll bring 'er down while 'Arry's on the organ. Righto, Mave, ta.' He replaced the receiver and turned to Mary. 'As soon as the pitture's finished, yer can go down. But I can't promise nuffin'.'

A short while later, Mary and Lennie were standing at the box office talking to Mavis, the cashier. As she waited to be called into the manager's office nearby, Mary was as nervous as hell, watching patrons arriving for the next performance, some of them hanging around the plush foyer to look over the posters for the coming attractions, and listening to the sound of Harry Percival at the Compton organ inside, playing to customers already seated for the continuous performance.

'Don't worry, darlin',' said Mavis, the middle-aged cashier, after she had dispensed two ninepenny tickets in the stalls. 'The ol' man won't eat yer. 'E can be a bit on the grumpy side from time ter time, but beneath it all, 'e's got a 'eart er gold.'

'Mary Trimble?'

Mary shuddered as she heard her name called from the open door of the manager's office.

'Good luck,' said Lennie. 'Remember, it's only a job.'

Mary smiled gratefully at him, and hurried into the manager's office.

'Nice girl,' said Mavis, peering through the cashier's window. 'Let's hope you have better luck with this one.'

Lennie threw her a look of thunder, and stormed off through the front entrance of the foyer. For a few moments, he stood at the top of the steps outside, and stared aimlessly at the passing traffic. Although it was only mid-afternoon, there seemed to be a lot of people around, most of them on the opposite side of Holloway Road where the main stores like Marks and Spencer's, Woolworths, Selby's and, further down, the ever popular Jones Brothers store, were. A lot was going through his mind, things that he never talked about to anyone, things that he

41

would certainly never talk to Mary about. The trouble was, however, it wasn't easy to bottle them up, especially after what had happened such a short time ago . . .

'So where did *this* one come from?'

Lennie swung around to find his dad lighting up a fag just behind him.

'D'you have to talk like that?' Lennie replied, irritably.

'I'm only askin,' said Ernie. 'I wouldn't've spoken up for 'er if I din't think she was worf it. Where d'yer meet 'er?'

Lennie sighed, subconsciously moved down one step, and watched a tram pulling alongside the bus and tram stop. 'She was on the Eaglet beano,' he replied reluctantly. 'They stopped near the house. Her young brother fell in the river, an' I pulled 'im out.'

Ernie pulled a face. 'Blimey,' he gasped. 'Did yer tell 'er how dangerous that river is? Did you tell her that girl—'

'Look, Dad!' snapped Lennie, swinging back on him. 'I don't need a cross-examination. Of course I told her, but by that time it was too late. Carole Pickard was stupid. Everyone knows that. She tried to ruin my life.' He could tell by his dad's expression that he didn't believe a word he was saying. 'I came down 'ere to tell Mary everything,' he calmed himself, 'that I was sorry for the way I talked to her, and to find out if her brother was OK after falling in the river.'

Ernie took out the pocket watch from his waistcoat, and whilst he was glancing at it, some of the audience inside were just leaving at the end of Harry Percival's intermission organ show. 'Well, let's 'ope she gets the job,' he said, taking a pull on his fag.

'It doesn't matter to me if she does or if she doesn't.'

Ernie flicked a critical look up at his son, and put his watch back into his pocket. 'Then why d'yer get me ter speak up for 'er?'

Lennie had to think about that, so much so that he didn't answer.

'So she doesn't know about Carole?'

Lennie froze. 'Don't you think it's about time you went back to work?'

Ernie grinned, dropped his fag on the step, stubbed it out, and started to go back inside. But he stopped briefly and turned to look back at the boy. 'Don't make the same mistake as me, son,' he said. 'It ain't worf it.' He turned, and hurried back into the picture house.

Mary was over the moon. The moment she left the manager's office the only person she wanted to see was Lennie. What he had done for her was beyond her wildest dreams. She had a second job which was not only going to help pay for the family's day-to-day expenses, but was also going to give her something to look forward to in the evenings. Mary had always loved going to the 'pictures', and the fact that she could watch them free of charge in between showing people to their seats every evening was such an exciting thought that she couldn't wait to get home to tell her sisters and brother. But as she made her way through the Marlborough's foyer, she was surprised to find that Lennie was not waiting for her.

''E's gone home,' said Mavis, the cashier, calling through the round hole in the window of her entrance desk.

'Gone home?' asked Mary. 'Why?'

Mavis shook her head despairingly. 'You don't ask Lennie Backer questions like that, dear,' she said. ''E's a funny boy. Does things at the drop of a hat, no rhyme, nor reason.'

'But didn't he leave a message for me?' asked Mary, puzzled and confused.

Mavis shook her head. ''E looked pretty grumpy ter me,' she said, with a wry grin. 'Somethin' must've upset 'im. But then somethin's always upsetting 'im. You hardly ever see a smile on that boy's face.'

Mary bit her lip anxiously.

'But did yer get the job?' asked Mavis eagerly.

Mary smiled, and nodded enthusiastically.

'Oh, that's wonderful, dear,' said Mavis. 'We'll be able ter have some lovely old chinwags.'

A few minutes later, Mary crossed Holloway Road and hurried past the Nag's Head pub into Seven Sisters Road. But she had hardly got there when the air-raid siren wailed out from the roof of the badly bombed Hornsey Road police station. She quickened her pace, turned off down Enkel Street behind the back entrance of Woolworths department store, all the while hoping that Granddad had got the kids into the Anderson shelter in the backyard. However, just as she had reached the corner of Roden Street, the air was pierced by the now familiar throbbing sound of a buzz bomb, its engines racing across the early evening sky, and when she saw everyone in the street lying flat on their stomachs on the pavements she had no alternative but to do the same. Within a few seconds, the deadly killer plane was passing right overhead, and when the chilling sound of the engines suddenly cut out, there followed the most heart-stopping silence as everyone tensed for the inevitable explosion. When it came, the whole street shook, with windows shattering and roof tiles smashing into the tiny front gardens below.

It seemed like hours to Mary, as she lay spreadeagled on the pavement, shaking with terror and apprehension, before she could relax, when she eventually heard the distant ringing of ambulance and fire-engine bells, and the panicked calls of alarm from her neighbours along the street.

'Here, Mary,' called the voice of someone standing over her. 'Let me help you.'

Mary turned over on to one side to find a hand lifting her up. 'Thank you,' she said with effort, her whole body still shaking with fright. She took hold of the hand, which gently eased her to her feet. But when she looked into the face of the person who was standing there, she was shocked to see that it was the Chinese woman who had been causing her such concern. 'You!' she gasped, quickly pulling her hand away.

'You have a cut on your forehead, Mary,' said Tanya Ling, whose jet-black hair, unlike Mary's, seemed to be completely unruffled. 'Here.' She took a small handkerchief from her pocket, and attempted to dab the small trickle of blood coming from a cut on Mary's forehead.

'You keep away from me!' snapped Mary, pulling away from her. 'You stay away from my family!' She turned and started to hurry off down the road towards home. 'I'm going to get the police,' she yelled as she went. 'D'you hear? I'm going to call the police. You're to stop following me!'

To Mary's astonishment, Tanya quickly followed her, her whole body moving as fast and as gracefully as a gazelle's. 'No, Mary!' she called, as she reached her and held on to her. 'You don't understand. You just don't understand.'

'Get away from me!' Mary was now shouting out loud.

'Wos up, Mary?' yelled one of the neighbours from a first-floor window. 'Wos she up to?'

Mary was about to shout back, but she turned her anger on to Tanya. 'Don't you understand?' she said forcefully, eyes glaring, a trickle of blood beginning to race down her face. 'You have no right to follow me – nor any member of my family. We don't like you, and we don't want you! Is that clear?' She didn't wait for an answer, but merely rushed off as fast as she could down the road.

It was only a short moment before Tanya called after her. 'That's not the way your mother felt,' she called.

This immediately brought Mary to a halt. She slowly turned round to cast an astonished look at the Chinese woman.

Tanya went to her. 'I loved your mother,' she said with a gentle, agonised expression. '*She* didn't hate me. She was my friend – my *best* friend. Don't you understand? I want to remember her. That's all, Mary. I want to remember her.'

Chapter 4

When Thelma, Dodo and Billy got home from school, they were a bit put out to find themselves barred from the front room just because their sister was deep in conversation with the Chinese woman. Needless to say, Billy's curiosity got the better of him, so he did his best to listen at the keyhole until Granddad grabbed one of his rather large ears and yanked him back into the back parlour.

'Your mother was a very special woman,' said Tanya Ling, who was sitting in the middle of the small two-seater sofa sipping from a cup of plain tea without milk. Mary was amazed how composed and serene her visitor was. Tanya's snow-coloured face was almost expressionless, like fine porcelain which looked as though it could suddenly break. 'The moment your mother came into my life, she was like a sister to me. At that time, I was very alone and without friends. My husband was away fighting in the British army.'

'But what was a Chinese man doing in the British army?' Mary asked naïvely. She had so many questions that needed answering she hardly knew where to start.

'Oh, Robert wasn't Chinese,' replied Tanya, putting down her teacup and gently dabbing the corner of her tiny blood-red lips with her handkerchief. 'He was as English as you are, born right here, just a few minutes, away, in Tollington Road. He and I met in London long before the war, soon after my family came here from Hong Kong. At the beginning of the war, my Robert and your father met on the troopship they were on, going across to France.'

Mary listened wide-eyed. 'My father?' she asked, totally astonished. 'You mean, my dad *knew* your husband?'

Tanya smiled, her dark eyes meeting Mary's with a look of strange affection. 'Oh yes,' she replied wistfully. 'The two of them became firm friends. In fact, they were inseparable.' Her spoken English was still faintly tinged with a soft Chinese accent, and the fact that she could not properly pronounce her 'r's made her sound even more attractive. 'It was during that time that I got to know your mother really well. Because my Robert had talked about how lonely I was, your father had written to your mother suggesting that she should come to see me. I was a little nervous at first. You and your parents were living over a furniture shop in Hornsey Road at the time, and I was sure there would be quite a few hostile glances from your neighbours, which is why I told your mother it would be better for me not to meet any of her family. But, from the moment I went to see her, we got on like "a house on fire".' Tanya smiled again, amused that over the years she had picked up such an English expression. 'We spent nearly two hours sipping tea and talking about our husbands. I remember she had such a lovely sense of humour. We laughed a lot together.'

Now it was Mary's turn to smile. Yes, she also remembered her mum's lovely sense of humour, always teasing Mary's dad whenever he was in a grumpy mood, always laughing when she'd burnt something on the stove. But this friendship between her mum and this Chinese woman baffled her.

'I know you're curious,' continued Tanya, the early evening light streaming through the lace curtains at the window behind her. 'And you have every right to be. You see, when your father came back home to England, my Robert was posted to Gibraltar where he went down with a terrible illness, and died.' She clasped her hands together forlornly, then rested them on her knees. 'The trouble was,' she said with difficulty, 'I then resented the fact that your father was the one who lived, and not my Robert. Oh, I know it was a stupid way to think – so wicked – and I've always felt so guilty about it. But your mother – *she* knew, *she* understood. "Everything is meant", she said. "Everything is decided by someone higher than us, someone who has their own reason why we must never understand.'"

To Mary, the Chinese woman suddenly looked vulnerable, and even though she was still a reasonably young woman, during those fleeting few moments, Tanya seemed to become several years older than her age.

Immediately composing herself, Tanya sat up straight. 'I've always remembered those words,' she said. 'In fact, they helped me to stop feeling sorry for myself and get some sleep at night. But then,' she stopped, and purposefully glanced across at a framed photograph of Mary's parents on the mantelpiece over the fireplace, 'then – I never saw them again – neither your mother nor your father. In fact, for years, I deliberately lost all contact with them. I moved out of the house in Tollington Road and went to live in Kentish Town. I had to get away, I had to break with the past, with anyone who might remind me of all the happiness I had shared with Robert. It was just too painful, more than I could bear.' She put down her teacup on the small table at the side of the sofa, and whilst staring at it aimlessly, she said, 'I met your mother again just a few months before she died in that terrible tube accident.' She looked up at Mary again. There was real anguish in her eyes. 'She came to visit me at my rooms in Kentish Town.'

Mary was finding it hard to take this in. 'But – if you hadn't met during all that time, how did she find you?'

Tanya smiled winsomely. 'She had seen a photograph of me at one of my exhibitions,' she said. 'It was in one of the local newspapers – the *North London Press*.'

'Exhibitions?'

'Oh, nothing important, I can assure you,' replied Tanya, with a chuckle. 'It's just that people fascinate me – the way they look, the way they move, their change of moods. That's why I sketch them. I've been doing it ever since I was a child back home in Hong Kong. Your mother had always known that. It's why she came to see me. I was so astonished when I saw her standing on my doorstep. I felt as though time had stood still, as though we had never drifted apart. It was a truly amazing experience. I remember I cried a lot!'

'This is all very interesting, Mrs Ling,' said Mary impatiently, 'but I don't understand why neither my mum nor dad ever mentioned you to me nor any of our family.'

Tanya lowered her eyes. 'Oh,' she sighed, 'your mother really *wanted* us to meet, but I was adamant. As it so happens,' she added ruefully, 'when I think how ignorant people can be, I'm sure I was right.'

'Then why did Mum come to see you?'

Tanya wanted to look up at Mary, but she just didn't have the courage. 'Mary,' she replied with difficulty, 'there is something you never knew about your mother – something no one knew, not even your father.' She finally found the strength to look up into Mary's eyes. 'When she came to see me that day, she told me that she was suffering from a terrible illness, and she was convinced that she hadn't long to live.'

Mary was shocked. 'Mum?' she asked with incomprehension. 'I don't believe it. I remember she had some rotten headaches—'

'She was dying, Mary,' replied Tanya earnestly. 'The reason she didn't tell your father, or you or the rest of your family, is because she couldn't bear the thought of all of you knowing what she was going through. She loved your father and all of you very much. But forgive me if I tell you that she had a very special place in her heart for *you*.'

Without realising it, Mary was shaking. For some reason or other, she felt resentment rather than gratitude. Who *was* this woman who had suddenly come into her life, purporting to know something about her mum that nobody in the world had ever known? 'Why should Mum have told *you* and nobody else? If what you say is true, what made her come to see *you* of all people, after all those years?'

Tanya sank back in the sofa and crossed her hands in her lap. 'Because she wanted me to do something for her, something I can only tell you about when the time is right.'

Mary was now more suspicious than ever. 'I don't know what you're talking about,' she replied tersely. 'What d'you mean – *when the time is right*?'

For a brief moment, Tanya remained silent. 'You have to trust me, Mary,' she said calmly, her lips hardly moving as she talked. 'You can be assured that I *will* know when the moment is right, and when I do, I shall do what your mother asked me to do. Until that time comes, all I ask of you is that you trust me.'

Granddad Trimble was not at all pleased when Mary told him that, in addition to her job as a waitress up at the restaurant, she had now got a part-time job at the Marlborough cinema, which meant that he would have to pull his weight around the house by getting the kids' tea ready for them when they got home from school each day. Work had never been one of Granddad's favourite pastimes. Even when his wife Winnie was alive, he had never lifted a finger to help her do anything even resembling work around their house up at Tottenham, and during the twenty years he had worked as a fitter at the Gas, Light and Coke Company in Seven Sisters Road, he had long held the record for being the employee who had taken more days off for sick leave than anyone else in the company. 'I'm not a bleedin' skivvy!' he snapped when Mary told him what she expected him to do from now on. But Mary was having none of it. As *she* was the only wage-earner in the family, it was her opinion that the least the old boy could do was to stop propping up the Eaglet's saloon bar and give her a bit of support.

Mary's two sisters and brother were not at all troubled that their big sister was not going to be around in the evenings. As long as they got their tea every night, they were only too happy that they could be left to do what they wanted without being watched and bullied and made to go to bed early. In fact, for Thelma, it was a dream come true.

Lennie Backer got off the Green Line bus on the fringe of Epping Forest. Although it was only a ten-minute walk home to the old farmhouse, it was a muggy late afternoon and, as he made his way through the forest, it wasn't long before he had to wipe the sweat from his forehead. At this moment, Lennie had a lot on his mind. He was thinking about Mary Trimble. He was thinking an awful lot about her, more than was safe for him to do so. After his one previous experience of having a relationship he had always told himself that he would never do anything like that again. But this was different. *Mary Trimble* was different. But if she *had* got the job at the picture house, would he go to see her again? He didn't know. He just didn't know.

The Backer farmhouse nestled snugly amongst tall oak and chestnut trees, which swayed gently back and forth in a light evening breeze. The old house was an early twentieth-century building made of brick and mortar, but because it was in bad need of renovation, it was a ramshackle place. Even the wrought-iron gate in the front garden was so rusty that it had remained wedged open for years. The garden itself, which was once a blaze of colourful summer stocks and English roses, was now a vegetable allotment, which, most days, Lennie toiled in as a way of providing fresh food for him and his mum. 'I'm home!' he called, as he approached the front door. This was a ritual he had grown used to over the previous few years, letting her know that he was home before he had actually entered the house. As the front door was locked only at night, he walked straight in. In the large open hallway with brown paint peeling from the walls, he was met by the familiar smell of soapsuds. 'Oh no,' he groaned, making straight for the washroom on the other side of the kitchen. Sure enough, a large aluminium tub was in the stone sink there, steaming with hot soapy water, one of Lennie's shirts on the scrubbing board waiting for attention.

'Ma!' he yelled, looking everywhere for her. But he knew where to go to find her, *exactly* where to go.

She was in the barnyard, hanging up clothes on the washing line, wearing the same dress and long apron she wore practically every day of her life, her straight, prematurely grey hair dangling wildly over her shoulders.

As soon as he saw her, Lennie sighed in despair. 'Oh, Ma!' he groaned. 'What d'you think you're doin'?'

Winnie Backer turned round to face him. Her large oval eyes which had once been a radiant violet colour, were now faded, and virtually bulged out of a thin, pale face. The moment she saw him she took out the peg she was holding between her teeth. 'Got to keep it all clean,' she said, slow and methodically. 'Cleanliness is next to Godliness.'

Lennie's reaction was irritable, but sensitive. 'I did all the washing yesterday. You don't have to do it all over again.'

He eased his arm around her waist and gently led her to a wooden bench outside what had once been a horse stable. Once he was sure that she was settled comfortably, he sat down alongside her. 'You know you don't have to do any of the chores. That's what I'm here for.'

Winnie smiled. It was a lovely, true smile. It made her look like she was really quite young, far too young to have lost a grip on things. 'That's what your dad said.'

Lennie looked at her warily. 'Dad?'

'Yes,' she replied confidently. 'He popped in to see me today. He said he was sorry he hadn't been home for a while, but that you'd make up for him. He's looking older these days. I told him so. I told him he must take more care of himself.'

This sudden rambling was something that Lennie had come to expect of his mum. It had been a long time since his dad had walked out on her; he hadn't set foot in the place since the great row took place on that fateful Easter Monday before the war. Lennie put his arm around his mum's waist. He still found it hard to believe that fate could have been so cruel as to attack her mind in such a way, a severe nervous breakdown which had led to premature senility. Under normal circumstances she was still young enough to have a full life, even to be attracted to other men, but something inside that poor, tired head just refused to allow her to blossom. It was as though she was sleeping whilst still awake. 'Why don't we go inside?' he said. 'I'll make you a nice cup of tea.'

'Still,' she said, talking as though she hadn't heard a word the boy had said, 'your dad likes that nice new girl of yours.'

Lennie's eyes flashed back at her. 'What?' he spluttered. 'Who – how did—'

'He says she's much better than the last one – that awful one who—' She suddenly broke off, and like a startled animal, shot a terrified look up towards the sky. 'Sssssh!' she gasped.

Lennie looked up with her, baffled, as always, by her sudden changes of mood. 'It's nothin', Ma.'

'Listen!'

Lennie watched, waited and listened, but could hear nothing but the leaves rustling in the trees, and a cheeky sparrow chirping impatiently for some scraps nearby. Apart from that, the silence was deafening. 'It's nothin', Ma,' he repeated after a moment's pause.

Winnie's eyes remained firmly focused on the sky, until just when Lennie was about to try and lead her back into the house, there came the distant sound that only *she* had heard. Gradually, high above them, the now familiar churning of the flying bomb's engines approached at speed.

'Oh God!' gasped Lennie, quickly grabbing his mum around the waist. 'Down, Ma, down!'

Pulling her to the ground, he immediately shielded her with his own body, keeping her face pressed to the ground. As he did so, the sound of the flying bomb, which was now only a short distance away, cut out abruptly, and was followed by a swish of air as the machine came crashing down into a nearby field. Winnie screamed out in terror as the explosion rocked the farmhouse, causing one or two tiles to slide off the roof. In a moment, it was all over.

Lennie waited for his mum to calm down, then gently eased her face and shoulders off the ground. 'You're all right, Ma,' he said, comforting her. 'No harm done.' But as he held her in his arms and brushed away the hair that had fallen across her face, he was astonished to see that she was smiling up at him.

'If you marry her,' she said, without any connection to what had just happened, 'will *you* leave me too?'

The next day, Mary turned up at the British Restaurant with mixed feelings. Although she had enjoyed working there as a daily waitress, she had decided that, with her new part-time job as an usherette, she needed more time during the mornings to do the family chores at home and so she had to resign. However, when she broke the news to Sheila Nestor, her supervisor, she was taken aback by her response. 'Makes no difference now, Mary,' she said, gloomily. 'They're closing us down next week.'

'Closing down?' asked Mary, with incomprehension. 'The restaurant?'

'The council say that as the war's nearly over, during the next few years there'll be no more use for places like this. What they really mean, of course, is they want to save money.'

Mary shook her head in disbelief. 'How can they say the war's over when these planes are coming down on us every day?'

'I know,' replied Sheila, who was smoking the last of her fags sitting in the open kitchen doorway. 'One of the cops on duty outside the tube station told me that ten of these damned things came down yesterday in the London area alone. I don't even know what we're supposed to call them – buzz bombs, flying bombs, doodlebugs? I mean, where the hell did they dig up a name like doodlebug?'

'My dad calls 'em a Jerry with 'is arse on fire!' called Mary's friend Maisie Stringer as she came into the kitchen carrying a pile of clean plates.

'Don't be so vulgar, Maisie,' chided Sheila. 'This is not a comic turn up the Finsbury Park Empire. This is people getting killed every day!'

Maisie shrugged her shoulders and quickly returned to laying tables in the restaurant.

'Still,' said Sheila, stubbing out her fag on the step outside, 'at least it looks as though we've seen the last of that woman who's been hounding you. She hasn't been in for days now.'

Mary was putting on her white apron.

'You haven't seen anything of her, have you?' asked Sheila.

'Yes,' Mary replied casually, 'as a matter of fact, I have. She came to see me at home. In fact, she's a very nice woman.'

Sheila watched her with astonishment. 'She came to visit you – in your own home?'

'Yes,' said Mary. 'Her name's Ling, Tanya Ling. But that's not her married name.'

Sheila was completely taken aback, so much so that she went to the restaurant door and stood there to prevent anyone coming in. 'How could you let a woman like that into your own home?' she hissed, lowering her voice. 'Knowing what her people have been doing to our boys out in the Far East?'

'Sheila!' spluttered Mary. 'What're you talking about?'

'She's from Japan,' retorted Sheila. 'Don't you know the Japs are our enemy? They're absolutely ruthless people.'

Mary clasped her forehead in despair. 'Sheila,' she said, going to her, 'Tanya isn't Japanese. She's from China. She was born in Hong Kong. She was married to a British man who died from cholera whilst he was serving in the British army in Gibraltar. They were both friends of my own mum and dad.'

Sheila stared at her. Suddenly she felt humiliated. She walked away from Mary and went to the serving table to start preparing food.

Mary went to her, surprised and puzzled by the woman's strange reaction. 'Sheila,' she said softly, 'Tanya is really a very nice woman.'

Sheila swung round on her. 'She's still a foreigner!' she snapped. 'You've only got to look at her eyes, to see how shifty they are, watching you, conniving. That's the trouble with this country. If we paid more attention to our own people there wouldn't be so many wars!'

Mary was completely taken aback by her supervisor's outburst. It was so irrational, so difficult to understand. 'There's nothing wrong with being foreign, Sheila,' she replied, almost defensively. 'As long as people get along with each other.'

'You see!' barked Sheila. 'That's what they do. She's twisted your mind. Well, if that's the kind of friend you want, then you might just as well get off to your posh new job today – right now. Take off your apron. I'll go and get your wages.'

'Sheila, please!' begged Mary. 'There's no reason for me to be unpleasant to Tanya. I blame myself for the way I talked about her. But

55

I was wrong. She's a good woman, Sheila. To my knowledge she hasn't done anything wrong in her whole life.'

'Is that so?' Sheila called from the restaurant door. 'Well that's not what *I* heard. Now please take off your apron and get out of here!'

Mary didn't have the energy to take a bus back home to the Nag's Head. All she wanted to do was to walk, to try and work out what had turned Sheila's head in such an aggressive way. Could that really have been Sheila Nestor, she wondered, the woman who had been so kind to her in the past, helped her, guided her through those first days when she had started at the restaurant after her mum and dad had been killed? But then, in one passing moment, she realised that Sheila had been a widow since the Great War, when her husband had been killed by a German bayonet in the trenches. To Sheila a 'foreigner' was someone who was automatically hostile, and she would be embittered for the rest of her days. Making her way down Holloway Road, Mary took a passing glance over her shoulder to where the usual midday queue had formed outside the restaurant where she had worked with such dedication and enthusiasm. It was a sad, unreal departure for her, and after all the distress she had endured by losing her parents and now all the things Tanya had told her about her mum's illness, her eyes were brimming with tears.

Crossing over the main Parkhurst Road, she wandered almost aimlessly towards the Marlborough cinema, where in a few days' time she would be starting a new job, meeting new people and making, she hoped, new friends. Pausing briefly on the kerbside in Holloway Road, she stared up at the portico high above the foyer of the old picture house. Squatting in a long row along the stone balustrade was a cluster of pigeons, all preening themselves in the morning sun. She stood there for a moment watching them, hoping that when she arrived to start her new job in a few days' time they would give her a better welcome than the one she had just received in the British Restaurant.

Lennie needed his gumboots for the trek across the field at the back of the farmhouse. In the distance, he could still see the frenzied activity

56

surrounding the wrecked fuselage of the flying bomb which had crashed with a loud explosion in the field. The large crater the bomb had caused was already half filled with muddy water, and small particles of debris were scattered around everywhere. Despite the fact that the Wardens from the Air Raid Post and Special Constabulary had sealed off the area with rope barriers, several local school kids, some of them wearing their dads' tin helmets, were gathered around like vultures searching for any souvenirs they could lay their hands on.

'Lucky you an' your mum weren't nowhere near this lot,' said Arthur Morris, a Special Constable from one of the nearby villages, but who actually lived in Woodford Green further down the road from the Forest. 'Blow you off ter kingdom come, that's fer sure.' Arthur was a grey-haired man, who had served in the Horse Artillery regiment during the Dardanelles campaign, but who was more active than some folks half his age. 'Must've upset 'er, though – bein' 'ow she is.'

'She's OK,' replied Lennie. 'Bit shook up, that's all.'

'Well, you'll be getting a bit er company later on today,' continued Arthur, his face bright red from a day standing around in the hot sunshine. 'The army's bringin' in some Jerry POWs from the camp other side of Haverhill. They're goin' ter put some of those buggers ter work on clearin' this lot. Since their mates sent the bleedin' things over, they can get on with it. Too many good folk've died, thanks ter these contraptions.' He sighed, adding cynically, 'And they tell us the war's nearly over!'

A few minutes later, the 'Specials' had cleared the area, leaving Lennie alone to wander around the mangled pieces of metal, and the remains of the swastika emblem on what was left of the fuselage. He turned to look around the field, and the first thing that came to his mind was the extraordinary way his mum had behaved at the time of the explosion. How did she know about Mary, when he knew only too well that his dad hadn't been to see his wife for years? Her mind never stopped baffling Lennie. Of course he was only too aware that she lived in a kind of dream world, where she could make things up in her mind and then believe them. But this was different. Apart from that Sunday afternoon when she had seen Mary through the window talking to him outside the house, how could she possibly know anything about her? There were times when Winnie Backer had no idea *what* she was doing, such as doing the same washing over and over again. Then there were other times, brief though they were, when she came out with something quite alarming, quite clear and succinct. It was cruel, so cruel that she had been robbed of so much, and at such an important period of her life. As he strolled aimlessly through the muddy field, he tried to work out what it was that first sent his mum over the edge. Yes, it *was* true that she *had* been spoilt all her life, but it was really the break-up of her marriage that was certainly the start of it all, and it hadn't helped that his dad had just walked out on her in the middle of the night without a word of warning. Yes, it was cruel, so very cruel, and it had been very difficult for him to cope with the aftermath of that broken marriage. If only he had had a brother or a sister, someone he could talk to. Someone like Mary. He came to a sudden halt, startled by the idea that he was giving some credence to a girl he hardly knew. For a moment, he stood there in silence, alone with his thoughts, alone with his despair, a gentle breeze ruffling his wavy sandy-coloured hair. High above, a lark fluttered its tiny wings in a dazzling display of joyful energy, whilst singing one of the many songs from its repertoire. There were many other birds skimming the fields too, swooping high and low, anxious to see what all the human activity had done to expose the grubs beneath the surface of the muddy field. Yes, they were all there – seagulls, pigeons, sparrows, lapwings, swallows. Especially the swallows.

Chapter 5

Most of the staff at the Marlborough Picture House knew the manager, Alfred Bickley, as 'the old man'. Not that he *was* particularly old, he was probably no more than in his mid-sixties, but he always seemed to give the impression that he was older than he really was. Mary liked him the moment she met him. When she sat in front of the desk in his tiny office behind the cashier's kiosk he was charm itself. Some folk said he had a bit of a roving eye, but if that was true, Mary had had no hint of it. And as he took her on a tour of the auditorium to 'show her the ropes', he couldn't have been more kind or considerate.

'Ever seen a pitture house without the audience?' asked Alfred, looking around the deserted auditorium. He was quite an ample little man, whose balding grey hair actually made him look quite distinguished. 'Not the same is it? This place only comes to life when there's something going on up there on the screen. But there's something else when the place is empty. No. There's nothing like the atmosphere of a pitture house.'

Mary followed him down the side aisle of the auditorium, admiring the plush red seats everywhere, despite the fact that many of them needed replacing. The 'old man' was right. There was no atmosphere like that of a picture house, right down to the lingering smell of cigarette smoke from the previous night's performance. Somehow her red usherette's uniform seemed to blend in with it all.

'Sorry we couldn't give you a brand *new* uniform,' said Alfred, as he reached the pit in front of the stage. 'Trouble is the company won't give us more clothing coupons to have any new ones made. Still, the young gel who was here before you was about your size. And just in case you're wonderin', my missus did wash and iron it over the weekend!'

Mary loved the way 'the old man' chuckled to himself. His large stomach shook so much so that it looked as though the strain would burst his collar button.

'Now, you take this stage,' continued Alfred. 'It's seen a few top-bill names in its time. In the ol' days, of course, it was all plays and things, but we've had quite a lot of variety stars here too. D'you know, we had George Formby here a few months ago?'

'Yes,' replied Mary enthusiastically. 'I'd love to have seen him.'

'Oh, you missed a lot, little lady,' said Alfred, gazing longingly at the empty stage and drawn, plush green curtains. 'He was a riot. The place was packed out to the gods, and they loved him! Had his missus, Beryl, playing for him on the piano. Right madam, that one! Every time she thought no one was around, she bossed the daylights out of the poor bloke. Can you believe, she wore a fur coat on the stage 'cos she said the place was freezin' cold! But George – now there's a real trouper!' To emphasise the point, he started to hum George Formby's famous song, 'When I'm Cleaning Windows'.

'Can I ask a question please, Mr Bickley?'

Alfred swung her a look as if she was going to ask for an increase in her wage. 'You can,' he replied peering over the top of his tortoise-shell spectacles, 'as long as it's not about money.'

Mary smiled. 'No, nothing like that,' she said. 'It's that I was wondering what I would have to do when there's an air raid?'

'Nothin'!' assured the 'old man' emphatically. 'I'm sure you've been here when the siren goes. Most people don't take a blind bit er notice. All they care about is seein' the pitture they've paid good money for. It takes more than Jerry's buzz bombs to empty the Marlborough!'

Although Mary agreed with what he had said, she still had a nagging feeling about what might happen if the place suffered a direct hit during a performance.

'No, dear,' continued Alfred, looking up at the Compton organ. 'As long as you make sure the customers know where the exits are, all you have to do is to shine your torch for them – and make sure they keep their voices down so the people inside can hear the pitture.' He turned his attention to the grand Compton organ at the front of the stage, where Harry Percival would soon be playing a popular musical extravaganza for the matinée audience. 'I'll get Alice to introduce you to 'Arry in between the double bill. 'Course, he's only temporary while our resident ol' Chuckbutty's away on sick leave.'

'Oh yes,' replied Mary. 'I've seen Mr Chuckbutty playing here lots of times. He's quite famous, isn't he?'

'Famous?' Alfred nearly choked on the word. 'Did you know that Wilson Oliphant Chuckbutty has played for royalty? *And* he's written a lot of his own music.'

Mary had very little time to be impressed before being interrupted by Alice, the stalls usherette, who was calling from the entrance door at the back of the auditorium. 'They're queuin' outside for the one and sixes, Guv'nor. Shall we start lettin' 'em in?'

'Five minutes, Alice!' returned Alfred, his voice booming out in the empty auditorium. 'Give Mary a chance to have a look round the circle.'

A few minutes later Mary was being given a lightning tour of the grand circle, which from now on was to be her 'patch'. Alice Thompson, who was in charge of the stalls, turned out to be a nice middle-aged woman and very helpful. In no time at all she had not only shown Mary how to use her torch when showing people to their seats in the dark, but also the location of the exits at the sides and back of the plush circle. 'Don't worry about a thing, dear,' said Alice reassuringly. 'It's as easy as pie. The only fings you 'ave to watch out for are too much 'anky panky in the back rows, an' young kids sneakin' in through the back door. You can always tell 'em. They're either tryin' to look as old as their mum 'n dads, or they hide under the seats when we flash our torches anywhere near 'em. If I catch the little sods, I usually give 'em a clout round the bleedin' ear'ole

61

an' chase 'em out quick as a flash. Uvver than that, just keep an eye on people comin' in in the middle of the pitture. If they break their bleedin' neck by fallin' in the dark, yer can bet yer life who gets the blame!'

Despite Alice's ripe language, Mary knew she would get on with her like a house on fire.

'Let 'em in!' The old man's voice boomed out from the stalls below.

Alice yelled back down to him. 'Comin', Guv'nor!' Before she rushed off to the rear exit, she called to Mary. 'Action stations!' She stopped briefly at the door and flashed her torch just once. 'Good luck, dear. And don't worry about the ghost. 'E's ever so friendly!'

Alice's parting remark sent a shudder down Mary's spine, and as the house lights slowly dimmed leaving her totally alone in the dark, Harry Percival let rip on the Compton organ on the front of the stage down below. The matinée performance was about to begin . . .

Later that afternoon, Thelma Trimble left Tollington Park Girls' School with her friend Amy Jenkins. The sun was still very hot, so once they were out of sight of the school, the first thing the two girls did was to take off their black school blazers, and unfasten the top two buttons of their white uniform shirts. Since she was nearly sixteen, Thelma hated wearing a school uniform. She had always maintained that if it hadn't been for the war and losing her mum and dad in that tube disaster, she would have been able to get a job just like any other sensible girl of her age. But then, not every girl of her age had an elder sister like Mary.

'Wanna fag, gels?'

Immediately recognising the voice behind them, Thelma and Amy came to an abrupt halt. They were being tailed by Jeff Bowman, who was the same age as Thelma, worked in a local sheet metal factory, and lived in Axminster Road just a stone's throw away from Thelma. The moment Thelma saw the packet of Woodbines being offered by the boy, she grabbed one without so much as a please or a thank-you. Amy was offered one too, but shook her head.

'Goin' up West this Sat'day, Thel?' asked Jeff cheekily, lighting up both their fags.

'What's it to you?' returned Thelma icily, taking a clumsy draw on her fag.

'Well, now your sister's got that job over the Marlborough, you can do what yer want – can't yer?'

Thelma glared at him. 'What I do with my time', she replied frostily, 'is nothin' to do with you, Jeff Bowman.'

'I just fawt yer might like ter come over ter *my* place for a coupla hours,' he said, with a knowing grin. He was a good-looking boy with long blond hair jutting out from beneath his flat workman's cap. 'My mum's goin' over ter see my aunt an' uncle in Waltham Cross on Sat'day afternoon. Fawt yer might like a change from chattin' up Yanks in Piccadilly.'

Amy bit her lip nervously. 'I'll see you termorrer, Thel,' she said, about to rush off.

Thelma grabbed her arm, and held her back. 'I prefer to spend my time in the company of people who know their place,' she growled haughtily at Jeff. 'People who have good manners, and who don't smoke *cheap* fags!' With that she threw down the hardly smoked cigarette he had given her, and twisted her heel into it on the pavement. She tightened her grip on Amy's arm, and led her off down the road.

Jeff watched them go with a wry grin. 'Better make hay while the sun shines, Thel!' he called, mockingly. 'Most of the Yanks are goin' off ter join the war over in France.' With no response from Thelma, he raised his voice. 'I've 'eard they much prefer the French gels!'

Refusing to turn around, Thelma merely carried on walking with Amy, but raised two fingers in a V-sign high above her head as she went.

'He really fancies you,' said Amy, as they continued walking.

'That's *his* hard luck,' replied Thelma dismissively.

'He's really good-looking,' persisted Amy.

'Then why don't *you* go out with him?' Thelma's acid reply stung Amy.

'I would in a flash, if he asked me.'

Irritated, Thelma shrugged her shoulders and walked on at a quicker pace.

'Are you *really* going up West on Saturday?' asked Amy, trying to keep up with her.

'That's *my* business!' came Thelma's terse reply.

'But what about your sister? What time does she finish round the Marlborough?'

'I don't *care* what time she finishes round the Marlborough!' snapped Thelma, now getting really annoyed with her friend. 'In a few weeks' time I'll be leaving school for good, I'll be earning my *own* living. From then on I make my own decisions about what I can and can't do. And that means I won't have to put up with stupid half-wits like Jeff Bowman.'

'The West End's a dangerous place, Thel,' warned Amy, anxiously. 'There're a lot of men round there who – who—'

'Amy Jenkins,' said Thelma, interrupting her, 'are you suggesting that I can't take care of myself?'

Amy hesitated. She had been friends with Thelma ever since they first went to junior school in Pakeman Street together, and she knew how headstrong Thelma could be. 'It's not that, Thel,' she replied with mounting concern. 'But what with the war and everything . . .'

'Haven't you heard, Amy?' replied Thelma icily. 'The war's nearly over. And when it is, I'm going to be out of this place, out of Holloway, out of Roden Street, just as fast my legs can carry me.'

Amy stopped at the street corner before turning off to go to her own home, leaving Thelma to walk on without her. 'Thel,' she called.

Thelma stopped briefly to look back over her shoulder.

'Be careful.'

Thelma threw her a haughty look, then hurried off.

Lennie Backer loaded the last of the strawberries into the back of his ancient Ford van, then went back into the house briefly to tell his mum that he would be back within an hour. As usual, the engine of the van took its time to start up, for spare parts were hard to come by, and because of the fuel ration, the vehicle could only be used for essential trips. As this was the height of the strawberry season, there was a good crop to sell to the fruit and vegetable wholesaler in nearby Epping Town, and Lennie had spent the past couple of days picking the ripe red strawberries in the allotment garden behind the house. Soon, the summer vegetables would be ready for harvesting in the last field that still belonged to the family, providing the only income for Lennie and his mum. Earlier that morning he had wandered across to the field where the flying bomb had crashed, where armed soldiers were supervising a group of German prisoners of war who had been given the task of clearing the wreckage from the site. It had been a curious experience for Lennie, for it was the only time he had come face to face with the enemy, a fact that had always made him feel guilty.

Despite the constant threat of flying bombs, the ancient town of Epping was as busy as ever. The wide High Street was bustling with shoppers, most of them there for the open-air fruit and vegetable market, which always helped to fill stomachs during the persistent wartime meat rationing. Once Lennie had delivered his crop of bright red strawberries to his usual market trader, he quickly pocketed the five pounds he'd been paid for them, and made his way back to the van. It was a hot morning, and as they struggled to weave their way in and out of the teeming crowds, most people wore as little as they could to keep cool. Behind him Lennie could hear the constant bellowing of market traders as they competed with each other for business, and from time to time their high-pitched patter produced roars of laughter from the war-weary shoppers. No one seemed to pay any attention to the thin white vapour trails which criss-crossed the clear blue sky above. The general attitude was that if one of those 'things' did get too close for comfort then they would all scatter like a flock of birds taking flight at a clap of hands. But the chat in groups everywhere was still about the war, and if and when it would ever come to an end.

'How are things, Len?'

Arthur Morris's husky voice brought Lennie to an abrupt halt just behind him.

'Fine thanks, Mr Morris,' replied Lennie, turning to greet him. 'Just got rid of the last of the strawberries. They've done very well this year.'

'I'm glad ter hear it, son,' said the old veteran, now serving as a special constable. 'You an' your mum could do with a bit of luck. How is she?'

Lennie shrugged, and put on a brave smile. 'Much the same,' he replied. 'Gets a bit confused from time to time, but on the whole, she's coping.'

'Well, I think it's wonderful the way *you* cope. Can't be easy for a young feller like you ter do all the chores *and* look after yer ma at the same time. Whoever hands out the medals should give you one too.'

The irony of the old veteran's remark did not pass unnoticed by Lennie, who merely smiled back blandly.

'Oh, by the way,' said Arthur, just as he was about to leave. 'Your Carole's over there buying tats at Charlie's barrer. She's got the baby with her.'

Lennie's eyes immediately flicked across through the crowds to where he could just see a young girl in a flimsy summer dress buying potatoes, helping the barrow boy to put them into a string carrier bag attached to the handle of the pram she had alongside. 'She's not *my* Carole, Mr Morris,' he replied, trying not to sound too terse, returning his gaze to the old veteran.

Arthur was flustered. 'No,' he replied quickly, a bit embarrassed. ''Course she's not. Sorry about that, son.' He turned to go. 'Give my best to your mum – if she remembers who I am. Cheers fer now!'

'Cheers, Mr Morris.' Lennie watched him go, but deliberately refused to look back at the girl buying potatoes at Charlie's barrow.

Back in the main part of the town again, Lennie paused briefly to take off his cap and pay his silent respects at the War Memorial. Fortunately, the High Street had not suffered excessively during the Blitz four years before, and so far the 'doodlebugs', as they were now

66

known, had not posed such a threat as they had to other districts closer to the nearby East End of London. However, just as Lennie was within striking distance of the kerb where his van was parked, he saw something dead ahead which immediately threw him into a cold panic. Strolling casually towards him were two army Military Policemen, who were scanning the male passers-by just in case one of them might look like a deserter from the lists they had in the top pockets of the tunics. Looking around for a quick retreat that would not attract their attention, Lennie casually turned around, and went into St John's church, where the doors were wide open.

Inside the church there seemed to be a fair amount of silent activity, with two ladies busily arranging vases of summer flowers at the altar, leaving the verger to distribute well-worn copies of the Bible and hymn books to the first ten pews. Clearly a service was about to take place there, which, as far as Lennie was concerned, with the MPs outside, would suit him fine. But his presence attracted the attention of the vicar, who came across to him from the vestry. 'The service doesn't start for another hour,' said the elderly man, with a welcoming smile.

'Service?' asked Lennie, as though he didn't know what the man was talking about.

'The funeral,' replied the vicar. 'We're laying a young soldier to rest today. Poor fellow. He survived the D-Day landings and then went down on a mine a few days later. Nineteen years old. Such a waste.' He sighed. 'I long for the day when our boys come home again, and we can have more weddings than funerals in this church.'

'I'm sorry, sir,' replied Lennie awkwardly. 'I didn't know.' He turned to go, now realising why the two MPs were lingering around outside.

'You're welcome to stay and pay your respects,' said the vicar. 'The boy's family need all the support they can get. If you don't know anyone, you can sit at the back. God's house is always open for anyone.' He moved on, and went to talk with the verger.

Lennie went to a back pew and sat for a while, contemplating, occasionally casting a discreet glance over his shoulder to the outside door, where the two MPs were on duty for the arrival of the young soldier's cortege. He had a lot to mull over in his mind, and to his surprise, the peace and quiet of the church proved to be the perfect place for him to be at one with himself. It had been a long time since Lennie had been inside a church, not since . . . that grim winter more than a year before. But the more he sat there in silent contemplation, the more he realised that there were very few people he could actually talk to, to confide in. Guilt had robbed him of his ability to make friends. There seemed to be no one he could trust. And yet, there *was* one person's image who kept flashing through his mind, and he couldn't understand why. After all, there was nothing extraordinary about Mary Trimble. She was a girl just like any other, and there was no way he was going to get involved with anyone else. After half an hour or so, the first of the mourners began to trickle in and were shown to their seats by the verger. When the coffin arrived, it was carried into the church by two soldier friends of the young victim and four civilians, with one of the two bare-headed MPs leading the procession behind the vicar, and the other following on behind. The moment the coffin had passed, Lennie got up from his pew and discreetly slipped out of the church.

By Saturday evening, Mary had completed her first few days as the new usherette at the Marlborough cinema. Despite the constant interruptions by Adolf Hitler's new 'toys', the building had remained unscarred by doodlebug explosions, which is more than could be said for some of the surrounding streets which had suffered spasmodic damage and casualties. Fortunately, the audience turnout for Noël Coward's *This Happy Breed* had been quite substantial, despite the fact that the 'B' feature second film, *The Falcon in Mexico* carried an 'A' certificate, which prohibited children attending the performance unless accompanied by an adult.

Not that this actually deterred *any* youngsters from seeing the films on their own, for a lot of them usually 'bunked in' the side doors, and hid under the seats whenever the usherette closed in on them. However,

Mary tried hard to keep clear of the back row which teenagers regularly used for hanky-panky. It would take her time to pluck up enough courage to tell them to behave themselves!

It was about 10.45 p.m. when the last house audience left the cinema. Soon after, Mary did the ritual clearing up of litter left behind by the patrons, and once the auditorium lights had been turned off, she quickly made her way out of the grand circle, and started to make her way down the dark gas-lit stairs. As she did so, she met Lennie's dad, who was just locking up the projection room. 'Well, at least it's Sunday termorrer,' he said. 'Three o'clock start. Only two performances.'

'It's funny showing two scary films on a Sunday,' replied Mary, following him down the stairs.

'People've seen more scary things in this war than they ever see on the pitture screen,' he called, his voice echoing up from the first-floor landing. 'They ain't nearly so scared of Frankenstein and Dracula as 'Itler and the buzz bombs.'

Mary waited for him to move on, astonished to see how well he managed to cope with the stairs, considering he was hobbling with one artificial foot; so much so, that she had difficulty in keeping up with him. When they passed through the door that led into the foyer, they found Alf Bickley, the manager, waiting there to lock up for the night. 'Come on now, little lady,' he said to Mary, hurrying her up. 'Mustn't keep your family waiting.'

'Oh, I don't think they'll worry about that,' replied Mary jokily. 'When the cat's away, the mice will play!' Although she, Alf and Ernie Backer chuckled, the thought quietly dawned on her that what she had said might not be all that far-fetched.

'Well, go and get yourself changed. We've got a good double bill termorrer. I reckon we'll be packin' 'em in.'

Mary waited for the old man to disappear into his office before walking with Ernie to the front entrance door. 'Have you seen Lennie lately?' she asked.

'Not since 'he brought you in last week,' replied Ernie. 'Why?'

'Oh – no reason,' explained Mary, a touch self-consciously. 'I just wanted to thank him for speaking up for me.'

Ernie grinned. 'Taken to 'im, 'ave yer?' he teased.

'Oh no,' she replied quickly. 'Nothing like that. But he was so nice to help me out. I'm so grateful to him.'

''E's certainly taken to you, I can tell. Mind you, 'e 'ain't a one ter show it. Not that 'e would, after all that went on.'

Mary gave him an enquiring look. 'That sounds very mysterious, Mr Backer. What d'you mean?'

Ernie became a bit more withdrawn, and made his way to the door. 'Oh, I've no doubt 'e'll tell yer – in time,' he replied, just as mysteriously. He reached the door, and opened it. 'All I can say is, don't rush into things, Mary. Lennie's a good boy, but 'e's very complicated. It's goin' to take time for 'im to get back on his feet again. Anyway, 'e's got a lot to wash out of 'is system before then. 'E's 'ad a rough time of it, and that's fer sure! Goodnight, gel. See yer termorrer.'

After Ernie had left, Mary went into the staff room where her fellow usherette, Alice Thompson, had just finished changing back out of uniform into her own clothes. 'So how d'yer feel after yer first week?' Alice asked. 'Fed up with the dark yet?'

'Not really,' chuckled Mary, quickly changing into her own clothes. 'Though it does seem a bit funny watching the same picture over and over again every single day.'

'Ha!' laughed Alice, who was quite a well-turned-out middle-aged woman, and who really looked quite good in her white blouse, navy-blue skirt and matching straw hat. 'I usually pass the time by sitting in one of the back seats, and imagining it's me up there dancin' with Fred Astaire, or fallin' into Clark Gable's arms.'

Mary laughed.

'Mind you,' continued Alice, 'if it's a good story, I don't care a bugger 'ow many times I see the pitture. I love war films! All that khaki and air-force blue. Aah ... sends me weak at the knees. Trouble is, no matter who they are, yer can't trust the buggers – specially the blokes. They all lie through their teeth. Just like that young Lennie Backer.'

It was too late for Mary to react. By the time she had thrown a startled look at her friend, Alice was already leaving the room.

'Come on, Mary,' Alice called. 'Time ter get out of this place for a few hours. The ol' man's waiting ter lock up.'

In the foyer, Alf Bickley was fitting up a billboard all ready for the following day's Sunday performances of the two popular detective 'B' features, *Charlie Chan and the Black Magic*, starring Sydney Toler, and an old favourite, *Mr Moto in Danger Island*, starring the redoubtable Peter Lorre.

'Night, Guv'nor!' called Alice, as she hurried out.

'Night Alice,' returned Alf, locking up the door of the cashier's kiosk. 'Don't be late tomorrow now.'

'As if I ever would!' called Alice from outside, knowing only too well that she was never on time.

'Goodnight, sir,' said Mary, as she passed through the foyer.

'Goodnight, young lady,' returned Alf, with a friendly smile. 'Don't forget, it's your day off on Monday.'

'Yes – thank you, sir.'

'And Mary.'

Mary paused briefly at the door.

'Well done this week,' said Alf. 'Keep up the good work.'

Mary beamed. 'Thank you, sir. Goodnight.'

Alice was waiting for Mary on the steps outside. 'Isn't it lovely,' she said, looking up at the sky. 'It's still not dark. I do love these long summer evenings – not that we see much of 'em stuck in there all that time.'

As they moved off together towards the main road outside, Mary immediately returned to the conversation she had been having with Alice in the staff room. 'Alice,' she asked breathlessly, 'what was it you were saying about Lennie Backer – about him lying? What did you mean?'

'Oh, I don't know,' replied Alice who kept on the move. 'It's just that 'e's a dark 'orse, that one. Wouldn't trust 'im no further than I can throw 'im.'

'But why d'you say that?'

'Well, somefin' must've 'appened when 'e went in the army, that's fer sure.'

Mary came to an abrupt halt. 'Army?' she gasped. 'Lennie was in the army?'

'Yes, 'course 'e was,' replied Alice. 'Not fer long, though. He was in and out like a dose er salts. Gord knows why. I always say never ask too many questions – just in case yer don't like the answers.'

After Mary had left Alice at her bus stop, she crossed Holloway Road, which was still blacked out, and made her way back home. She walked briskly, her mind now battered by what Alice had just told her about Lennie. Surely she had heard him say that he had been exempt from the army so that he could care for his mum, who was mentally unstable? Why would he want to lie about such a thing? And in any case, he could only be about eighteen or nine-teen years old, so what time could he have had to serve if he *had* been called up?

Although the pubs had been closed for over half an hour or so, there were still groups of high-spirited middle-aged and elderly men hanging around outside, putting the world to rights, not caring a damn that some people in the houses nearby were trying to get some sleep. As she turned into Herstlet Road, a tough-looking cream-coloured mongrel dog with a brown patch over one eye was up on his hind legs trying to force his nose into one of the few remaining pigswill bins, watched timidly by a jealous scattering of moggie cats. Just then, the peace of the late evening was pierced by the shrill call of the air-raid siren. That was enough for the dog and cats to scramble for their lives, and for Mary, worried about the kids at home, to break into a trot.

By the time she got home, the house was in darkness, so the first thing she did was to rush upstairs to see if Thelma, Billy and Dodo were safe and sound. But the moment she took the torch and shined the beam on to Thelma's bed, she realised that it was empty. Quickly making sure the blackout curtains were drawn, she switched on the light and yelled at Dodo and Billy who had been fast asleep in their own beds. 'Where's Thelma!' she ranted.

Dodo immediately sat up in bed and rubbed her eyes. 'What's up?' she moaned.

'Your sister!' Mary yelled again. 'Where *is* she?'

'Turn off the light!' called a bleary-eyed Billy from his own put-you-up bed, quickly covering his head with the bedclothes. 'I'm tryin' to get some sleep.'

Mary rushed across to him and angrily pulled back his bedclothes. 'Where is she, Billy?' she shouted. 'How long has she been gone?'

'I don't know!' Billy yelled back.

'Has she gone up West again?' persisted Mary furiously. 'Has she?'

Billy grabbed the bedclothes back, and angrily covered himself again.

Beside herself with rage, Mary rushed downstairs and burst straight into the front room where Granddad slept. The place smelt of brown ale. 'Where's Thelma?' she yelled, switching on the light.

Granddad, who a moment before had been snoring his head off, looked up, squinted, and tried to raise himself up on his elbows. 'Wos goin' on?' he spluttered.

'Where – is – Thelma?' barked Mary.

''Ow should *I* know?' returned the very cross old man.

'Well, you *should* know!' insisted Mary, glaring at him. 'It's *your* job to know, instead of spending all your time propping up that counter in the Eaglet. If I have to go to work, the very least you can do is to keep an eye on the family!'

'Don't you talk to me like that!' growled Granddad, blurring his words. 'If your mum and dad were alive they'd—'

'If Mum and Dad were alive, they'd be ashamed of you!' yelled Mary. 'You can't even—'

As she spoke, she heard the key go into the latch of the front door. Rushing out into the passage, she was just in time to see Thelma coming in. 'You!' she roared. 'Where've you been?' Her voice was now loud and shrill. 'I've had enough of this, you little cow! Tell me, Thelma! Tell me where the hell you've been?'

73

Thelma would not allow herself to be ruffled. She quietly closed the door behind her, and remained still. 'You *know* where I've been,' she answered, quite unconcerned. 'It's Saturday, remember? I always go over to Amy's place on a Saturday. So what's all the fuss?'

Chapter 6

Nutty Nora was hanging her washing out on a makeshift washing line stretched across her two top-floor windows overlooking the street below. Most noticeable to the residents below were the two gigantic pairs of bloomers hanging there alongside two dishcloths, a pair of her brother's long john underpants, and one of his shirts. It was not exactly a pretty sight, and Mary had told her as much on countless occasions.

'I do wish you'd stop hanging stuff out on the line at the front of the house,' Mary called to her when she came out to scrub the front doorstep. 'You know how Mr Cotton's told us about not doing it.'

'To 'ell with ol' Cotton,' yelled Nora, peering down over the top of her pink pair of 'passion killers', as the neighbours had called them. ''E may be the landlord, but 'e don't tell *me* 'ow ter run my life!'

'But you've got a perfectly good washing line in the backyard,' persisted Mary. 'You know very well you can use it any time you want.'

'If you fink I'm going to go up an' down them stairs with my rheumatics just to hang up me bits 'n' pieces, yer've got anuvver fink comin'!' As usual, her return was shrill and cross. She said no more, but went inside and slammed the window.

Mary sighed. She couldn't remember how many times she'd gone through this same exchange with the upstairs tenant, so she knew that the old girl would never give in to criticism. Fortunately, however, it wasn't Mr Cotton's day for collecting the rent, so she just shrugged her shoulders, and went back inside. It was her first day off from her new job at the Marlborough, and with the kids at school, she at last felt that she could have some time to put her feet up and listen to the wireless. However, first she had to get breakfast ready for Granddad, but once she'd done that she went back to her own small bedroom on the first floor, and lay down on her bed. She had a lot to think about; everything Tanya had told her about her mother, and now the added concerns about the way her sister Thelma seemed to be getting out of control. Despite Thelma's assurances that she had spent the whole of Saturday with her friend Amy Jenkins, Mary still felt uncomfortable, and was really concerned that working at the Marlborough had given Thelma the opportunity to go anywhere she wanted. But as she lay there listening to 'Music While You Work' on her ramshackle old wireless set, she tried to think more realistically about her sister. After all, Thelma *was* almost sixteen now. If it hadn't been for the war, she should really have left school more than a year before, for it was quite obvious that Thelma was not going to pass her school exams. No. It was time for a radical rethink about Thelma's future, and she tried to work out in her mind what her mum and dad would have done about the girl if they were still alive. Times were dangerous for young people, especially if they went wandering up to the West End on their own. Once Thelma left school the following month, she would just have to get a job. But what could she do? She had shown no interest in anything except trying to make herself look grown up and glamorous like the film stars she saw in magazines. There was no denying that Thelma was a real dilemma for Mary, and she didn't know how to deal with her. If only there was someone around she could talk to, to confide in about the girl. Someone like Tanya.

Later that morning, Mary joined the queue outside Lipton's the grocer's shop in Seven Sisters Road. A rumour had gone around that they were selling some pig's trotters, and as they were one of Granddad's favourite meals, she thought she would give it a try. Not that she owed anything to her grandfather. He was the meanest old goat alive, and only thought of himself. He was so different to Mary's dad, who had been kind and generous to a fault. Nonetheless, Granddad was an old man, and Mary looked after him not for himself, but for her dad. However, whilst she was standing there, with the sun burning the back of her bare neck and the queue moving forward more slowly than a tortoise, she found herself facing another problem.

'Oy, you!'

Mary turned with a start to find a rather unkempt-looking woman, glaring at her from the side of the queue.

'Your name Trimble?'

Embarrassed, Mary answered, 'Yes?'

'I want a word with you,' growled the woman, who was probably in her late thirties, and had long straggly curly hair the colour of golden syrup.

'What about?' asked Mary, who thought the woman spoke as common as muck.

'I'm Amy Jenkins's muvver,' barked the woman, making no effort to keep her voice low. 'An' if yer know wot's good for yer, yer'll come an' listen ter wot I've got ter say.'

Now highly embarrassed because everyone had turned to look at them, Mary left the queue and followed the woman to the kerbside nearby. 'Would you mind telling me what this is all about?' she asked angrily.

'You know who Amy Jenkins is?' asked the woman bossily, her voice husky from smoking too many fags.

'Of course I know who she is,' snapped Mary. 'She's a friend of my sister, Thelma.'

'Not any more, she ain't!' returned the woman, wiping sweat from her neckline. 'I've told my daughter that if she ever goes near that snotty-nosed little madam again, I'll beat the livin' daylights out of 'er!'

Mary took after her mum when it came to dealing with people like this. She was simply not prepared to take insults from this woman. 'If you're going to call my sister names, then don't expect *me* to listen to you!' she replied. 'Now tell me what this is all about, or you can go to hell!'

The woman reached into the pocket of her dress and took out what appeared to be a small cutting from a magazine. 'What d'yer fink of this, then?' demanded the woman, holding it out to Mary.

Mary took the cutting. Her face stiffened with shock. It was a photo of a naked man lying on top of a naked woman. Mary squirmed at the photo, and quickly gave it back to the woman. 'What it's got to do with my sister?' she asked defensively.

'She give it ter my gel,' growled the woman.

'Who said so?' asked Mary, desperately trying to avoid eye contact with the woman.

'Amy said so,' the woman replied, putting the photo cutting back in her pocket. 'Amy never lies.'

'You believe everything she says?'

'I 'ave no reason not to,' returned the woman haughtily, as though butter wouldn't melt in her daughter's mouth. 'She said your Thelma cut it out of a magazine she got up the West End. Seems that's one of your sister's favourite places she always makes for — 'specially on Saturdays.'

Mary tensed; she could feel her spine tingling with anger. 'As far as *I'm* aware, my sister and your daughter spend an awful lot of time together – *especially* on Saturday nights.'

The woman roared with laughter. 'An' the rest!' she spluttered.

'Thelma told me she spent all of Saturday with Amy at your house.'

The woman shook her head. 'Amy was with *me*,' returned the woman, with a knowing grin. 'I took 'er over ter see her gran an' granddad over at Stoke Newington. Amy's not interested in goin' up West an' mixin' with a whole lot of yanks an' their tarts.'

Mary's inclination was to punch the woman right in the face, but she didn't want to lower herself to the same kind of gutter behaviour as the woman herself. Her mum had always taught her never to argue with people who had no manners. 'I shall ask Thelma what this is all about,' she replied calmly, turning to go.

'Just keep your sister away from my gel!' snapped the woman, who certainly didn't know anything about manners. 'I'm sure the authorities would like ter know that you ain't fit ter be lookin' after 'er.'

'As you say, Mrs Jenkins,' replied Mary, 'Thelma is my sister, not my daughter. She doesn't have the burden of a mother like *you*.'

The woman's face had a look of thunder, and she automatically raised her hand as though she was going to slap Mary's face. But when she saw Mary's ice-cold expression, her hard, determined eyes glaring defiantly at her, she quickly lowered her hand, turned around, and strode off.

Mary waited for her to go, then returned to the shop. But the queue had dispersed, and on the inside of the window an assistant had fixed a notice which read: ALL TROTTERS GONE. SORRY.

Letty Hobbs was scrubbing her doorstep. In fact, to most of her neighbours in Roden Street she was *always* scrubbing her doorstep. But then, she was that kind of woman; someone who cared for her husband, her family and her home, a woman who wanted everything to be right, because her own upbringing had been overshadowed by a domineering mother. Nonetheless, Letty was, in her own way, domineering too, but in a calm and reasonable way, and only because her husband Oliver was a passive sort of man who had been seriously wounded in the army during the First World War, losing not only a leg but also his confidence. Letty and Oliver were a model couple – two people who had been in love with each other since the day they met, and Letty desperately wanted her three boys to grow up with the determination to make the best of themselves. Mary thought the world of her, mainly because Mary's mum and Letty always confided in each other, but also because Mary knew that Letty Hobbs was someone she could trust.

'When you've finished here,' Mary said, as she stopped at the Hobbs's front garden gate, 'you can come and do my doorstep too!'

Letty looked up from the mat she was kneeling on. Her face lit up the moment she saw Mary. 'Any time, Mary dear,' she said. 'You know that.'

Mary chuckled. 'Oh no, Mrs Hobbs,' she replied. 'I was just joking. You've got quite enough on your plate with your own family.'

'Yes, but I don't have to go out to do a full-time job,' said Letty, getting up and going to the garden gate. 'Anyway, that's what neighbours are for.' She paused a moment and looked hard at Mary. 'So what's up, dear?' she asked.

'What d'you mean?'

'Mary, I've seen that look on your face too many times,' replied Letty. 'Just like your mum – storing up everything inside. Come on in and have a cup of tea.'

A few minutes later, Mary had poured her heart out to Letty. Sitting in the Hobbs's back parlour over a cup of tea, Mary told her everything that Thelma had been getting up to – the visits up to the West End, the disgusting cutting from the magazine, but most of all, the way Thelma was getting completely out of control.

Letty was disturbed to hear all Mary was telling her about the girl. She had had problems in her own family, and she had had to learn the hard way how to deal with them. 'Well,' she sighed, once Mary had finished telling her, 'I can't say I'm surprised. Your mum once told me that if there was going to be a problem child in the family, it was going to be Thelma.'

'She said that?'

'Oh yes,' replied Letty. 'There was one time when she told me how she'd caught Thelma smoking with a boy behind the toilets in the school playground. This was some years ago, before the war. Thelma could only have been about eleven or so. Your mum was really upset about it, but she never told your dad. She always said that Thelma had a will of her own.'

As she slowly took this in, Mary looked pale and tense. 'What am I going to do about her, Mrs Hobbs? What *can* I do?'

Letty stood by the old pine dresser and took a passing look at a framed photograph of her own family. 'The trouble is, Mary,' she said, 'when your kids make up their minds to do something, whatever you say, they'll do it.' She went to the parlour table and sat opposite Mary. 'Let me tell you something that happened to my eldest brother, Nicky, when he was about the same age as your Thelma. Although my father ran our household in a very strict Victorian way, he was very shrewd when it came to how I and my two brothers were brought up. One day, he caught Nicky putting a cigar butt in his mouth and admiring himself in the mirror in our sitting room. The cigar wasn't lit, but the way Nicky was behaving made him feel as though he was grown up. Father let him off that time, but when he later caught him doing the same thing again, he made Nicky put the cigar back into his mouth, and then lit it. In a way, it was an awful thing to do, because Father made him smoke the cigar, and in no time at all, Nicky felt so sick he had to rush off to the lavatory.' She smiled wryly. 'He never smoked cigars again!'

Mary laughed. 'How cruel!' she said.

'Yes,' replied Letty, 'but it did the trick. The trouble with kids – and I include what *I* used to be myself – is that they're born stubborn. Let them learn by their mistakes, I always say – as long it's not too late to put things right.'

'But I'm so angry about what Thelma's doing behind my back,' said Mary. 'Now I've got this job at the Marlborough, she can do anything she wants.'

'What about your granddad? Can't he help out?'

'Granddad?' Mary snorted in frustration. 'Granddad has never helped anyone in his life. Ever since Grandma died and he came to live with us, he's just been waited on hand and foot. And it's got worse since we lost Mum and Dad. I just wish he'd go and live with Dad's brother and sister-in-law. Him and my Uncle Cyril and Aunty Gladys are three of a kind – they never helped me out when Mum and Dad were killed, and mean as hell!'

'Well, I think it's so unfair,' said Letty, leaning back in her chair and sipping her tea. 'It's not right that a young girl like you should have to take on the responsibility of looking after a whole family on your own. You should be having boyfriends, and a life of your own. I only wish *I* could help out, but I've got all my time cut out looking after *my* lot.'

'Oh, I'm OK, Mrs Hobbs,' said Mary, who was suddenly aware of the smell of freshly washed clothes hanging across the room on the ceiling rack. 'I have no real problems with the other two. Billy's a bit cheeky at times, and Dodo's a bit of a grizzler, but they're too young to get into any *real* mischief. But Thelma . . .' Once again she sighed. 'I just hope things will get better when she leaves school and gets a job of her own. But then, you can never tell. With money in her pocket, she could get up to anything.'

Letty leaned across the table to her. 'There must be *someone*,' she added. 'Someone you can turn to for help, someone you can *really* trust?'

'Oh, I wish there was, Mrs Hobbs,' replied Mary gloomily. 'I only wish there was.'

Ernie Backer had just finished the first house showing of *The Keys of the Kingdom*, a new epic religious film with Gregory Peck. The audience was pretty thin, as it usually was for a Monday matinée, and it wasn't helped by the fact that the copy of the film had a tear in one of the reels, which added ten minutes to the showing whilst Ernie did a quick patching-up job. However, the slow handclap from the few impatient patrons in the auditorium was soon forgotten once Gregory Peck had reappeared on screen in his role as a Scottish pastor posted to a tough rural community in late nineteenth-century China. Fortunately, despite his difficult mobility, Ernie was one of the best projectionists on the Islington picture-house circuit; much admired both for his skills and his courage. But in his time, Ernie had had a lot of problems to contend with, not least with his own family. The break-up of his marriage to Winnie Backer had been inevitable, not because she was no longer desirable, but because she never stopped attacking him for the most absurd reasons. It was some time before he learned that her mind was not all it could be, but when the doctors diagnosed her with a form of premature senility, he found it difficult to feel any guilt. If there *was* guilt, it was because he had left Lennie to pick up the pieces and look after his mum. On top of that, the tragic episode that followed in Lennie's life only made things worse.

What with being called up for the army, only to be discharged in disgrace, followed by the boy's reckless relationship with Carole Pickard, it had been a difficult few years.

Once the feature film had come to an end, Ernie had a fifteen-minute break to thread up the film stock on to the second projector for a couple of The Three Stooges' comedy 'shorts', which formed the bulk of the accompanying programme. Once he had done that, and made sure that Harry Percival was entertaining the customers on the Compton organ, he left his projection room and went downstairs to have a quick fag outside. It was a hot day, and his shirt was damp with perspiration, but he loved his work, and it never disturbed him to spend each day in a small, airless room with two monster film projectors. In fact, that cinema projection room was his domain, and he resented the fact that his stand-in used it on Ernie's one day off every Wednesday.

At the front of the house, patrons were already queuing for the late-afternoon continuous performance, many of them clutching sand-wiches, vacuum flasks of tea, and lemonade for their kids. It gave him a smug feeling to know that without him, there would be no 'pittures' for them to look at.

'Hello, Dad.'

Ernie turned with a start to find Lennie approaching him from the main road. 'Len?' he called. 'What you doin' 'ere, son?'

'Need to talk to you.'

'I've only got another five minutes or so.' Ernie held his fag between his teeth and straightened his braces. 'Anyfin' wrong? Who's lookin' after yer mum?'

'She's OK,' replied Lennie, stiffly. 'The WVS woman's with her. That's what I want to talk to you about. I think it's about time you came to see her. I've got a feeling she's getting worse.'

Ernie pulled on his fag. Now it was *his* turn to stiffen. 'Why d'yer say that?'

'She's got to wandering off the moment I'm out of sight. I can't keep my eyes on her the whole time. You've got to do something.'

Ernie shrugged. 'Come off it, boy,' he replied awkwardly. 'What can

I do with me stuck upstairs in that projection room day after day, night after night?'

'Not *every* day, Dad,' insisted Lennie. 'You get Wednesdays off. I think you should at least make the effort.'

Despite the heat, a cold shudder went down Ernie's back. The idea of seeing his wife again after all this time filled him with horror. As far as *he* was concerned, his break-up with Winnie had had nothing to do with the state of her mind. It was simply because he had fallen out of love with her. 'You know I can't do that, son,' he replied uneasily. 'Yer know very well yer mum hates the sight of me. How many times did she tell me that she never wanted ter see me again as long as she lived? How many times did she tell me that she wished she'd never met me? If I come up ter see her now, it'd probably makes fings worse. I've told yer that so many times.'

'That's fine for you, Dad,' replied Lennie, 'but what about *me*? Have you ever taken into account that *I* have a life of my own to live, that I need some time of my own to breathe, to do some of the things that *I* want to do? Come home and see her. For Christ's sake, she *is* your wife.'

'Not any more she's not!'

'She's still your wife until you make it legal!'

Angry, Ernie threw down his unfinished fag and twisted it into the ground with his one good foot. Then he reached into his trouser pocket, took out a ten-shilling note, and offered it to the boy. 'Here!' he snapped.

Lennie looked with contempt at the note in his dad's hand. 'If you don't make some attempt to help out,' he said angrily, 'I swear to God I'll get Mum put away in a home. Then it'll cost you more than ten bob to get rid of her!' With that, he strode off back towards the main road.

Ernie watched him go, suddenly wishing he hadn't said all the wrong things. But what could he, Ernie, do about it? He just couldn't feel the same for the woman he had once loved, even though she had given him a son, a son he was proud of, despite the problems the boy had heaped upon himself. So what *could* he do?

'Ernie!'

Ernie turned to see Alice Thompson, the stalls usherette, calling to him from the main entrance of the cinema.

''Arry's almost finished,' she called. 'Five minutes to curtain!'

'Be right with you, Alice,' he returned, before hurriedly making his way up the back staircase, back to his projection room, back to the only life he knew, to the only life he cared for.

22 June 1944   *27 B Fortess Road*
                                                Kentish Town
                                                NW5

My dearest Mary,

Since we met so very cordially, and drank tea together in your front room, I have been thinking so much about you, thinking so much about what we had to say to each other, about your lovely parents, about the past, the present, and now, I hope, the future. As I told you, your mother wanted us to be friends, and for that reason, I would like to see you again. I would like you to know more about me, about my life, and what I do with myself. In that way, I hope I can build a trust in you, to get to know you more, as you can get to know me. So, then, when you next have the time, I would like to invite you to visit me at my home here in Kentish Town. It's not too far for you to come – maybe one Sunday morning before you go to work at the cinema? There is so much I want to tell you, but only if you feel you can trust me. Please let me know if and when you can come.

Your friend,

Tanya Ling

Mary was furious that Granddad had not told her about the letter from Tanya, which the postman had delivered three days before. But, as much as she wanted to tell him how angry she was, she was more interested in the contents of the letter itself. It was true that her last meeting with the Chinese woman had been cordial and absolutely fascinating, but it also left her with some questions of her own that needed to be asked. Still ringing in her ears was Sheila Nestor's scathing comment when she had sacked Mary from her job at the British Restaurant, for insisting that Tanya hadn't done anything wrong in her whole life: *'Is that so?'* She could hear Sheila's words loud and clear. *'Well that's not what I heard!'* By the time she had read Tanya's letter and put it safely into her dress pocket, Mary had already made up her mind to visit her in Kentish Town.

Once she had finished the family's washing, and swept and mopped the linoleum floors, Mary felt she had devoted enough time to chores on her first day off. However, she still had to tidy up the bedroom shared by her two sisters and their young brother. As usual, it looked more like a pig sty; none of them ever thought about putting clothes away once they'd worn them. Thelma was the worst, with clothes and half-opened women's magazines left on her bed and all over the floor. She got quite a shock when she cleared away some of Thelma's belongings and replaced them in the top drawer of the chest of drawers her mother and father had bought her the year before they died. Tucked away in between a clean school shirt and her underwear, was a tin containing a bright red lipstick, an eye pencil and a tin of mascara. Mary had seen none of this before, and had certainly never seen Thelma made up with any of it. But worse was to come when she discovered a large envelope hidden at the back of the drawer. Inside was a collection of snapshot photos of young men in military uniform, some American GIs, some British Army, and one navy rating. Posing with each of them was Thelma, almost unrecognisable in her provocative white low-cut blouse and skirt, her face plastered with make-up. Mary was beside herself with shock. She had never seen either the make-up or that blouse before. Where *did* Thelma get the money to buy such things? How *did* she manage to keep them secret without Mary ever knowing about them? Mary clutched her head in panic and despair.

So it was true. Everything Amy Jenkins's mother had told her was true. Thelma, barely sixteen, was finding ways to go up to the West End to mix with men who were desperate for the company of women. Oh God, she gasped. What if – what if . . . she could hardly bear thinking about what Thelma had been getting up to. In a sudden fit of anger, she pulled the drawer right out and tipped all the contents on to the floor. Everything was scattered there, including the open tin with the lipstick, eye pencil and mascara.

'You bloody cow!'

Mary swung round to find Thelma, purple with anger, standing in the open bedroom doorway.

'You've got no right!' screamed the girl. 'This is *our* bedroom! You've got no right to be in here!' She rushed straight across to the upturned drawer on the floor and started to throw her personal belongings back into it.

Mary grabbed hold of the girl's hair and yanked her to her feet. 'How *could* you?' she barked, holding Thelma's face to her own. 'How *could* you do these things?'

Thelma pulled herself free and glared back at her sister. 'I'm a woman now!' she yelled. 'I don't have to ask you for *anything*! I do what I want!'

'Does that include being a whore, Thelma?' said Mary, trying to restrain herself. 'Does it?' She moved closer to the girl. 'D'you think Mum would have been proud to know that she had a whore for a daughter?'

'Mum wouldn't've cared less what I do!' Thelma snapped back angrily. 'You can bet your life that when she was my age *she* was no saint!'

This provoked Mary into such a fury that she slapped the girl hard around the face. 'Don't you ever say such things about our mum again, d'you hear!' she yelled.

Thelma reeled back and burst into tears. 'I hate you, I hate you!' she screamed hysterically, rushing out of the room, and thumping down the stairs.

Mary waited a moment, then heard the front door open and slam. She was too overcome to move. All she could do was to perch down on the edge of the bed, and try to take in what had just happened. She had never used force with any of her sisters and brother before, but this time her mind had no control over her emotions. Thelma's outburst was unforgivable, and Mary would never forgive her for what she had said about their mum. But what could she, Mary, do about it? Through no fault of her own she had been given the responsibility of trying to bring up a family, a sister who was completely out of control. What *could* she do about it? Was there no one in the whole world who could teach her how to deal with all the trials and tribulations of being a mother? Without realising it, tears were welling up in her eyes, and she used her knuckle to clear them away from her cheeks. Just then, she remembered the letter in her dress pocket. She took it out and clutched it. Maybe, after all, there *was* someone who knew her mum well enough to help her shed this terrible burden . . .

Chapter 7

During the nineteenth and early twentieth centuries, Kentish Town had been known as the home of many famous piano and organ manufacturers. It was an area of great dignity and elegance, with Victorian and Edwardian houses gracing many of the cobbled backstreets and main roads. Mary was glad that she had decided to walk from the Nag's Head rather than take a bus, for it would have meant changing at the Archway and, in any case, it gave her the chance to take in a part of North London she had never seen before. At first, she'd been in two minds about whether she would accept Tanya Ling's invitation to visit her, but after reading what the Chinese woman had said in her letter, the temptation was too great: '*I would like you to know more about me, about my life, and what I do with myself. In that way, I hope I can build a trust in you, to get to know you more, as you can get to know me.*'

The walk from the Nag's Head to Fortess Road took her along the side of the majestic Gaumont Cinema in Holloway Road, and down fashionable Tufnell Park Road with its tall Victorian houses, which fortunately had escaped any heavy damage during the Blitz a few years before. However, the war was never far away, for the first thing she noticed on the newsvendor's board outside Tufnell Park tube station were the dramatic scrawled headlines: HITLER'S NEW SECRET WEAPON. Mary averted her eyes as quickly as possible. Hitler's dreaded flying bombs were already wreaking chaos and destruction on so many parts of London and the Home Counties. The thought of yet another new weapon was too horrific to contemplate. Fortess Road turned out to be far longer and far busier than Mary had expected. Although the terraced houses were elegant reminders of a bygone age, there were quite a lot of them, with many of the residential dwellings poised above shops. It all seemed to be such a hive of activity, so lively and colourful. But as she paused briefly to look in a womens' clothes-shop window, which displayed a yellow beret-style hat which she absolutely adored, she was suddenly reminded that the war was still very firmly all around her. Fortess Road became as still and silent as the grave, but for that terrifying sound of an approaching buzz bomb in the sky above. As she stood with her back pressed rigid against the residential door at the side of the shop, everything and everybody came to an abrupt halt, with all eyes turned towards the sky. A brewer's horse and cart remained static, the few cars and vans along the road slowed down, and even a rather cross mongrel dog stopped barking at every passer-by. It seemed much longer than the few moments it took for the hated flying machine to pass overhead, its engines droning menacingly, cracking the air with impatience. Mary closed her eyes and prayed. The flying bomb passed right over without its engines cutting out. There was no explosion. That sound would come when the dreaded thing reached its innocent target in just a few minutes.

'Hey, mate! Got a fag?'

Mary opened her eyes again. She couldn't believe that the road had returned to normal, and standing before her was a young scoundrel of a boy, aged no more than eight or nine.

'Come on, mate,' repeated the boy cheekily. He seemed to be wearing his dad's shirt and trousers, they were so big for him. 'I ain't got all day. 'Ave yer got a fag, or ain't yer?'

Mary came to a halt with a start. 'No, I haven't!' she replied crossly. 'And even if I had one, I wouldn't give it to you.'

'Why not?' asked the boy, his face all crumpled up in indignation.

'Because you're far too young to smoke.'

The boy came right back at her. 'My sister weren't too young. Me and 'er used ter like smokin' a fag.'

'Then your sister's a very naughty girl,' replied Mary, trying to sound as maternal as she could. 'Now be a good boy, and go back home.' She started to walk on.

'She can't be naughty, 'cos she's dead.'

The small boy's voice went straight through Mary. She came to a dead halt and turned to look at him. 'What d'you mean?' she asked.

'She got killed by a doodlebug,' said the boy. 'On 'er way 'ome from school. That's why I won't go ter school.' He walked on, but called back over his shoulder. 'I much prefer to 'ave a fag!'

Mary watched him go, almost paralysed with sadness and disbelief.

A few minutes later, she reached number 27 Fortess Road, which was actually a newspaper shop. A door at the side of the shop window showed the number 27 B, so she pressed the bell and waited.

Within seconds, a first-floor window opened above, and Tanya Ling's excited voice called out. 'Mary!'

Mary looked up.

'It's wonderful to see you!' Tanya called. 'Here, take the key. First floor.'

Mary picked up the key Tanya had thrown down to her, and went inside.

The moment she entered, Mary was aware of the strange exotic smells coming from upstairs, smells unlike anything she had experienced before.

'Oh, Mary!' called Tanya, as she came hurrying down to greet her. 'It's wonderful to see you!' She hugged Mary and lightly kissed her on both cheeks. 'Come upstairs. I'm just making some green tea.'

Mary followed her up into a room on the first-floor landing. She expected to find something very different and Oriental, but the moment she went in she was astonished to find a very ordinary parlour room not so very different from her own front room. She was immediately astonished by the tall potted plant in one corner of what was really a good-sized room.

'I hope you like plants?' asked Tanya, quickly scuffing up a cushion on an oval-backed chair. 'There are more upstairs. Now just make yourself comfortable, and I'll bring us some tea.'

As soon as Tanya had left the room, Mary sat down, but got up again almost immediately when she suddenly noticed some framed photographs on a highly polished mahogany table with Chinese carvings. One of the photographs was of Tanya with a man who was most probably Robert, her late husband. They had their arms around each other's waists, in happier times on a pebbled beach somewhere. However, the other two photographs really took her breath away, for one of them was a snapshot photo of Tanya standing between Mary's mum and dad; they were all clasping their arms around each other's waists and laughing ecstatically at the camera. But the third framed photo was the real eye-opener. It was of Mary herself in a group picture with her mum and dad, Thelma, Dodo and Billy. If ever she needed any proof that Tanya had been close to Mary's parents, she had it now.

'You've no idea how I treasure those pictures,' said Tanya, coming back into the room carrying a small tray with two cups of green tea. 'It reminds me of what good people your parents were – not that I really need reminding. But I do miss them, especially your mother. In many ways she taught me so much.'

Mary was quite perplexed. 'Really?' she asked.

'Oh yes,' replied Tanya, with a faint smile. She put the tray down on the table, and offered a cup and saucer of green tea to Mary. The cup was small, and painted green with Chinese symbols. Mary looked suspiciously at the hot, green liquid in the cup. She had never seen anything like it before. 'Taste it,' said Tanya. 'I know it's different, but it really is very good for you. It's from a herbal leaf in China. It will help to make your blood pure and without tension.'

When Mary sipped it, the face she was pulling gradually relaxed. 'It's very nice,' she pronounced, bravely.

'Ah!' exclaimed Tanya, victoriously. 'Your mother liked my tea. Whenever she came here, it was the first thing I gave her.'

'Why did you ask me to come to see you?' asked Mary.

Mary's sudden, direct question took Tanya by surprise, so she lowered herself down slowly into an oval-backed chair just opposite her. 'You know, Mary,' she replied, 'one half of my body is all Chinese dragon, but the other half is a quiet English lady. I am proud of both parts of my body, of course, because it gives me an insight into two different worlds.' She sipped her tea delicately, with her little finger outstretched. 'However, I have to say that the Chinese part of my body is more capable of looking inside a person, of knowing what is troubling that person, than the gentility of my English adoption. When your mother first told me about her illness, I already knew. In the village outside Hong Kong where I was brought up, my knowledge was called *Chu Fa Ya* – foresight. I knew she was troubled, and I felt honoured to know that she trusted me. It was the same when you and I spoke for the first time the other day. I knew there was something wrong. It is in your eyes. But there was no way I could help because I knew you had to know more about me. That's why I asked you here.'

Mary suddenly felt very self-conscious, and struggled to drink her tea.

Tanya watched her and smiled. 'Would you like to come and see my studio?' she asked.

Mary looked up with a start. 'Studio?'

On the top floor, Mary was shown into a large, bright room, bulging with an array of large potted plants, and lit by a huge, arched fanlight. Around the walls were black-and-white sketches of so many different people, some of them Chinese working in what looked like a paddy field in another country, but most of them ordinary men, women and children – even dogs and cats – doing the very casual things of life such as walking, sitting, getting on to a bus, laughing looking grim-faced, happy, sad. It was an extraordinary conglomeration of a whole range of faces. 'It's amazing,' gasped Mary, quite taken aback by it all.

'They are all my family,' said Tanya, adjusting the shades on the arched window. 'I don't know any of their names, but I *do* remember their faces. They are all *here*' – she placed her hand gently on her forehead – 'and *here*.' She moved her hand to cover her heart.

Mary followed her around the room, watching her pick up one large-sized sketch after another – first of a child in a pram, then two women chatting over a garden fence, then a group of men smoking fags and pipes outside a pub. They were all fascinating slices of everyday life.

'Every picture tells a story,' said Tanya. 'Every one different. Look at this one.' She picked up a sketch of a small Chinese child being held in a cradle on the back of his mother, who was working in a rice field. The child's eyes were big and inquisitive, as though it wanted to say something but didn't know how. 'This is a picture I drew from memory,' said Tanya. 'Although I was very young when I left Hong Kong, I remember this child vividly. He had such a round, cherubic face, but he was very grumpy, so much so that he kept pulling off his little skull cap and throwing it into the paddy – much to his mother's intense irritation!'

Mary laughed.

'The evening I drew the sketch,' said Tanya, 'I thought a lot about that child. I thought so much about him that I made up a little story about him. It was all fiction, of course, but to me it was real, and it helped me to bring his little face back into focus. It was the same with the old chap.' She moved on to the far side of the room, and picked out a smaller sketch of an old man in a flat cap, with no teeth, staring into the lake up at Finsbury Park. 'This old gentleman must have been over eighty years old, for in his eyes were the memories of his entire life. I remember how every so often he grunted to himself, then grinned, then wiped a tear from his eye. There was so much emotion in the old chap. I adored him!'

Mary took the sketch and looked at it in admiration.

'So many of them!' continued Tanya. 'I feel as though I've got them all living with me, right here under my own roof!' She smiled to herself, as though the dawn of a new day was reflected right there in her eyes. She moved away again, and went to look at something mounted on an easel, something that, until that moment, Mary hadn't noticed. 'My dear,' she called gently, holding out her hand, 'I want to show you something.'

Mary went to her.

'This is my Robert,' said Tanya, showing Mary the large sketch

94

mounted on the easel. The picture, in black crayon, was of a man in his late twenties, in soldier's uniform, and with a huge, dazzlingly attractive smile on his face. But what Mary noticed more than anything was that Tanya had captured his expression of pure love. 'This is how I shall always remember him,' Tanya said, smiling with such affection at the sketch. 'He was a man of wisdom, understanding and great humour. We laughed and loved together so much.'

Quite unconsciously, Mary found herself putting her arm around Tanya's waist.

'The sad thing for both of us,' continued Tanya, 'is that I was never able to give Robert the child we both wanted so badly. But he never made me feel a sense of guilt or shame. He said it was an act of God, and we would just have to accept it.' She turned to Mary, her pale face the colour of snow in the sun's rays which were streaming through the great arched window. 'It was so wonderful having a man like that in my life, Mary; someone who knows how you feel without asking, someone you can share your problems with, to talk them over, someone who could make you realise that they are not nearly so difficult as you think. I wish *every* woman was blessed with a man like Robert.' She paused a moment, looking straight into Mary's eyes. 'It's what *you* deserve too, Mary,' she said fondly. 'You're far too young to take on an inherited family single-handed. Your mother knew it too. When she told me about how serious her illness was, she expressed the hope that you would never have to bear such a burden. The death of your parents was a tragedy not only for them, but also for you.'

Mary lowered her eyes and went across to the window. Tanya waited a moment, followed her, and then gently turned her round to face her.

'This boy,' said Tanya, softly. 'The one you met in the countryside . . .'

Mary looked up with a start. 'How did you know ab—?'

'What do you know about him?' replied Tanya, without offering any explanation of how she knew about Lennie.

Mary shook her head. The light through the window was turning her hair into the soft yellow of a wheat field. 'All I know,' she replied awkwardly, 'is that he seems to be carrying around the weight of the whole world on his shoulders. When I first met him he told me that he was exempt from doing military service because his mother was an invalid and couldn't be left alone. But then the other day, someone at the cinema told me that he *had* been in the army, but that he'd been discharged.'

'Discharged?' asked Tanya, with curiosity. 'Why?'

Mary shook her head again. 'I wish I knew,' she said. 'He's not the sort of person who wants to talk about his life. One thing I do know, however, is that he's full of bitterness. He blames his father for the break-up of his marriage to this poor woman. He's so very complex, Tanya.'

'But you *are* attracted to him?'

Mary waited a moment before answering. 'I don't know, Tanya. I just don't know.'

Both women were now staring aimlessly out through the massive window. In the road below, the brakes of an army truck skidded to a halt when it nearly knocked down what looked like a large terrier dog who was barking madly at them. A soldier with a rifle climbed out of the back of the truck, went to the dog quite fearlessly, stooped down, and stroked him behind the ear. His mates, who were peering out from the back of the truck, broke into wild cheers and applause. The dog, quite oblivious to what he must have considered his tormentors, fluttered his tail haughtily and plodded off to the other side of the road, straight past a newsvendor's billboard which showed a headline about a setback for the British forces in Normandy. The soldier climbed back aboard, and the truck drove off.

Looking down at them from above, Mary and Tanya showed no amusement at what they had just seen. 'How can I help?' asked Tanya.

Mary turned to look at her with some surprise. 'Help?'

'Would you like me to try and find out something about this boy?'

'Oh no, Tanya!' returned Mary, shaking her head vigorously. 'I would never spy on *anyone*! I would never want to know about Lennie's private life unless he wanted to tell me.'

'I wouldn't spy on him, Mary,' Tanya assured him. 'I would merely make a few discreet enquiries. I could at least find out why he was discharged from the army.'

'It's not only the army, Tanya,' replied Mary, staring straight at her. 'There's something else. There was a girl . . .'

That afternoon, Mary became quite alarmed when the cinema was shaken to its foundations by a doodlebug which was shot down by anti-aircraft guns who managed to target it as it passed over nearby Highgate Woods. During most cinema performances patrons rarely left because of an air raid, but the incessant rumble of gunfire outside brought patrons rushing to the exits to see what was going on. Mary's concerns immediately turned to her family at home. She hoped that her granddad had made them take cover in the Anderson air-raid shelter in the backyard, and she breathed a sigh of relief when she realised that most of the activity was nowhere near home in Roden Street, nor near the Nag's Head across the road. Once the crisis had passed, all the patrons returned to their seats to find that 'The Three Stooges' were in the middle of their usual zany antics on the screen, which immediately provoked gales of laughter in the auditorium. With only a scattering of people watching the show, Mary found a few rare moments to rest her weary feet by sitting down on an aisle seat in the back row, which, apart from an old lady sucking Zubes medicated sweets, was quite empty. This gave her a chance to mull over the conversation she had had with Tanya when she had gone to see her in Kentish Town during the morning, a visit that had helped to raise her confidence not only in the Chinese woman, but also in herself. Tanya's advice on how to deal with Thelma had given her a lot of food for thought. 'If she gets into trouble,' Tanya had said, 'then she will realise that the only person who can help her is you. That's the time when she will know that she needs you more than you need her.'

Mary was suddenly snapped out of her thoughts by the loud sound of someone snoring in a seat a couple of rows down in front of her.

She was about to get up, when a man appeared from the side entrance door and made straight for her. She got up quickly, only to discover that the man beside her in the dark was Lennie.

'Got to talk to you,' he said in a low voice.

'What are you doing here?' she asked nervously.

'I said I've got to talk to you,' he repeated, impatiently. 'Now!'

'Lennie, I'm working!' she replied, her voice higher than she realised. 'I can't talk in here!'

'Sssh!' called the old lady further along the row, before popping another Zube into her mouth.

Although her voice and Lennie's were no competition for the laughter around the auditorium, she said hurriedly, 'No, Lennie!'

To her shock, Lennie grabbed hold of her hand, yanked her away from the seat, and dragged her to the entrance door. They came to a halt in the circle lobby outside.

'Lennie!' she gasped, panicking. 'What are you doing? If Mr Bickley comes up here . . .'

Lennie held on to her hands. 'I have to talk to you, Mary,' he insisted. 'Once I've left here I'm going home. But there are things I have to talk to you about, things I *want* to talk to you about.'

'But why now, Lennie?' replied Mary, now really quite nervous of him. 'Why can't it wait till I'm not working?'

To her absolute astonishment, he said nothing, but leaned forward, pinned her back against the wall, and kissed her hard on the lips.

Whilst this was going on, Alice Thompson, the stalls usherette, came up the stairs and stopped dead. 'Whoops!' she gasped. 'Excuse me!' With that, she rushed straight back downstairs again.

Mary finally managed to push Lennie away. 'What the hell d'you think you're doing, Lennie?' she spluttered. 'Are you mad or something?'

'I want to tell you the reasons why,' he replied, unremittingly, but letting her break loose. There was desperation in his voice. His entire body seemed incapable of keeping still. Everything that had been bubbling up inside since he had spoken to his father earlier in the day was now coming out. 'I can't do this thing on my own any longer!' he murmured, partly to himself, partly to Mary.

'What can't you do, Lennie?' she pleaded. 'What are you talking about?'

'I can't look after that woman any longer!' he barked, plodding up and down the lobby in great agitation. 'I've had too much to cope with, too little time to think about how I'm going to face up to the rest of my life.' He came back to her. 'I helped *you*, Mary, now it's time for you to help *me*.'

'It seems we *both* need help, Lennie,' she returned. 'But this is not the way to go about things, especially if it means I have to pay you back for getting me this job.'

'To hell with the job!' he growled, eyes glaring at her.

'Then why did you get it for me?'

He turned away from her and stopped. 'All I ask is that you give me time to tell you the truth. Is that too much to ask?'

'The truth about *what*, Lennie?' she asked, trying her best to lower the tension.

He turned around slowly to look at her. 'Will you come and visit me at the farmhouse?' he asked, his eyes pleading and soulful.

At that moment, Mary thought that he was one of the most beautiful people she had ever seen. With his usual casual appearance, unshaved face, glowing blue eyes and ruddy complexion, he looked so vulnerable, so helpless, so lost. 'I work six days a week,' she replied. 'You know that, Lennie.'

'You have a day off every week,' he reminded her.

'In case you've forgotten, I *do* have a family to look after,' she replied firmly, but with compassion. She turned with a start as voices were heard in the front-entrance lobby downstairs. More patrons were arriving for the start of the feature film. She turned to go back inside to wait for them in the circle. 'Lennie, I have to go.'

He rushed across, and prevented her from opening the circle door. 'Say yes, Mary,' he begged. 'Say you'll come and see me on your next day off – on Monday. Please Mary – *please*.'

For one brief moment, Mary looked at him in total bewilderment. 'Lennie?' she asked intensely. 'Why did you kiss me? Why?'

Behind them, the first patrons were beginning to appear at the top of the stairs.

Lennie wanted to say something, but lost his courage. Without another word, he strode off, leaving Mary to show the new arrivals to their seats.

Chapter 8

By the end of June, the war against Germany was building up on all fronts. In the Cherbourg peninsula in France, thirty thousand German troops were trapped by units of the US Ninth Division, and Field Marshal Montgomery's British Second Army was launching fierce attacks on the beleaguered infantry and tanks of Field Marshal Rommel. Ever since the D-Day invasion by Allied forces on 6 June, the determined advance against the German war machine had been slow but relentless, and on the Russian front, war was progressing dangerously close to the borders of the German fatherland itself. However, despite the Allied successes, aerial attacks by Hitler's 'revenge weapon number one', now known more familiarly as 'the flying bomb' as well as by several other nicknames, continued aggressively, with no respite for the civilian population who lived in daily fear of their lives. Each day came the fervent hope that the Allies would soon discover where the deadly pilotless planes were being launched from, and that they would be destroyed before they caused any more death and destruction.

One of the many affected was Mary, who not only bore the daily brunt of anxiety about how to ensure the safety of her young brother and sisters, but also worried about how to keep them out of mischief whilst she was at work at the Marlborough cinema. Thelma was, of course, her main concern, although since their confrontation over the indecent magazines Mary had found in her sister's chest of drawers, there seemed to be no evidence that she was still making her Saturday afternoon trips up to the West End. Perhaps Tanya had been right about the girl when she suggested that if Thelma ever got into real trouble, then she would know that the only person she could ever turn to would be Mary. Well, so far, Thelma hadn't got into trouble, for she seemed to have taken on board her elder sister's angry outburst about her behaviour. However, it had to be said that Dodo and Billy were not exactly saints for, on more than one occasion, there had been complaints from some of the neighbours about their rowdy behaviour when leaving school in the afternoons, like the time when Billy directed his buttocks up towards Nutty Nora who nearly fell out of her top-floor window with rage and indignation. Then there was Dodo ('that dear, sweet little girl,' as some misguided passer-by once described her), with Fred Parfitt from next door wanting to wring her neck when she started playing 'Knock Down Ginger' through his letter box. Yes, Mary had a lot on her plate, and she was beginning to think that what Tanya had said about getting a man in her life was true. The trouble was that the *only* man in her life was a bit of a problem too. That kiss – that strange, unexpected kiss in the dress circle of the cinema, had puzzled and disturbed her. Nonetheless, much against her better judge-ment, she decided to do what Lennie had begged her to do. On her next day off, she got on the Green Line bus outside the Astoria cinema in Iseldon Road, and took the forty-five minute journey out to Epping.

Lennie was waiting for her at the bus stop. It was a glorious morning, and Mary was dressed accordingly in a knee-length floral cotton dress, together with cream-coloured half-heeled shoes and a black shoulder bag that once belonged to her mum. The moment she saw him she suddenly realised something she hadn't really noticed before, namely that he was one of the most ruggedly handsome men she had ever seen. With his usual light growth of stubble on his face and chin, his ruddy complexion seemed to set off his bright blue eyes, which glis-tened like sapphire stones in the bright sunshine. But the one thing that Mary noticed more than anything else was the fact that he had actually combed his hair, and his white shirt looked as though it was freshly ironed, which perfectly complimented his grey flannel trousers and well-polished shoes, all of which gave her the feeling that he had spruced himself up especially for her.

'Thanks for coming,' he said, as he helped her off the bus.

'I wasn't sure if you'd got my letter in time,' she replied rather coyly.

'Came first post Sat'day morning,' he replied, awkwardly. For one brief moment his eyes unintentionally met hers. 'You look – very nice,' he ventured bravely, before flicking his eyes away in panic.

'So do you,' she replied.

He scratched his head vigorously, as though he'd already gone too far. 'I didn't think you'd come,' he said, as matter-of-factly as he could manage.

'Why wouldn't I?' she returned.

'Well,' he shrugged, 'after the way I carried on last week.'

Mary gave him a reassuring smile. 'It didn't worry *me*,' she replied. 'I understood perfectly. In any case, we both have problems with our families. I'm looking forward to meeting your mum.'

'Sure you don't mind?'

She stretched out her hand to him. 'Come on,' she said.

His face lit up, and he took her hand, which felt warm and smooth.

They walked briskly off into the woods, which to Mary seemed to be much thicker than the last time she had been there on the day of the pub beano, with the lower branches of massive oak, elm and chestnut trees drooping lazily across the narrow, winding path. Every so often they stepped over clutches of wild lavender, coloured foxgloves, pink ragged robins, and pink and white campions, and as they came out into the light again, small patches of white mead-owsweet nestled comfortably in the thick green hedgerows. By the time they had reached the front garden gate of the old farmhouse, Mary was quite overwhelmed by the sheer beauty of the surrounding scenery. In the sunshine, everything seemed so clear and bright, something that she was so unused to back in Roden Street, where a view of the sun over the rooftops or in between the terraced houses was a luxury.

Once inside the house, Lennie's first task was to make sure his mum was there. He had got so used to her wandering off on her own into the woods that he could never be sure that she would be around. 'Mum!' he called. He knew only too well that it would take more than that to get her attention.

Mary waited in what looked like a small hall which had a faded red-brick floor, wattle-and-daub walls, a timber-beamed ceiling and an old inglenook fireplace which had some large logs already laid in the grate ready for winter. Above the fireplace was a narrow framed painting of farm labourers toiling in a hay field in the sun, and there were brass wall hangings of working horses pulling carts. But it was the musty smell of the place that she noticed most of all, probably caused by the fact that the hall room was dark, having only one small lead-framed window. But then there was another smell, more inviting, and coming from what must have been the kitchen.

'Mum! Where the hell are you! Mary's here!'

Standing alone in the entrance hall, Mary felt quite unnerved, listening to Lennie calling out for his mum, hurrying from one room to another, downstairs and then upstairs.

When he returned, Lennie looked quite flustered and irritated. 'Sorry about this,' he said apologetically. 'She drives me mad. I only have to leave the house for a few minutes and this happens. Come on. I'll make us some tea.'

Mary followed him into what turned out to be an old-fashioned timber-beamed kitchen, where, to her surprise, a kettle was already steaming on the hob, and by the succulent smell coming from the oven, something was cooking there. Without being asked she plonked herself down at the pine kitchen table, which had been set for three. 'It's a lovely place, Lennie,' she said. 'How long have you lived here?'

'All my life,' replied Lennie, busily making tea. 'It's been in Mum's family for donkey's years, right back to when my gran and granddad used to farm here. It's a bit run down now. Hasn't been done up since before the war. Can't afford the paint, even if we could get it.'

As he talked, Mary was enchanted to see two small birds fluttering on to the window frame, tapping at the glass there. 'Look at those birds!' she exclaimed excitedly. 'What are they doing?'

Without so much as a glance up at the window, Lennie replied, 'Wagtails. They're always on the cadge for tit-bits. So are the robins in winter. Sometimes they sit on my shovel while I'm digging. They prefer a nice juicy worm.'

'You have a lot of birds here?' asked Mary, fascinated as she listened to the tap-tap of the birds' beaks on the window pane.

'We've got our fair share,' replied Lennie, bringing her a cup of tea. 'At least they're company.'

Mary was curious. 'You get lonely living here?' she asked with some trepidation.

'Me?' replied Lennie. 'Nah. I prefer animals and birds to people any day of the week. At least they don't answer back.'

This remark made Mary even more curious. If he was so indifferent about people, why did he ask her to visit him? She watched him pour himself a glass of brown ale, and put it down on the table opposite her.

'Give me a mo,' he said. 'I'd better go out and find Mum. I'm always worried that she'll get down to the river. Make yourself comfy. I'll be right back.' He went to the back kitchen door and opened it, but as he did so, his mum's voice called from the open door of the hall. 'Hello, Mary.'

Mary swung with a start to find Winnie Backer coming across to her. She immediately stood up to greet her.

'Don't listen to anything he says,' said Winnie, whose large violet-coloured eyes were gleaming bright with vitality. 'He's not really a country boy at heart. He much prefers the bright lights of London.'

'Mum!' Lennie gritted his teeth and came across to her. 'Where the hell have you been?' he snapped irritably. 'I told you never to leave the place when I go out.'

Winnie's face crumpled up. 'I only went to pick these,' she replied sheepishly, holding up a small bunch of wild flowers. 'We've got to have something nice for the table,' she said, almost like a small child who had just been scolded.

Mary turned to look at Lennie, who sighed and took the flowers from his mother. 'Come and sit down, Mum,' he said, as calmly as he could, trying to show that he wasn't angry with her.

Winnie sat down opposite Mary, and couldn't take her eyes off her.

'I think the flowers are lovely, Mrs Backer,' said Mary, mustering a warm smile. 'It must be lovely to be able to go out into your own garden to pick flowers.'

'Oh they're not from *our* garden, dear,' replied Winnie. 'I got them down by the river, near the forge.'

Over Winnie's shoulder Mary could see Lennie freeze. She felt so sad as she looked at his mum's prematurely aged face, and the strands of grey amongst hair which must once have been a pretty brown colour. 'They're still lovely,' she said, as Lennie came back to the table having put them into some water in a vase.

'I'm serving up dinner in a minute, Mum,' Lennie said. 'As soon as we've finished, you must go up and have your rest.'

Winnie ignored him, and concentrated on Mary, smothering her with warm, admiring smiles. 'Do you like living in London, Mary?' she asked, her chin resting on both fists on the table.

Mary was a bit taken aback by the question, but did her best to answer it. 'It's my home,' she replied. 'It's where I was brought up. I don't know anything different.'

'My Ernie always used to say that living in a town was far better than living in the country.' Winnie's eyes were still glued to Mary. 'He said that there were more people to talk to, and that you didn't have to listen to the birds every day.'

Although it was a curious remark to deal with, Mary coped with it calmly. 'I would have thought that the sound of birds singing in the morning would be lovely to listen to,' she replied.

Lennie, unsettled by his mum's conversation, quickly removed a hot enamel dish from the oven.

Winnie shook her head, and leaned closer to Mary. 'Don't believe everything the birds tell you,' she replied, voice lowered. 'Especially the swallows.'

Before Mary had a chance to get the woman to explain what she meant, Lennie, using two tea towels, placed the hot dish on to the

106

table. 'Hope you like cottage pie,' he said. 'It's about the only thing I can make. We practically live on it, don't we, Mum?'

'I'm very impressed,' said Mary. 'I don't usually think of boys doing the cooking.'

For some reason or other, Mary's remark seemed to have offended Lennie, who dropped the hot dish on to the table with a thump. 'Someone has to do it!' he snapped.

Mary, wounded by his response, slumped back in her chair.

Winnie watched her. She hunched up her shoulders and grinned, as though she enjoyed her son's irritation.

Lennie, realising how unnecessary his response had been, stopped what he was doing, and looked across at Mary. 'What I mean is, needs must. I don't let Mum do the cooking. I'm afraid she might burn her hands or something.'

Mary let it pass, and by the time all three had started to eat, the atmosphere was relaxed and without incident. Mary loved the fresh peas and cabbage. Although the vegetables she queued up for at Hicks, the fruit and vegetable greengrocer's in Seven Sisters Road were always good, they were no replacement for vegetables that had been dug up just an hour or two before eating. How lucky country people were, she thought to herself.

Winnie ate her meal so daintily that she could have been a guest at a high-class dinner party. After every bite, she dabbed her lips with her handkerchief, and when she accidentally dropped a small piece of mashed potato from her portion of cottage pie, she quickly retrieved it from her lap and returned it to the side of her plate. Her manners were impeccable. But Mary was completely taken aback by the lovely baked rice pudding Lennie had made for afters, especially as it came with custard made with farmyard fresh milk, and not the powdered milk she and the family were so used to back home in Roden Street. But just when Mary had thought the meal had passed so pleasantly, she was puzzled by a strange question from Lennie's mum.

'Mary,' asked Winnie, her chin resting on her elbows again, as she stared straight into Mary's eyes, 'do you ever have dreams?'

Before answering, Mary flicked a quick, enquiring look at Lennie. 'Sometimes,' she replied casually.

'*I* have lots of dreams,' continued Winnie, excitedly. 'The other night I dreamed that Ernie, Lennie and me were all driving in a horse and cart to Epping. And d'you know what happened when we got there?' Mary shook her head.

'The Mayor was waiting to greet us! Can you believe it, Mary? The Mayor of Epping coming to meet the likes of *us*! And d'you know what he said to me as I got out of the cart?' She didn't wait for a response. 'He said, "Mrs Backer, you look fine, you look beautiful! Don't listen to what they all say. There's nothing wrong with *you* – absolutely *nothing*!"'

Mary saw Lennie tense, and get up from the table. 'Time for your nap, Mum,' he said hurriedly.

'But I'm not tired,' protested Winnie.

Lennie was already easing her up from her chair. 'Forty winks'll do you the world of good,' he said with affectionate persuasion. 'When you come down you can have your tea and a piece of that jam sponge Mrs Honer made for us.'

Reluctantly, Winnie allowed herself to be led up the rickety old wooden staircase that led to her bedroom.

Whilst they were gone, Mary turned over in her mind the extraordinary conversation she had had with the poor woman. It made her realise just what duty to one's dear ones really meant, for in some ways, she and Lennie were caught up in the same kind of situation. After all, there was not really so much difference between looking after a mother whose mind was prematurely unwell, and looking after a young brother and two sisters who had lost their mum and dad. The responsibility placed upon some young people was enormous. Where and when would people like her and Lennie have the chance to live their own lives without being tied down by such a huge burden? And yet, if anyone truly loved their family, how could they have it any other way?

★

Fred Parfitt, Mary's neighbour in Roden Street, had had enough of Nutty Nora's ranting. All she ever did was complain about anything she could think of, such as him having his wireless on too loud next door, and burning too much wood in his laundry copper in his back scullery which sent smoke out of the window and, so she said, made her cough. Then there was the time when she complained about him coming home drunk from the pub late at night, and waking her up by singing out loud the words of some dirty song he and his mates round the Eaglet were very fond of. Fred and Nora did *not* get on well, which was all too clear at this precise moment, for they were in the middle of a flaming row about who should clear the shrapnel that had fallen from the anti-aircraft shells that exploded practically every night in the sky during endless attempts to bring down the doodle-bugs. Within minutes, the row had spread, for the noise had brought other neighbours to their windows with cries from angry women yelling out, 'Why don't you two shut yer 'oles!' and 'Ain't you got nothin' better ter do with your time!' and 'I'm tryin' ter get my bleedin' kid ter sleep!' However, the squabble took a turn for the worse when the law suddenly intervened.

'What's all this, then?' The elderly bobby who approached was well known in the neighbourhood for cutting people down to size. 'So who's ter blame this time, then?' called PC Jones, who had a handlebar moustache that made the old Kaiser's face look like a baby's bottom.

'I've told this *person*,' called Mary's irate lodger from her top-floor window, 'that it's time 'e cleared out that gutter. Look for yerself. It's goin' ter crack any minute with all that shrapnel stuck in it!'

'I've done my best to clear it out!' countered Fred, who was at the end of his tether with the old bag. 'I've tried over an' over again to shift it with a broom, but it won't budge.'

'Then get a bleedin' ladder!' yelled a near hysterical Nora.

'Watch your language now, Ma,' PC Jones called up at her.

'If she thinks I'm goin' to climb up a ladder an' break *my* bleedin' neck,' snapped Fred, angrily, 'she's got anuvver think comin'!'

'That goes fer you too, Fred Parfitt,' warned Constable Jones. 'Now why don't you two settle this whole thing and get on to yer landlord.'

'What d'you take me for?' Nora yelled down at him. 'Yer can't get any of the landlords ter do anyfin' 'round 'ere! They're too busy linin' their bleedin' pockets!'

'I've warned you, Ma!' called PC Jones, pointing a finger at her.

With a loud sigh of utter frustration, Nora withdrew back into her upstairs castle, and slammed the window.

'That woman!' Fred shook his head in despair, then went back into his own house. He knew beter than to challenge the law.

The law, represented by PC Jones, also had little time to waste on such trivial matters. He had more important business to attend to on the ground floor of Nutty Nora's house.

Granddad Trimble was pretty shocked when he opened the front door to find the law waiting there. 'Wos up?' He scowled, peering round the half-open door.

'Your granddaughter home?' asked the Constable.

'Which one?' As usual, the old boy thought he was being too clever by half. 'I've got three of 'em.'

'The lady of the house.'

Granddad's face dropped. 'Mary?'

'Mary Trimble,' returned the bobby. 'Is she in?'

'What she done?' asked the old boy, eyes popping out of his head. 'Robbed a bank or somefin?'

'I hope not,' replied PC Jones. 'Is she in, or isn't she?'

'No, she's not!' grunted the old man, brusquely. 'She's gone off on the Greenline bus to Eppin', ter see some young hot arse. And don't ask me what time she's comin back, 'cos I don't know.'

The bobby pondered for a moment. 'Right, then,' he said. 'When she comes back, tell her to come round as soon as possible to the station. Tell her to ask for Sergeant Hopkins. He wants to have a word with her. Tell her it's urgent.'

For one brief moment, Granddad was at a loss for words. The idea of his granddaughter being wanted by the flatfoots was a bit of a turn up for the books. 'What's it about?' was all he could ask.

'Just give her the message,' returned Constable Jones, sternly, before making his way back out to the street.

Mary had not enjoyed herself so much for a long time. Despite the rather strange conversations with Winnie Backer during the midday meal, she felt invigorated by the bracing air of the Essex countryside. As she and Lennie strolled through what had once been a wheat field at the back of the house, her cheeks glowed in the early afternoon sun. Even the stubble that had crept up through the hard Essex clay had a beauty all its own, long thin lines of fresh green grass nestling side by side with so many different varieties of weeds which were determined to claim their place as the dominant force in the field. The young couple spoke very little until they had reached the site where the flying bomb had crashed, the massive hole now filled in by German Prisoners of War. But they thought a lot, mainly about each other, about the extraordinary circumstances that had brought them together. Now, as they came to a halt in silence, two tiny specs against a vast blue horizon, they stared up at the sky and marvelled at the peace of it all.

'You're so lucky,' Mary said. 'It's like a different world. Out here I feel I can actually breathe.'

Mary's exhilaration gave Lennie the courage to gently slip his arm around her waist.

She looked up, smiled, and snuggled against him.

'What *do* you dream about?' Lennie asked, echoing his mum's earlier question.

'It's always the same,' she sighed, contentedly. 'I dream about going away on a holiday.'

'You mean, like going to Southend?'

Mary chuckled. 'No, of course not, silly,' she replied. 'I love Southend, but I want somewhere different, somewhere a long way away, where I can take off my shoes and walk barefoot along a sandy beach.' She suddenly swung a look at him. 'I'd love to go to Devon.'

'Devon?' replied Lennie in astonishment. 'But that's miles away.'

'Not really,' she said. 'You can go on a coach from Victoria Station. It's called the Blue Coach, and it takes all day to get there.'

'To get *where*?'

'Oh, I don't know,' she replied, slipping her own arm around his waist. 'They say once you get past Exeter, the coast is lovely down there, all the rocks are red, with long stretches of white sandy beaches. And you can hear seagulls swooping down into the sea all the time.' Even as she spoke, they suddenly heard the screeching of seagulls in the far distance ahead of them. 'What's that?' she asked excitedly.

'You want seagulls?' said Lennie with a grin. 'Well, we have them.' He pointed into the distance to where a farmer and his workhorse were tilling an adjacent, unplanted field, followed mercilessly by a hoard of gulls. 'That's old Percy Ruggles. He's getting his land ready for the autumn sow. All the birds love that soil. Plenty of grub for them.'

For a few moments they just stood there, watching the pure-white wings flapping excitedly over the horse and plough, swooping down on to the unsuspecting creatures in the soil who would soon be their food. And high above them a lark sang energetically.

'Tell me something, Lennie,' asked Mary, as though waking up from her dream. 'What did your mum mean about not believing everything the birds tell you?'

Lennie's mood changed, and his eyes looked up towards the sky. 'See those up there – those small birds with the forked tails and long pointed wings? They're swallows.'

'Swallows?' Mary looked up to see the small feathered creatures diving towards the ground and shooting straight up into the air again. 'I've always wondered what they look like.'

'They're actually known as songbirds,' he said. 'They migrate every year from hot climates down south somewhere. When Mum was first taken ill, she used to say that she hoped she'd live long enough to see the swallows come again.' He smiled wryly to himself. 'So far, so good.'

Mary hugged his waist hard and looked up at him. 'Don't you worry,

Lennie,' she said. 'Your mum's just a bit frail, that's all. She'll go on for a long time yet.'

Lennie shrugged. 'Maybe,' he replied with some irony. 'But I wouldn't want her to go on if she didn't have at least *some* quality of life. I wouldn't want her to go on if she wasn't happy.'

Mary waited a moment before asking the all-important question. 'Are *you* happy, Lennie?'

He looked down at her and gradually his frown relaxed. He leaned forward and kissed her gently on the lips.

Despite all the questions she needed to ask, Mary was beginning to feel more relaxed. However, there was still that nagging worry that he was keeping things from her, things that she had to know if they were ever going to have any kind of relationship. But in time. All in good time. Only when *he* was ready.

In the field beyond, the seagulls swooped down for their meal, whilst the swallows high above sang their songs and frolicked together in a dazzling bright-blue sky.

Chapter 9

Sergeant Jim Hopkins was an amiable sort of chap. When he first joined the police force at the tender age of twenty, he had been a bit of a street thug, knocking around with the lads in the East End of London, showing off like mad, getting drunk at the weekends and scaring the life out of innocent old ladies who crossed the road rather than walk past the pub door. But once he'd seen the light, being put out on foot patrol proved to be a big plus, not only for the police, but also for himself. Yes, after battling out on some of the most dangerous streets in London, Jim Hopkins knew all the ropes, and also all the villains who tried to rule those streets. But in so doing, he had learned about tolerance and compassion, and how to tell if someone was a liar or an innocent. He had also learned a lot more when, three years earlier in 1941, he had been transferred from the East End to the makeshift building in Holloway which was being used after the Hornsey Road police station had been bombed during the Blitz, with the loss of six police officers. It was a harrowing experience to follow in the wake of those six dead colleagues, but he was determined to carry on their tradition of professionalism, of treating everyone with fairness and lack of intimidation. That's why Mary felt perfectly comfortable in his company when, following the visit by PC Jones to the family home in Roden Street, the sergeant had called for an urgent meeting with her. The interview room was small and bleak, and the sound of voices talking even in hushed tones, echoed eerily up on to the corrugated-iron roof of the police station, producing a very scary sound indeed.

'So how long have you known this Chinese lady?' asked the sergeant, sitting opposite Mary at a small, well-used wooden table.

'Hardly any time at all,' replied Mary, who still found it hard to believe that she was being questioned about someone who seemed to her to be the essence of goodness. 'I first came into contact with her after . . . well, after she talked to my young sisters and brother. She's an artist. I went to see some of her drawings up at her flat . . .'

'Her flat over the newspaper shop, in Fortess Road?'

The sergeant's question took Mary completely by surprise. 'You – *know* where she lives?' she asked.

'Oh yes,' replied the old-timer. His white hair was a complete contrast to his uniform, and his face was lined, but still handsome for a man in his sixties. 'We know about Mrs Rawsthorne.'

'I know her as Tanya – Tanya Ling.'

'That's her maiden name.' The sergeant sorted through some papers in a file on the table. 'She was born in Hong Kong. Mother Cantonese Chinese, Father from mainland China. She met her husband when the family emigrated to England before the war.'

Mary found it hard to take all this in. 'But – why are you telling me all this?' she asked, clearly bewildered and confused. 'Has she done something wrong?'

'I don't know, Mary,' replied the sergeant, closing the file in front of him. 'But when you get a complaint from someone, it's our job to investigate it.'

Mary sat up straight in her chair. 'Complaint? From whom?'

The sergeant paused for a moment, then loosened his collar and got up. 'Gets so hot in this place,' he said, going to a small metal-framed window. 'These prefabricated things are all very well, but they're always either too hot or too cold.' He continued his questions whilst opening the window. 'I understand you've been working at the British Restaurant, up at the Archway?'

'Yes,' Mary replied quickly, 'But I left there and—' Suddenly the penny dropped. 'It's that woman, isn't it?' she snapped. 'Mrs Nestor – the manageress at the restaurant. What's she been saying to you?'

The sergeant stood with his back to the window. 'You must let *me* ask the questions, Mary,' he replied, with a fatherly smile.

'But Mrs Nestor *hates* Tanya! She was so nasty about her, and all because she came to have tea with me at home.'

'My information is that Mrs Rawsthorne visited the restaurant on a regular basis. Why *was* that, d'you think?'

'Well, hasn't she the right to go there?' asked Mary, indignantly. 'It's a public place.' Suddenly aware that she was being a bit uptight, she softened her attitude. 'She only came to sketch people. She loves looking at people, studying their faces. There's nothing wrong with that – is there?'

The sergeant returned to his chair, but stood there, leaning his hands on the back of it. 'Mary,' he said softly, 'you don't think Mrs – you don't think Tanya Ling would have gone to the restaurant for *other* purposes, do you?'

Mary stared at him in astonishment. 'What do you mean?' she asked, transfixed.

'Our information is that she was often seen there meeting up with – shall we say – *different* men.' He raised his hand, to prevent her saying anything. 'Have you any idea who these people were, Mary?'

Mary felt as though she was about to explode. 'I don't know what you're talking about!' she snapped. 'I never saw Tanya sitting with anyone – not once. She was always alone, always sketching people.'

The sergeant studied her carefully, then sat down again opposite her. 'Mary,' he continued, uneasily. 'Do you know what opium is?'

Mary looked genuinely mystified.

'It's a drug, taken from the poppy seed. It's very dangerous, and it's illegal.' He sat back in his chair. 'My information is that – Tanya Ling – was seen collecting cash from these men, and passing small packets of opium to them.'

The seriousness of this accusation suddenly gripped Mary. The idea that the woman who was so close to her parents was some kind of criminal was, in her mind, cruel and false. 'I won't listen to this!' she growled, getting up from her chair.

The sergeant stayed where he was. 'Sit down please, Mary,' he asked, quietly.

'I've told you,' insisted Mary emphatically. 'That woman at the restaurant is wicked and evil. She doesn't like anyone who's even in the slightest bit different to her. She hates foreigners. She has a chip on her shoulder as big as — as — Big Ben! She got rid of me because I said I like Tanya. It's a wicked lie, I tell you!'

The sergeant, still seated, now used his words as an order, not a request. 'I said please sit down, Mary.'

Although the sergeant's response was calm and sympathetic, Mary knew that she could not disobey his warning.

The sergeant waited for her to sit down again before talking. 'Now Mary, I want you to know that no one is accusing *you* of doing anything,' he continued quietly. 'But you must know that since we received this information, we have been keeping a close watch on Tanya Ling, and, at some time, it may be necessary for us to issue a search warrant.'

Mary clutched her hand to her mouth. She was totally distressed. 'But you can't *do* that,' she cried, quietly, close to tears. 'Tanya's done nothing wrong, I know she hasn't. She was a friend, a very close friend of my mum and dad. They wouldn't've had *anything* to do with her if they thought they couldn't trust her. I just can't believe she's ever done anything wrong.'

The sergeant slowly lowered his head, then raised it again. 'I wish I could say to you that that's true, Mary,' he said, with a sigh. 'But I'm afraid it's not. You see, a couple of years ago, she spent a week in prison.'

Granddad Trimble hated responsibility. Even when his wife was alive, he much preferred an easy life, which meant being waited on hand and foot, having three square meals a day, reading the *Daily Mirror* newspaper from end to end, spending as many evenings and Sunday opening hours in the Eaglet pub as he could, and having a kip whenever he was bored with his wife's company. Of course he did have to go to work, but unfortunately that was the only way he could get

117

money to pay for his food and drink, although he made sure his presence at the Gas, Light and Coke Company was restricted to as few hours as he could possibly manage without being found out by his Works Supervisor. Therefore, the idea that he was now having to act as chaperone to his grandkids was something that had riled him, right from the moment when Mary had got a job first at the British Restaurant, and now at the Marlborough cinema. Not that he had to do any cooking; Mary did all that before she set off for work every early afternoon. But the thought that he was being treated as some kind of housewife, looking after a family, clearing the table after they had eaten, and making sure they got to bed on time every night, were just not the kind of things that should be expected of a man in his position. And try as he might, there were times when he just couldn't bear that Thelma. She was almost sixteen years old and *she* should be the one to be looking after her young brother and sister. After all, in a few weeks' time she would be getting the results of her Matriculation exams up at her school, and since it was perfectly obvious to everyone that she hadn't a chance in hell of passing any of them, the old man felt it was about time she took on the burden of responsibility – well, at least some of it. He had told Mary this time and time again, and in his view, it was about time she listened to him. But Thelma was no walkover. She had a mind of her own, and if she wanted to go on the prowl up West, nothing and no one in the whole wide world was going to stop her. 'The least you could do is to help me get your dinner out the oven,' he growled irritably, when Thelma came down from her bedroom expecting to find the meal ready and waiting for her on the table.

'I'm not a skivvy!' she replied, snidely. 'In case you've forgotten, I'm still a schoolgirl.'

'Hah!' snorted the old boy. 'Some schoolgirl! Yer mum and dad must be turning in their graves.'

'If they're turning in their graves,' came her retort, 'it's because you've turned out to be a useless old sod!'

Outraged, Granddad raised his hand to slap her. 'You cheeky little cow!' he yelled. 'You talk to me like that again an' you'll get *this* round yer face!'

'Oh yeah?' scoffed Thelma, taking her usual place at the table. 'You and whose army?'

Eyes blazing, Grandad was only stopped from giving her a hard whack when Dodo and Billy burst into the room.

'What's for dinner?' asked Dodo, immediately plonking herself next to Thelma at the table.

''Ope it's not scrag end mincemeat again,' blubbered Billy, sitting next to his younger sister. 'I'm getting fed up with leftovers from Sunday.'

'Well it *is* scrag end mincemeat!' blurted out the old man, tetchily. Both Dodo and Billy groaned.

'An' if yer don't like it, you can blame yer sister!' Casting an angry look at Thelma, he stormed out of the back parlour into the scullery.

As he went, Thelma made a rude gesture with two fingers at him behind his back.

'What's up with Granddad, then?' asked Billy, who was already holding his knife and fork ready for some grub.

'Probably as fed up as us about having yet more mincemeat,' proffered a grumpy Dodo. 'What was you having a barney about with him, Thel?'

Bored with the ritual mealtime with her brother and sister, Thelma leaned her head against the wall. 'I don't know what you're talking about,' she sighed dismissively.

'You *was* having a barney,' Billy said, smugly, ''cos we heard you.'

Thelma turned on him. 'Then you should mind your own business and stop listening to other people's conversations!'

'Was it about that bobby who came to see Mary yesterday?'

Thelma immediately sat up straight. 'Bobby?' she asked, darting a look at her young sister. 'What bobby?'

'He turned up at the front door,' said Billy. 'My mate Freddy Wilcox said he saw her going into the cop shop in Hornsey Road.'

'What the hell are you talking about, you little turd!' grunted Thelma.

'It's true!' insisted Billy, wiping his nose on the back of his hand. 'She went this mornin' – before she went to work. Dunno what it's all about, though. P'raps she's killed someone.'

Thelma glared dismissively at him.

'P'raps it's got something to do with her boyfriend.'

'*What* boyfriend?' asked Thelma, getting caught up in what she usually took to be her brother and sister's rubbish talk.

'That bloke who got me out the river,' replied Billy, now putting the fork impatiently into his mouth as though he was starving. 'The one who lives out in Epping Forest.'

Thelma took this in. It was gradually dawning on her what was going on. 'She went all the way to see him, out at Epping?'

'It *was* her day off,' said Dodo, who was now so bored, she was making patterns with her fork on the clean tablecloth.

'She went on the Green Line bus,' said Billy.

'How d'you know all this?' asked Thelma, somewhat skeptically.

'I've got ears,' returned Billy, cheekily.

'*Big* ears!' said Dodo, laughing at her own joke.

This set the two of them locked in battle across the table. Whilst this was going on, Thelma was miles away. Not that she ever believed a word her young brother and sister ever said, but if it was true that Mary *had* been called to the police station that morning, then whatever it was must have been serious. If what the two brats had said was true, then the one person who would know what was going on would surely be Granddad. Leaving Dodo and Billy in a battle to the end, she quickly eased herself up from the table, and went out to the scullery.

'Granddad!' To her astonishment, the old man was at the sink, dabbing his eyes with his handkerchief. He was sobbing profusely. She went to him quickly. 'What's the matter?'

The old man turned his head away from her. 'What d'yer think what's the matter?' he said, falteringly. 'You lot treat me like a bit er dirt!'

For one moment, and for probably the first time in her life, Thelma felt guilty. She didn't know why, because she had never really had any interest at all in her granddad. In her mind, and just like everyone else in the family, she felt no affection for him at all. But it was his own fault, for he was a mean and grasping old man, who never had a thought of concern for anyone but himself. He had always wanted to be the centre of attention, using his age to gain respect rather than trying to be someone that his family could look up to. But in the few seconds that she stood there beside him, watching him sob his heart out because of something she had said to him, it did actually cross her mind that in some ways, *she* was no different to *him*. 'I'm sorry, Granddad,' she said. Despite her sudden feelings of remorse, the words stuck in her throat. 'I didn't mean what I said, you know I didn't.'

'Oh yes,' spluttered the old man. 'Like 'ell yer didn't!'

She turned him round and gently raised his head. 'I said I'm sorry,' she repeated. 'I promise I won't talk to you like that again.'

He looked up at her, tears streaming down his unshaved cheeks. 'Why d'you 'ave ter mock me?' he blubbed. 'Why d'yer 'ave ter say things that yer don't mean?'

'Look,' she continued, trying another approach. 'If I get the food out the oven and put it on the table, will you believe that I *am* sorry?'

The old man paused a moment before answering.

'Depends,' he replied.

'On what?' she asked.

He dabbed his eyes, and looked straight at her. 'On what you're after,' he replied.

Thelma looked back him. She knew he had seen right through her. 'Why did Mary have to go round Hornsey Road police station this morning?' she asked.

Alf Bickley was standing at the back of the stalls watching the British Movietone News, which was showing vivid accounts of British ground troops of the Second Army locked in a violent battle with Field Marshal Rommel's panzer divisions in the Caen area of north-western France. With his hands in his pockets and a cigarette dangling from his lips, the manager of the Marlborough cinema looked grim and anxious.

From the pictures on the screen, it was clear that the Allied invasion since the D-Day landings a few weeks ago still had a long way to go, and with reports coming in that, alongside the doodlebugs, the Germans had developed another secret weapon to use on the civilian population of Great Britain, he was only too aware that although the Marlborough hadn't yet suffered too much from bomb damage, there were still anxious days ahead for him and his patrons.

'Excuse me, Mr Bickley.'

Although Mary's voice was low, Alf turned around with a start.

'Sorry to disturb you, sir, but I was wondering, since it's an all-"U" programme this week, would it be all right to bring my young brother and two sisters in to see the show on Saturday afternoon? I'd make sure to keep an eye on them.'

'Of course you can, Mary dear,' he replied, his voice only just audible over the sound of the bloody military battle on the screen. 'I told you when you joined you could bring 'em in any time. You can always get 'em to the air-raid shelter over by the Savoy cinema if there's an air raid.'

'Thank you very much, sir,' said Mary, turning to go.

Alf followed her out to the lobby. 'Mary.'

Mary came to a halt at the foot of the stairs leading up to her pitch in the grand circle.

'Make sure you lock up well tonight,' said Alf. 'The Gaumont along the road had a break-in to the manager's office last night. They got away with the day's takings. Sounds like it's an army deserter on the run. Must be desperate if he's down to breakin' into pitture houses. Mind you, I'm not surprised it was the Gaumont. Swanky place like that looks as though it's full of stuff the Black Market would give a pretty packet to get its hands on.'

'I'll make sure I lock up, sir.'

'Good girl.' Alf disappeared into his office behind the cashier's cubicle.

Mary went upstairs and waited outside the entrance doors of the grand circle, just in case there were any more patrons for the main feature, which this week was part of a return double bill of Walt Disney's *Bambi* and *Dumbo*. However, as this was the last performance of the evening, there weren't many kids in the audience, which mainly consisted of adults. But to her consternation, sitting in the back row was a young couple, a sailor and his girlfriend, indulging in what Mary thought was going quite a bit further than the usual slap and tickle she usually associated with those who wanted to sit in the back row. This kind of thing hadn't happened before, but she knew she had to stop it before one of the patrons nearby complained, so summoning up all her courage, she quickly made her way behind the back row and shone her torch on to the startled couple. 'Come on now, you two,' she whispered. 'Save that till you get home.'

The girl panicked, and quickly adjusted her dress. The sailor merely sat upright in his seat, and grinned. 'Spoilsport!' he whispered.

When the couple got up and left, Mary did indeed feel like a bit of a spoilsport. After all servicemen had been through during the war, it seemed churlish to deprive them of *anything* they wanted to do in the back row of a cinema. Her mind went back to the sinking of the battleship *HMS Hood* three years earlier, with the loss of a thousand and three hundred lives, and the terrible tragedy of *HMS Royal Oak*, one of the great British battleships torpedoed by a German U-boat back in 1939, with the loss of over eight hundred lives, and taking place before war had even been declared. As she watched the young couple leave the circle, she felt a sense of despair. However, rules were rules, and not even *she* could break them.

At the end of the last showing of the feature film that evening, the audience stood to attention as the National Anthem was played, then filed out in an orderly procession. Some of the women, and even one or two of the men, were dabbing tears from their eyes after the emotional end of one of Disney's most popular animated films. It always surprised Mary how people, including herself, always cried in the cinema. After all, what happened on the screen was only make-believe, so why did people identify so much with the characters and situations? Not that there was anything wrong with showing how you felt. She had seen so much pent-up emotion during the reality of the war. Thank God for the pictures, which helped people escape from that reality.

It was whilst she was going along the empty rows in the grand circle, picking up bits of litter left behind by the patrons, that Ernie Backer called to her from the side exit door. 'I'm all done, Mary,' he called.

'Right you are, Mr Backer,' she called back. 'See you tomorrow.'

'Isn't it about time you called me Ernie?' he said, his voice echoing around the empty cinema.

From down below, Alice Thompson called up. 'I know what I'd like ter call you, Ernie Backer!' she joked, her voice bouncing along the bare lino floors which had replaced the lush apple-green carpet from the cinema's more opulent past.

Both Ernie and Mary laughed. 'I bet you would, Alice Thompson!' he called back.

Mary came up the circle stairs to the side exit, carrying her paper bin full of litter. Ernie was waiting for her.

'So how was your day with my son yesterday?' he asked.

Mary, surprised, came to a halt. 'How did you know about that?' she asked.

'Oh, walls 'ave ears, y'know,' he replied. 'Did 'e cook a meal for you?'

Mary could hardly believe she was having this conversation with Lennie's dad. When she had agreed to go out to Epping, she was under the impression that Lennie would be the only one who knew about it. She did not, however, count on Mavis, the cashier, one of the biggest gossips the world had ever known. 'Yes,' she replied, 'he gave me a lovely meal. He's a better cook than me.'

'And what about his mum?'

Mary didn't really know how to answer.

'I take it you *did* meet her? Or did he lock her up in her bedroom?'

Mary was a bit startled by his remark. Looking back at those moments after they had eaten at the farmhouse, all she remembered was Lennie taking his mum upstairs for her afternoon nap. She certainly didn't realise that he was locking the poor woman into her room. 'Mrs Backer was very nice,' was all she was prepared to say.

'Poor Winnie,' he said, seeming to be genuinely sad. 'I wish I could have given her what she deserved. But . . . well, things just didn't work out between us, so there weren't much I could do about it. When two people don't love each other any more, I s'ppose all yer can do is to go your separate ways, ter try and pick up your lives all over again. It's the same with Lennie. *He* deserves a break – especially after what happened between him an' that . . . oh well, that's up ter him to tell you.'

Mary listened to what he was saying with rapt attention, but she was determined not to pry any more information out of him than he was willing to give.

'All I'm sayin' is that Lennie's a good boy.' He took the remains of a dog-end from behind his ear, put it between his lips, and lit it. 'Over the years, him an' me's had our fair share of slaggin' off each other, mainly 'cos I weren't prepared to keep in touch with Winnie. But I tip my hat to the way that boy's looked after his mum. I'm not proud of the way I've left him to it. One way and another he's had a pretty rum ol' time. That thing in the army . . . I s'ppose he's told you about that, has he?'

Mary merely shook her head.

Ernie puffed hard on his dog-end. 'Well, it's no use him carryin' on like *that*. The longer he bottles things up inside him, the worse it'll be for the two of you.'

Mary looked up at him. With most of the lights now turned off in the cinema, his face was little more than a shadow. 'I'm not sure I know what you mean, Mr Backer,' she said.

Ernie smiled knowingly back at her. 'Oh you will, young Mary,' he replied. 'You will.' He turned towards the door. 'See yer tomorrow. G'night.'

'Goodnight.'

After Ernie had left, Mary stared at the door for several moments. He was such a strange man, so full of things he wanted to tell her, but, like Lennie, he was unwilling to do so. She turned and looked around the grand circle. The stall lights had now been turned off, and there were now only two dimmed wall lights left for her to turn off. After a last-minute check for more rubbish, she started to make her way back towards the side exit. When she got there, she switched off the lights, plunging the grand circle and the remainder of the cinema into the dark. As she did so, however, she heard the door creak open at the back of the auditorium above her. Thinking it was Ernie returning for something, she stopped and turned to look up towards the projection room, once the gallery of the old live theatre. 'Mr Backer?' she called.

The silence was complete, compensated only by a light coming from the door at the back.

'Mr Backer,' she called again. 'Is that you?'

But her whole body was chilled with fright as she suddenly saw what looked like the figure of a man in Victorian clothes, bathed in a thin film of fluorescent light.

'Mr—' She was too frozen to the spot to switch the lights back on.

The figure stopped, and briefly looked down at her before slowly moving across the back of the auditorium.

In a flash, Mary fumbled for the light switch and found it. But when she turned on the dim lights, there was no sign of the mysterious figure. Shaking with fear, she rushed out of the auditorium, stopping only briefly to lock the doors behind her.

As she did so, a barrage of anti-aircraft gunfire thundered out across the sky in the distance.

Chapter 10

That night, Mary didn't sleep a wink. The very thought that she had actually seen a ghost in the grand circle of the Marlborough cinema sent constant shivers down her spine. But she had seen it, all right, plain as daylight. Even so, when her usherette friend Alice Thompson ridiculed the idea when Mary told her what she'd seen, she knew that it had not all been in her imagination. As she lay in bed, her head covered tightly with her sheet, she could still see the way that the strange figure had turned towards her, as though he wanted to say something to her, but the moment Mary turned on the circle lights, he disappeared.

'Oh, I know what they all say about it,' scoffed Alice as she locked up the main entrance doors for the night, 'but I still say it's only psychic people who can see dead people.'

'How d'you know I'm *not* psychic?' asked Mary, dreading the reply she might get.

''Cos you've got more sense, that's why,' insisted the ever-practical Alice. 'When people die, they die, and that's all there is to it. You mark my words, that stupid woman Alf Bickley brought here to sort it all out was a real loony. All she wanted was to get on the front pages of the newspapers.'

'*What* woman?' asked Mary, apprehensively.

'Mrs Blackwell,' replied Alice, adjusting her tortoiseshell spectacles and lighting up a fag. 'She's a teacher at that school near where you live. Calls herself a spiritualist.' She scoffed at the idea. 'Hah!' They came down the front entrance steps of the cinema and made their way towards Holloway Road, which, in the continuing blackout, looked dark and curiously quiet as the grave. 'A mate of hers got into a right ol' pickle. She's supposed to be one of the leading spiritualists in the country, but she ended up at the Old Bailey – somethin' about fakin' a séance.'

Mary shivered at the very mention of the word séance. She had seen such scary things at the pictures, and she always kept her eyes shut and put her hands over her ears.

''Ol Ma Blackwell was called as a witness to help out the woman, but it cut no ice with the jury. She still landed up in the clink.' She suddenly caught a sight of her all-night bus approaching the bus stop. 'See you temorrer, Mary. Don't 'ave nightmares!' She rushed after her bus.

'Alice!' Mary called, as Alice was just getting on to the bus as it moved off. 'Who *is* that thing I saw inside?'

'An actor!' Alice called back. 'So they say!' The bus sped off with her clinging to the handrail. 'Don't think 'e gets much work these days!'

An actor. Mary mulled this over in her mind as she tossed and turned in her bed that night. What kind of actor, and why was he still roaming what once used to be the old gallery of the Marlborough? She shivered again, and suddenly felt very lonely, wishing she had moved in with her two young sisters for the night. As it was, the night passed very slowly, and by the time daylight was streaming through the side of the blackout curtains, her poor battered mind had raced through so many of her problems, not least the worrying concerns about Tanya Ling.

The journey up to Kentish Town took only a fraction of the time it had taken Mary the last time she had walked there from the Nag's Head. This was thanks to the old bicycle which used to belong to her mum, who often cycled the long distance across London to the Mile End Road, to visit Aunt Gladys and Uncle Cyril. After the interview she had had with Sergeant Hopkins at the police station the previous day, her return trip to see Tanya Ling seemed completely different. Even Fortess Road looked drab and uninviting, whereas before she had admired the old four-storey terraced houses and little shops. And the people she passed on the way seemed so preoccupied with walking with their heads down, staring at the pavement, it made them look, to Mary at least, dour and grumpy. However, as she approached the door of the small newsagents' shop above which Tanya had her flat, she felt a gradual glimmer of hope that, once she had spoken with Tanya again, all the accusations against her would soon prove to be false and malicious. As it was, whilst she was cycling the ten minutes or so up Tufnell Park Road, all she could think about was that hateful Sheila Nestor, the manageress of the restaurant, who was obviously causing mischief just because of her own personal prejudices. However, there was one burning question that Tanya needed to answer, a serious question that could affect the trust Mary's mum and dad had had in the Chinese woman. What *was* all this about her spending a week in prison?

By the time she got off her bicycle and leaned it against the wall by the side of the shop door, she was brimming with a mixture of confidence and uncertainty. After straightening her hair beneath the black beret she was wearing, she rang the bell of number 27 B, and waited there for Tanya to call down from the first-floor window. After a moment or so, there was no reply, so she rang again, and then looked up towards the window. With still no reply, she decided to use the door knocker, just in case the bell wasn't working. Once again there was no response, so she tried calling out through the letter box. 'Tanya! Are you there? It's me – Mary Trimble!'

'She's not there, dear.'

The voice calling from the open door of the shop caused her to jump. When she turned to see who it was, she found the shop owner, a middle-aged woman with a turban around her head, peering round at her.

'She hasn't been there for three or four days now,' said the woman, a fag dangling from her lips.

'Have you any idea where she's gone?' asked Mary, tentatively.

'Gord knows, dear,' replied the woman, holding the shop door open. 'Tanya keeps herself to herself. Sometimes she stays out half the night, don't come back till the early hours of the mornin'. Strange woman. But then she *is* a foreigner, in't she?'

'Have you any idea where she goes to?' persisted Mary.

'Haven't the foggiest, dear,' came the first sign of irritability from the woman. 'You from the bobbies or somethin'? They've been round twice askin' about her. I'm telling you, if she's been up to no good, she can pack her things and get out! I don't want no trouble in *my* place.' With that, she closed the shop door, and went back inside.

Mary was now becoming despondent. For a moment or so, she stared up at the first-floor window, still hoping that Tanya would suddenly appear there. But the fact gradually dawned her that calling on Tanya unexpectedly was not a good idea. The Chinese woman clearly had a life of her own, a life that Mary and quite a few other people knew nothing about. It was a depressing thought to know that Tanya might not be altogether the person Mary had imagined her to be.

On Saturday afternoon, Lennie was digging up onions in the allotment at the back of the house. Stripped to the waist, and wearing an old pair of torn, knee-length army shorts and Wellington boots, from time to time he took off his flat cap and wiped the sweat from his face with it. As it was now coming into July, the weather was really hotting up, and because there had been very little rain since the beginning of the previous month, the ground was so hard that he could hardly get his shovel into the soil. After working on the land since he was a youngster, Lennie was a well-built young man, with rippling muscles and a body that was tanned a deep brown. But since getting out of the army, he had grown to hate the work, and, as his mum had told Mary, he yearned for the bright lights of London town, a dream that was not likely to come true, at least not whilst his mum was still alive.

Winnie Backer's eyes opened with a start. She had no idea how long she had been asleep. All she knew was that she hated having a forced nap every afternoon. It made her feel so fuzzy in the head, so much so that she couldn't think straight when she woke up. Once the room had come into focus, she gradually eased herself up in the bed, and sat there for a moment or so. Sun streamed through the window, which was shut, and as the curtains hadn't been drawn, Winnie felt stifling hot. She slowly got out of bed, stood up, went to the window and looked out. In the allotment at the back of the house, she could see Lennie toiling in the sun. She smiled in admiration; he was such a fine figure of a lad, and always so good to her. So different to his dad, so different to that terrible Dr Simmons who had been treating her for so long, so different to all those people who thought there was something wrong with her. Winnie went to her dressing table and, for a moment, stared at herself in the mirror there. Although she didn't like the way her hair had grown out straight and was flecked with grey, she still thought she didn't look too bad for her age. The only trouble was, she couldn't remember what that age was. But Lennie knew. *He* would tell her. Yes, that's what she'd do. She'd go down and ask him. Lennie knew *everything*. He would tell her. But when she went to the door, it was locked. She tried to turn the handle, and then to pull it, but it wouldn't budge, so she turned away in frustration. What did it mean, she asked herself? Why was the door locked again? Suddenly, she felt unsettled, restless, disoriented. She paced around the room, around in circles, not knowing what to do. Her bedroom seemed to get smaller and smaller, and she became breathless, as though she couldn't breathe. She was now desperate to find a way out into the open, into the light, into the world outside. She went to the window, and tried to open it, but it was shut tightly, and she didn't have the strength to raise it. Her only hope now was the small lavatory that Lennie had converted from a boxroom beside his mum's bedroom. Winnie went in there, but the window was positioned a little too high in the timber-framed wall for her to reach, so she went back into her bedroom, and brought the chair from her dressing table. Climbing up on the chair was a risky business for it was very old, and had already been repaired several times. However, Winnie finally managed to reach the window, which was not locked, and by some extraordinary will-power rather than strength, she managed to push open the window, and lever herself up.

In the allotment outside, Lennie, gradually digging up an ample supply of onions, was at the same time trying to work out in his mind how he could tell Mary about the things she had to know if there was ever going to be a chance of them getting together. But, despite the fact that he had rehearsed in his mind what he was going to say to her many times, he knew only too well that he might never be able to actually say them all. But then, he asked himself, was Mary the kind of girl who could shrug her shoulders and tell him that she didn't care about his past? It was the present and the future that was important. Although Lennie took comfort from that possibility, he was not at all sure that it could be a reality. The tragic events of his short time in the army was one thing, but what had happened between him and Carole Pickard was something else, something that any girl would find difficult to understand. Snapping out of his thoughts, he picked up the bunch of onions, put them into his wheelbarrow, and took them off to the old barn to start cleaning the soil off them.

On Saturday afternoon, Mary had a busy time, for not only was the cinema full of kids and their parents who had packed in to see the all-'U' Walt Disney double-bill, but, with Alf Bickley's permission, Thelma, Dodo and Billy were to be let in free of charge. The only problem was that when Dodo and Billy turned up before the start of *Bambi*, Thelma wasn't with them.

'Why didn't she come?' Mary asked anxiously, as she met her youngest sister and brother in the foyer of the cinema.

Both kids shrugged their shoulders. 'She said she doesn't like cartoon films, that they're only for kids.'

This angered Mary, particularly as it meant Dodo and Billy would have had to cross the dangerous Holloway Road all on their own. 'Follow me,' she said, leading the excited youngsters up the well-worn carpeted stairs, after getting the all-clear from Mavis the cashier.

'This *your* gang, then?' called Alice Thompson, who was just coming out of the stalls after showing some patrons to their seats.

Mary stopped on the stairs. 'The wicked witch of the West and her brother, Frankenstein!' she replied, acidly.

Dodo and Billy pulled faces.

Alice laughed.

'Dodo, Billy,' said Mary. 'Say hello to Mrs Thompson.'

The two kids simultaneously reluctantly mumbled, 'Hello,' and then continued to rush up the stairs.

'Sorry, Alice,' apologised Mary. 'At least I hope to get a few hours' rest from them!'

'I shouldn't bother if I were you, dear,' returned Alice, laughing. 'The place is full of the little rotters. You won't be able to hear much of the pitture once *they* start yelling and cheering!'

Mary quickly followed Dodo and Billy up into the grand circle, where she immediately plonked them down into the two seats she had earmarked for them, on the side at the end of the row, which put them near the exit just in case she had any trouble with them. They were excited to see Harry Percival thumping out some of the songs from *Snow White and the Seven Dwarfs* on the organ, and they immediately joined in with the other kids in the audience singing out loud the tunes which had been played on the wireless so many times.

'Now I'm warning you two,' said Mary, threatening them with a wagging finger. 'One peep out of you, and I'll get that ghost to come down and sit with you!'

Both their heads swung her a startled look. 'Ghost?' they spluttered, in terrified unison.

Once Mary was satisfied that the two of them were settled down, she quickly showed late-arrival patrons to their seats, leaving Harry Percival to take a thunderous ovation from the house full of kids. It was more like a football match.

Once the house lights were dimmed, and the stage curtains had parted for *Bambi*, the place went silent, which gave Mary the chance to wait outside in the circle lobby, just in case there were more late

133

arrivals. But whilst she was standing there, torch at the ready, she suddenly felt consumed with anger that Thelma had not turned up. It was Saturday afternoon, and the fact that not only were Dodo and Billy not at home, but also that Granddad had gone off for the weekend to stay with one of his old drinking partners over at Edmonton, meant that Thelma could do what she wanted, and there was absolutely nothing Mary could do about it.

'If you want to bring the kids up in the interval,' called Ernie from his open projection room door in the gallery, 'I'll give 'em a look round.'

Mary called back up to him. 'That's very kind of you, Mr Backer,' she replied. 'Depends if they behave themselves. I've told them that if they don't, I'll get the ghost to come and sort them out.'

Ernie laughed. 'I'd be careful, if I was you,' he replied. 'Yer never know when the Toff's going to pay us a visit.'

'Not in the afternoon though?'

'I wouldn't bank on it,' replied Ernie. 'Lennie saw him once when he was helping me to load the film on my number two projector. It was soon after he come out of the army. Scared the wits out of him.'

'Lennie actually *saw* the ghost too?'

'Oh, he's not the only one,' Ernie assured her. 'The ol' Toff gets around and about when he wants to. We all reckon he must have been an actor from when this place used to be a theatre, 'cos he loves to show 'imself off.'

'The Toff?' she asked. 'Why d'you call him that?'

'Ah, it's just a kind of kind of nickname, that's all. We all reckon he must've been a toff if he was an actor. But Lennie saw 'im longer that anyone else. He swears the Toff tried to talk to him, but I think that's pushin' it a bit. Still, Lennie *was* feelin' down in the dumps at the time, especially after those kids got drowned in the river back home.'

Mary had no time to ask questions, for there was a stream of late-comers who came rushing up the stairs to catch up with the exploits of Disney's most famous young deer.

★

134

Once he'd left the onions to dry off, Lennie left the old barn and made his way back to the house. As soon as he reached the kitchen door, he took off his Wellington boots, and left them outside. He quickly used a soiled kitchen towel to wipe the sweat on his chest, then left it on the floor for the next wash day. At the old stone sink, he found a chipped enamel mug and pumped himself some water up from the well outside in the courtyard. He drank the mug of water right down, and wiped his mouth with the back of his hand. As he did so, he noticed that it was after four-thirty on the old kitchen wall clock, and realised that it was time for his mum to be let out of her bedroom after her afternoon nap. He quickly filled the kettle, and put some tea from the caddy into the teapot, which was always kept upside down on the draining board. On the way through the entrance room, he stopped briefly to collect his sleeveless pullover, which he put on whilst going up the stairs. The key was in the lock on the outside of his mum's bedroom, and he turned it and let himself in.

'Cup of tea downstairs for you, Mum,' he said, going in.

He stopped in horror as he saw the bed empty, and both the lavatory door and window inside wide open, with his mum's dressing-table chair propped up beneath the window. 'Christ!' he yelled, rushing back to the window in the bedroom. With tremendous force, he pulled open the window and scoured the fields around. 'Mum!' he called, his voice trembling with panic. 'For Christ's sake, Mum!'

His voice was so loud and deep that it thundered across the court-yard, and out across the fields beyond the back of the house. But, try as he may, there was absolutely no sign of her anywhere, only a scattering of swallows, hovering in the sky above.

For the past few hours, the Marlborough cinema had taken quite a bashing. The kids who had accompanied their parents to the matinée performance had shouted and cheered their heroes *Bambi* and *Dumbo* so much that the plaster above the auditorium was in grave danger of collapsing.

Mary was very relieved when it was time to show Dodo and Mary down the stairs to the front foyer, no matter how well behaved they had been during the two films. Fortunately, the two kids were able to cross over Holloway Road with all the other families, but just as they were doing so, the air-raid siren suddenly wailed out over the rooftops. What had started as an orderly audience exit from the cinema now turned into a mad scramble to make for home or the nearest air-raid shelters. Mary anxiously watched Dodo and Billy rush down Seven Sisters Road, knowing that the two of them would be home within the next few minutes, but before she went back inside the cinema, she scoured the sky for any sign of an approaching flying bomb. However, nothing happened until she went into the front entrance lobby, where the new audience was already queuing at Mavis's ticket kiosk for the next continuous performance. An explosion from somewhere nearby rocked the place, bringing down flakes of plaster from the ceiling, and resulting in everyone throwing themselves on to their stomachs on the floor.

'Hold on, everyone!' Alf Bickley's reassuring voice was calling from the open door of his office. 'Everythin's OK!' By the time he appeared, the sudden emergency had passed, and people were already getting to their feet again. 'Don't worry, folks!' he called to the crowd gathered there. 'It's not come down anywhere near. Get your tickets. The next show's about to begin. Tickets at all prices!'

Mavis the cashier slowly re-emerged above her desk in the kiosk, where the patrons were already rushing to form a queue again.

Alf helped Mary to her feet. 'You OK?' he asked anxiously.

'OK, thank you, sir,' replied Mary, still trembling. 'That was close. Where was it?'

'I dunno,' said Alf, keeping his voice low. 'Sounded like up Highbury somewhere. Just carry on as normal. I don't think we'll get any more.'

Even as he spoke, the All Clear sounded, and Mary quickly made her way up the stairs to collect tickets at the doors of the grand circle.

'By the way,' Alf called up to her, 'did your kids enjoy the show?'

Mary stopped briefly and called back to him. 'Oh yes, they did,' she said. 'And thanks very much, sir.'

'Any time,' returned Alf, before turning to the patrons still crowding into the foyer. 'Seats at all prices! One and threepence on your left, one and ninepence on your right. Hurry now. Show's starting in five minutes!'

By the time Mary had shown the last of the ticket holders into their seats, Harry Percival at the organ was just finishing off his ten minutes' curtain raiser with a rousing chorus of 'There'll Always Be an England!' Then the lights dimmed, and the curtains parted as the beam from Ernie's projector illuminated the screen with the start of *Bambi*. Whilst this was going on, Mary went across to the seats where Dodo and Billy had been sitting watching the previous show. As she expected, they had left behind the screwed-up newspaper from which they had been eating the fish-paste sandwiches she had made them before she left home that morning. And stuffed under Billy's seat was an empty bottle of Tizer, which Mary quickly retrieved. As she was doing so, her shoe stuck on some chewing gum on the floor. At first, she was just plain furious, and resolved to give both Dodo and Billy a piece of her mind when she saw them the following morning. However, it wasn't until she started cleaning up the mess that she realised the significance of the two of them having chewing gum at all, something that was extremely hard to get in the shops.

'Mary!'

Alice Thompson was standing there in the flickering light from the screen.

'Somebody left this for you with Mavis during the afternoon.' She handed Mary an envelope. 'Sorry, I meant to give it to you earlier, but it's been like bedlam downstairs.'

Mary took the envelope and slipped it into the skirt pocket of her uniform. Once she'd scraped up the remains of the chewing gum with some of the newspaper, she went out into the circle foyer and opened the envelope, which was plain, and not addressed. Inside was an undated note, with no address, but she immediately recognised the handwriting:

My dear Mary,

I'm sorry I haven't been in touch with you for a while, but I'm away from home at the moment dealing with a personal problem. I just wanted you to know that I've been doing a bit of asking around about your friend Lennie Backer, and I'd like to pass on to you what I've found out. I know you told me not to, but when I got to thinking about what you had told me about him, I didn't want you to be hurt. Forgive me?

I'll get in touch with you as soon as I can.

Much love,

Tanya.

Mary was furious. After all she had gone through at the police station, she didn't like the idea that Tanya was behaving in such a mysterious way. And the idea that Tanya was spying on Lennie when she distinctly asked her not to was very unsettling. She folded the note up again and slipped it back into the envelope, just in time to meet a group of late arrivals for the show that had already begun.

Lennie was half out of his mind with worry. How had his mum managed to get out of her bedroom without him noticing? Where had she gone? She was not safe to go *anywhere* on her own. She was like a child, who had to be watched night and day. He practically leapt over the fence into the field at the back of the house, then ran as fast as he could in his Wellington boots which were still muddy from his afternoon digging up onions.

'Mum! Where are you?'

His frantic yells echoed across the hedgerows, and when he came to a brief stop, a squabble of seagulls took flight in panic from the stubble all around him. How could he have been so careless? Surely he should have realised that someone as mentally sick as his mum had the craftiness of a fox. Hadn't Dr Simmons told him that many times before? Hadn't he told Lennie that someone with his mum's tragic illness was capable of heightened powers that were difficult for most people to understand? Oh, how could he have been so stupid? He vowed there and then never to leave his mum alone in the afternoons. She had to be watched at all times. As he swung round and round in the field, looking in every direction, he also vowed that things were coming to a crunch with her. Dr Simmons had told him that this time would come, that sooner or later the poor woman would need the sort of constant attention that he, Lennie, could never provide. Now beside himself with worry, he turned his attention to the woods, suddenly feeling an ice-cold chill racing up his spine. The old forge!

He found her down by the river's edge. She had just taken off her dress and carpet slippers, and was standing there in her petticoat. Below her, the surface of the river was rippling with anxiety, as though it was trying to tell her not to do what she was about to do. She moved as close to the edge as she could and looked down, but before she could jump, Lennie was upon her, throwing his arms around her waist, tackling her to the ground. 'No, Mum, no!' he shouted.

Startled, Winnie struggled to break loose.

'*Please!*' begged Lennie. '*Please!*' His face was crumpled up, and tears were welling in his eyes.

Winnie, pinned on the ground on her stomach, slowly turned to look round at him. 'But I only wanted to have a swim,' she mumbled, her eyes shining and vacant. 'There's nothing wrong with *that* – is there?'

Chapter 11

The results of Thelma's school exams did not, as expected, make happy reading for either Thelma or Mary. In nearly all subjects her grades were just about as low as she could get, so much so that Mary decided there and then that as Thelma was now of school-leaving age, she would see to it that her sister got a job as soon as possible. However, after the results of her exams, Thelma's grandiose ambition to become a reporter on the BBC was dismissed by Mary as a non-starter; if Thelma couldn't even write the King's English properly, how could she ever expect to get a job which involved at least a certain standard of education?

Anticipating that such a situation would arise sooner or later, Mary had already taken the steps to get Thelma applying for a variety of jobs. These included a trainee hairdresser at a salon in Seven Sisters Road, a receptionist in the Emergency Department of the Royal Northern Hospital in Holloway Road, and as a shop girl in Woolworths and Marks and Spencer's stores, also in Holloway Road. But every interview Thelma went to, she behaved as though the prospective employer would be very lucky indeed to have such a person like herself on their staff. However, with the prospect of the girl ending up as an office cleaner or something, Mary finally persuaded a friend of their mum's, who worked in the accounts section of Jones Brothers, to get an interview for Thelma for a vacancy as a junior sales assistant. Jones Brothers, an old established and much-loved department store, was just a stone's throw away from where the Trimble family lived in Roden Street, which meant that if Thelma was able to get a job there, she would be close enough for Mary to keep an eye on.

On the morning of the interview, Mary gave Thelma the strongest talking to, warning her that this was an opportunity she should grab with both hands. As ever, Thelma took everything her elder sister told her with a pinch of salt, even down to wearing a skirt, blouse and make-up to try and give the impression that she was a woman and not a child. But Mary put a stop to all that, so that by the time she and Thelma left for the interview, she was looking more like a school-leaver who would be willing to learn a trade.

Jones Brothers, situated in a highly favourable position on the corner of Tollington and Holloway Roads, was gradually replenishing stock that had been missing in the store for the best part of the war. Even though some of the shop-front windows were boarded up after damage following the most recent doodlebug explosion down the main road near Highbury Corner, the place still retained an air of charm and elegance. The moment Thelma entered the place, she loved the smell of eau de Cologne and the different perfumes, things which had virtu-ally disappeared from the stores in wartime.

On the second floor, they reached the Personnel Department, where they were told to wait until Miss Bennet, the Personnel Officer, was available to see Thelma. Whilst they waited, Mary felt more anxious than her sister about the interview, watching every minute tick by on the clock on the wall above the secretary's desk, praying that, just for once, Thelma would stop trying to be a madam, and behave like someone who wanted to get on in life.

The door of the Personnel Officer's room opened, and a smartly dressed young woman in white blouse and black skirt appeared. 'Miss Trimble?' she asked, with the sweetest of smiles.

Both Mary and Thelma stood up.

'Which one of you is the applicant?'

Reluctantly, Thelma slightly raised her hand.

'Please come in,' said the woman, who beamed politely at Mary as she stood back to let Thelma enter her office.

Mary watched the door close behind them. She feared the worst.

'Please sit down, Thelma,' said the woman, indicating a chair in front of her desk. 'It *is* Thelma, isn't it?'

Thelma shrugged grandly.

'I see you've just left school?' said the woman, sitting at her desk and referring to Thelma's application form there.

Thelma looked all around the room at anything she could see, but deliberately avoided the woman's gaze.

'Thelma,' said the woman, 'my name is Miss Bennet. I'm responsible for enrolling staff for Jones Brothers. Have you ever visited the store before?'

Thelma shrugged. 'Sometimes,' she answered, casually.

'What d'you feel when you come into a place like this?'

Thelma's boredom threshold was very low. 'What d'you mean?' she asked.

Miss Bennet sat back in her chair, carefully awaiting Thelma's response. 'I mean,' she said, 'do you feel excitement when you see all the things we sell here? We have so many interesting departments, for men *and* women. Do you ever look at the lovely clothes and wish you could buy at least some of them?'

Thelma was a bit baffled by the woman's question. 'Yes,' she replied, tentatively. 'I like clothes.'

'So would you know how to sell them to a customer?'

Thelma paused to consider this. ''Course!' she replied, confidently.

'And would you be able to do the same if you were selling – let's say – a bar of soap, or a tube of toothpaste?'

Thelma sat up straight in her chair. 'I wouldn't want to sell a bar of soap or a tube of toothpaste.'

'Why not?'

''Cos it's boring.'

'But customers need a bar of soap just as much as clothes. Why should that be boring?'

Again Thelma shrugged. ''Cos it is, that's all,' she replied, indignantly.

Miss Bennet waited a moment, then leaned forward across her desk.

'Thelma,' she said softly, but firmly, 'your examination results are not exactly first class, are they?' She did not wait for an answer, but again referred to Thelma's application form. 'There is nothing on this form that tells me how suitable you would be to sell a bar of soap or a tube of toothpaste. To do that you must have the urge to make a sale, the ability to convince your customer that you know what you're talking about. Looking at your application form, I see nothing here that convinces *me* that you would be an asset to Jones Brothers. Do you think I'm right, Thelma?'

'I could do the job as well as anyone else,' replied Thelma, bombastically. 'Better!'

'Well, if you couldn't do it in your school work, if you didn't take an interest in learning, how do I know that you would be interested in doing a good day's work *here*?'

For the first time, Thelma was so taken aback by this woman's approach, she just didn't know what to say.

'Thelma,' said Miss Bennet, whose sweet-natured smile disguised a shrewd sense of observation, and who calmly picked up Thelma's application form and put it into her desk draw, 'one of our staff here, someone I believe you know, assured me that the position we are offering here would be perfect for a school-leaver like you. Well, I have to say that, at the moment at least, I cannot agree with her.' She got up from her chair, and stood behind it. 'So tell me. Can you say one single thing that can convince me that I am wrong?'

Waiting in the secretary's office outside, Mary sat with her head bowed low, trying to work out in her mind what she would do if Thelma failed yet another interview. Thelma was a major problem in Mary's life. Although the girl was now old enough to take on some of the responsibilities in the home, she was intent on creating as many difficulties as she could. Yes, she was going through all the mysteries every teenager had to face as they grew up, such as exploring things that could be potentially dangerous, but Thelma was stubborn and, at times, deeply unpleasant, and if she didn't grow out of it soon, there was no doubt in Mary's mind that it was going to lead the girl into real trouble. By the time twenty minutes had passed, Mary had convinced herself about the outcome of Thelma's interview. Just then, Miss Bennet's door opened, and a very chastened Thelma came out. 'Well?' Mary asked despondently, having convinced herself of the outcome.

Thelma closed the door behind her, and shrugged. 'I got the job,' she said.

Lennie was distraught. After finding his mum on the river bank about to jump in, he felt the only thing he could do was to chat to her doctor, for although he didn't want to face up to what Dr Simmons was bound to tell him, he now accepted that, for his mum's sake as well as his own, the time had come to take drastic action.

'I'm sorry, Len,' said the aged doctor, who had been attending Winnie Backer ever since the first symptoms of senility appeared some years before. 'Make no mistake, what happened to your mum is going to happen again and again. In the back of her poor old tired mind is a desperation to do away with herself. After all that's happened to you, that's not something you should be expected to cope with.'

They were walking together in the courtyard behind the house, Lennie clutching a pamphlet Dr Simmons had given him to read. In the far distance they could hear the sound of anti-aircraft gunfire which signalled the approach of more flying bombs over the Thames Estuary.

'And that's another thing,' continued the doctor, bringing them to a halt at the fence shutting off the courtyard from the field beyond. 'What happens when you're away somewhere and those things come over? It's not fair to expect a stranger to deal with seeing that your mum is protected. There's no doubt about it, Len, the time has come when your mum needs expert, twenty-four-hours-a-day care.'

'That's all very well,' replied Lennie, flicking though the pages of the pamphlet, 'but where's the money coming from to get Mum into a place like this?'

'Holly Manor', said the doctor, taking the pamphlet from Lennie, 'is run by a Church charity. As I remember, your mum was a regular churchgoer in her younger days, so I don't think she'll have much trouble in getting a place there.' He flicked through the pamphlet. 'As you can see, the bedrooms are small, but they're really very comfortable.'

'It's not the bedrooms I'm worried about, doctor,' replied Lennie. 'It's my own conscience. Do I have the right to lock my own mother away in a strange place, a place that she may not like?'

'You lock her away in her bedroom every afternoon, Len,' replied the doctor, with a frankness that Lennie found very unsettling. 'At least in a place like this she'll be with other people whom she can talk to, with trained staff to look after her and give her a quality of life.'

'Dr Simmons,' replied Lennie, grimly, 'do you know how old my mum is? She's not sixty, seventy, eighty years old. She's only forty-seven. Is it really right for someone to be locked away for the rest of her life – at *that* age?'

The doctor sighed, and considered Lennie's question. 'What's the alternative, my boy?' he asked, handling the pamphlet back.

A few minutes later, Lennie watched the doctor go back to his banged-up Austin car, which was parked outside the courtyard, before disappearing out on to the fringe road around the forest. Taking such a decision about someone he loved was clearly a dilemma that was going to haunt Lennie for the rest of his life. But, as he turned to go back into the house, something occurred to him very strongly. Surely that decision was not his alone to take? Although his mum and dad had separated some years ago, they had never divorced, in which case surely his dad would have to take at least some of the responsibility for what happened to his wife? Deep in thought as to what he should do, he strolled back into the kitchen, unaware that his mum was at her bedroom window, looking down at him . . .

Tanya Ling got off the bus which was just a few minutes' walk from her flat in Fortess Road. She moved gracefully, her long thin legs not visible beneath her flowing, pale blue ankle-length dress. Beneath one arm she carried her treasured sketchbook, which, by the way she held on to it, had been put to good use during the past day or so. She seemed happy enough, but the smile on her face betrayed what she was really feeling inside. Ever since those mischievous remarks made by the manageress of the British Restaurant, she had become something of a recluse, staying away from home at night, only returning during the day when it was absolutely necessary. Thank God for her distant elderly aunt in Bermonsey, who had allowed her to stay in her spare room whenever she wanted, not that she *wanted* to stay away from home. After all, *what* had she done wrong?

When she reached the newspaper shop, she panicked to see a police car parked in the road outside, and when she reached the door, she found it open.

'Mrs Rawsthorne?'

The deep-throated voice behind her brought her to a nervous halt. Standing there was Police Sergeant Hopkins from Hornsey Road police station.

'Or is it Miss Tanya Ling?'

'What's all this about?' Tanya asked, trying her best not to sound too anxious.

'We'd just like to have a few words with you,' said the sergeant. 'Let's go inside.'

Reluctantly, Tanya entered through the open door and into the passage. With Sergeant Hopkins following on behind, she went up the stairs, where, to her horror, she found a police constable just coming down from her studio on the top floor. 'What – what's going on?' she spluttered, indignantly. 'What are you people doing in my—'

Sergeant Hopkins held up an official-looking document. 'We have a search warrant, madam.'

'A – search warrant?' Tanya was overcome with shock. 'What on earth are you talking about?'

'It's perfectly legal, I can assure you,' said the sergeant. 'Issued at Kentish Town Magistrates' Court first thing this morning. Let's go upstairs, please.'

Shaking with nerves, Tanya led the way to her studio. Up there the shock was even greater, for her sketches were spread out all over the floor. 'What's the meaning of this?' she demanded.

'I'd like to know the names of these people,' asked the sergeant. '*All* of them.'

Tanya shook her head with disbelief. 'I don't *know* the names of them all. To me they are just faces – people in the street, in pubs, in the park . . .'

'In the restaurant?' added Sergeant Hopkins, provocatively.

Tanya glared at him. 'Will you please tell me what this is all about?'

'I'd like to know if any of the people – the men, that is – are the same people you met up with in the British Restaurant over the past few weeks?'

Tanya was bewildered. 'I've not met most of the people in these sketches,' she insisted. 'To me they are just faces. As I told you, they could be anywhere. I wouldn't know who these people are or where they come from. That doesn't interest me.'

'I see,' replied Hopkins, staring down at one of the sketched male faces on the floor. He hardly believed a word she was saying but, for the time being, was willing to give her the benefit of the doubt. 'Then am I correct in saying that you didn't meet any of these people in the restaurant over midday lunch, and that you didn't take cash from them in exchange for something *you* had to offer?'

Tanya was so taken aback, she could hardly talk. She knew what Sheila Nestor the restaurant manageress had probably been saying about her, because she had threatened to inform the police about her idling away her time at the same table every day, but she had no idea that she was spreading malicious gossip like this. 'I never ever met one single person who sat at the same table as me! If that is what that dreadful woman has been telling you, then it's a lie!'

'Mrs Rawsthorne,' said the sergeant, his eyes still scanning the sketches lying around on the floor. 'In 1941 you were charged at Highbury Magistrates' Court with being found in the possession of opium. You were fined five pounds, and were sentenced to one week in Holloway Prison.'

147

Tanya clutched her forehead in disbelief. 'In case you didn't know,' she said, truly distressed, 'at that time my husband had just died of a terrible disease, in the British Army, in Gibraltar. It was a painful experience for me, and, as I explained to the court at the time, I needed something to relieve that pain. I know it was a reckless thing to do, but when you are in a state of grief such as *I* was at that time, you will do anything – anything at all.'

Hopkins listened carefully. What she had said was true. He had already read the minutes of her appearance in court, and knew that, despite calls from the prosecution to throw the book at her, the magistrate had given her an extremely lenient sentence. And that sentence had carried a particularly unusual warning from the Magistrate not to take against the accused simply because she was Chinese. In court, Tanya had been described as a woman of good character, a woman who had adored her English husband so much that his untimely death had robbed her of her reason to live. Her taking of a miniscule amount of opium from a Chinese acquaintance in London had been a mistake, but a release. But even though the sergeant knew that she had paid the price for that mistake, it was his duty to investigate these latest allegations from a witness who had claimed to have seen her passing an illegal drug for cash. 'If what you say is true, Mrs Rawsthorne,' said the sergeant, 'why do you think these allegations have been made against you?'

Tanya suddenly saw her sketch of Sheila Nestor propped up untouched against the wall. 'Because,' she replied, going over to the sketch, 'because one person has a grudge to bear. A grudge that is futile and unjust.' She picked up the sketch, and threw it on the floor on top of the other sketches there. 'I can't help being what I am, sergeant. I can't help where I come from. You can search this place from top to bottom, but I can tell you that I did *not* do any of those things. And if you don't believe me, ask anyone who knows me. Ask Mary Trimble.'

★

Just before the end of the last evening performance at the Marlborough, Mary could hear Ernie having a row with someone up in the projection room. Fortunately, none of the audience heard what was going on as they filed out of the grand circle and, as she didn't want to get involved with whatever was going on in the projection room, once she had cleaned up underneath the seats and turned off the lights, Mary quickly made her way down to the foyer. Mavis the cashier had already gone home, and Alf Bickley was patiently waiting for Alice Thompson to finish off her duties down in the stalls.

After she had bid Alf goodnight, Mary left the cinema and made her way across Holloway Road. Because the double bill of two thrillers were shorter than usual, every night that week, she had managed to get home early. However, just as she had got to the other side of the road, and was making her way towards a short cut down Bovay Place, she heard someone call out to her.

'Mary – wait!'

Swinging round, she was surprised to see who was hurrying towards her. 'Lennie!'

'I saw you leave,' he said, breathlessly. 'Thought I'd missed you.'

Mary looked bewildered. 'What are you doing here at this time of night?' she asked, totally flustered. 'It's after ten o'clock.'

As soon as she finished talking, he kissed her lightly on the lips. 'I can't tell you how glad I am to see you,' he said. 'I came down to see Dad. It was urgent.'

'So it was *you* having that row upstairs? What was it all about?'

'Oh, it's a long story,' replied Lennie, slipping his arm around her waist as they walked. 'He told me to stop being a mummy's boy, to get a life of my own. I told him that he was an uncaring old git, who'd made my life a living hell.' For the next few moments he told her how the doctor had advised putting his mum into a Church-run nursing home.

'And did your dad agree?' Mary asked.

'Oh yes, he agreed all right,' replied Lennie, bitterly. 'In fact, he suggested it some time ago. As far as he's concerned, the sooner Mum's out of the way the better. Anyway, he's signed the consent form, so when I get back tomorrow, I'll start making all the arrangements. Dr Simmons seems to think he can get her in by the weekend. Luckily, our neighbour Mrs Honer's staying at the house tonight.'

'And then what?'

'I don't know, Mary,' he said. 'But I think I want to get rid of the house. Trouble is, while the war's on, there's not much chance of selling it. But I've had enough of the place. It's been like a millstone round my neck.'

'I don't know how you can say that, Lennie,' she replied, with some surprise. 'It's such a beautiful place, so quiet and peaceful.'

'That's the trouble,' he sighed. 'It's too quiet. I need to see more people. People like you.' He leaned across and kissed her neck. 'Let's go and have a cup of tea somewhere.'

Mary was worried. 'I can't ask you home, Lennie. It's too late, and the kids might—'

'I don't mean *that*,' he said quickly. 'I mean somewhere else.'

'There isn't anywhere – not at this time of night.'

'There's the all-night stall near the Regent,' he said.

Hand in hand they made their way up Holloway Road towards Highbury Corner, past Jones Brothers department store, beneath the mainline railway bridge and the underground station, and finally to the old Regent cinema, which had always looked as though it had seen better days. Nearby was the all-night stall which had formerly been set up for the use of the emergency services during the Blitz, but was now a favourite stopover for the long-haul truck drivers who travelled on the Great North Road. Lennie quickly paid for two cups of tea without saucers, and the two of them then squatted down to drink them on the steps of the old nearby cinema. For several moments, neither of them said anything. They just sat there watching two old tramps munching through some cheese sandwiches and sipping hot cuppas, thanks to the generosity of the middle-aged bloke behind the counter. Both Mary and Lennie seemed miles away, but when they did talk it was because Mary was determined to get him to be frank

150

and honest with her. 'Lennie,' she asked suddenly, 'why did you leave the army?'

He quickly swung a glare at her. 'Do we have to talk about that now?' he asked, tersely.

'No,' she replied. 'But we'll have to – sooner or later. If we want to get to know each other, Lennie, we shouldn't bottle things up inside. I promise I'll tell *you* everything you want to know about me, but if we're going to be open with one another, we *must—*'

'I killed a man.'

His sudden outburst cut right across what she was saying. It was a real shock for her. 'How?' she asked, falteringly.

'I was in the Royal Engineers,' he continued, dourly. 'I had a mate called Joey. We both worked in the transport section. We were based up near Norwich. We used to take turns driving this heavy-duty truck, back and forth between two camps. Most of the load was for the gunners on coastal defence, catching enemy raiders before they could get too far inland.' He took a gulp of his tea as if to give himself the energy to carry on. 'We both liked to drink, but me more than him. One trip was overnight. I drank too much and Joey begged me to let him take over the wheel. I said he must be crazy. I said I knew how to hold my drink, and we were safe as houses.' He stopped talking for a moment, trying to pluck up enough courage to continue. 'It was a very narrow country lane, no moon – pitch dark. We came to this bend. Two horses came running straight at us out of nowhere, right into the headlights. I couldn't think quickly enough to avoid them, and I hit them dead on. Somehow my door got flung open and I got thrown out of the driver's seat ending up in a hedge. But the truck carried straight on, with Joey still trying to get out.' He lowered his head. 'I can still hear him screaming out, "*Len! Get me out of here! For Christ's sake, get me out of . . .*" It was too late. The truck smashed into a tree and went straight down a slope on to a railway line. It was full of ammunition. It exploded. Joey was blown to pieces.' He sighed and looked up at the moon. 'They only just managed to stop a train coming from Norwich.'

Mary put down her teacup, and gently put her hand around his waist.

'I got put on court martial,' continued the now chastened Lennie. 'They put me away for nine months for manslaughter, followed by what they called "a dishonourable discharge".' He drained the last of his tea, and held the handle of the cup on one finger. 'So I went back to Epping and looked after Mum.'

Mary held on to him, but he suddenly broke loose and stood up.

'OK! So you've got what you wanted!' he ranted. 'Are you satisfied now?'

Mary stood up, and tried to hug him. 'It wasn't your fault, Lennie,' she insisted, illogically.

'What the hell are you talking about?' he barked. 'Of *course* it was my fault! I killed Joey. I killed him as if I'd pushed a knife right into him.' He glared with such anger at her. 'Don't you understand? It wasn't on my roster to drive that night, but *I* insisted. Joey begged me not to, but *I* insisted. If it wasn't for me, he'd still be alive!' By now his voice was croaking and faltering. 'He was nineteen years old. He had a girlfriend. They were going to get married.' He swung round on her, and pushed her away. 'Are you satisfied now, Mary Trimble?' he shouted. 'Are you?' With that he strode off.

Lennie's raised voice caused the man serving at the stall counter to look over at him. 'Everythin all right, mate?' the man called anxiously.

'Everything's all right,' Mary called back, reassuringly.

Although not entirely convinced, the man withdrew back behind his counter. But the two old tramps were alarmed, and scuttled off as quickly as they could.

Mary quickly returned the two cups to the tea stall, then rushed after Lennie. She caught up with him just as he was about to disappear down Hornsey Road. 'Lennie!' she pleaded, turning him round to face her. 'Listen to me – *please!*'

'No!' he yelled. 'You made me tell you something that I've never told anyone else before. What happened is something *I* have to live with – not you, not anyone – just *me!*'

'You're wrong, Lennie,' she insisted, firmly. 'If we're going to trust each other, if we're going to have any chance at all of loving each other, what happened to you is not something you have to live with alone for the rest of your life. Can't you understand that, Lennie? Can't you understand?'

Lennie went quite still. Although the general street blackout still hadn't been lifted, the summer moon was so bright, Mary could see every feature of his anguished face. It was a luminous white, eyes full and questioning. But as she pressed herself against his masculine form, and felt the sheer power of his heart racing, her heart was racing too. They held each other, her head resting on his shoulder, their breathing slight and warm. Then they slowly walked together towards the station.

Chapter 12

Mary hadn't seen Tanya Ling now for more than a month. Despite the fact that Sergeant Hopkins had assured her that no charges were being brought against the Chinese woman, Mary was concerned that Tanya seemed to have just disappeared into thin air. Nonetheless, she was told by Sergeant Hopkins that, until Sheila Nestor withdrew her allegations about Tanya being involved with drug dealing in the British Restaurant, the police investigation was still ongoing. With this in mind, Mary decided to do some investigating of her own by paying a visit to the woman who had given her the sack so unceremoniously from her job at the restaurant.

Sheila Nestor lived in a ground-floor flat in Duncombe Road, which was two or three stops on the number 14 bus from the North London Drapery Stores in Seven Sisters Road. Under normal circumstances, Mary would have walked the journey, but she had so little time to spare in the mornings before she went to work at the cinema, that she decided to cut her journey time and take the bus.

After months of flying-bomb attacks, people were still carrying on as though the war was virtually over, despite Mr Churchill's warnings in Parliament that the Germans had another rocket-propelled machine called the V-2, which was just waiting to compliment its cousin, the doodlebug. Nonetheless, the noose seemed to be getting tighter and tighter around the necks of the Nazi generals, for whenever Mary passed a tobacconist's shop, there were newspaper placards outside proclaiming that the Allied Forces were winning one battle after another in Northern France.

The house where Sheila Nestor lived looked pretty run-down to Mary, but at least the small front garden of the rather imposing looking three-storey Edwardian house was neat and tidy, and contained quite a colourful array of summer flowers. Mary first of all checked that the number on the front door was the one her friend at the restaurant, Maisie Stringer, had given her, then opened the garden gate, and rang the bell to the downstairs flat. For a minute or so there was no reply; she was unaware that someone was looking out at her through white lace curtains at the downstairs window. She rang again, and waited, but just as she was about to go, the door was suddenly flung open, and Sheila Nestor appeared, with a look of fierce rage on her face. 'What are *you* doing here?' she roared, her voice gruff and threatening.

'Mrs Nestor,' replied Mary, 'I have to talk to you.'

Sheila, a dumpy little figure with a shock of white hair, refused to come out, and kept her hand firmly on the door. 'Who gave you my address? You got no right . . . I'll get on to the police . . .'

'Only a few minutes, Mrs Nestor,' argued Mary. 'After what you've done to Tanya Ling, it's the least you can do.'

Sheila slammed the door in her face.

'You can't just ignore the truth!' yelled Mary, her face pressed against the door. 'You can't just destroy someone's life without asking yourself why.'

The door remained firmly shut. Mary raised her voice even louder. 'You're a wicked woman, Mrs Nestor!'

With no response, Mary turned and started to leave. But as she did so, the door opened behind her. 'You – Trimble! Come in!'

Mary turned around, and saw Sheila holding the door open for her. She hesitated.

'Well, if you're coming, come!'

Mary, held herself straight, and went into the house, following Sheila into the front parlour where she had been watched through the lace curtains. It was at once a depressing room, with peeling cream wall-paper which had at one time been covered over with light brown varnish, and an overhead light shade with frayed tassels. But at least the mantelpiece was crammed with framed sepia snapshots of her husband in uniform, together with family photos of the two children Sheila had had in her early twenties.

'So let's have you!' growled Sheila, who was a ferocious little woman, with horn-rimmed spectacles that seemed too small for her rather bloated face. 'Evil, am I?'

'I'm sorry I talked to you like that, Mrs Nestor,' replied Mary, who was conscious that she was deliberately climbing down. 'But you've caused a great deal of pain and suffering to my friend because of false information you gave about her to the police.'

With arms crossed defiantly, it was clear that Sheila was not going to invite Mary to sit down. 'I *know* what I saw, and no one can say otherwise.'

'I'm afraid *I* can,' replied Mary, herself calmly defiant. 'And I'm not the only one. Maisie Stringer—'

'*Her!*' Sheila bellowed, collecting her half-smoked cigarette which was still burning in the ashtray. 'That girl hasn't got a brain between her ears!'

Mary found it hard to accept this woman's unpleasantness. It was so difficult for her to reconcile the way she was behaving now to the way she used to be when Mary first got her job at the restaurant, when she was helpful and kindness itself. For some unknown reason, these days the woman was eaten alive with bitterness. 'Neither Maisie nor I ever saw Tanya sitting with different men at her table. Whatever people joined her were shown to that table by either Maisie or I.'

'Then why did she sit at the *same* table every single time?' demanded Sheila, blowing out a rush of smoke.

'Because', Mary returned emphatically, 'it was the best position for her to get a good view of all the people eating in the restaurant. Tanya's an artist, Mrs Nestor. It's her job, her profession. She's had exhibitions of her work.'

'A restaurant is a place to eat,' grunted Sheila, 'not to draw pictures in a book, *and* all over the paper tablecloths which we had to throw away!' She turned her back on Mary, and stared out aimlessly through the lace curtains at the window.

Mary found it difficult to bring this woman into focus. 'Mrs Nestor,' she asked, 'who told you Tanya had once been in prison for a drug offence?'

Sheila reacted without turning. 'You don't run a restaurant without having contacts,' was her sinister response.

Mary went across and stood behind her. 'Do you know *why* she took that opium, Mrs Nestor?' she asked quietly.

'Because she's a drug addict,' replied Sheila, but not quite so ferociously. 'Because they're all like that down Chinatown in the East End.'

'She took it because of the pain she felt after her husband died in Gibraltar,' Mary said. 'He was a serving soldier in the British army.' She hesitated briefly. 'The same as *your* husband, Mrs Nestor.'

Sheila stood quite motionless, still staring out through the lace curtains, cigarette smoke curling out from her mouth above her head.

'I *know* how painful it must have been for you, too, when you lost your husband in the last war – the terrible way he was killed by that German soldier.'

Sheila still didn't respond.

'I can see by all these pictures how much you loved him,' Mary said, compassionately. 'To be a widow all these years can't have been easy. It isn't easy for Tanya either. I'm sure someone like you would understand that only too well.'

Sheila turned her head just enough to look up at an oval-framed sepia photograph of her husband taken during the previous war.

'Tanya told me that after her husband died,' continued Mary, 'because she wasn't born in England, the authorities wouldn't pay for her to go out to visit her husband's grave. If it hadn't been for the British Legion, it was something she would never have been able to do.' She continued talking to Sheila's back. 'I think that's a pretty unfair attitude to take, don't *you*? I mean, when someone you love dies, you feel as though your whole world's fallen apart. I know it was like that for me when my mum and dad were killed in that tube disaster. Tanya's a human being just like anyone else, Mrs Nestor. Yes, she made a mistake taking that drug, but she's never taken it or had anything to do with drugs

157

since. She's not a criminal. She's no different to any of us. Tanya is just someone who suffers – just like you and me, Mrs Nestor. Just like you and me.'

After a moment, Sheila turned around to face Mary. Her face was like stone. 'Please go,' she said quietly.

Feeling utterly defeated, Mary turned, and quietly left the room.

Sheila waited to hear the sound of the front door open and close, before turning to look out the window as Mary went off down the road. For a moment she just stood there, deep in contemplation. Then, slowly, she went to a small built-in cupboard at the side of the tiled fireplace. From there she brought out a folded piece of flimsy table-cloth paper, which she took to the polished table, and spread out. She stared down impassively at the sketched face of a woman there. It was a drawing of her own face.

To everyone's surprise, not least Mary's, her sister Thelma was doing quite well in her job as a junior assistant at Jones Brothers. By the end of July she had settled in nicely in the haberdashery department, living up to what she had told Miss Bennet about wanting to get a job so that she could help her sister with all the expenses around the house. Even though nothing could have been further from the truth, having money in her pocket gave Thelma a new sense of freedom. The only problem was that she had to work every Saturday, which somewhat curtailed her forays up into the West End. However, it was a problem she soon got over, for the one day of the week that she did *not* have to work was Sunday.

Thelma got off the number 14 bus in Piccadilly Circus. It seemed strange to her to be in the West End on a Sunday afternoon, for so many things were closed, although the pubs were open for a couple of hours at lunchtime. As she strutted down Shaftesbury Avenue, she made directly for Rainbow Corner, which, after the time that the Americans had entered the war against Germany, had become a popular social club for homesick GIs. It was also a honey pot for bees; young girls from every walk of life who were looking for a good time and the chance of a better life on the other side of the Atlantic. Today, however, with so many of the American combat forces fighting in France, the Rainbow Club was somewhat depleted of available young men, much to Thelma's great disappointment. However, the West End was always a good breeding ground for potential boyfriends, and Thelma certainly looked older than her years. There was no doubt that if Mary could see her now, with her frilly low-cut white blouse, short, black satin skirt, Jones Brothers drop earrings, high-heeled clog shoes, and her hair piled on top of her head, the sparks would fly back home in Roden Street. Over the past year she had been keeping any real knowledge of her trips up West from Mary; concealing the outfits she had acquired, thanks to the generosity of two different service boys, a young sailor from Norway and an older US airman, who was based out at an airfield in Essex. The only miracle so far was how she had managed to play the field without having to pay her admirers with the one thing they wanted most.

As she passed by the Rainbow Club and found it completely devoid of any activity, Thelma was determined not to go home without having the kind of good time she craved, and that meant the kind of company she was looking for. The opportunity came when she was strolling at a snail's pace through Leicester Square, trying to give the impression to all the passers-by that the only thing she was interested in were what films were on at the giant Odeon cinema, or the Empire cinema across the square. For a few moments she stopped briefly to look at the posters outside the pocket-sized Ritz cinema next door to the Empire, where a queue was already beginning to form for the first showing of the day of *Gone With the Wind*, which had been playing at the same cinema for the best part of the war years. Whilst she was doing so, she was distracted by the voice of a young bloke who had come to stand alongside her.

'It's a terrific picture. I've seen it twice,' he said, in a rather posh voice.

Thelma turned to look at the boy, who was about eighteen or nineteen, with a single lance corporal's stripe on a soldier's khaki uniform. 'Yes,' she replied, grandly. 'I've heard it's good.'

'Wanna come in?' asked the boy, quite brazenly. 'I'll treat yer.'

'I've got my *own* money, thank you very much,' she said haughtily, lying through her teeth. 'In any case, the picture's far too long for me. It's too nice a day to sit in the dark in a picture house.'

'Wanna come for a drink, then?'

His quick approach took even Thelma by surprise. 'You're a quick worker,' she replied, clearly flirting with him.

'No time like the present,' replied the boy, with a grin. '"Tomorrow is another day," Scarlett O'Hara says that in the picture.' He moved in closer, his voice low. 'So – feel like havin' a drink with me?'

Thelma thought about it for a moment, then turned to look at him. He was certainly presentable, more than presentable in fact; he was good-looking, with lovely blue eyes under the brim of his army cap, and a radiant smile that would melt the heart of *any* young girl.

'It may have escaped your notice,' she replied, patting the back of her upswept hair, 'that today is Sunday. The pubs are closed till tonight.'

The soldier boy looked around to make sure that no one could hear him. 'We don't have to go to a pub,' he said. 'I know a place.'

'Where?' asked Thelma, suspiciously.

'A private pub,' he replied confidently. 'Don't worry, it's all above board. Of course, it's not as well stocked up at the Yanks' place, but it does good business for us Tommy Atkinses.' He paused, waiting for her answer. 'Wanna give it a try?'

He held out his arm for her, and after looking him over just one more time, she took hold of his arm, and let him lead her off. Oh, what the hell, she told herself, wryly. Live for today, gone tomorrow.

'By the way,' the boy said as they strolled through Leicester Square and along Charing Cross Road, 'my name's Chris. What's yours?'

Thelma thought for a moment. The last thing she ever did was give out her real name to *anybody*. She never could understand why, so that when anyone asked, she always used her favourite false name. 'Loretta,' she replied.

'Loretta!' The boy glowed with excitement. 'She's my favourite actress. Loretta Young! Did you see her in *Bedtime Story*? She was fantastic!' His excitement ran away with him, for he slipped his arm around her waist. 'I knew from the moment I saw you, we were going to get on like a house on fire!'

When Mary got back home, she found Nutty Nora waiting at the top of the stairs for her.

'Oy! You down there!' she yelled. Her voice sounded peculiar. 'That brother of yours has bin up 'ere again! I told you I'd 'ave 'is guts fer garters if I ever catch 'im up in *my* place!'

Mary sighed, and called back. 'What's the matter now, Mrs Kelly? What's Billy done *this* time?'

'I'll tell yer what 'e's done!' With that, she hobbled down the stairs as fast as she could. 'Look at this!'

It was not a pretty sight that Ma Kelly was showing Mary, for she was baring her gums. 'He's nicked my bleedin' teef again!'

Mary wanted to burst out laughing, but it was not the first time that her young brother had been up to Nutty Nora's rooms and taken her false teeth from the glass of Miltons that she always kept at the side of her bed. It was funny the first time he did it, but now it was becoming a joke too many. 'I'm very sorry, Mrs Kelly,' said Mary. 'Have you any idea where he's hidden them?'

The old girl was on the point of hysteria. 'If I knew that I'd be wearin 'em! But I'm tellin' you this, if I don't get them back when that little sod gets back from school, I'm goin' ter get my bruvver ter go round the bobbies! That boy's a little rat-bag! Between 'im and 'is sister and 'im next door, I don't get a minute's peace round this place!'

'Once again, I'm terribly sorry, Mrs Kelly,' Mary called. 'I'll have a look round before I go to work and see if I can find them.'

'You'd better!' yelled the old girl, going back up to her room and slamming the door so hard the house shook from top to bottom.

Mary was just about fed up with Billy's pranks. She charged off up to the first floor and went straight into her brother and sisters' bedroom to search for the old girl's false teeth. It wasn't the first time Billy had done this, so in her rage she angrily stripped off his bed and looked under his mattress. Then she looked on the window sill which was one of his favourite hiding places, where, he said, the cats would be scared stiff by Nutty Nora's false teeth. Finally she looked in his cupboard where he kept most of his junk and a few of his badly treated clothes.

'Yer won't find 'em up 'ere.'

Mary turned with a start to see Granddad standing in the open doorway.

'He took the teef off to school.'

Mary straightened up and glared at him. 'And you let him do it?' she growled, keeping her voice down in case Nutty Nora upstairs heard her.

'I'm not 'is dad!' returned Granddad. 'That boy does as 'e likes. They *all* do. He once nicked my walkin' stick, hid it outside in the Anderson. I don't know 'ow I've put up wiv it – the way everyone treats me in this 'ouse.'

'Well, I'm surprised you've managed to suffer us for so long, Granddad,' Mary snapped, acidly. 'If you hate it so much here, why d'you stay?'

'That's a good point,' replied the old man. ''cos I ain't stayin here any longer.'

Mary stopped dead. 'What d'you mean?' she asked, without trying to sound too rattled.

Before replying to her, Granddad went out on to the landing, and looked up the stairs to make sure Nutty Nora wasn't trying to listen in. Then he came back into the kids' bedroom and closed the door. 'I've decided ter move on,' he said grandly.

If Mary was taken aback, she was determined not to show it. 'Oh yes?' she replied, as though she'd been expecting it.

'My ol' mate 'Arry Watts said I could go an' bunk in wiv 'im any time I want,' he said. 'He's got a nice spare room no one ever uses, and I've got plenty of room for all me bits and pieces. In any case, I like Edmonton. They got some nice pubs over there.'

'Fine,' said Mary, tersely. 'Then you must do what you *want* to do,

Granddad. The last thing *we* would want to do is to keep you away from some decent pubs.' She started to move off past him, but he stopped her.

'Don't get me wrong, Mary,' he said, trying to pacify her. 'I don't really fit in 'ere – *you* know it, and so do the kids. I'm too old for all of yer. You want ter get on wiv your lives, and so do I. In any case, when yer mum an' dad died I only stayed on to help you out.'

This remark made Mary so indignant, she could have slapped him. 'I beg your pardon, Granddad?' she asked, utterly bewildered.

'Well,' he continued, quite oblivious to the nonsense he was talking, 'I knew you was takin' on a big load, trying to do all the fings that yer mum and dad used ter do – looking after yer bruvver and sisters an' all that. If it hadn't been fer that, I'd've gone long ago.'

'Well, it's a pity you didn't,' replied Mary.

The old man did a double take. 'What did you say?' he asked, completely taken aback.

'I said,' she repeated, 'it's a pity you didn't go before now. I don't know if it's ever occurred to you, Granddad, but ever since Mum and Dad died, you haven't lifted one finger to help your grandchildren. In fact, you never did when they were alive!'

'That's a lie!' he blurted, scarcely able to take in what she had said. 'I've always done what I could fer this family, but all I've ever had is cheek and disrespect from all of yer! I've got feelings, yer know.'

'If you've got feelings, Granddad,' she returned, with no holds barred, 'then you should have shown some for your family. Not a penny have you ever contributed to your board and keep.'

'Oh, so that's it, is it?' replied the old boy, trying to show how hurt he was. 'It's all about money.'

'Money?' asked Mary, raising her voice. '*What* money? I'm the one who brings the wages home here. I'm the one who has to clothe and feed everyone. And yet you even moan about getting the food out of the oven when I'm not here, you moan about looking after the kids whilst I'm at work – you moan and groan about *everything*! But not the pub – oh no, Granddad, when it comes to your regular trips round the

163

pub, there are *no* complaints. So – yes, I think you're doing the right thing. It's obvious you'll be far happier living with your mate in Edmonton, and it's obvious you'll be far more appreciated there than here, so – the sooner you go, the better!'

Granddad lowered his eyes in disbelief as, without another word, Mary swept straight past him and left the room.

Mary rushed down the stairs into the back parlour, and then out into the scullery. For a moment or so she stood over the empty kitchen stove. Without realising it, tears were streaming down her cheeks. What she had just said to her granddad had come out of the blue, and she felt thoroughly ashamed of herself. A few minutes later, she heard the door of the front parlour open, and knew that the old man must have been collecting his few things together.

A short time later, she heard the front door open and close, and when she rushed to look out through the front-parlour window, she saw the old man, a small suitcase in his hand, making his way determinedly down the street.

London in the rain has always had a certain charm, and, despite the ravages of wartime bombing raids, the notorious West End Streets at the weekends were still thriving with day-trippers, tradesmen and servicemen from many different countries. Being picked up by a serviceman was nothing knew to Thelma. However, on the Saturday afternoons that she had managed to slip away from home, she had usually had encounters with American GIs, who had flattered her with gifts, such as chocolates, silk stockings, make-up, and also chewing-gum, which she usually passed on to Dodo and Billy. But now that the Allied invasion of France was in full swing, today there were few US servicemen around. Nonetheless, Thelma, arm-in-arm with her young lance corporal, whom she knew only as 'Chris', was perfectly happy to spend the Sunday afternoon with a British serviceman who at least seemed to have enough money to buy her a drink.

Although the plain brick wall of the tall Victorian house just behind Frith Street was only a stone's throw away from the theatres, cinemas, and other bright lights, the quiet small mews had a seedy look about it. A pigswill bin was overflowing on the corner, a group of cats were growling at each other over a discarded chicken bone on the kerb, and two over-made-up, underdressed girls were standing in the open doorway at the side of a rundown tobacconist's shop nearby, their eyes glued to the end of the street to see what prospective customers might appear at any moment. By comparison to the two girls, Thelma's outfit was pretty tame stuff, but by the time she and her lance corporal had reached the house they were making for, the fine summer afternoon rain had left her feeling damp and clammy.

'What *is* this place?' she asked apprehensively.

'It's a private pub,' he replied, quite cheerily. 'Reserved for servicemen on leave.'

'Then why are all the windows boarded up?'

'They've taken quite a pounding round here,' he replied. 'There was a buzz bomb down Charing Cross Road last week.

Thelma followed him warily down a dimly lit staircase. From somewhere below she could hear the sound of a gramophone record of a sultry female singer doing her own version of a popular blues number. When they finally reached the bottom of the stairs, they were in what was a small, sleazy bar with just two tables and chairs.

'Hello, mate,' called the middle-aged barman, who looked about as scruffy as you could get, with a half-smoked fag behind his ear, and a plain black shirt which was open to the waist. 'What'll it be?'

The lance corporal looked to Thelma for an answer. 'Loretta?' he asked. 'Beer? Or would you like something stronger?'

Thelma looked worried. 'Er – I'll have a shandy.' For a brief moment, she really didn't feel as grown up as she'd imagined she was.

'A shandy?'

'I don't feel like too much alcohol on a Sunday afternoon,' came her fumbled reply.

The lance corporal looked across at the barman and shrugged. 'I'll have my usual please, Pete.'

165

They sat at one of the tables. 'You've been here before,' said Thelma, taunting him.

''Course,' replied the lance corporal. 'Every time I get home on leave.'

'Where d'you live?' she asked.

He didn't seem too pleased to answer the question. 'Oh – down Lambeth,' he replied casually.

'"Doin' the Lambeth Walk"?' she asked, airily singing the first line of the popular song.

His laughter was forced. When the barman brought the drinks, he gave him a ten-bob note, but didn't seem to get any change. 'Cheers!' he said.

Thelma half raised her glass to his, and took a gulp down to steady her nerves.

'D'you know somethin', Loretta?' he said, leaning across the table to her. 'You're a real good-looker. How old are you?'

'As old as I want to be,' came her cocky reply. 'How old d'you think?'

He studied her briefly. 'Eighteen?'

'Nineteen,' she returned, curling a few strands of hair back on top of her head.

'Mmmm,' he replied, leering at her. 'Bet *you* know a thing or two.'

'Why is the place empty?' she asked, ignoring what he had just said.

'Oh, it gets busy later,' he replied. 'I always prefer it in the afternoon. It's much quieter.'

Behind the counter, Pete the barman was smirking.

'Hey!' the lance corporal said quite suddenly. 'Have you ever seen a talking parrot?'

Thelma stopped adjusting her hair. 'A *what*?' she asked, puzzled.

'A parrot who talks,' he continued. 'His name's Barney. If you say hello to him, he says it right back. It's amazing how he can copy the human voice.'

'Pull the other one,' scoffed Thelma.

'Well, if you don't believe me, come and see for yourself.' He looked across to the barman. 'Barney still in the back room, Pete? Can we go and see him?'

''Course!' returned Pete. 'Help yourself.'

The lance corporal stood up, and held out his hand to Thelma. 'Wanna come?'

For a brief moment, Thelma sat where she was. For some unknown reason her heart was beginning to thump. Such a thing had never happened to her before, and even though she knew why, she was doing her best to ignore it. In those few split seconds all she could think about was what she was doing there, a dingy little place with plain brown walls, and hardly any lighting. Then she thought about Mary, and what she would say if she knew that her kid sister was in such a place, sharing an afternoon with a soldier boy she'd never met in her life. But then the other side of her mind told her that she wasn't a kid any more. She was now a woman, a woman who was earning her own living in a department store, a woman who had the *feelings* of a woman, and deserved to be treated like one. 'I haven't finished my drink,' she said.

'It'll keep,' said the lance corporal, still holding out his hand to her.

Knowing only too well that there was no way she could trust this bloke, she nonetheless took a last gulp of shandy to fortify herself, then took his hand, stood up, and followed him into the back room.

Chapter 13

Now that Winnie Backer had been admitted as a full-time resident in a nursing home in Epping, by the first week in August, Lennie was spending more time in Holloway meeting up with Mary. Since Granddad Trimble had left the family home in Roden Street, Lennie was becoming a popular visitor to the house, especially as he occasionally stayed overnight, sleeping on the put-you-up in the front parlour, recently vacated by Granddad. Billy and Dodo particularly enjoyed his company, for, during the evenings whilst Mary was working at the Marlborough cinema, he was more of a friend than Granddad had ever been, sharing party games with them, and even helping them with their school homework. The one person who had become strangely withdrawn, however, was Thelma, who pretty much kept herself to herself. After her experience with Chris the lance corporal, she decided not to make any more visits 'up West', mainly because it had shattered her confidence, and left her nervous and aware that an exciting life carried risks that she had never taken into serious consideration. Her primary concern now was if and how she would ever be able to tell anyone about what had happened in that seedy Soho club. In a few days' time she would be sixteen. On reflection, lying about her age to strange men now seemed a wild and dangerous thing to do; it had been a sharp lesson in how not to grow up.

Over at the Marlborough, Alf Bickley was concerned about rumours that the Germans were naming various targets in London that were on a list of those that would be destroyed by their V-1 flying bombs. The rumours were emanating from regular broadcasts over German radio by the Irish traitor, known as Lord Haw-Haw, who warned that within the next few days one of those targets would be the flagship Gaumont cinema in Holloway Road. Nobody who had been listening to the broadcasts quite knew why the cinema was being targeted, but it certainly sent nervous signals to everyone in the vicinity of the cinema, not least Alf Bickley and his staff. However, the manager of the Gaumont told all his own staff to keep their nerve, assuring them that no Nazi propaganda was going to close down *his* cinema, which had kept up the morale of the people of Holloway throughout the dark days of the Blitz. Alf was taking no chances, and he warned both his regular and part-time staff to be vigilant during an air-raid alert, and to make sure that all doors were kept fully open in the eventuality of a hurried mass exodus by the audience.

Mary's constant concern continued to be about the disappearance of Tanya Ling. After her confrontation with Sheila Nestor in Duncombe Road, Mary had hoped she had fired a strong enough warning shot over her former manageress's head about lying to the police. But since she had not heard from Tanya for such a long time, she was beginning to question everything Tanya had told her. Preying on Mary's mind was the conversation she had had with Tanya when she had first come to the house back in June. What *did* she mean when she talked about Mary's mum wanting to do something for her, but only when the time was right? Was Tanya *really* telling the truth when she told Mary how close she was to both of Mary's parents? Tanya was such a mysterious woman, gifted, talented, and charming to be with – but mysterious.

On Sunday, the Marlborough was showing its usual double bill of horror films. This time is was the blood–curdling, *Sweeney Todd*, coupled with *The Face At the Window*, both starring the irrepressible Tod Slaughter, who, for the best part of his career, had scared the living daylights out of theatre and cinema audiences. During the last house, Alf Bickley came to talk to Mary in the foyer behind the grand circle. He was in a sombre mood. 'So what you up to for the Bank Holiday?' he asked her, realising that the following day was her day off.

'Nothing special,' replied Mary, as he sat down beside her on a rather tatty old sofa. 'Well, that's not quite true,' she corrected herself. 'Actually, Lennie Backer has asked me and the family to spend a day with him at his place in Epping. If the weather stays nice, I'm really looking forward to it.'

'Well, he's a good lad, is our Lennie,' said Alf, leaning back with his hands behind his head. 'Now he hasn't got to worry about looking after his mum, he deserves to have a bit of fun in his life. Reckon you two are going to make a go of it?'

Mary was a bit embarrassed. 'It's early days yet, Mr Bickley. We hardly know each other.'

Alf grinned. 'Doubt you'll *ever* get to know young Lennie,' he said, lightly. 'He's got so much locked up inside him, that one. He's just like his dad – blow a fuse as good as look at you – both of 'em.' He took out his pipe from the top pocket of his jacket, and started prodding it with the sharp end of a pipe cleaner. 'Did you know that a few years ago I nearly gave Ernie the sack?'

Mary looked at him, shocked.

'Oh yes,' continued Alf as he struck a match and lit his pipe. 'He got a bit too cocky with me, and all because I told him how sorry I was about his wife. Flew at me! He said the way he treated his wife had nothin' to do with me, that I should mind my own business and get on with lookin' after the cinema.'

Mary gasped.

'Yes,' continued Alf. 'Well, I wasn't going to take *that* from one of my own employees, was I? I mean, he's a first-class projectionist, there's no doubt about that, but when he came out of the army after the last war with that kind of disability, he was lucky to have a job to come to, I can tell you. He was just one of thousands of blokes with terrible war wounds who couldn't get a job. Wonderful, isn't it? You fight for your country and nearly get killed, and what happens – there are no jobs to come back home to. You mark my words; it'll be just the same if and when this war ever comes to an end.' He puffed hard on his pipe, sending plumes of smoke up to the ceiling. 'Anyway,' he continued,

170

'I let it pass.' He turned to look at her. 'D'you know how long Ernie Backer's been working in this pitture house?'

Mary shook her head.

'Nearly twenty-seven years!' With his pipe in between his lips, he put both thumbs behind his braces and stretched them. 'And I'll tell you this much. Apart from that one incident, I've never had a day's trouble with him in all those years. Even when I know he's been in pain with his foot, he's never been late for work once, which is more than I can say for the bloke who covers for Ernie on his days off.' He let his braces go. 'Can I give you a word of advice from an old timer, Mary?' he asked.

Mary smiled back at him, and nodded.

'Young Lennie may be a bit of a nut some of the time,' he said, keeping his voice low, 'but he's pure gold. Don't be put off by what happened between him and that girl, and that thing in the army. The thing about Lennie is that his heart's in the right place. All he needs – dare I say it – is a girl like you.'

Mary had no time to answer what he had said, for they were suddenly distracted by the sound of the National Anthem coming from inside the auditorium. Both of them sprang to their feet, and as the first youngsters came rushing out to try to avoid standing for their King and country, Alf quickly tapped the hot tobacco from his pipe into a nearby brass ashtray and slipped the pipe back into his jacket.

'Goodnight, sir! Goodnight, ladies. Hope you enjoyed the show. Hope you don't have too many nightmares! Good night, young feller!' Alf's polite farewell to his patrons was just as courteous as his greeting when they arrived. He started to join them all as they flooded down the stairs. But then he stopped briefly, and called back over his shoulder. 'Mary! Forgot to give you this!' From his jacket pocket he took out a folded copy of a newspaper and waved it at her.

Mary hurried her way through the departing audience and took the newspaper.

'Something in there might interest you,' said Alf. 'The advert on the back page.'

Once the patrons had cleared the grand circle, Mary did her usual rounds of clearing up the rubbish from beneath the seats. Then she switched off the circle lights and went out into the foyer. Before she turned off the lights there, she unfolded the newspaper Alf Bickley had given her. Quickly turning to the back page she found the advertisement he had referred to:

HOLIDAY OF A LIFETIME

Only eight hours from Victoria Coach Station to the
sun-drenched beaches of Devon. Travel by five-star luxury on
THE BLUE COACH

Forget about Hitler's doodlebugs, forget about ration coupons,
forget about the war. Start the peace with a trip on a journey
that you will *never* forget.
Book now!
You won't regret it!

For several moments, Mary just stared at the advert, which appeared just below a photograph of the luxury long-distance coach. It was everything she had dreamed about, the thing she had been saving three-pence a week for, ever since she had got her job at the Marlborough. This was what she wanted, and as soon as she had enough money saved, this was what she was determined to have.

The river was as grey as the morning sky. After rescuing young Billy from drowning during the Eaglet beano outing, Lennie had vowed never to let either Billy or Dodo near the river again. However, since he had invited Mary and the family to spend Bank Holiday Monday with him at the old farmhouse, there was very little he could do but to keep a close eye on them. Fortunately, Mary's youngest brother and sister seemed more interested in chasing after butterflies and rabbits than strolling anywhere near the river, which suited Mary and Lennie just fine, for it gave them the chance to spend more time together. To save Lennie from cooking a midday meal, Mary suggested they all have a simple picnic in the woods near the river, and this consisted of tinned spam, cold boiled potatoes and salad, and bread and margarine. There was also a bottle of lemonade and a bottle of Tizer for the kids, and a vacuum flask of tea for Mary and Lennie.

From the time the family had set out on the Green Line bus in the morning, Thelma's absence had caused great concern to Mary. 'I don't like it, Lennie,' she said now, as they set out the things for the picnic on a small, open stretch of ground. 'For this past week or so, something's been worrying her. It can't be anything to do with her job, because only the other day, she told Mrs Hobbs down the road how much she was enjoying working at Jones Brothers.'

'Maybe she just didn't want to come out here to the country,' said Lennie, trying to make light of Mary's concerns.

'I doubt that,' replied Mary. 'Thelma likes *you*, I know that. She's asked many a time when we'd be coming out here to visit you. No, it's something more. Something that's she's brooding about.'

'Isn't there someone she can talk to?' asked Lennie. 'Some older person she'd listen to?'

'The only person Thelma could ever talk to,' replied Mary, 'is me. She doesn't know it, of course, but it's true.'

Lennie lay down flat on his back on the grass. 'Can't you just ask her what's wrong?'

'Not easy,' she said, lying alongside him. 'There are some people whom you could ask that kind of question,' she replied pointedly, 'and others you can't. Thelma is just about one of the most obstinate people I know. Mum always used to say that, but it's not until this last year that I've noticed it.'

Behind them, Dodo and Billy were making a hell of a noise whilst they tried to climb a tree. On hearing them, Lennie sat up and leaned on his elbows. 'Watch it, you two!' he called.

Dodo and Billy stopped what they were doing, and changed to a game of chasing each other around the trees.

'They think the world of you,' said Mary, staring up at the dark clouds. 'You know that, don't you?'

'I hate to say it,' replied Lennie, still keeping an eye on the kids, 'but I've taken quite a shine to *them*, too.'

'Thelma too?'

Lennie suddenly went quite silent.

Mary noticed this. 'Lennie?'

He turned to look at her.

'She's OK,' he replied, with little enthusiasm.

'Just OK?'

He shrugged.

Mary sat up. 'Have you been having any trouble with her?'

Lennie thought carefully before answering. 'Look, Mary,' he replied, awkwardly. 'Thelma's a good-looking girl – nothing like *you*, of course. But I – well, I don't get on with her in the same way as I do with –' he nodded towards Dodo and Billy.

Mary twigged on immediately. 'Has she been making a pass at you?' she asked anxiously.

He slowly eased himself up, leaning on his elbows.

'Not exactly,' he replied, none too convincingly. 'It's just that I – well, after all that . . . I just don't want to take any chances, that's all.'

Mary thought carefully about what he had said. Suddenly, she felt panic. 'Lennie,' she asked, 'are you trying to tell me something?'

'Now don't start *that* all over again,' he replied, irritably. 'D'you *have* to keep asking questions?'

'Yes, Lennie, I do,' she insisted firmly. 'Especially when it concerns my own sister.' She tried hard to make eye contact with him. 'If she's trying to make a play for you, I want to know.'

'Thelma's only trouble is that she's growing up,' he replied, evasively. 'She trying to find out about things.'

'About boys? About you?'

Mary's direct question clearly struck home, for Lennie turned away and pretended to watch Dodo and Billy racing each other near the woods. 'Look, Lennie,' she said. 'Thelma is only a few years younger than me, a few years younger than you. I have to take her seriously. She has no one to guide her but me. If she's making a play for you, you have to tell me.'

He still avoided her question.

'Is it because of – that girl?'

Lennie swung a look at her.

She smiled sweetly at him, and gently rubbed her hand through his hair. 'Darling,' she said in a rare moment of affection, 'how many times do I have to tell you that you don't have to keep secrets from *me?* And *I* don't have to keep secrets from *you.*' For one brief moment she thought he was relenting, and this gave her the courage to pursue what she had asked. 'Who *was* she, Lennie? Why don't you want to talk about her?'

Lennie remained like a block of stone.

She smiled again. 'You know, in the past, I've had boyfriends. I'm no saint.'

To her astonishment, he suddenly got to his feet, and stood looking up at the sky. Dodo and Billy were now playing a game of cricket with the bat that Lennie told them he had used when he was their age. 'I wish I hadn't got you that job at the Marlborough.'

His remark came like a bolt out of the blue for Mary. 'Lennie!' she said, bewildered, quickly getting up. 'That's a terrible thing to say. *Why?*'

'Those things,' he replied, nodding up towards the sky, 'those bloody things that are killing people everywhere. If one came down on the Marlborough . . .'

She stood beside him, and slipped her arm around his waist. 'Don't talk like that, Lennie,' she said lightly. 'Don't even *think* like that. I'll be quite safe. Nothing's going to happen to the dear old Marlborough. You're forgetting the "Toff", our ghost, our guardian angel. And in any case, once the Allied troops find the sites where they're firing those horrible things from, the war will soon be over – for us, at least.'

'Won't be long before the swallows are on the move again,' he said, ignoring what she had said, staring up at the sky.

High above them, a flight of swallows were actively chasing flies and other winged insects, diving low then shooting straight up into the air again.

The swallows reminded Mary of exactly what was on his mind. 'Why don't we go and see your mum?' she suggested.

He turned to look at her. 'Why?' he asked.

'Because she's your mum,' she replied openly. 'Now she's settled in at the home, I'd like to see her again.'

'No point,' replied Lennie, dourly.

'Why not?' she asked, disappointed by his changing mood. 'I'm sure she'd love to see you. It would cheer her up.'

'Lennie!'

Billy's shouts caused them both to turn with a start.

'Come and play with us! We need a wicketkeeper! You too, Mary!'

'Oh, come on, Lennie!' yelled Dodo, grumpily.

Lennie started to move off, but Mary held on to him. '*Please*, Lennie,' she pleaded. 'Let's go and see her. We could go in your truck. It's not far to Epping. Or we could go by bus. And if you don't want Billy and Dodo to go in, we could take turns in keeping an eye on them outside.'

Lennie thought about it for a moment, then, without giving an answer, rushed off to join the kids.

Mary watched him go. Whilst the swallows circled high above, she couldn't help dwelling on what he had told her the last time they were out together in the fields: '*When Mum was first taken ill, she used to say that she hoped she'd live long enough to see the swallows come again.*'

Sheila Nestor, now reduced to living off her late husband's First World War widow's pension, rarely did her shopping in Seven Sisters Road. Although it was only a short journey by a number 14 bus from her ground-floor flat in Duncombe Road, she much preferred to use some of the smaller shops closer to her own patch. In fact, she didn't like visiting the Nag's Head district, mainly because her late husband had been born in Muswell Hill which, in Sheila's mind, was a much more 'refined' district. However, today was different. Today she had to make the short journey because she had a very specific reason for doing so. Mary Trimble's visit to her some days before had given her a great deal of food for thought. For a start, the visit itself was impertinent, and Sheila would be having a few sharp words with Maisie Stringer if and when she ever saw the girl again. In any case, she had never cared for Maisie, and had always regretted employing her at the restaurant in the first place. However, what had to be done had to be done.

Being the first day of the working week, there was plenty of traffic around, but it had to be diverted due to the clearing of debris from a block of terraced houses which had been hit by a doodlebug over the weekend. Sheila had been at home when she heard the explosion, and the place had shook from top to bottom, reminding her of the terrifying days and nights of the Blitz. If it hadn't been for the important visit she had to make now to Hornsey Road police station, she would definitely have postponed her journey which now had to be undertaken on foot, and which included one very upsetting diversion around the bomb damage itself. By the time she had got as far as the public baths, Sheila, being a fairly small, plump woman, was exhausted. Like everyone else, she had also been at home during the time the police station had been bombed back in 1941, and she had even been in the crowd of sightseers when the King and Queen had visited the site within just a few hours of the tragic incident.

And, like everyone else, she still hadn't got used to the temporary corrugated iron construction that was housing the new police station.

'Yes, madam?' asked the Special Constable who was on clerical duty at the reception desk. 'Can I help you?'

'I wish to see Sergeant Hopkins, please.'

'Is he expecting you?'

'No,' replied Sheila. 'But I think he'll want to see *me*. I have something very important to tell him.'

Holly Manor was a beautiful red-brick building in the district of Epping, set in its own grounds laid well back from the main London Road, and reminiscent of the setting of every detective thriller Mary had ever seen. The outside walls were draped with creeping ivy, and an abundance of tall, multicoloured hollyhocks swayed to and fro in front of the ground-floor windows. There was a rather imposing entrance hall, which suggested that the building had only been built a few years before the war, giving the immediate impression of somewhere much more modern than those elegant Tudor and Elizabethan stately homes. Inside the building, the inevitable smell of old age pervaded most of the corridors and rest areas, although it had to compete with the far fresher smell of carbolic soap which was clearly used widely on all the linoleum floors.

Mary and Lennie sat with Winnie Backer in the large garden at the back of the house. Matron Beatrice had allowed Dodo and Billy to be there too, but they fidgeted so much, watching and listening to someone who, to them, was just an old lady, that they were allowed to spend most of their time exploring the stone fountain with its cupids and mermaids. Lennie's mum was clearly enjoying herself, for she was bright-eyed and very attentive to all that was going on around her.

'They're very nice people here,' said Winnie, talking to Mary in a low voice as though it was something she shouldn't be saying. 'The trouble is, they either sleep all day, or they read every page of the news-papers over and over again.' She looked from Mary to Lennie and then back to Mary again. 'I suppose it's because of the war,' she asked. 'Is it over yet?'

'Not yet, Mrs Backer,' replied Mary. 'But it won't be long now.'

'I hope it'll be over soon,' continued Winnie. 'I would love some sweets again. Liquorice All-Sorts are my favourites.'

'I promise I shall get you some, Mrs Backer,' said Mary. 'As many as you can eat.'

Winnie's face lit up. 'Thank you so much, dear,' she replied. 'But my name's Mum, not Mrs Backer. Isn't that right, son?'

Mary threw a quick glance at Lennie, then back to Winnie. 'Mum is a lovely name,' she said.

'You're so much prettier than that other girl,' said Winnie right out of the blue. 'She had freckles. I've never liked freckles. They look like pimples.' She changed the subject as quickly as she had started it. 'Is your dad coming today?' she asked Lennie.

'Not today, Mum,' he replied, awkwardly. 'He said he'll try and come on one of his days off.'

'He told *me* he'd come and see me every single Sunday. I must keep a look out for him.'

Sitting beside Winnie on a stone bench, Mary held her hand and gently smoothed it with her thumb.

The two kids finished their fountain exploration, and came back to talk to 'the old lady'.

'How old are you?' Dodo asked directly.

'Dodo!' scolded Mary. 'That's a very rude thing to ask.'

Winnie chuckled. 'I'm older than you, dear, but younger than God.'

'How d'you know how old God is?' Dodo persisted, cheekily.

Again Winnie lowered her voice. 'Because He talks to me every night,' she said.

'What about?' asked Billy.

'Oh – all sorts of things,' said Winnie. 'He once told me that birds in the air are just like little children. They like to keep on the move the whole time. But I love birds. I used to watch them from my bedroom window in the afternoons. Lennie thought I was fast asleep, but I wasn't. I was miles away, up in the air with them, floating through the clouds, watching the world below, thinking how small it all was to the world up above. I watch the birds now.' She looked up at the sky, still grey and threatening rain, but with a gentle warm breeze that from time to time ruffled her greying hair. 'They remind me of home.'

Quite unexpectedly, Dodo leaned forward, and gave Winnie a quick kiss on the cheek, then rushed off with yells of, 'I'll race you to the gate, Billy!'

As they went, Winnie, eyes wide, slowly felt with the tips of her fingers, the place on her cheek where Dodo had just kissed her. It was a touching, poignant moment, and even though it took her by surprise, it brought a beaming smile to her face.

At that moment, the air was pierced by the sound of the air-raid

179

siren, wailing out from the distance. Within moments, Matron turned up with one of the nurses. 'Come on now, Winnie,' she called. 'Let's get you into the shelter.'

From all around, elderly residents were being hustled away in their wheelchairs.

'You're welcome to come down with us,' said Matron, once the siren call came to an end. 'There's plenty of room down there.'

'No,' said Lennie. 'I think we'd better get back home. Thanks all the same.' He leaned down to Winnie, kissed her on the cheek, and helped her to her feet. 'We'll be in to see you again, Mum,' he promised.

Then Mary kissed her. 'I'll see you again too – Mum,' she said.

Although startled by all the hurried activity, Winnie beamed at her. 'I hope you'll give me a grandchild,' she said, bewildered and confused. 'The other one doesn't count.'

Mary was completely floored by Winnie's parting words. She watched her being led off to the air-raid shelter by Matron and the nurse, then turned to Lennie, but he had rushed off to collect Dodo and Billy.

From the distance came the first buzzing sound of an approaching doodlebug.

Chapter 14

'*I hope you'll give me a grandchild. The other one doesn't count.*'
Those few parting words from Winnie Backer as she was being led off to the air-raid shelter at the nursing home, had given Mary several sleepless nights. What did they mean, and why had Lennie persistently refused to discuss what his mother had been trying to say? However, once again Mary decided to let him explain in his own good time. She didn't know why. All she knew was that if the air was going to be cleared between them, sooner or later he would *have* to tell her.

A few days later on Friday, it was Thelma's sixteenth birthday, but as Mary had to work during the evenings, a party was planned for the family on Mary's next day off, the following Monday. During the past week or so, Mary had been quite concerned about Thelma's dark moods. She only talked to people when she had to, and showed little or no enthusiasm at all for her forthcoming birthday celebration. Another thing that had started to worry Mary was Lennie's unwillingness to talk about the way Thelma had obviously been showing an interest in him, a situation that had become precarious now that Lennie was quite regularly staying overnight, sleeping on the put-you-up in the front parlour. When finally he admitted to Mary that Thelma had several times come into the parlour late at night and sat talking to him, perched on the edge of the put-you-up, Mary decided that the time had come for her to bring the matter out into the open with her sister. The opportunity came over breakfast on Friday morning, just as Thelma was leaving for work.

'Mind if I walk with you?' Mary asked, as she left Lennie, Dodo and Billy to clear away the breakfast things. 'I've got a bit of shopping I want to do in Holloway Road.'

As usual, Thelma shrugged, indicating that she couldn't care less if Mary joined her or not.

With two more flying bombs down somewhere in the district overnight, the sound of ambulance and fire-engine bells once again echoed in the distance. Fortunately, it was a lovely morning, with the promise of a heatwave over the next few days, which meant that both Mary and Thelma were dressed in only the most comfortable summer clothes. As Thelma always took the short cut to Jones Brothers, entering through the back entrance to the store in Jackson Road, the journey would only take about ten minutes, which meant that Mary had little time to say the things she had to say. 'We're very lucky to have Lennie around the place,' she said, quite casually. 'Don't you think so, Thelma?'

'Why *lucky*?' Thelma asked in return.

'Well,' continued Mary, 'with Dodo and Billy on school holidays, it takes the pressure off – knowing that there's someone to keep an eye on them.' She waited a moment before getting to the point. 'I mean, at least you have a good job now. No need for anyone to look after *you*.'

Thelma didn't reply. She had not yet guessed what Mary was leading up to.

'Lennie's so nice – don't you think, Thelma?'

Thelma shrugged. 'He's all right.'

'But you *do* like him?'

'Who cares if *I* like him or not?' replied Thelma, dismissively.

'*I* do, Thelma.'

This remark brought Thelma to a dead halt. The penny had dropped. 'What are you talking about?' she asked warily.

'Why do you get up in the middle of the night and go down to talk to Lennie?' Mary asked, directly.

This made Thelma really angry. 'What's he been saying about me?' she snapped.

'What d'you *think* he's been saying?' asked Mary. 'Is there anything you want to tell me, Thelma?'

Thelma swept off, only coming to a halt before crossing the busy Tollington Road.

Mary came alongside her, waiting for the traffic to clear. A brewer's dray horse and cart seemed to take for ever to pass. 'You're sixteen today, Thelma,' she said, with affection. 'You're not fully grown up yet, but you're getting there. What's been wrong this past week or so?'

The brewer's cart passed, and Thelma immediately stepped out into the road. Mary had to grab hold of her arm as an army motorcyclist seemed to come from nowhere, and nearly knocked her down. Once they had reached the other side of the road she repeated her question. 'Thelma,' she asked, 'what's been wrong this past week or so? Is it something to do with Lennie?'

Thelma stopped dead. 'What's the matter with you?' she growled, angrily. 'Lennie Backer's *your* bloke, not mine. If *you've* got problems, then don't blame *me!*' She stormed off, closely followed by Mary.

'Thelma,' said Mary, grabbing hold of her sister's arm. 'Ever since you started work at Jones Brothers, you've been going out somewhere on Sunday afternoons.'

'That's a bloody lie!' Thelma retorted, coming to a defiant stop.

'There's no need to swear at me, Thelma,' replied Mary, calmly, aware that passers-by were giving the two of them questioning looks. 'Over these past few weeks, it's been perfectly obvious that something's upset you. Now I know I'm only your sister, but if Mum and Dad were here, you know very well they'd be asking you the same question. You've got to learn to listen to me, Thelma. You've got to learn to *trust* me, not just for *your* sake, but for *their* sake, too.' She drew closer. 'Just tell me,' she pleaded. 'Are you involved with someone?'

Thelma's eyes shot up at her. They were glassy, and her face was beginning to crumple up.

'Is it a boy?'

Thelma suddenly rushed off into Jones Brothers' backyard, but instead of hurrying in through the staff entrance of the building, she hid out of sight behind the big yard doors that were usually kept locked every night.

Mary followed quickly, to find her leaning her face against the wall. 'Thelma!' she pleaded. 'What is it?' She gently turned her sister's face towards her. The girl was quietly sobbing. 'Oh my dear Thelma,' she said. 'What is it? Please tell me.'

It was a moment or so before Thelma was able to talk. By the time she did, tears were streaming down her face. 'I met this . . . he's in the army. He took me to this pub, this place . . . I thought he was so nice, not at all like some of the idiots at school. I . . . just wanted to have a good time, that's all.'

Mary's heart began to sink. 'When *was* this?' she asked, making sure they both kept their voices low.

'A couple of weeks ago – up West,' replied Thelma, trying to rub the tears away with the back of one hand. 'He seemed to be so nice. I didn't think he'd—'

Mary's eyes closed, then flicked open again immediately. She hardly dared ask the question: 'He'd do *what*, Thelma?'

Thelma's face crumpled up again. 'He took me into this room . . . he turned off the light . . . he tried to . . . it was my own fault, I told him I was nineteen. He didn't . . . I didn't let him. You've got to believe me, Mary, I didn't let him. I ran out and came straight back home . . .' She dissolved into tears.

Mary threw her arms around her, and hugged her. 'It's all right, Thelma,' she said, reassuringly. 'If what you've told me is true, then I *do* believe you. I suppose we all have to learn lessons the hard way.'

The two of them stood there clutching each other for a moment or so, unnoticed by the drivers of the trade vehicles coming in and out of the yard. Mary then gave Thelma her handkerchief to dab her eyes.

'D'you know something, Thelma?' Mary said, with affection. 'Today you're sixteen years old. I promise you, this is the day when things are going to change for you. I'm proud of you, Thelma. We're *all* proud of you, proud that you're doing so well in your job, proud that you're bringing money back home to help out your family. So let's make it a new start – all right?'

Thelma, tears now wiped away from her eyes, nodded, and even tried a weak smile. Then she left Mary, and went off into the building.

'Thelma.'

Thelma stopped and looked back.

'Happy birthday!' called Mary, with a supportive smile.

Thelma smiled back and disappeared through the staff entrance, but as she did so, Mary's smile faded. In her mind, only time would tell if she could now *really* start trusting her sister.

Tanya Ling's studio now looked much better than it had after the police had been with their search warrant. All her sketches had now been tidied, and were neatly leaning in piles against the walls, or bundled up in the two cupboards on either side of the fireplace. The new picture she was working on had undergone many changes, which she mainly put down to the changes in mood of the subject. However, it was a sketch that she was finally quite satisfied with, not exactly happy with, but satisfied. The one sketch that had remained the same was that of Sheila Nestor. After all the lies the former manageress of the British Restaurant had told about Tanya, there was no getting away from the reality of that hard, plump face, the tiny eyes behind horn-rimmed spectacles, and the permanent, determined expression. Even so, Tanya didn't hate Sheila; she was sorry for her, sorry that she had developed so much bitterness, so much so that she wanted to destroy another person's life. But there was one sketch that would always remain close to her heart.

The August sunshine was streaming through the Venetian blinds at her windows, casting strange, shadowy lines across the walls of one side of the room. For a few moments Tanya stood in the middle of the room, listening to the voices of all the people in those sketches, but each time two voices dominated those sounds. This prompted her to go to her 'special' corner of the room which was curtained off from all the rest of her work. From there she brought out a large sketch wrapped in brown paper and tied up with string. After leaning it against the wall for a moment, she went to a trestle table which was placed in between the two windows, and cleared to one side the charcoal pencils, notepads and other materials that were scattered there. Once she had made a big enough space, she collected the large sketch she had placed against the wall, lifted it on to the table, untied the string, and exposed what was wrapped there. A warm smile came to her face. In her mind, the two people she had sketched were talking to her. '*It's up to you now, Tanya. At least we know we can trust you. Don't let us down, dear friend. Don't let us down.*'

Whether those were the words she could *really* hear was quite immaterial. To her, Mary Trimble's mum and dad were as real as if they were standing beside her right there in that room. To Tanya, they would always be alive, and no, she would never fail them – never. When the time was right she would do what she had to do – but *only* when the time was right.

Her concentration was suddenly broken when she heard a car door being slammed just beneath her window. She carefully covered the sketch over with the brown paper and peered down to the street below.

Getting out of the police car, accompanied by a special constable, was the formidable Sergeant Jim Hopkins.

Trafalgar Square was bathed in the hot sunshine of an August afternoon. Although there were not all that many sightseers around, the pigeons were as fat as ever, billing and cooing every time they fluttered down on to Billy's and Dodo's outstretched hands to collect a few more dried peas from the small penny packets Lennie had bought for them from a stallholder in the square. It had been quite a boisterous morning for Lennie. When he set out to give the two kids a treat by taking them on the double-decker tram up to the West End, little did he know that they would make it a point not to obey one single word he said to them. In fact, it was quite the reverse, for on two occasions they just disappeared, only to re-emerge playing tag with each other, especially whilst they were strolling along the Victoria

Embankment by the River Thames. As usual, Billy showed off like mad, posing like a camel in front of the obelisk of Cleopatra's Needle, whilst Dodo applauded him and laughed hysterically. Looking after kids was clearly not something that Lennie was in tune with, but at least he was doing something practical to help Mary. However, it was only whilst he was in Trafalgar Square watching the kids being bombarded by hungry pigeons, that he realised just how domesticated he was becoming. Did this mean that he was falling in love with Mary, he kept asking himself? Did it mean that he was at last putting to one side all that had happened with Carole Pickard? Even the very thought of the girl's name sent a shiver down his spine. And yet, he couldn't just ignore what she had done to him – or *tried* to do to him. If he was ever going to have a chance of settling down to a normal relationship with Mary, then sooner or later he would *have* to tell her.

The one thing that unnerved Lennie, however, was the Army Recruitment tent that had been set up in one corner of the square. Although he had tried to dismiss it from his mind, it was Billy who suddenly started to grate on his nerves by asking awkward questions.

'Why aren't *you* in the army, Lennie?'

Lennie swung the boy an angry glare. 'Because I don't want to be!' he snapped.

'But I thought *all* blokes have to go in the army?' Billy persisted. 'If *I* was old enough, *I'd* go in the army.'

'Then we'd be sure to lose the war!' added Dodo, a remark that immediately got her a clout from her brother.

As the tussle between the two kids followed, the pigeons all around them took flight, their wings flapping wildly until they reached safe positions on top of Admiral Lord nelson's head. On the other side of the square, Lennie caught a glimpse of two Military Policemen strolling aimlessly in his direction. It immediately unnerved him, and he automatically looked away from them and sat down on one of the rickety bench seats beneath the main road in front of the National Gallery. He didn't know why he always felt so guilty when these aggressive

187

looking military types appeared, for he had nothing to fear from them. He had paid the penalty for what he had done, so why should he feel so anxious whenever he saw one of these military thugs? But guilt for taking another man's life was deep, and ingrained in his very soul, and he would never forgive himself for what he had done. For quite some time he sat alone, watching Dodo and Billy chasing some of the poor bewildered winged creatures they had just been feeding, but most of all he started thinking about Mary, about what and how he was going to be able to tell her about Carole Pickard.

'Good morning, sir.'

He looked up with a start to see the two army MPs standing over him.

'Wonder if I could trouble you for your Identity Card?' asked the burley one of the two, who was smiling politely. 'It's just a formality. I'm sure you know that we have the powers of the civilian police during the emergency.'

'Emergency?' asked Lennie, who was incensed that his privacy was being intruded upon. 'What emergency?'

'The war isn't over yet,' replied the other, thin man. 'We're here to keep our eyes and ears open at all times. Plenty of Jerry's keeping an eye on us, I can tell you. Especially in a place like this.'

Resentfully, Lennie reached into the pocket at the back of his trousers, and handed over his ID card to Burley.

'Thanks a lot, Mr –' he referred to the card, 'Backer?'

Lennie didn't answer.

'I see you're from Essex?'

'What are you doing here in these parts?' asked Thin. 'Never been registered for call-up?'

'I'm exempt,' Lennie replied quickly. 'Ill-health.'

'Oh, I'm sorry to hear that,' said Burley, in a rather sinister way.

Even before the accident during his short period in the army, he, like so many other ranks, despised the Military Police. It wasn't fair really, as they were only doing their job. But somehow, their very appearance was always intimidating.

'That's a pity,' joked Thin. 'We were rather hoping we could persuade you to join up!'

Lennie wasn't amused. The man's pathetic little joke fell on deaf ears.

'Thanks anyway, sir,' said Burley, handing back Lennie's Identity Card.

The two men turned to leave. As they did so, they stopped dead to find Dodo and Billy standing side by side staring in bewilderment at them.

'Hello, hello,' said Burley. 'And what have we here?'

'These belong to you, sir?' asked Thin.

Lennie stood up. 'In a manner of speaking,' he replied, dourly.

'Wanna join the army, young man?' Burley asked Billy.

'I'm too young,' replied Billy, with the confidence of a trouper.

'Well,' added Thin, 'one of these days, eh? Bet you'll do your country proud.'

Both men chuckled at their own joke. As they did so, the air-raid siren echoed out over the rooftops of the West End, sending the entire pigeon population there into panic, scattering them from the square and from the top of Lord Nelson's head and shoulders.

'Better get to the shelters!' called Burley as he and Thin rushed off. 'There's one just behind the Haymarket over there. Those ruddy things don't take long to get here!'

'Dodo! Billy!' yelled Lennie, grabbing the two kids and yanking them out of the square. 'Go, go, go!'

Even as he spoke the ominous chugging sound of the doodlebug was heard in the distance from the direction of the Mall, and before people could get away from the square, the dreaded black pilotless plane streaked across the sky, tail blazing, passing straight over, high above the National Gallery, narrowly missing the defensive electric wires of the barrage balloons floating up from St James's Park. Everyone, including Lennie and the two kids, threw themselves flat on their stomachs on the ground, and waited for the explosion, which came just a moment or so after the engines had cut out. Then everyone got up again and brushed themselves off, and with Admiral Lord Nelson at the helm, the pigeons returned, and Trafalgar Square was once again shipshape and back to normal.

Thelma hadn't had much of a birthday. For a start, an elderly woman came into the haberdashery department and spent nearly an hour trying to choose the right colour embroidered ribbon she needed to replace the one on her sofa, and even when she had chosen the right one, she discovered that she had left her purse at home. Then Thelma found that black cotton was out of stock, two boxes of men's trouser buttons were wrongly labelled and, as if that wasn't enough, there were two air-raid alerts which meant sitting for ages in the store's air-raid shelter, crammed with customers and staff. But she did get a nice birthday card and a jar of face cream from Ivy Murphy, one of the girls she had befriended on the ladies' cosmetics counter, and in between air-raid alerts the two had a midday meal together in the staff canteen. However, just before closing time, she had an unexpected customer.

'Hello, Loretta.'

Thelma froze. To see the lance corporal standing in front of her at the counter was a complete shock. When she had got away from him that day in the private Soho club, she had thought it would be the last she would ever see of him. 'What're *you* doing here?' she growled, looking all around hoping no one could hear her. 'How did you know where to find me?'

'You said you worked in Jones Brothers,' he replied. 'It just needed a bit of detective work.'

Thelma was just about to deny that she had told him anything of the sort, when she suddenly remembered that, in an unguarded moment, she *had* in fact told him where she worked. 'You've got no right to come here,' she snapped, her voice low. 'I'm supposed to be working.'

'I went all over the store trying to find you,' he replied quietly. 'Nobody knew someone with your name who worked here. So I just went from one department to another.'

He smiled at her, that same smile that had won her over in the first place. To Thelma, he still looked immaculate in his uniform, with his blue eyes, round, slightly chubby face, and blond hair which was only just visible beneath his army cap. His lips were so full and red that if he hadn't been a bloke, she would have sworn he was wearing lipstick.

'So what do you want?' she asked tersely, remembering how and why she had got away from him in that dark room at the back of the club.

'You've been on my mind ever since you rushed off,' he replied, awkwardly. 'I don't know why you did that. I – wasn't going to do anything.'

Thelma grunted dismissively then looked around the department anxiously. 'You shouldn't've come here,' she repeated. 'I told you . . . I told you . . .'

At that moment, a buzzer sounded closing time.

'Will you at least come and have a walk with me?' he pleaded. 'Just give me a chance to explain.'

'There's nothing *to* explain,' she insisted. 'I have to get home. I don't want to see you again, I just don't!'

Chris, the lance corporal, looked crushed. 'D'you mean that?' he asked. 'Do you *really* mean it?'

Thelma turned her face away, and pretended to be tidying and polishing the counter.

'You probably won't see me again,' he said. 'I'm being posted in the next few days.'

She stopped what she was doing and looked up at him.

During the interval at the Marlborough, Mary and Alice Thompson took the opportunity to take a breather outside. It hadn't been a full house as word had got around that the feature film was a bit of a dire comedy that had produced few laughs and plenty of snoring patrons.

'I wonder if the day'll ever come,' remarked Alice dreamily, 'when we can look up there and feel safe?'

Mary looked up at the patchy red sky, which was now heavily reflected on their two faces. She shook her head. 'Not until they get rid of those horrible things,' she replied sceptically.

'Plenty more where *they* came from,' yawned Alice, her arms crossed. 'I just hope that git in Berlin hasn't got anythin' more up 'is sleeve for us.'

'It's a pity the nights are beginning to draw in again,' added Mary. 'You can notice it more every night now.'

'Oh well, we ain't done badly, I s'ppose,' replied Alice. 'Not that *we* see much of the sun stuck in *this* place each day. Still, when my George gets demobbed, it'll be nice to snuggle up with 'im in front of the fire again.' She turned a brief look at Mary. 'Which reminds me, how's it goin' now with you and Lennie?'

Mary flicked a quick, embarrassed glance at her. 'I'm not sure yet if it's actually "going",' she replied. 'There are still a couple of skeletons in the cupboard to dig out. But – he *is* a wonderful help around the house, especially with Dodo and Billy. I don't know what I'd do without him.'

'The thing is – do you *love* 'im?'

Mary thought about this for a moment. In fact, she had been thinking a great deal about it of late. She had asked herself so many times how she could possibly love someone who just couldn't be open with her. Ever since that parting remark from Winnie Backer about a grandchild, she had been desperate to know whether Lennie had fathered a child by this woman in Epping Town. She didn't know *what* to think. However, despite her misgivings, she couldn't help herself replying: 'Yes, I suppose I *do* love him, Alice. I love him very much. And the silly thing is – I think he loves *me* too.' She looked away again. 'Funny, isn't it? I was beginning to think I was getting too old for all that stuff!'

'Old! *You?*' Alice roared with laughter. 'It don't matter 'ow old or 'ow young you are, ducky, if the urge is there, 'ang on to it!'

Thelma and Chris strolled together along Holloway Road. This time, however, they were not arm in arm; Thelma was determined that once bitten, twice shy. She had agreed to meet him on the other side of the road once she had finished work for the day, and for the first few

192

minutes they said very little to each other. But when Chris broke the uneasy silence, he was determined to clear the air between them. 'Loretta,' he said clumsily, 'I never wanted to do what you thought I wanted to do . . . no, what I mean is . . . Look, I knew you weren't the age you said you were.'

Thelma brought them to an abrupt halt. She felt very offended. 'What d'you mean?' she asked, indignantly.

'I just – *knew* – that's all,' he said, sheepishly. 'The trouble was – *is* – that I still wanted you. Not for – oh, you know what I'm trying to say.' His posh voice seemed to be getting even posher. 'I want to tell you something, Loretta,' he continued. 'I told you I'm eighteen. But I'm not. I'm seventeen.'

Thelma was puzzled. 'But how come you're in the army? I thought you couldn't get called up until you're eighteen?'

'I lied,' replied Chris, quite openly. 'Let's just say I forged a few papers.'

They walked on. As every minute passed, Thelma was thinking more and more about this boy. He was unlike any boy she had ever met before, especially like that stupid half-wit, Jeff Bowman, who used to harass her every time she came home from school.

'So you see,' continued Chris, 'I don't mind your not telling me your right age. It's the person that counts.'

'Is that why you took me into that back room?' she asked, acidly. 'I told you then that I wasn't old enough for . . . what *you* wanted to do.'

'Are you too young to be kissed?'

Again Thelma brought them to a halt. She turned and looked him.

'Did I try anything?' he asked. '*Did* I?'

Thelma found herself looking straight into his eyes. And gradually those few moments in that back room came drifting slowly back to her. No, he *hadn't* tried anything with her. Of course he hadn't! Everything she had told Mary had been nothing but pure fantasy. The whole thing was in her mind, like a scene in any film she had seen a million times; a poor young girl at the mercy of a foul-minded stranger.

She was still staring into those eyes, those beautiful blue eyes that were pleading, begging for forgiveness and understanding. Those moments in the dark room were a figment of her imagination, of her own stupid wishful thinking. Without saying a word, right there in the middle of the Holloway Road, she suddenly leaned forward and kissed him gently on the lips. 'It's my birthday today,' she said with a lovely, sweet smile. 'I'm just sixteen. And my name's not Loretta. It's Thelma.'

Chris's face lit up. '*Sweet* sixteen!' he beamed. Then he hugged and kissed her. 'Why don't we celebrate?' he asked, pulling away from her.

'What d'you mean?' she asked, sceptically.

'Let's go to the pictures!'

Chapter 15

The explosion rocked the house. It woke Mary, who sat up in bed with a start to find plaster coming down from the ceiling. In the next room, Thelma, Dodo and Billy were out of their beds in a flash, Dodo screaming and crying, Billy rushing excitedly to peer out through the blackout curtains, and Thelma, shaking with fear, getting out on to the landing outside as fast as she could where Mary came bursting out of her own bedroom.

'What is it?' asked Thelma, trembling all over. 'Have we been hit?'

'No,' replied Mary, putting a comforting arm around her sister. 'But it's close.' As she spoke Dodo, in tears, came hurrying out and straight into Mary's arms.

'Are you all right?' called Lennie, rushing up the stairs to them. 'Anyone hurt?'

'I don't think so,' replied Mary, breathlessly. Then she yelled out upstairs. 'Mrs Kelly!'

There was immediate concern when Nutty Nora did not reply.

Lennie rushed up the stairs to investigate. 'Mrs Kelly!' he called, banging on her bedroom door. 'Are you OK?' With still no reply, he went straight in and turned on the light. To his dismay the old girl was not there, but large clumps of plaster down from the ceiling were scattered all over the place. 'Mrs Kelly?' he called.

'Don't yell at me!' came the reply. The old girl was sheltering underneath her bed. 'I'm not bleedin' deaf!'

'Are you OK?' he asked, taking her hand and practically dragging her out from her instant shelter. 'You're not hurt?'

'Of course I'm not hurt, yer stupid bugger!' she replied as Lennie helped her to her feet. She had her hairnet on, and was wearing her long flannelette nightie. 'Bleedin' 'ell! Look at the state of the place!' She went to the window, and regardless of the fact that there was no glass left in any of the panes there, she drew back the blackout curtain, opened the window and shook her fist. 'You bleedin' Adolf!' she yelled, as though Hitler was in the road outside. 'I'll get yer fer this!'

Ignoring the old girl's furious language, Lennie put his arm around her waist, and led her out of the room. 'Be careful of the bit of broken glass, Mrs Kelly,' he warned. 'Have you got a pair of carpet slippers around anywhere?' But she had no need to answer for Lennie found the slippers, which were full of glass and plaster.

Mary and the family were waiting on the first-floor landing for her, and Lennie got them all to go downstairs.

'Where's your brother tonight, Mrs Kelly?' Mary asked the old girl, only too aware that the old boy was more like a recluse, hardly ever at home, and that when he was, he was always dodging out of sight so that he didn't have to talk to anyone.

'I don't know, and I don't bleedin' care!' grunted the old lady. 'Probably locked up with some floozie up King's Cross, if I know *him*! And good riddance!'

Thelma and the two kids had plonked themselves down at the table. Dodo was still sobbing and shaking with fright, although Billy was clearly loving all the excitement, and was having the time of his life.

'I'll just go out and see if I can find out where it's come down,' said Lennie, who had just reappeared from the front parlour, having got his trousers on in double-quick time.

'I'll come with you,' said Mary. 'Thelma, can you make some tea for us all? And you, Billy. Make yourself useful. Put the kettle on.'

Billy groaned, and disappeared out into the kitchen, leaving Dodo with a very tetchy Nutty Nora.

In the street outside, it seemed that everyone had come out in panic on to their doorsteps, all of them togged out in nothing more than their nightgowns, pyjamas, hairnets, and long johns. The road was littered with broken glass, and roof tiles were down as well as one or two chimney stacks. The smell of burning rubber, gas and blazing timbers pervaded everywhere, causing the neighbours to cough and splutter.

'Where is it, Mr Parfitt?' Mary asked her next-door neighbour, who was sporting rather flashy striped pyjamas.

'Must be Holloway Road,' replied 'Mr Know-it-All', with his usual self-confidence. 'I'd lay a fiver it's over the Nag's Head somewhere.'

'That's nasty!' spluttered Lennie, who, with horror, was watching a huge cloud of black smoke spiralling up into the sky beyond the rooftops of Roden Street.

The neighbours had noticed it too, for they were all pointing and yelling out that the doodlebug must have come down somewhere along Holloway Road, which was just a stone's throw away.

Lennie suddenly made a dash back inside the house, rushing straight out into the backyard. The sight he saw was devastating, a vast plume of black smoke covering the entire area, and looking far too close for comfort. In Mayton Street at the end of the yard, there were terrifying sounds of people leaning out of their smashed windows, yelling and coughing and shouting out to each other about what had happened.

'Can you see anything?' bellowed Mary from the scullery as she came hurrying out into the yard. 'Oh my God!' she gasped, the moment she saw and smelt the foul-smelling smoke, and heard the chaos and mayhem going on just a few streets away, together with the clanging of fire, ambulance, and police bells as they all rushed to the scene, and the hysterical barking and wailing of dogs all around the neighbourhood.

'I think all of you had better think about getting out of all this,' said Lennie, trying to disguise his own anxieties with a sense of firm authority. 'First thing in the morning, pack up all your things and we'll go back to my place in Epping.'

'Don't be absurd, Lennie,' replied Mary, eyes still glued to the dark, grim sky. 'Me and Thelma can't just give up our jobs. And what about Dodo and Billy? Their summer holidays are over next month. They can't just give up school like that.'

Lennie was now getting impatient with her. 'So d'you all want to get killed?' he bellowed, more through anxiety than anger. 'Like your own mum and dad? The bloody buzz bombs are far from finished. There'll be more, and they'll all have our names on them.' He tried to calm down. 'Look, Mary,' he pleaded, 'I don't want to be disrespectful, but your parents should have evacuated the whole family at the beginning of the war!'

'Don't be so stupid, Lennie!' she yelled back. 'D'you really think we could've just packed up everything and run away? Families have to stick together!'

Lennie was just about to turn away in frustration when Fred Know-it-All shouted down the passage from the open front door. 'It's the Marlborough!' he yelled.

Hearing Fred's voice, Mary froze with a start. 'Oh God!' she gasped.

She and Lennie rushed back into the house and met Fred at the front door, where a crowd of neighbours were gathered.

'It's the Marlborough, all right,' said Fred, gloomily.

'Must've bin a direct hit by the sound of things,' added one of Mary's female neighbours from the other side of the road.

'It was bound to 'appen sooner or later,' said a neighbour next door but one, leaning out of her ground-floor window. 'I mean pitture 'ouses are one of the first things they go for.'

Mary felt as though her stomach had collapsed.

It took her only a few minutes to get changed. Lennie was waiting for her, and they practically ran up to the end of Roden Street. As they turned into Herstlet Road, their hearts were in their mouths, for there was pandemonium everywhere. Mary was deeply distressed that the old cinema she had grown to love so much had taken a hit from one of the deadly doodlebugs, and as she and Lennie made their way along Seven Sisters Road to the Nag's Head, she dreaded the thought of what they were about to see on the other side of Holloway Road. However, despite the fact that there were fire-engine hose pipes snaking along the pavements and gutters everywhere, when they eventually reached the junction of Seven Sisters and Holloway Road, their eyes widened in astonishment at what they saw.

Standing imperiously as it had done ever since it first opened in October 1903, the Marlborough picture house was untouched.

Mary and Lennie were in shock. How *could* they have been fed such wrong information? Why was it that people jumped to conclusions without knowing the facts? And the facts were that, as far as they could see, not a brick of the dear old Marlborough cinema had been touched. But even as they stood on the pavement looking across at the building, their attention was very soon drawn to where the flying bomb *had* come down.

'Oh no!' Mary gasped. 'It can't be.'

She and Lennie crossed to the other side of the road, then across Parkhurst Road. Just ahead of them were floodlights which were lighting up the majestic exterior of the magnificent Gaumont cinema, roof disintegrating from a fierce blaze within the building, and debris from the foyer and walls scattered all over the surrounding area.

They reached as close as they could to all the activity, but they and a crowd of anxious, grey-faced onlookers were held back by a cordon that had been placed around the entire building.

'Wouldn't get any closer if I were you, mates,' said one of the firemen, who, with two other firefighters, was toiling with several hosepipes at the same time. 'It's a bit of a mess inside, might cave in at any minute.'

'Anyone in there?' asked Lennie.

'Not sure yet,' replied one of the special constables who was doing his best to keep the sightseers behind the cordon. 'We know the manager and his wife sometimes sleep in one of the dressing-rooms backstage. Trouble is, the water mains have been hit, and there's a danger that everything behind the safety certain might be flooded.'

One of the firefighters inside the cinema's formerly grand foyer shouted to his mates outside. 'Fractured water main backstage! The place is flooding! The two of them may be holding out in one of the dressing rooms!'

Mary clasped her hand over her mouth in dismay.

Some yelled at the top of their voice: 'Look out!'

At that moment, a gigantic piece of masonry came crashing down on to the pavement at the Tufnell Park side of the building.

Everyone immediately ran for cover and waited for the dust to settle. Considering it was halfway through the night, there was an enormous amount of traffic around, but most of it from the emergency services which had been called in from neighbouring boroughs. There were also Alsatian tracker dogs inside the building who were being led over the debris by their military trainers, searching the place for anyone who might be trapped. Although the surrounding buildings had escaped serious damage, most of the windows at the old Empire Theatre on the opposite side of the road, and also the nearby Royal Northern Hospital, had been blown out.

'I can't believe this has happened,' said Mary, who was by now close to tears. 'I mean, ever since this place opened it's been the number one cinema in this area. Have you ever been to a picture here, Lennie?'

'Not really,' he replied. 'But I remember the crowds that turned up when it opened up a few years back.'

'So do I,' Mary recalled, wistfully. 'It was like Hollywood – ladies in long dresses, men in black bow ties and dinner jackets. And lots of famous people. D'you know, they used to have on the wireless the man who played the organ – what's his name now . . . Edward O'Henry. Funny little man with glasses – but he played so beautifully. It's terrible, just terrible to think what's happened to this lovely place, that beautiful auditorium.'

'And for *what*, I ask myself?'

Both Mary and Lennie swung round to find Alf Bickley, the manager of the Marlborough cinema, hands in his pockets, staring mournfully up at the building.

'Oh, Mr Bickley,' sighed Mary. 'Isn't it awful? What good can they do by bombing a cinema?'

Alf shook his head. 'Well, they said they were going to do it. Or at least, old Haw-Haw said they would.'

'But *why*?' asked Mary, unable to fathom it all.

'The bloke who does my job in there,' replied Alf.

'The manager?' asked Mary, confused.

200

'And his missus,' said Alf. 'They're both good mates of mine – rivals, but good mates.'

Mary exchanged a puzzled look with Lennie. 'You mean – it was a personal thing.'

'So the rumours say,' replied Alf.

'But *why*?'

Alf slowly looked up at her. He looked really shattered. 'They're Jews,' he replied.

Mary's face crumpled.

'Whether it's true or not, I don't really know,' said Alf. 'But old Goebbels has always been one to keep a grudge. I still reckon that's the reason Leslie Howard copped it when Jerry shot down his plane on the way back from Lisbon last year. Goebbels never forgave him for makin' those anti-Nazi films, like *The First of the Few* and *Pimpernel Smith*. I don't know if my mate inside had ever done anything to upset that lot in Berlin, but if he did you can bet your life they weren't going to let him get away with it.' He sighed despairingly, and looked up at the blazing building. 'At least those beautiful walls are still standing.'

Mary took the bold step of putting a comforting arm around Alf's waist. 'Well, the Marlborough's still there to carry on the good work, Mr Bickley,' she said. 'Those awful people can send over as many of their rotten bombs as they like, but they won't rob the people of their picture night.'

This cheered Alf up no end. 'You're a good girl, Mary, that's for sure,' he said, giving her an appreciative smile. Then he turned to Lennie. 'You don't know how lucky you are, young Len.'

From inside the cinema foyer, someone shouted out excitedly: 'We've got them! They're alive!'

Alf's face lit up. 'So up yours, Goebbels!' he yelled out at the building, as he made the V for Victory sign with two fingers.

Before she left home to go to work on Saturday afternoon, Mary received a visit from Police Sergeant Hopkins. At first she was inclined not to let him through the front door, but when he told her why he had wanted to see her, she calmed down and took him into the front parlour.

'All I can say is,' he said, having taken off his cap, 'I'm really sorry for the pain and inconvenience this situation has caused you. You have to understand that we acted in good faith, and if someone makes those kinds of allegations, it's our duty to follow them up.'

Mary was still confused as to why he was there. 'What exactly are you trying to tell me, sergeant?' she asked in as polite a way as she could muster.

Sergeant Hopkins found himself fumbling for words. It was something he was not used to. 'I've come to tell you', he said, falteringly, 'that the allegations made against your friend, Mrs Rawsthorne, have proved to be completely without foundation.'

Mary stared hard at him. Oh why, she asked herself, did policemen always have to talk as though they were reading aloud from a book? 'I see,' she replied, taunting him. 'So what have you found out that made it quite unnecessary for you to question me?'

The sergeant did his best not to look as though he had been made to look like an absolute idiot. 'We had a visit,' he replied, slowly, cautiously. 'Mrs Nestor. She came to tell us that she'd made a mistake about the allegations.'

'A mistake?' snapped Mary. 'Are you telling me that Sheila Nestor called what she said – a *mistake*?'

The sergeant moved his weight from one foot to the other. 'I suppose – on the whole – you could call it – an error of judgement.'

'An error of judgement?' It was clear that Mary was not going to let him off easily. 'So is it an error of judgement when a perfectly innocent person could go to prison for however long, and all because someone can make up anything she wants, and get away with it?'

The sergeant shook his head. 'Mrs Nestor hasn't got away with it – well, not altogether. We're charging her with giving false evidence, and she'll have to answer to a magistrate's court.'

'And what punishment will she get?' Mary asked outright.

'Oh, she'll get a fine, there's no doubt about that.'

'How much?'

'I couldn't possibly tell you that, Miss Trimble,' he replied awkwardly. 'That's a matter for the court. But I'd not be surprised if she had to cough up five quid or so.'

'Five pounds?' replied Mary calmly, but with irony. 'Five pounds for trying to destroy someone's life, a woman who has had to live with the pain of knowing her husband died for a country that didn't accept her? Sheila Nestor is a disgusting woman! She ought to be locked away for life!'

'Can I say, Miss Trimble,' said the sergeant, cap in hand, his face betraying his true feelings about what had happened, 'you have every right to feel the way you do. It's not the first time we've had to deal with petty allegations like this . . .' – he put his hand up to stop her replying – 'oh, I know it's not petty to you. But the fact of the matter is that this world is full of little people like Mrs Nestor. Because of their own pent-up emotions, they cling to whatever mischief they can get up to; they cling to ways they can get their own back for something that doesn't mean a brass farthing. In her case, it riles her because Mrs Rawsthorne is different to her. She's got a bee in her bonnet, and she doesn't know how to get rid of it. You know, in some ways, we have to feel sorry for someone like that. They have a lot to live with.'

After listening to what the sergeant had to say, Mary changed her mind about him. He wasn't quite the fool she had taken him for. 'Have you told Mrs – have you told Tanya?'

'Oh yes,' replied the sergeant. 'She was the first to be told. We went to her flat to tell her.'

'You mean, she's now back at the flat – in Kentish Town?'

'Back amongst all those pictures,' said the sergeant, putting on his cap again. 'I hadn't realised she's such a talented lady. D'you know, she even did one of me. I was quite impressed. I gave it to my wife, and she said that for the first time in my life I actually look quite hand-some!'

Mary found herself laughing with him. But she hesitated when he held out his hand for her to shake. Finally, however, she relented.

'Once again,' he said, looking her straight in the eyes, 'I'm sorry.'

After he'd left, Mary went to the window and watched him stride off down the street. She knew only too well that all the lace curtains would be fluttering, especially old Fred Know-It-All next door. And she could hear all the gossip as the bobby disappeared around the corner: '*What's she been up to now?*' and '*It's that Thelma*' or '*It's that Dodo and Billy.*' Insinuations, made-up stories, jealousies, dislikes – Mary was only too aware that they were all part of life in any town, any city, any street behind the curtains. How well Tanya could capture all those faces in her sketchbook . . .

That same afternoon, despite optimistic forecasts in the newspapers that more and more V-bomb sites were being located and captured in northern France, and that Allied soldiers were now only fifty miles from Paris, two more doodlebugs streaked across the sky over Islington. Where they came down nobody knew at first. After what had happened at the Gaumont cinema during the night, the moment anyone in the street caught sight of one of those 'things', their eyes would remain glued to the sky whilst they waited for the engines to cut out, those few chilling moments of silence, and then the inevitable explosion – somewhere. And every time, during that terrible silence, Mary would pray to herself and say, '*Please God, don't let it be me or those I love,*' knowing only too well that if it *wasn't* her turn, then it would be someone else's.

On the way to work, Mary decided to make a short detour to take a look at what was happening at the Gaumont. Although in the full light of day it was a sorry sight, the overall structure of the building was intact, with most of those striking fawn-coloured tiles on the outside walls still clinging on as in the hallowed days when they were first put up. A steady stream of sightseers were shunting past the imposing front entrance, all of them straining to catch a glimpse of what had once been the grand foyer and was now a mass of tangled iron beams, charred wood, piles of fallen plaster from the once greatly admired ornamental ceiling, and broken glass from the huge central chandelier. Mary could also just see what was left of the majestic winding carpeted staircase which had led up to the Gaumont's much-loved afternoon tearoom, all now exposed to the daylight from the roof of the building which had been struck by the flying bomb, bringing it down on to the cinema's vast stage and luxurious auditorium. Mary had no idea who had designed the building, but whoever it was had given the area something to remember. However, as she stood there in the sunlight, the one thing she was grateful for was that the bomb had not struck during the last evening performance, when Thelma and her lance corporal had been sitting in the back row of the grand circle.

On her way to the Marlborough, Mary thought a lot about what Thelma had told her that morning, about her extraordinary meeting with the young soldier, about whom she had initially feared so much. Mary was immensely proud and relieved that her sister had now told the truth, and that relations between the two sisters had improved so much. If Thelma really did have feelings for this boy then Mary had made up her mind not to try to deter her. After all, the way *she* saw it, *true* love was not just the prerogative of older people.

Once she had arrived at the cinema and changed into her uniform, Mary went around her 'patch' in the grand circle, checking to see that the cleaners hadn't missed anything, especially discarded cigarette butts in the ashtrays, and she found an empty Zubes tin, medicated pastilles that were a poor wartime substitute for sweets. Whilst she was doing so, she stopped at the front row of the circle to look around the entire auditorium which would soon have to take on the hordes of extra cinemagoers who would normally be regulars at the nearby Gaumont. For some unknown reason, the place suddenly seemed quite ominous to her. Maybe it had something to do with the fact that the vast area was deserted, waiting for the onslaught of the crowds who had begun to form queues for the matinée performance out front. But the more she thought about it, the more she feared what would happen if the Marlborough should share the same fate as the Gaumont. Lennie was right about London not being safe for her and the kids. Maybe she *should* do what he had suggested, pack up everything and move out with him to his farmhouse in Essex. After all, there was plenty of room out there – for Granddad as well if he wanted to get out of London – and the kids would have a life that they had never experienced before; plenty of space, fresh air, food that country people had but which was completely unattainable without ration coupons in London, and, most of all, the knowledge that their lives would not be in constant danger. It was a hard decision to make, one that she could not make easily. However, if the onslaught of the flying bombs continued, she would have to think first and foremost about the safety of her young brother and sisters.

'Pity about the poor old Gaumont.'

Mary swung round with a start to find Lennie's dad, Ernie Backer, calling from the back of the circle behind her.

'It's just terrible,' said Mary, going back up the stairs to meet him. 'I still can't believe it's happened. It was such a beautiful place. Thank God nobody was killed.'

'It's a bloody miracle, if you ask me,' replied Ernie. 'A few hours earlier and it would have been carnage, hundreds killed.'

With Thelma and her lance corporal in mind, a cold shiver went down Mary's spine.

Ernie said nothing for a moment or so, and sat down in one of the seats. 'So – how are things with you and Lennie?' he eventually asked. 'Is he looking after you?'

'I don't need looking after, thank you, Mr Backer,' she replied, indignantly, her voice raised just enough to echo around the empty auditorium. 'I've learned to do that for myself. But Lennie is being a wonderful support.'

Ernie grinned. 'Well, *he's* certainly learned a lot in the last year or so,' he replied. 'He's had to learn how to grow up the hard way.'

'I'm not sure I know what you mean,' she said.

'Oh – takin' on responsibility. Doin' all the things to look after his mum that *I* should've done.'

206

'Lennie's a *very* responsible person, Mr Backer,' replied Mary. 'If it hadn't been for *him*, his mum could never have coped.'

Ernie took her implied criticism without responding to it. 'How's Winnie doin' in that home she's in?' he asked.

'As well as can be expected,' she replied. 'It's a comfortable place, and they look after her very well.' She hesitated a moment. 'Have *you* been to see her at all?'

Ernie sniffed. 'No, not really.'

'Well *she* seems to think you have. Whenever we go to see her, she tells us you've been to visit her. But that's her condition, of course. It's so sad.'

Ernie was embarrassed, but looked away. 'I'll try and pop down to see her on one of my days off,' he said awkwardly.

'I'm sure she'd appreciate it,' said Mary, pointedly.

'Of course, I'll have more time to meself when I leave this place,' he said quite suddenly.

Mary did a double take. 'Leave?'

'Can't go on forever, Mary,' he said. 'All good things have to come to an end. In any case, there's more to life than bein' stuck in a projection room. I want to get out and do things. Thought I might move up north somewhere. I'm fed up with Islington. I could do with a change of scenery.'

'Away from Lennie?' asked Mary, acidly. 'Away from your wife?'

'Away from meself,' he replied with a wry grin.

'Mary!'

Mary looked round to see Alice Thompson calling to her from the circle entrance door.

'There's someone come to see you downstairs,' she said. 'They're queuing up outside, so she's waiting round the back door.'

'Who is she?' Mary asked, with some trepidation.

'Couldn't say, dear,' replied Alice. 'Looks Chinese ter me.'

Mary's face immediately lit up, and without saying another word, she left Ernie, and, bursting with excitement, rushed straight out through the side exit.

The moment she got outside into the back alley, she saw her. Although the woman was standing with her back to her, she knew immediately who it was. 'Tanya!' she called.

Tanya Ling turned with a start. She was beaming, but there were tears in her eyes.

'Forgive me! Please forgive me! Damn Sheila Nestor! Damn the police! I was stupid to believe them, Tanya – stupid! Oh, please forgive me?'

Chapter 16

In the early hours of the eighth of September 1944, Hitler's latest secret weapon, which became known as the V-2 rocket, came thundering down on the West London borough of Chiswick. The explosion left an enormous crater, which, probably because of its depth, helped to contain the damage to surrounding properties. However, when the second rocket exploded on the same day on wasteland in Epping, Mary had no hesitation in ruling out evacuating herself and the family to Lennie's farmhouse. Nowhere was safe. Despite the horrors of the new weapon, life for Mary and her family continued as normally as possible, even though it meant taking added precautions every time the vapour trail from the deadly rocket was seen streaking across the sky. On Guy Fawkes Night in November, there was panic and consternation when a V-2 dropped on to Boothby Road near the Archway Underground Station, causing a massive loss of life, and severe damage to the surrounding area. The huge explosion also rocked the very foundations of Roden Street and all the other neighbourhoods around the Nag's Head, where Lennie, Thelma, Dodo and Billy had to throw themselves to the floor under the back-parlour table to escape flying glass from broken windows. The war, everyone was told, was gradually drawing to a close, but the battle would not be won until Hitler's now not-so-secret weapon had been eliminated for ever.

On Christmas Day, the Marlborough was closed, and this enabled Mary to spend the time with her family. Lennie had managed to scrounge some black-market petrol to drive his old truck down to London, so early in the morning he drove them all to the farmhouse, where he and

Mary roasted the chicken he had got from under the counter at Dan's butcher's shop in Epping Town. For Mary, it was a day of absolute bliss. Not only did she have the best Christmas Day meal she had had since her mum and dad had died, but also Lennie was at his best, doing everything in his power to make both her and the kids happy. Thelma too was loving and helpful, so different to what she had been for the best part of the year, mainly because, in the lance corporal, she had found her first real boyfriend, whom she wrote to at least three times a week whilst he was away on active service. Billy was overjoyed to get his Christmas present from Lennie, which turned out to be a do-it-yourself make-up kit of the Spitfire fighter plane, and Dodo was equally thrilled to be given a toy nurse's outfit, complete with a first-aid kit. Even Thelma was not forgotten. Mary and Lennie had combined to buy her a cosmetic pack, which she had seen and loved in Jones Brothers. Lennie's present to Mary was not only unexpected, but also just what she wanted. It was a travel book which concentrated on glossy photographs of Devonshire and its beaches, bringing her dream of visiting those exotic places one day just a little bit closer. Mary's present for Lennie was more personal, and she waited until they were having a stroll along the back lane behind the house after the midday meal with the family.

'It's beautiful,' said Lennie, as they came to a halt so that he could open the small parcel, which contained a shiny brown wallet. 'Where did you get it?'

'I bought it for Dad's birthday just a few months before he died,' she replied, pulling the collar of her topcoat up snugly around her neck. 'It's hardly been used.'

'I can see that,' replied Lennie gratefully. 'I'll treasure it.'

'I was going to give you his pocket watch,' continued Mary, 'but I thought it was only right to hold on to it until Billy gets a bit older.'

'I really like this,' said Lennie. 'It's just what I need.' He opened the wallet, his face lighting up when he saw what was inside. It was a small snapshot photo of Mary. He looked up at her. '*This* is just what I need, too.' He leaned forward, put his arms around her waist, and gently kissed her.

'Lennie,' said Mary, her expression gradually more serious, 'is there somewhere we can talk?'

He looked uneasy. 'What about?' he asked.

'Us,' she replied. 'I don't want the kids to hear.'

Lennie took her hand and led her to the old barn in the backyard. They were wrapped up as warmly as possible, for there had been a hard frost that morning, and now it had melted there was plenty of mud around.

The barn itself had timber beams and a high loft. It hadn't been used for a long time because it was no longer a working farm. 'When I was a kid and I'd been cheeky to Dad, I used to come in here to hide,' he said. 'In those days the place was full of hay, because we kept two horses and some chickens in here. Dad always caught me, of course, and I ended up getting quite a few whacks – not on my head, but because I wore shorts, it was always on my calves. I remember climbing out of my bedroom at night and sleeping down here, just because I couldn't take the way Mum and Dad used to shout at each other. Many a time I just wanted to run away and forget all about them. I wish I'd had a brother or sister to talk to.'

'Well, you can talk to *me*, Lennie,' said Mary.

He looked at her with trepidation. 'What about?'

'About the things I have to know if we're going to have any chance of staying together.' She sat down in one of the wooden stalls where Lennie had once groomed the two horses. 'Tell me about this girl.'

Lennie immediately turned away.

'No, Lennie,' she said immediately getting up again. 'It's Christmas Day. Let's make this the time when we cleared the air once and for all. Who is she?'

Lennie took a long time to answer. He walked around and around, agitated and clearly in turmoil. Finally, he stopped at the door, leaned one hand on the timber-pannelled wall, and stared out into the back-yard. 'Her name's Carole,' he began, 'Carole Pickard. We met at a dance in the Town Hall. It was soon after I got out of the army. I was in a pretty bad way, dark moods, all that kind of thing. She had a great

211

sense of humour – at least I thought she did at the time. But I was wrong. She treated me like a toy, like I was someone she could just have a bit of fun with.'

'What kind of fun, Lennie?' asked Mary.

He hesitated, and looked back at her. 'She wanted to have a baby.'

Mary went quite cold.

'I never wanted that,' he said firmly. 'I never wanted that at all.'

'But you slept with her?'

Put so bluntly, he had no choice but to tell the truth. 'Only once,' he said.

'Where?'

This angered him, and sent him pacing up and down the barn, constantly running his fingers through his hair as he went. 'For Christ's sake, Mary!' he snapped. 'Does it matter *where?*'

'Yes, Lennie,' replied Mary. 'It *does* matter.' She hesitated. 'Was it in here?'

'Yes, for Christ's sake – it was in here!' He stopped dead, and looked across to see how she would react.

Her back was turned towards him, her arms crossed, and she was staring up at the sunlight streaming through a hole in the hay loft.

He wanted to go to her, but he had gone this far, and couldn't do so until he had finished what he had been forced to start. 'Yes, Mary,' he said, with conviction. 'She *did* have a baby . . .'

Mary turned, and made for the door.

As she went, he grabbed hold of her. 'It wasn't *my* baby, Mary. It wasn't *mine.*'

She slowly turned to face him. There were tears in her eyes.

'You've got to believe me,' he begged. 'For a long time, she convinced me that I was the father, that I was the one who had to look after her. She comes from a lousy family. All they ever think about is money. That's what Carole wanted. She saw this house, the land that was in my mum's family for years, and she wanted it!' He went to one of the two horse stalls, and stood there leaning with both hands against the frame around the half-door. 'She wanted me to marry her. I said "no", but she said

212

that if I didn't, she'd get her dad to sue me for the upbringing of the baby. I still refused, and when the baby arrived two months premature, they filed a case in some court up at Epping. I didn't get a wink of sleep – I wanted to do away with myself because I knew that she'd forced me into doing what I'd never wanted to do in the first place.' Clearly now in great distress, he turned around to look at her.

She was standing in the middle of the barn, quiet, impassive, but watching every move he made.

'Two days before the court hearing in Epping,' he continued, 'someone came to see me. His name was Des Thomas. I remembered him straight away, because he went to the same school as me. Good-looking bloke, straight as a dye.' He held back for a moment. 'He told me I had no right to Carole's baby. He said it was his – and not mine.'

Mary looked at him in astonishment.

'Only then did it all make sense to me,' continued Lennie, now with some difficulty. 'What he told me was that he'd been having a relationship with Carole long before I got to know her. He said that he'd slept with her several times, and that there was no way that *I* could be the father of her child.' He paused just long enough to sneak a look at Mary. 'That was the reason she'd had the baby two months before *I* was told it was due. Des said he'd always told Carole that he'd never marry her. When he got called up, he hadn't got a penny to his name. That's where *I* came in.'

Clearly shocked by all she was hearing, Mary went to the open barn door. Now it was *her* turn to look out into the yard. It was difficult for her to take in everything he was telling her.

'The night before the court hearing,' Lennie continued, 'I went to see her. I told her everything Des had told me, and that if she went ahead with taking me to court, Des agreed he'd be a witness. She flew at me, called me every name under the sun, told me that her dad would sort me out, that I'd never be able to show my face in Epping ever again. But in the end, she had to withdraw. It wasn't until after it was all over that I'd heard she'd taken the baby to show to my mum. I couldn't believe it. She knew that Mum was mentally ill.'

213

It seemed to Lennie an eternity before Mary spoke to him. When she did, her look seemed hard and unforgiving. 'Let's go and see your mum,' she said.

Lennie was shocked, completely taken aback. 'Why?' he asked.

'For God's sake, Lennie,' she replied. 'It's Christmas!'

The sitting room of Holly Manor was big enough to accommodate around forty residents. However, today there was a Christmas party in progress, and some of the visitors had packed the place out. Not that there were many visitors – there never were. At the best of times, most families found it a chore to have to spend an hour or so with their elderly relatives, especially on Christmas Day when they were too busy getting the big meal ready, having a snooze in the afternoon, and playing party games and joining in sing-songs in the evening.

When Lennie, Mary, Thelma, Dodo and Billy arrived at the home, Winnie was sitting in a comfortable armchair, joining in with her fellow residents a rousing sing-song of Christmas carols. For obvious reasons the favourite was 'The Holly and the Ivy,' and although the other residents didn't exactly lift the roof off, they were vocal enough to drown out the piano playing of the Matron. Dodo and Billy thought it was all great fun, especially when one of the nurses gave them paper hats to put on, making them look even more comical than some of the old folk. Once the sing-song came to an end, some of the residents went off to have a nap before they launched into their special Christmas evening supper of tinned pink salmon and cucumber sandwiches.

'You're looking well, Mum,' said Mary, once she and Lennie were alone with her. It was not, however, what she really thought, because since the last time Mary was there, the look in Winnie's eyes seemed to have become even more distant. 'Looks like they're feeding you well here.'

'Oh, they haven't given us any food today,' replied Winnie, vaguely. 'Still, I expect sooner or later they'll give us *something*.'

Mary exchanged a quick, knowing look with Lennie. She knew

what Winnie had said wasn't true, because Matron had already told them that, thanks to the generosity of some of the local farmers, the residents had had a slap-up Christmas lunch of roast turkey, baked potatoes, brussel sprouts, carrots and cauliflower, which had been followed by Christmas pudding and mince pies.

Lennie drew closer to her. He still felt guilty about leaving her in such a place, but by the way she was gradually deteriorating, it seemed to be the only solution. 'Are you happy, Mum?' he asked, quietly.

Although she looked almost poignant in her party hat, turning to look at Lennie brought a great smile to her face. 'Oh yes,' she replied. 'The only thing is I can't see the swallows from my window.'

Despite Mary's somewhat less enthusiastic feelings for Lennie at the moment, she gave him a quick, reassuring smile.

'The swallows have gone for the winter, Mum,' Lennie said. 'You'll see them when they get back in March or April.'

Winnie gave him a strange, distant look, almost as if she didn't believe a word he was saying.

On the other side of the room, Dodo and Billy were admiring the decorations on the Christmas tree, whilst Thelma was wandering around the room looking at all the photographs on the walls, including a framed letter from Winston Churchill, who, as Member of Parliament for nearby Woodford, had written to congratulate the opening of Holly Manor before the war. When Thelma joined Mary and Lennie, they found Winnie staring hard in bewilderment at the girl.

'Mum,' said Mary, 'this is my sister, Thelma. She's just sixteen years old, and she works at Jones Brothers.'

'Where?' asked Winnie, puzzled.

'Jones Brothers,' repeated Mary.

'I don't know them, do I?'

Thelma was about to laugh, but quickly thought better of it.

'It's a department store, Mum,' said Lennie. 'You went there a few times when you used to go down to Holloway to see Dad.'

'Dad?' asked Winnie. 'Oh yes! I must remember to tell him that when he comes to see me. What's the time? He should be here soon.'

Lennie's face crunched up, but Mary gave him a reassuring look. She remembered how Ernie Backer had called Lennie a 'mummy's boy', which, even when he said it, she found a cruel thing to say – and not true at all. She wondered how *she* would have felt if she had seen her own mum or dad gradually drifting off into a world of their own. Saying goodbye to someone you loved was hard enough, but when they were still alive, looking straight through you with empty eyes that penetrated deep into your very heart and soul, must be very difficult to cope with. And yet, the more she looked at this sad woman, the more she felt that Winnie Backer knew more than those eyes revealed. The brain was such a strange mechanism. Who really knows *exactly* how it works?

Most of the residents had now gone off for their afternoon nap, and the room was empty.

'I think we'd better go,' said Lennie. But quite suddenly, his mum started humming one of her favourite songs. It was called 'Irish Lullaby', and although she couldn't remember the words, she hummed beautifully, and swayed to and fro to the sound.

On hearing Winnie, Dodo and Billy hurried across, and before anyone knew what was happening, the two of them were joining in a song which their own mum and dad used to sing to them at every family get-together. Then Thelma picked up the chorus, followed gradually by Mary. Whilst this was going on, Lennie slipped away to the other side of the room, where, to Mary's absolute astonishment, he sat down at the upright piano, and accompanied the singing. Mary took hold of both Winnie's hands, and sang the song softly to her. Then Thelma, Dodo and Billy cuddled up to Winnie, and made the song a very poignant event. However, Mary was puzzled to see that Winnie's attention seemed to be focused in blank bewilderment on something on the other side of the room. When Mary turned around to look, she saw Ernie Backer standing in the open doorway. She got up immediately, and Lennie stopped playing the piano.

Ernie's eyes met Winnie's.

Lennie went to him. 'Did you tell her you were coming?' he asked.

Ernie shook his head. Then he crossed the room and crouched down in front of the woman he had once loved.

The chances of a white Christmas soon receded when ice-cold rain started to fall just as the family got back to the farmhouse. It was now bitterly cold, and it took a while for Lennie to get the log fire burning in the fireplace in the hall. But once it got going, the glow it produced was so comforting. The kids loved it, for it gave them the chance to play with their Christmas presents, and whilst Mary made some sandwiches in the scullery, Lennie helped Billy to assemble his model aircraft Spitfire, and Thelma to be the patient to Dodo's nurse.

A short while later, Lennie went into the scullery to join Mary. The anguish she felt about all the things he had told her about Carole Pickard and her baby was still uppermost in her mind. Despite the fact that this was Christmas evening, the words would not come easily.

'How did she know?' Lennie asked, who set about slicing the bread for her. 'Dad told me that he definitely didn't get in touch with either Mum or the home, so how could she have possibly known that he was coming to visit her?'

'The main thing', replied Mary, 'is that he *did* come. And it was his own decision.'

'Dad hasn't ever made a decent decision in his entire life.'

'Well, he did this time,' said Mary. 'People don't always do the things that are expected of them. Just like you.'

Lennie stopped slicing the bread. 'What's *that* supposed to mean?' he asked, puzzled.

She looked up at him. 'Where did you learn to play the piano?'

Lennie was embarrassed. 'Oh that.' He slowly resumed slicing the bread. 'I can't really play it,' he said. 'Mum used to play by ear a bit, and I watched her. Just a few songs, nothing more. I've never thought of myself as Paderewski.'

'You don't have to be Paderewski to enjoy playing a piano,' replied Mary, who was now spreading a scrape of margarine on to the slices

217

of bread. 'But I just never thought of someone like you *wanting* to do something like that.'

'Is that a criticism?' he asked.

'Just an observation,' she replied.

As far as Lennie could make out, there was no doubt in his mind that a frosty atmosphere had developed between them. In some ways he blamed himself. He should have told Mary about himself and Carole Pickard long ago. He should have told her that she *did* have a baby, but that he wasn't the father. For the next few minutes they concentrated on what they were doing in silence. Eventually, the silence became too much for him. One way or another he had to clear the air. 'Mary,' he blurted out, 'do you want to split up?'

Mary tried not to look surprised. 'Why?' she asked.

'Well – after what I told you this morning. I mean, I know what you must feel.'

'Do you, Lennie?' she replied, scooping salmon out of the tin and spreading it on to the sliced bread.

This lack of communication was beginning to get him down. 'Oh, for Christ's sake, stop playing games with me, Mary!' he snapped. 'You've hardly said a dozen words to me since I told you.'

'I think going to see your mum was more important than us,' she replied, still without looking at him. 'Don't you?'

He suddenly exploded, and threw down the bread knife. 'D'you want me to take you home?' he growled, turning her round to face him. 'If so, I'll get the truck out. I can get you all home in an hour or so.'

'I know how long it takes to get home, Lennie,' she replied, infuriatingly calm. 'But don't you think we should at least think of the others? It is Christmas, you know.'

'Sod Christmas!' he said. 'It's obvious you hate the sight of me, so why don't you just say so, and let's call it a day.'

'You mean, you don't want us to spend the night in your house. Is that it?'

'That's *not* what I said,' he replied, angrily. 'I've already told you, there are enough beds for everyone, but if you can't bear to sleep under the same roof as me, then what's the point?'

'When did you last see that girl, Lennie?'

Her question only riled him even more. 'For goodness' sake, Mary!' he bellowed. 'Do we have to go through all that again?' Thoroughly agitated, he started to pace up and down. 'I saw her a few months ago – yes, the baby too! If you must know, she was buying vegetables in the market.'

'Did she speak to you?'

'No, she didn't speak to me,' he snapped, 'and if she had, I'd have walked away from her. How many times do I have to tell you that, Mary? How many times?'

'All I have to know, Lennie,' she said, with some difficulty, 'is if what you're telling me is the truth.'

This stopped Lennie dead in his tracks. He slowly came back to her. 'Are you telling me – you don't trust me?' he asked, earnestly.

'I don't know, Lennie,' she replied. 'I just don't know.'

It took Dodo and Billy a long time to get to sleep. From the moment Lennie showed them into their bedroom, they were so excited that they kept Thelma awake, so much so that she was on the verge of strangling the pair of them. For kids from the big city, sleeping for the first time in a strange bedroom, with not a sound outside except the hooting of owls, was an experience they were savouring. It was exciting for Thelma too, although she wouldn't dream of showing it to her rowdy young brother and sister. What *she* loved was the dark, and the feeling of being tucked up in bed with a hot-water bottle. The only thing she regretted was that she still had to share a bedroom with Dodo and Billy, but at least the room was big enough to keep them at arm's length, and once they had settled down, she really began to feel the luxury of being away from home.

Mary too was very comfortable. Lennie had let her use his mum's bedroom, which had a fireplace to keep the place so warm that she didn't really need a hot-water bottle. However, she was still very unhappy about the angry quarrel she had had with Lennie earlier in the evening. Every so often she would toss and turn, and think of the way he had given up his own room to her brother and sisters, whilst he slept downstairs on a camp bed in the sitting room. And gradually, she felt the guilt seeping through her entire body. Hadn't Lennie done what she had asked him to do? Hadn't he opened up and released all those gremlins that were lurking inside? Could she really keep thinking of Lennie as a liar? After all, it would be very easy for either herself or Tanya to find out what really happened between him and that girl. During the summer Tanya had done some asking around about Lennie, and had come up with nothing but praise for the way the boy had looked after his mum, the way he had carried on with the family business. No one had even mentioned his brief relationship with Carole Pickard. She was an unknown quantity.

Right up until the early hours of the morning, Lennie lay wide awake on his camp bed in the sitting room. The blackout curtains were drawn back, because it gave him the chance to see the moon, bobbing in and out of dark night clouds, throwing a bright fluorescent light on his face, moving around the pupils of his eyes like little stars. How he hated the way he had talked to Mary during the evening. It was so rash, so typical of the way he flared up over the slightest thing. After all, Mary had the right to know the truth. She had the right to know if he was the kind of bloke she could trust. But it was all over now, he was quite sure of that. After he had taken the family back to Roden Street in the morning, Mary would ask him to collect his things together and leave. He couldn't even bear to think about it. He loved her; he was *in* love with her. If she was no longer in his life, he didn't know what he'd do. Go away? Go and live in some remote place where the sun never shone, where the birds never sang?

Finally, he managed to close his eyes. He dreaded waking up in the morning. Suddenly, as he lay there, he heard something move. He didn't know what it was, but it was enough to make him open his eyes with a start. Was it an owl, or was it a bat that sometimes found a way into the house? He slowly sat up, and kept absolutely quiet. His heart was pounding, but he didn't know why. After a moment, he got up. As he did so, he felt a pair of arms gently embracing him. And then the warm breath on the back of his head, followed by equally warm lips pressing lightly against his neck.

'I love you,' whispered Mary, turning him around to face her. 'I don't know why, but I love you so much.'

Lennie looked in awe at her face, flooded by the cold white light of a winter moon. Then he smothered her with kisses . . .

Chapter 17

Granddad Trimble was not really enjoying his move to Edmonton. It was nothing to do with the district, which suited him just fine, but more to do with his old mate, Harry Watts, who was turning out to be a bit of an old granny as far as keeping his house clean and tidy was concerned. The trouble was, Harry, now in his late sixties, had never married, so he had never known what it was like to share his house with anyone. When Granddad had first arrived, it was all good old mates, but once the honeymoon period was over, Harry started to complain about keeping the place spick and span, with comments like '*A tidy home is a happy home,*' and '*I don't know how your wife put up with you all these years.*' Needless to say, it didn't take Granddad long to get fed up with all the petty rules and regulations, and, apart from the local pubs where he spent whatever was left of his meagre weekly pension from the Gas Light and Coke Company, he wished he'd never left Roden Street. However, it was too late to do anything about it now, because, after living in Harry's house for a few months, he realised just how much he had not pulled his weight with his own family, whom, despite that ugly row he'd had with Mary before he left, he was still very fond of.

Harry's house was really quite small, more like a cottage, built on two floors in a quiet cul-de-sac just off Wilbury Way, just a stone's throw away from Tottenham Grammar School and the North Middlesex Hospital. As it was quite a way from the nearest pub, Granddad was allowed to use Harry's old Raleigh bicycle to get back and forth, although the forth part of it could sometimes be quite hazardous, especially after downing a few pints of bitter. Just occasionally, the two men went to the pub together, which meant that they had to walk to their local, which did not suit Granddad at all, for it was nearly half a mile away.

The saloon bar of the the Green Parrot was full that night. With so many of the local young men now called up and on active duty overseas, most of the regulars, including Granddad and Harry, were quite elderly. But their age did not restrict them from having opinions of their own, and after a few hours of 'tippling' they were all quite vocal in their condemnation of the Government for practically *everything*. Spread along the bar counter some of the customers were poring over newspapers that contained graphic front-page reports and photographs of the progress of the Allied invasion, together with the Russian army's advance into Germany. But the main talking point tonight was the massive bombing attack on the German city of Dresden by one thousand, four hundred planes of RAF Bomber Command.

'Well, I think it's disgustin',' croaked one rather tipsy customer, who happened to be the only woman in the bar. 'Killin' all those people is a crime against 'umanity.' She could only just get the words out.

'A crime against 'umanity?' spluttered Granddad over his pint of bitter. 'Was it a crime against 'umanity when Goering bombed the daylights out of poor ol' Coventry?'

'I 'ad a sister-in-law livin' up there,' said one of the customers named Ted, who had his wits about him because he was only on his first glass of draught ale. 'She lost everythin', her mum, the house, her two kids, *and* her dog. When my bruvver came home on compassionate leave, he nearly had a fit. They didn't tell him exactly what had happened, only that a member of his family had been killed. He naturally thought it was his missus, but it turned out to be the old gel. His missus was living in a Salvation Army hostel. It broke him up, I can tell yer.'

'Yer see!' said Granddad, aiming his fire at the female customer. 'An' are we s'pposed ter be upset becos a few hundred huns got what they deserved?'

'A few thousand, more like!' growled the woman. 'It's mass murder, if yer ask me.'

She was so angry with Granddad that she gulped down half her glass of pink gin, then turned her back on him.

Granddad did the same to her.

'As a matter of fact,' said Harry Watts, who always wore a trilby hat, summer and winter, and rarely took it off, 'I think Elsie's got a point. I don't believe in "an eye for an eye, a tooth for a tooth." No matter what or where, human life is precious.'

'You wouldn't say that if it was *your* life, 'Arry Watts!' murmured Granddad. 'Just remember, we din't start this bloody war!'

There were rumbles of agreement from all around the bar. Harry didn't like that. He never took well to criticism of any sort, and the fact that it came from Granddad only made him more indignant.

The feather in the woman's hat wiggled angrily. 'Well, I'm off!' she called, downing the last drops of her gin. 'I'm clearly outnumbered by all you mass murderers!' With that, she swept off haughtily, and left the pub.

'Good riddance, too!' burped Granddad. 'One for the road please, Jim!'

Jim, the guv'nor, pulled up another pint for him.

'Trouble with Else,' said Ted, 'is she can't take a joke. She nearly blew her top when she saw in the paper that some WAAF gel mechanic was workin' on the tail of a Spitfire when the pilot took off.'

This produced a roar of laughter from the customers.

'What 'appened?' asked Granddad.

Ted was laughing so much he could hardly speak. 'She clung on fer dear life, only got down again when the pilot noticed he was carrying too much weight!'

Another roar of laughter from the customers.

'I don't think that's very funny,' said Harry, who was not renowned for his sense of humour. 'She could've been killed.'

'Serve her right fer tryin' ter do a man's job!' yelled one of the half-cut regulars on the other side of the bar.

'Don't think that's fair,' said another customer. 'If it wasn't for the gels, we wouldn't be able to fight this war. When yer think how they kept us all goin' durin' the Blitz – doing men's jobs in the fire service, drivin' ambulances, and Gord knows what else.'

There was reluctant agreement from all round.

'I mean,' continued the same customer, 'think what they did durin' that disaster down at Bethnal Green tube. I hear they saved a lot of lives.'

More murmurs of agreements such as, 'That's true.'

At the mention of the Bethnal Green tube tragedy, Granddad suddenly seized up. 'Think I've 'ad enough,' he announced.

'What about your drink?' asked Jim, the guv'nor.

'Give it to one of the needy,' replied Granddad, sourly. 'See yer back 'ome, 'Arry.'

Everyone watched him go in silence. Only after he had gone did Harry remind the regulars about Granddad losing his son and daughter-in law in the tube disaster.

It was pretty cold outside, and as Granddad staggered his way back to Harry's place, he soon found that the pullover and jacket that he wore without a topcoat was not adequate. It was dark as well; pitch-black, in fact, with not a sign of either moon or stars. The old boy's eyes weren't all that good either, and as he was too vain to wear the spectacles the optician had prescribed for him, he had to be very careful where he was walking. Behind him, he could hear some rowdy singing and shouting going on in the Green Parrot, a loud and drunken version of 'She'll Be Coming Round the Mountains'. He moved on as quickly as he dared.

On the way he felt pretty lousy about all the bad feeling he had caused since he went to live with his own family. In the dark, all the events of the past few years flashed before him, culminating in the terrible tragedy of Bethnal Green tube station, when so many people had been killed all because someone tripped on the escalator during an air raid. Losing his son and daughter-in-law was bad enough, but he had never taken into consideration how devastating it must have been for Mary, Thelma, Dodo and Billy. Every step of the way, he felt guilty, guilty because he had never done one single thing that could have helped to relieve the grief his family were feeling, especially Mary. But what could he do about it now, he asked himself? After all the family had done for him, he had just walked out on them, leaving Mary to cope single-handed. He felt ashamed. There was only one thing he could now, and he would make sure he attended to that first thing in the morning.

At that moment, he saw the outline of someone approaching him in the dark. It brought him to an abrupt halt.

'Hello, hello, hello,' came a heavy voice, shining a torch beam straight into Granddad's eyes. 'An' what are *you* up to, old timer?'

'What d'yer think I'm up to?' Granddad snapped back. 'I'm on my way back home from the pub. An' I'll be obliged if you'd turn off that light. It's blindin' me.'

The special constable who was making Granddad so tetchy took a good look first, then switched off the torch. 'Where's home, then?' he asked.

'I'm stayin' with my friend 'Arry Watts,' replied the old chap, indignantly. 'Other side of Wilbury Way. Why? What's it to *you*?'

'No need to get uppity,' replied the constable, firmly. 'Just checkin', that's all. What's yer name?'

'Trimble,' replied Granddad, tersely. '*Mister* Trimble to *you*.'

'Well, when you get back home,' said the constable, who, without his torch beam, remained just a faceless figure in the dark, 'make sure you don't turn your lights on till you've drawn your blackout curtains. We've got one or two prosecutions in the pipeline – people being careless, sending their lights right up so Jerry can see them.'

'Lot of ol' rubbish,' scoffed Granddad. 'The war's nearly over.' In fact, this was true. It was February 1945, and as the number of rockets falling on London seemed to be getting fewer each day, people were beginning to regain their confidence. 'They said on the wireless the other day we can start thinking about relaxing the rules a bit. They've already started taking the masks off the car headlights. Let's face it, doodlebugs and rockets don't need pilots. It's stupid ter go on panicking about petty things.'

'Nothin' petty about gettin' your head blown off,' replied the constable, firmly. 'So just be a good lad, and keep your lights down. OK?'

Granddad was too indignant to answer, so he said nothing and went on his way, mumbling to himself about bureaucracy and quite unnecessary regulations that should now be scrapped. However, he had only just reached halfway, when he heard what sounded like a plane's engines. Before he had had enough time to throw himself to the ground, he was engulfed in an almighty explosion, the force of which knocked him off his feet, catapulted him into the air, and dumped him unconscious into a nearby hedge.

Tanya Ling stood back and looked at her charcoal sketch of Lennie. Although it was not yet quite finished, she felt that she had captured him in a way that she had rarely captured anyone before. In this case, it was because of the mood he had been in when she had decided to embark on something more ambitious. Her portraits of the people she sketched only came to life when they spoke to her. As she looked at Lennie, she could hear what he was saying: '*I love Mary. I just hope she loves me too.*' When she heard him say that to her, his mood was quite unlike the way he looked most times, which was generally edgy and lacking in confidence. The nice thing about *this* portrait was that not only was he not scowling, but he was also actually smiling, showing just what a good-looking boy he was. Of course, there was another reason why she wanted to capture Lennie in a portrait, but that was something that she would not be able to discuss with Mary until she saw if and how their relationship was going to develop. Nonetheless, she was on tenterhooks as she waited for Mary to see the sketch for the first time.

'Oh, Tanya,' said Mary, as the portrait was uncovered on the easel in Tanya's studio. 'It's – wonderful. I've never seen Lennie look so good. Just look at that smile!'

'Yes,' said Tanya. 'I had to wait rather a long time to get *that*!'

Both of them chuckled.

'I can't wait for him to see it,' said Mary. 'When are you going to show it to him?'

'Well, that's something I wanted to talk to you about,' replied Tanya. 'I've managed to get a new exhibition of my work, and I want to include this one in it. D'you think he'd mind?'

Mary was overcome with excitement. 'Oh Tanya,' she gasped, 'I think that's wonderful, absolutely wonderful. Of course he won't mind, and if he does I shall tell him that he has no say in the matter! Where and when is the exhibition going to take place?'

'Oh, not for six weeks or so. But you'll never guess. Islington Borough Council are going to sponsor the exhibition, and they're going to let me use the old church where you used to work – in the British Restaurant.'

Mary's face dropped. The thought of returning to the place that had given her so much unhappiness took away the joy of knowing that Lennie's picture would be hanging on the wall there.

'The most interesting thing about it,' continued Tanya, 'was *how* the Council were persuaded to do this for me.'

Mary was puzzled. 'How?' she asked, sceptically.

'Our good friend Mrs Nestor.'

Mary was thunderstruck. 'Sheila Nestor?' she gasped. 'After all she did to you?'

'I know,' replied Tanya, who covered over Lennie's portrait again and put it into the cupboard at the side of the fireplace. 'It *is* extraordinary, isn't it? But when she saw all my work here, she suddenly came up with the suggestion. Apparently, she knows someone fairly high up on the Council, and she offered to speak to her for me.'

Mary could hardly believe what she was hearing. 'Sheila Nestor – came *here* – to this studio?'

'I found her waiting on the doorstep one day,' said Tanya. 'She said she wanted to talk to me, so after what she'd done in clearing my name with the police, I asked her up to have a cup of tea – *Chinese* tea!' She chuckled to herself.

'Incredible!' said Mary.

'We sat in the kitchen,' continued Tanya, 'talking about all kinds of things – mainly about her losing her husband, and me losing mine. She opened her heart to me, saying how confused and stupid she had been, and would I forgive her. She told me that after her husband had been killed during the last war, she closed herself up to the world. The only thoughts she had about people were very negative, especially foreigners like me. I watched her carefully, taking in every line, every feature of her face, her eyes, her hair, her mannerisms. After a time, we were like old friends. She asked me if I could show her some of my pictures, and I took her up here to the studio. She became very excited, like a child with her toys. It was then that she came up with the idea of my holding an exhibition. A few days later it was all arranged. She's an extraordinary woman, Mary. Isn't it strange how one can misjudge somebody? We human beings are *so* complicated.'

A short while later, Tanya cooked Mary some Chinese noodles. It was quite an experience for Mary as she had never tasted any foreign food before. At first she was sceptical about tasting the vegetables and sauce that went with the noodles but she eventually took quite a liking to it.

Tanya decided to walk with Mary part of the way to the Nag's Head, where Mary had to start work at the Marlborough by two in the afternoon. On the way, Tanya started asking questions about Lennie. 'How do you feel about him now, Mary?' she asked. 'Are you in love with him?'

After the night she and Lennie had spent together at the farmhouse, Mary was a bit shy talking about him. 'I think', she replied, evasively, 'that he's very special.'

'*How* special?' asked Tanya. 'I know you probably think I'm being rather forward, but I do have a reason. If you remember, when we first met I told you about something your mother wanted me to do for her, that I could only tell you when the time is right. Well, the time is still not quite right – yet, but your relationship with Lennie does have a bearing on what I'll eventually tell you. I know this all probably sounds very mysterious but, believe me, Mary, this is what your mother wanted.'

They were just coming up to St George's Church, when Mary brought them to a halt. 'I must say,' she said, 'I don't understand how my relationship with Lennie can have anything to do with Mum. I mean, I didn't even meet him until at least a year after they died.'

As they stood there, a few snowflakes started to flutter down, sending passers-by scurrying for shelter. But Tanya and Mary were unperturbed, and merely turned up their coat collars. 'Your mother was a very shrewd woman, Mary,' said Tanya. 'She always looked to the future, not the present or the past. The only thing I *will* tell you, though, is that I think your mother would have liked Lennie. Yes, she would have liked him very much.'

A moment or so later, Tanya turned back to go home. For a short while, Mary watched her go, not at all worried by the snow which was now coming down fast, and beginning to settle. Tanya moved so delicately, striding out with such feminine poise, snowflakes quickly covering her jet-black hair. But what her Chinese friend had told Mary had clearly worried her, and as she finally turned to make her way to the Nag's Head, she couldn't help wondering what this was all leading up to.

With the Gaumont cinema now permanently closed because of severe damage caused by both V-1 and V-2 explosions, the queues at the Marlborough stretched right round the back of the building. With so much extra work, Alf Bickley took on two extra girls to help out, whilst his wife Ethel also came in to help Mavis in the cashier's kiosk, mainly because there were evenings when there were so many people queuing for tickets that some had to be turned away.

When Mary arrived at the cinema to get ready for the matinée performance, despite the snow now falling quite heavily, there was already a queue forming outside. The attraction this week was a double bill featuring the immensely popular Deanna Durbin, whose singing films, like so many others, always seemed to raise the spirit of Londoners during the dark days of the Blitz, especially as the songs nearly always sent them home humming the tunes. However, just as Mary was getting into her uniform to usher in the afternoon queues, Alf Bickley knocked on the door of the changing room, waiting to give Mary some rather worrying news: 'Sorry to trouble you, Mary,' he said. 'Just had a call from a man up in Edmonton, a man called Harry Watts. He says your granddad got injured in a bomb blast up there last night.'

Mary's blood went cold. 'Oh my God!' she gasped. 'How bad is he?'

'No idea,' replied Alf. 'He's in the North Middlesex Hospital, and you can visit him any time. You push off and get up there. One of the two new girls can cover for you.'

A few minutes later, Mary was on the top of the number 659 trolley bus heading for Edmonton. It was a perilous journey for, although the snow had settled an inch or so, in the busy city streets it was turning into a slippery black slush. The most distressing sights en route were the bombed-out buildings, the interiors of which which were totally exposed to the elements, and it was an odd experience for Mary to look out at what were once familiar sights such as kitchens with gas stoves, and front parlours with sofas and chairs still dangling precariously over the edge of demolished upstairs floors. But the thing that was uppermost in her mind was her granddad, and how seriously hurt she would find him when she got to the hospital.

As the bus slowly passed through the districts of Finsbury Park, Manor House, and Tottenham, her anxiety gradually turned to guilt. Over and over again she kept asking herself why she had been so cruel to him. After all, he *was* her own grandfather, her own kith and kin, and he was an old man. How could she have allowed him to go off in such a manner? Why didn't she just accept that no matter how tetchy and bad-tempered he was, she should never have allowed either herself or the kids to make him feel unwelcome. If anything were to happen to him now she would never forgive herself.

She got off the bus just near the vast Regal cinema in Silver Street, where many of the windows in the upper part of the building had been boarded up because of previous bomb blasts. Despite the intense

cold, there were queues everywhere – the greengrocer's, where potatoes were in short supply, a butcher's shop, and the Express Dairy, where,
after complaints from all over London that the morning deliveries of
bottled milk were either frozen before people got up, or that sparrows
had been pecking at the foil caps, people were queuing with their
ration books to get their own jugs filled with some unfrozen fresh
milk. Mary passed one of the longest queues she had ever seen outside
a fresh-fish shop, and some women had even formed a queue outside
a women's clothes shop, which specialised in wedding dresses. Before
she turned off the main road she caught a glimpse of a placard outside
a stationer's shop with the scrawled banner: EDMONTON HIT BY
RUNAWAY BOMBER.

It was a short walk to the North Middlesex Hospital, and when she
got there she went straight to the Emergency Wing where the nurses
on the reception desk soon located Granddad on a list of the previous
night's casualties. Mary feared the worst. Hurrying up the stairs, her
stomach started churning, and by the time she reached the ward where
Granddad had been taken, she was a shivering mess.

'Wos all the fuss?' said the old man, the moment she saw him, lying
on top of a bed at the far end of the ward, filled with men who had
only slight injuries.

Mary was astonished and relieved to discover that, apart from a bruise
over his right eye, her granddad looked no worse after his experience
in the dark the previous night. 'But what happened?' asked Mary,
anxiously. 'The message I got was that you'd been seriously injured.'

'Bleedin' bunkum!' spluttered the old man, whose teeth were in a
glass of water on a bedside cabinet. 'That's 'Arry Watts for yer – always
tryin' ter make a mountain out of a mole 'ill! It was just bad luck that
I was out at the wrong time. This bleedin' Jerry come over from
nowhere, dropped his bomb, and buggered off. But they brought 'im
down over the coast, so they tell me. After what he done to that poor
ol' bobby, I 'ope he rots in 'ell!'

'What bobby?' asked Mary.

'I was on me way 'ome from the Parrot, and he stopped me to 'ave a few words. I think he thought I was one of 'Itler's spies or somefin'. Anyway, a coupla minutes after he left, this thing come down. I don't remember anythin' more, only this big blue flash. When I come to, they was just pickin' me out of a hedge. Funny thing is, I din't 'ear no plane comin' over – no sound of an engine – nothin'. It was just there an' – whoosh! I thought the bleedin' war was s'pposed to be over.'

'What happened to the policeman?'

The old man turned his face away. He looked genuinely upset.

'Oh God,' Mary sighed, 'how terrible. But at least I'm grateful to know that you're alive.'

Mary's response seemed to take the old man by surprise. 'You are?' he asked.

'Well, of course I am, Granddad,' she replied, amazed that he should even have questioned what she had said. 'If anything had happened to you—' She stopped talking, and suddenly gently placed her hand over his hand. 'We wouldn't *want* anything to happen to you, Granddad.'

For one brief moment, the old man didn't quite know what to say. Not only was he surprised that Mary had made the journey to see him, but he was also strangely moved by her show of affection. 'You shouldn't've come all this way ter see me,' he said. 'When I see that 'Arry Watts, I'll give 'im what for!'

'It's no problem to me, Granddad,' she said, convincingly. 'In any case, I don't like you being over here all on your own – well, more or less on your own. If you should feel like coming home when you get out of here, you can have your bed back in the front parlour.'

The old man was truly taken aback by Mary's offer. But although it sent a warm feeling right through him, he was determined not to show it. Granddad was a proud man. He wasn't going to admit that leaving her and the kids had been a great mistake. 'That's – very – good of you, Mary,' he said, fumbling for words. 'But I'm quite all right where I am. As a matter of fact, 'Arry Watts ain't such a bad ol' fool. He means well. Nah, I'm all right. You need the room, gel. Don't you worry, I'll be on me feet in no time. They said I'll probably be out of this place terday some time.'

Mary straightened up. 'If you like,' she said, tentatively, 'when you're back at your friend's place, I could come over and see you sometime?'

Granddad thought about that for a moment. He looked up at her, and gave her one of his non-committal smiles. 'Wait and see,' was his reply. 'You've got a job ter get on with – *and* the kids to look after.'

'They sent their love,' she replied.

'That's nice,' he said, rather stiffly. As she was leaving, he said, 'Don't work too hard.'

Mary smiled, and kissed him gently on the forehead.

His eyes followed her all the way to the exit at the end of the ward. He'd forgotten what a slip of a girl she was. After she had gone, he lay back on his pillow and closed his eyes. In his mind, he could still see her, the living image of her mum, and just as caring. He felt so rotten that he had been nasty to her. There was *nothing* about Mary, about his grandchild, that deserved it. She was one of the best. His family were the best, and he could kick himself for not having realised it before. But it was no use moping about the past, about the mistakes, about the old ratbag he had become. No. Now it was time to do something positive, time to show how grateful he was, and how much he loved the family that he had treated so badly.

Chapter 18

If it wasn't bad enough to have V-2 rockets still shooting across the sky and causing havoc and destruction, London also had freezing fog to contend with. Fortunately, Dodo and Billy had only a few minutes' walk to get to school at the end of the road, but both Mary and Thelma had to allow more than three times longer to get to work. Despite the bonfires that were lit on street corners both day and night, it was a hazardous time for everyone, with transport in chaos, and everyone ill and gloomy, never knowing from one minute to the next whether a rocket would suddenly come dropping out of the sky and blow them and their houses to pieces.

Nutty Nora was in a bad way. Her chilblains played up something awful, and for weeks she had stayed at home, wrapped up in a shawl, coughing and sneezing and complaining of everything from rheumatism to a boil on her neck. Whatever illness anyone ever had, Nutty Nora had it too. Fred Parfitt next door called her a walking medicine chest, but felt sorry for her because, in his own words, her lazy sod of a brother either sat on his fat arse most of the time, or went off on one of his nightly visits to a known whore house in Caledonian Road. Fortunately for Nora, Mary was around to help out with her shopping, but she was nonetheless very ungrateful.

During this bitterly cold winter, the Marborough, like all the other cinemas in London, was feeling the crunch, with audience attendances down, mainly due to fog seeping into the auditorium and making it difficult to see what was going on on the screen. It was made worse by the fact that there were severe fuel shortages, which meant that central heating in the auditorium had to be rationed – none at all during matinée performances, and only two hours during the evening. No wonder that many people brought blankets and hot-water bottles with them, together with flasks of hot tea, and, in the case of the scattering of men in the audience, a few tots of the hard stuff! It was also not easy for the staff to cope, and Alf suggested to them all that they wear coats over their uniforms, and, if they wanted, scarves around their necks. In the case of Mavis the cashier, she sat in her kiosk so wrapped up in woollies and a fur hat that she looked just like an Eskimo.

Mary was now missing Lennie. On the day that the fog really took a hold, he was out at the farmhouse, and as the Green Line bus service to London had to be suspended, there was no way he could get back to Roden Street. It was now more than three days since Mary had last seen him, and she was beginning to feel very frustrated. 'If I know my son,' said Ernie Backer, smoking a dog-end to great risk in his projection room whilst the beam from his projector was doing its best to penetrate the fog to show the glamorous Technicolor of a new Betty Grable musical called *The Dolly Sisters*, 'he'll be like a bear with a sore thumb. He goes all moon-eyed every time your name's mentioned. Sounds like you've tamed him, that's for sure.'

Mary, sitting on a high stool beside him, felt a warm glow inside. 'Lennie doesn't need taming, Mr Backer. He just needs a decent start in life.'

'Well,' said Ernie, 'let's hope he gets it, if and when he sells the house. Though I doubt there'll be much chance of that till the war's over. Trouble is, he should be getting a decent job. Sounds like you're the one that's earning all the bread in the family.'

'I don't mind doing that,' she replied. 'While I'm at work, Lennie looks after the kids, and that's a great help to me.'

Ernie took a deep puff of his fag, which added smoke to the haze of fog. 'I wouldn't bank on that for too long if I were you,' he said, ominously.

This disturbed Mary. 'What d'you mean?' she asked.

'Oh, I dunno really,' replied Ernie, trying not to sound too serious. 'But Lennie's funny when it comes to being asked to do something that, in *his* mind, makes him look inferior.'

'What!' gasped Mary, trying to talk over Betty Grable's singing. 'I wouldn't ask him to do anything that he didn't want to do. In fact, *he* was the one who offered to look after the kids in the first place.'

'I know that, Mary,' replied Ernie, taking a quick look through the projection hole to make sure that the beam was functioning well. 'I only say that because of something that happened a few years ago, before he ever got called up. He got a job markin' out tickets or something at the bagwash up Holloway Road. He was only sixteen at the time, but the woman in charge there took a shine to him, so much so that she took him for granted, made him do all sorts of jobs that he wasn't engaged to do, like ironing shirts and women's dresses and things. Anyway, one day he objected, and told this woman that he was a man, and didn't do women's work. The result was, she got real nasty with him, told the bossman that he tried to make a pass at her. Well – that was it. He got the push, and it left him with a chip on his shoulder the size of the rock of Gibraltar.'

'I would *never* take Lennie for granted,' Mary insisted, 'not for *anything*. I respect him too much for that.'

'*I* know that,' said Ernie, 'but I just thought I'd warn you.'

Mary left the projection room and stood outside for a moment or so. For some reason, she was furious with Ernie for his so-called warning about Lennie. She was sick to death of Ernie's criticisms of his son, who had done more for his mum than her husband had ever done. Nonetheless, as she stood there, the doubts remained. *Was* she taking Lennie too much for granted?

Holly Manor was engulfed in freezing fog. It was not a night to go out, and the Matron made quite sure that there were good log fires burning in all the grates, and that every resident had a good meal in their stomachs. In the Grand Lounge, as it was called, there were a lot

237

of laughs as everyone gathered there listening to the hugely popular radio show *It's That Man Again*, with Tommy Handley. A few of them, however, were fast asleep, their heads on one side, way off in another world.

Winnie Backer had decided to go to sleep early. The radio didn't really interest her, unless it was some nice popular classical music that she could hum to. As she sat there, a lot of things were going through her poor, confused mind. She thought a lot about the people who came to see her on Christmas afternoon, especially Lennie. Or *was* it Lennie? And who was that man who came in when the others left? Then everything seemed to become muddled, and she couldn't really remember anything. Why can't the swallows come and sing to me? she asked herself over and over again. Who was it who promised they would soon be back? She rubbed her forehead, hoping it would provide the answers. And then a thought came to her. It wasn't a very clear thought but gradually it seemed to make sense. If the swallows couldn't come to *her*, then why shouldn't she go to *them*?

There was no one in the corridor when Winnie came quietly out of her room. She was wearing her favourite blue cardigan and the carpet slippers with the white bobbles on top. She could see a lot of people gathered together in that room at the end of the corridor, but they were all laughing so loudly that they didn't even notice her. She stood perfectly still for a moment, waiting for Matron to disappear into her office in the nearby annex, then looked around to see where she wanted to go. Eventually, she noticed the exit door just behind her, on the other side of the lavatory. She didn't have to think twice. Thinking played no part in her life now. She merely turned around, pushed down the safety bar on the exit door, and quietly slipped out of the building.

The biting cold cut right into her. She tried to look from left to right, but her face was pressed up against a grey wall of fog. There was no sound, not a single sound – and yet, for one brief moment she thought she *did* hear *something*. It was quite a long way away, right out there ahead of her – somewhere. She wasn't entirely sure what it was until she heard it again. A bird? A very small bird by the sound of things. Shouldn't it be in bed by now, in its nest, with its mother? She started to move, very slowly, one foot precariously in front of the other. Then again, she heard the sound. It gave her encouragement. She knew what it was. They were back. They were waiting for her.

Slowly, methodically, the tiny, slight figure disappeared into the ice-cold, murky grey fog, heading towards those friends she loved so much, and whom she knew were waiting for her . . .

Lennie was waiting for Mary when she came out through the front entrance of the Marlborough. For obvious reasons, the evening performance had been poorly attended, and she was glad to be getting home.

'You shouldn't have turned out in this weather,' said Mary, taking his arm. 'I've got cat's eyes. I can see further than you think.'

'I don't like you moving around on your own in this fog,' he replied, shining his torch beam which produced a wall of light that was really no help at all. 'You never know who might be tailing you.'

Mary loved the way he talked to her. He was so protective, so firm and decisive. As they struggled along blindly, she started to sing softly: '*I've Got My Love to Keep Me Warm*.' To her surprise, he knew the words, and quietly joined in. He also knew why she had chosen to sing the song.

With no light to guide them, when they eventually reached the main Holloway Road, which was usually no more than two minutes' walk from the Marlborough, they stopped at the kerbside in between a trolley bus and a tram, which had come to a dead halt in the appalling conditions. Then they crossed the road, hand in hand, hoping they would be able to see some lights coming from the windows of the Nag's Head pub, but as the blackout restrictions still hadn't been fully lifted, they had to quite literally feel their way along the wall along Seven Sisters Road. They stopped with a start when they reached the side entrance of Woolworths department store, for they bumped into a boy and a girl who were taking advantage of the fog to enjoy themselves in the sheltered doorway. The girl giggled, but the boy, whoever he was, said, 'Sorry, mate. Right ol' pea-souper!'

Mary and Lennie chuckled, but didn't hang around to get in the way. However, when they got to the corner of Herstlet Road they were greeted by a glaring wall of crackling flames from a huge bonfire, one of many that had been lit around the district to act as markers. Standing around the bonfire were the shadowy figures of people who were huddled as close as they could to the flames to keep warm. Mary soon identified the voice of Fred Know-it-All, her next-door neighbour, so she whispered to Lennie to make as wide a detour around them as possible. However, they left behind a lot of laughter, and the smell of steaming hot cocoa, which was a sure sign that the neighbours were making the best of a bad job.

At Holly Manor, the Matron and her assistant Eleanor Johnson went around turning off lights, leaving on only the few low-voltage safety bulbs that were necessary if any of the elderly residents should wander around during the night. After all the laughter the ITMA show had produced earlier on in the evening, the place was now so quiet, that all that could be heard was old Vera in room number seven on the ground floor, who was, as usual snoring her head off.

'What's it like out there now?' asked Matron, her voice a low whisper.

Eleanor tiptoed as quietly as she could on the linoleum floor, and peered out through one of the blackout curtains in the sitting room. In contrast to Matron, who was quite full and plump, Eleanor was tall, lanky, and rather awkward in her movements. 'Can't see a bat,' she whispered.

'Just as well,' returned Matron. 'Can't bear the horrible things!'

They moved on to the ground-floor corridor. 'Don't worry, Matron,' said Eleanor. 'I'll do the check. Why don't you turn in?'

'Are you sure, Ellie?' asked Matron. 'I must say, I'm dead on my feet tonight. It's been one hell of a day.'

'Of course,' replied Eleanor reassuringly. 'I'm on tonight, so it's no problem for me. Goodnight, Matron. See you in the morning.'

240

'Goodnight, Eleanor dear,' called Matron, quietly, as she went off to her own quarters in the annex.

Torch in hand, Eleanor immediately started her night rounds, which meant peering in, as quietly and as discreetly as she could, into every bedroom. She never ceased to wonder how incredible it was that some elderly people slept all through the day in their armchairs in the Grand Lounge, then slept all the night without waking up once. But then there were those poor souls who just couldn't sleep, and laid with their heads on their pillows, eyes wide open, staring aimlessly in the dark up at the ceiling. Winnie Backer was one of those who seemed to be awake from morning to night. Not that she was any trouble; in fact, she was one of the sweetest residents, who just seemed to watch everything that was going on all around her with a fixed smile, without really knowing what it was all about.

'Winnie, dear.' When she reached Winnie's door, Eleanor tapped as gently as she could. 'Coming in, Winnie.' Her voice was soft as she could manage, and she actually succeeded in easing open the door without letting it creak. But when she went in and directed her torch beam on to Winnie's bed, she found it deserted. Not yet panicking, she quickly checked Winnie's own little lavatory, one of the few of the resident's bedrooms that actually had such a luxury. But when she turned on the light, Winnie wasn't there.

'Oh my God!' she gasped, before rushing straight out into the hall.

The next morning, Mary had every intention of sleeping late. It was not something she could do very often, for most mornings she had to get Thelma off to work and Dodo and Billy to school. But as she had sat up late talking to Lennie over two cups of cocoa in the back parlour, she saw no reason why she should not get up until the last possible moment. However, when she did eventually get up and drew back the blackout curtains, she was relieved to see that the fog had completely disappeared.

As she came down the stairs in her topcoat over her nightie, the first thing she could smell was fried bread, and when she went into the back parlour, she found the family tucking into their breakfast treat which had been cooked for them by Lennie. 'My God!' she cried. 'What d'you think this is – the Ritz?'

Everyone was enjoying their fried bread so much that they just ignored her and carried on eating.

'Lennie,' she called. 'You're spoiling them!'

Lennie suddenly came in from the scullery carrying the frying pan. 'Sit down,' he said. 'This is *yours*.' He plonked a slice of fried bread on her plate, another slice on his own plate, then sat down beside her.

'Come off it, Lennie,' Mary said, remembering the conversation she'd had with Ernie the night before, about taking Lennie too much for granted. 'You're not a skivvy.'

'Doesn't take five minutes,' replied Lennie, already tucking into his own breakfast. 'Mum used to make it for me when I was a kid.'

'Well, don't think you lot are going to get this *every* morning!' she joked with all of them, but they were far too preoccupied to take any notice of what she was saying. She turned to Lennie with an affectionate smile. 'Thanks, Lennie,' she said. 'I don't know what we'd do without you.' As she spoke there was a hard knock on the front door. Everyone immediately looked up. 'Oh no,' she sighed. 'Not at this time. Billy, see who it is.'

'Why always *me*?' he groaned, slamming down his knife and fork.

''Cos you're fat and lazy!' spluttered Dodo, her mouth full of fried bread.

Billy was about to whack her, before Mary stopped him.

'Billy!' she growled. 'Door!'

Glaring at his young sister, Billy reluctantly got up from the table, wiped the grease from his lips and chin with the back of his hand, and went out to the front door.

'I hope to God it's not that stupid woman down the road, about you two being rude to her again.' Mary was scowling at Dodo, who completely ignored her. 'Because if it is . . .'

'Mary!' Billy's shout from the front door echoed along the passage outside. 'Someone to see you!'

Mary sighed, and put down her knife and fork. 'One of these days, Dodo,' she warned, 'I'm going to kill you and your brother!' She left the room, wiping the grease from her lips with her handkerchief as she went. When she got to the door, she was shocked to see who was standing on the front doorstep.

'Miss Trimble,' said PC Jones, his handlebar moustache looking even fuller than the last time Mary had seen him. 'Sorry to trouble you, but we've just had a phone call from a place called Holly Manor. Have you got a Len Backer staying here?'

Shocked, Mary immediately swung a look back at Lennie, who was standing watching her from the open back parlour door.

With the wartime fuel shortage, and the truck out at the farmhouse, it was nearly three hours later before Lennie and Mary could reach Holly Manor. Because of the thick fog that had blanketed the area for the past few days, there was a backlog on all transport services throughout London, and the wait for the Green Line bus at the Isledon Road bus stop was not only interminable, but also freezing cold. However, by the time they had got there the fog had more or less disappeared, ending up as a thin, grey haze struggling in the midday sun. Mary was so grateful to Alf Bickley for readily agreeing to call in one of his standby staff to cover for her so that she could go out to Epping with Lennie. Alf was just as distressed as she was that Winnie Backer had disappeared during the night from the nursing home.

'I don't understand it,' said Matron, who had clearly been up half the night looking for Winnie. 'One moment she was there, the next she was gone. It gave my girl Eleanor such a shock. We have always been so very careful about your mother, Mr Backer. We know what a wanderer she is.'

Lennie knew that too. There were so many times when his mum had managed to slip out of the house, only to be found either down by the river, or sitting crouched in the bushes like a rabbit. 'It's all right, Matron,' he said. 'I'm not blaming you.'

'We have such strict regulations about not leaving doors open,' added

243

Eleanor, Matron's second-in-command, who was very distressed. 'Unfortunately, she got out through the emergency exit, which we're not allowed to lock at night.'

'We've had people out all night in the fog searching for her,' continued Matron, 'but someone with that type of condition always seems to have such an elusive way of keeping out of sight. Anyway, the police will be coming in to talk to you later. They've had people out in the search squad, of course, but with these damned V-bombs coming down all the time, their resources are very overstretched.'

'I'm going out to look for her,' said Lennie, in a sudden burst of activity. 'She used to come with me to town in the truck sometimes. It's possible she's hiding out somewhere that she might just remember.'

'In the fog?' asked Eleanor, utterly exhausted after not sleeping a wink all night. 'I checked in her wardrobe. She didn't even have a coat on.' She was close to tears.

Matron comforted her. She knew only too well how conscientious poor Eleanor was, and how she would be blaming herself for what had happened. 'Would you like one of the staff to come with you, Mr Backer?' she called, as he rushed out.

'No,' he called back. 'Mum knows my voice. If she's still alive, I'm the only one she's likely to respond to.'

Mary automatically hurried after him.

Epping Town was brimming with shoppers. After the appalling weather conditions that had confined them to their houses for the past few days, there was a mad scramble to buy some fresh food and vegetables, but the first thing Mary noticed was that the queues outside butcher and fish shops were not as long as back home in Holloway. It was still bitterly cold, and everyone was wrapped up in heavy overcoats, scarves and mittens, literally anything that could keep out the biting wind that was coming up. Lennie knew the place well. As a kid his mum used to drag him around the shops for hours. The local bus took only ten minutes to get there, and what he remembered most was carrying heavy shopping bags whilst trying to help his mum on and off the bus. What he also remembered was that his mum never failed to reward him for his help. Every time they came to Epping, she would always buy him one of his favourite water ices from the Italian shop near the church, and that evening the meal was always very special, with some home-made meat or fish dish, together with freshly cooked country vegetables.

'It's difficult to know where to start looking,' said Mary, not holding Lennie's arm whilst they hurried along because she knew how tense and upset he was. 'I mean, what direction would she take after leaving the Home in dense fog?'

'I blame myself,' was all Lennie could say. His stomach was so churned up he felt like punching into a brick wall with his fist. 'How could I have done this to her? How could I have been so stupid? I knew this would happen sooner or later – it was bound to. How could I lock my own mother away in a strange place, with strange people who have nothing in common with her?'

'Lennie!' Mary brought him to an abrupt halt, and grabbed hold of his arm. 'Don't talk like that. Don't ever let me hear you talk like that. Nobody loves your mum more than you do. Nobody has done as much for her as you have. It would have been wrong for you to have given up your life just to look after her.'

'*Just* to look after her?' he exploded. 'She's my mum, for goodness' sake! If *I* don't look after her, who on earth will?' He rushed on.

'Listen to me, Lennie!' she called, hurrying to keep up with him. '*Please* listen to me! Has it ever occurred to you that your mum may have *wanted* to get away from you?'

Lennie came to an angry stop. He looked at her in absolutely bewilderment.

'To get away, because she wanted you to have a life of your own.'

His face nearly crumpled up with remorse, but he controlled it sufficiently to let her hug him.

'Where are the most likely places we might find her?' she asked.

Lennie quickly composed himself and with Mary at his side, searched every back alley, every small lane behind the shops, the church graveyard, and even the inside of an old mill house which had been badly damaged during the first wave of flying bomb attacks. Finally, however, he led them to the woods on the other side of the road to the nursing home. It was tough going, made more difficult by the fact that there was at least an inch of soft snow still lying there and, as they went, their feet sank into the slushy mud.

The moment they reached the first clearing, Lennie starting yelling out: 'Mum! Where . . . are . . . you? It's me . . . Lennie . . . Mum!'

The lack of response was deafening. Even though they stood still for a few moments, all they could hear were the twittering of birds in the thickest part of the bushes and trees. They moved on, and whilst they were winding their way along a narrow path through the under-growth, Lennie came to a sudden anxious halt. 'Stop!' he shouted, his hand held up to prevent her from going forward.

'What is it?' she stuttered, trembling.

'Butterfly bomb,' he replied. 'During the Blitz, the Germans dropped a lot of these bloody things in forest areas to try and get people to step on them, especially kids. They're a kind of booby trap.'

'Oh my God!' gasped Mary. 'That's so wicked!'

'Just follow me closely,' he said, moving off, carefully avoiding the strange metal object half buried in the mud just in front of them. 'Just keep your eyes open.'

A few minutes later, they reached a small pond, which, at the back of Lennie's mind, was the sort of place he was dreading. Whenever his mum had got out of the house in the past, the one place she always seemed to make for was the river. Somehow, the water fascin-ated her, and every time he found her she was standing on the river bank just staring down at the waves as they came tumbling down from a small nearby waterfall. 'Mum?' he called out as loud as he could.

This time his voice sent a whole battalion of sparrows fluttering up into the air from the trees in panic, and the noise really started to unnerve Mary.

'Mum!' The booming sound reverberated around the woods, and

246

sent several muscovy ducks scurrying along the surface of the water to the other side of the pond.

'I think we're wasting our time here,' said Mary, uncomfortably. 'If she was here she'd answer you.'

'*If* she's still alive,' Lennie returned, grimly. For the next few minutes, his eyes scanned the entire area, every nook, every clearing beneath the bushes and in the undergrowth. He even stooped down to look around the entire circumference of the pond just to make sure that Winnie was not floating in some inaccessible corner beneath the reeds.

As they stood there, both of them hoping for some clue, some ray of hope, they were sharply distracted by the sound of a man's voice calling them from the outer fringe of the woods. 'Mr Backer! Are you there?'

'Here!' Lennie shouted back. 'What is it?'

'We've found her!'

A few minutes later, Lennie and Mary, accompanied by an elderly Special Constable, passed through the huge iron gates of Holly Manor. They were met by Matron, who was dabbing her eyes with her hand-kerchief. They were led round to the back of the Manor, where the beautiful green lawns and well-stocked garden beds were such a feature of fine summer days. As they approached the far end of the garden, there was a small stone fountain that had not been used since the start of the war. Gathered around it was a small group of people, most of them nurses from the home, but also a couple of police constables. Mary gripped Lennie's arm as tightly as she could as he went forward to take a look.

Yes, Winnie was there all right, crouched in front of a stone orna-ment that seemed to have given her a few last moments of joy, for there was a smile on her face, a smile of release and not of pain. Lennie slowly stooped down, and with the tips of his fingers, delicately outlined that smile, that same sweet smile that he knew so well. Then he drew close to the small, lifeless figure, and kissed her forehead. He wanted to cry, he wanted to cry so badly, but he knew that that was the last thing his mum would want him to do. What was it she always used to tell him? '*Boys musn't cry, Lennie. That's the job of us girls.*' He stood up again, and took one last look at her, and at the tall, crumbling garden ornament where she had decided to spend her last moments. It was a bird bath. In his mind, he could almost hear the swallows coming home again.

Chapter 19

According to the BBC, the winter of 1944/45 was proving to be the harshest for fifty years, and no one believed how true that was more than Granddad Trimble. In early March he was getting really fed up with the way his mate Harry Watts was skimping and saving on his household bills, which meant that he only put money in the gas meter when it was absolutely necessary. The old man was furious because, although his mate Harry wasn't charging him any rent, the least he could expect was a bit of warmth from the gas fire in his own bedroom. But no, he had to shiver and shake all night, under two thin blankets that wouldn't keep a cat warm, let alone an elderly man like him, who suffered more aches and pains than a human lunch inside a crocodile's stomach. Thank God for his hot-water bottle! However, at least it was getting safer to go out these days. By all accounts the Allied Forces were gradually getting rid of the V–2 rocket sites, and there was no doubt that those that *were* still coming over from the remaining sites were definitely getting few and far between. With that in mind, he decided that he'd get out of the house for a while by walking up to the post office.

Although the weather was still quite nippy, the sun was shining, which, if nothing else, always helped the morale. It was at times like this that Granddad missed being back home in Roden Street. Despite the fact that he had always been such a 'grumpy old bugger', as the cheeky Billy had once called him, he was much happier with his own kith and kin around him. Unfortunately, however, that was never the impression he ever gave to any of them, and that was something that had troubled him every night as he lay in his cold bedroom, and equally cold bed, in Harry Watt's dreary little town cottage. Still, now he'd had time to think, he was determined to put things straight with his family, not right away, but in good time. From now on, things were going to change.

It had been almost a month now since Lennie had lost his mum during that tragic night in the fog out at Holly Manor. On the whole, he had dealt with the trauma pretty well, but mainly because of Mary, who had stood at his side every inch of the way. The worst part, of course, had been having to go through the police investigations, the post-mortem, the coroner's inquest, and then Winnie's funeral, which had been held in the Epping cemetery. Ernie refused to go to the church service, but he watched the interment from a distance, head bared, face grave and pale, his eyes welling with tears. It was a poignant event, with only a few mourners present, but with Mary's help, Lennie stood up to it all in a way that would have made his mum proud. The whole business had been a hard blow, and it would take quite a while for him to get over it. However, soon he would have to start thinking of the future, of what he was going to do with his life. 'You do realise, don't you?' he said to Mary as they lay clutched in each other's arms on her bed after making love together. 'I've got to think about getting a job. I can't go on just living off you for ever.'

'You're *not* living off me, Lennie,' she said. 'The help you give me in looking after the kids is absolutely amazing.'

'I'm not talking about that,' he replied, getting up from the bed. 'Looking after kids is a woman's job – it's not for a man. But earning money to keep my head held high is important to me.'

Mary watched him as he collected his trousers and started to put them on. Only then did she remember Ernie's warning: '*But Lennie's funny when it comes to being asked to do something that, in his mind, makes him look inferior.*' But why should he think that looking after the kids was a woman's job? Did he think it was unmanly or something, and if so, did he think the same thing when he was looking after his mum all those years? 'Oh Lennie,' she replied with a sigh, 'as long as we have enough money to keep us going, what does it matter?'

He turned round on her. 'It matters to *me!*' he replied, irritably. 'Dad has told me that I can have the house out at Epping, that he doesn't want any part of it. That's all very well, but as far as I'm concerned, the place is a white elephant.'

Aware that she could not reason with him, she got up and put on her top coat, which felt cold over her naked body. 'Look, Lennie,' she said, going to him. 'One day, you'll be able to sell the house and keep all the money for yourself. God knows you're entitled to it.'

'For Christ's sake, Mary,' he snapped, 'why can't I make you understand? It doesn't matter who you talk to, everyone knows it's going to be years before anyone will buy a broken down old ramshackle of a place like the farmhouse. When the war's over, people are going to need *new* houses, buildings to replace the ones they've lost during the bombing. I mean just look at all those prefabricated things that have sprung up all over the place. They're quick and serviceable. No.' He had now put on his vest and shirt. 'If we're going to get married, if I'm going to look after you and the kids, then I need money and I need it now, and the only way I'm going to get it is to earn it, to go out and find a job before all the blokes start coming back home from the war. It's nothing but a pipe dream to say that I'll be able to sell the house and keep all the money for myself.'

'There's nothing wrong with having dreams, Lennie,' she replied, defensively.

Now he was really irritated. 'Oh yes, I know,' he snapped, snidely. 'The Blue Coach to those far-away beaches, lying in the sun, the kids leaping in an' out of the sea. It's all make-believe, Mary. You need money for things like that. If I don't go out and earn some money, you won't ever get any further than the end of the road!'

Mary, stung by that remark, stood back from him. 'As a matter of fact,' she said with dignity, 'in my money box at the bottom of my wardrobe, I've already saved six pounds eleven shillings and threepence for the trip.'

'And how much d'you think it's going to cost you to take yourself, Thelma, Dodo and Billy on a luxury coach trip all the way to Devonshire, plus board and lodging for a week or so?'

Mary was beginning to feel crestfallen. 'I don't know, Lennie,' she said. 'But I'll do it eventually. And I was kind of hoping that you'd be coming with us.'

He turned away impatiently and looked out of the window. 'You live in a dream-world, Mary,' he grunted. 'It's just not real to think that you're going to save up all that money single-handed.'

'Then why did you buy me that travel book for Christmas?' she asked.

Lennie froze, suddenly aware of the selfish things he'd been saying to her. He turned around and saw her sitting down on the edge of the bed, a funny little thing all wrapped up in her topcoat. He had clearly hurt her, and being the awkward creature that he was, he didn't know how to take back the stupid things he had said. But then he noticed the travel book she had mentioned, the one about the wonders of family holidays in the West Country. He picked it up, and slowly went across with it, perching on the bed beside her. 'I wonder how many seats they have in these things?' he asked, looking at the front cover of the book, which contained a coloured photograph of the Blue Coach luxury charabanc.

Mary was too upset to look up and, with his fingers, Lennie moved her face around to see the front cover of the book.

'What d'you think?' he asked again, softly. After a quick glance at the photograph, Mary started to cry, so he threw his arms around her, and gently eased her face against his chest. 'Tell you what we'll do,' he said, softly. 'On your next day off, we'll go up to Victoria Coach Station and take a good look at this so-called Blue Coach. You never know, until you see something for real, it might not even exist.'

She pulled her face off his chest, and looked up at him. She was half laughing, half crying. Then she threw her arms around him in a tight, loving embrace.

★

252

Granddad Trimble was on top of the world. That very morning, just before he left for the post office, he had had a letter in the post to say that he had won ten bob on a sweepstake ticket he'd bought at the Eaglet pub in Holloway months ago. OK, so it wasn't a fortune, but it was going to be a good addition to his Post Office Savings Account, a nice little nest-egg he had great plans for. To cheer him up even more, the moment he left Harry Watts's house, the sun came out and, for the first time in ages, he could feel the strengthening warmth of the sun, reminding him that the start of spring was just around the corner.

Once he had reached Silver Street, he paused at a pedestrian crossing where the Belisha beacon was flashing excitedly, but he didn't wait for the traffic to pass before he crossed, he merely held up his walking stick, waved it with great authority, and brought the traffic to a skidding halt. With drivers cursing him like mad, he crossed in his own time, waving false thanks to them all. For those few minutes, all his many ailments seemed to have been forgotten.

Tilly Raglan, the postmistress, had got used to Granddad trying to push in front of the queue at her services counter. From the first day he came in, she could tell by the way he kept straining to look around the person in front of him that he was one of the more impatient of her customers. Despite this, she liked him, for when she had time to chat to him he was always very interesting about his past, about his family, and particularly about the tragic loss of his son and daughter-in-law in the Bethnal Green tube disaster. At times, also, he was very amusing, always making jokes about people he had no time for, and making her laugh with mischievous jibes about what a nice lump of woman she was, a real 'Merry Widow', and how her black and white spaniel dog must have seen her getting up to quite a few naughty things in her time. Fortunately, today there were not too many people in the queue, maybe four or five, most of them elderly, but one young woman there with a baby in its pram. However, the topic of conversation amongst them was certainly not about Merry Widows and spaniel dogs.

'It's all over,' said one old lady named Ethel, who was second in the queue. 'My 'usband 'as it on good authority that Churchill's going to declare the end of the war some time next week.'

There was an immediate bubble of excitement around the small, well-loved shop on the corner of a quiet back street.

'How come he knows about that, then, Ethel?' asked a tall, bespectacled man named Mr Braithwaite, who was standing just behind her. 'He in the know or something?'

'Of course 'e's in the know, Cyril Braithwaite,' sniffed Ethel, indignantly. 'You know very well he works for the Government.'

'Inland Revenue — that right?' asked Harold, the man standing in front of Granddad Trimble at the back of the queue, who was wearing a bright yellow woollen scarf around his neck.

Amongst ripples of muffled laughter, Ethel haughtily turned her back on them all, whilst Bessie the spaniel dog, up on her hind legs, peered over the top of the counter from inside, and barked crossly.

'Down, Bess, down!' scolded Tilly, the postmistress, pulling her spaniel's paws off the counter. 'Bad dog!'

Granddad listened to all this with detached disinterest. He spent most of his time scanning the same old posters on the walls, which must have been there since the start of the war: MORE COAL FOR THE WAR DRIVE; MAKE-DO AND MEND; A.R.P: SERVE TO SAVE.

Granddad had read those slogans on the walls so many times over the past few months that he knew them all by heart.

'Well,' said Mr Braithwaite, who was sporting a new brown-check flat cap and brown patent shoes. 'I s'ppose if anyone knows, it must be Churchill. Though I don't think we should start pulling down the air-raid shelters till Hitler's out of the way.'

'It may not have occurred to *you*', said old Ethel snootily, directing her remark to Mr Braithwaite without turning to look at him, 'that we've had hardly any rockets over in the last week or so.'

'An' we won't!' added Harold, the man in front of Granddad. 'Our boys've captured all the sites. We won't see any more of those bleedin' things!'

254

'Don't speak too soon, Harold,' commented Tilly, who was making a bit of a din slamming her rubber post-office stamp down on some postal orders for the young woman with the baby at the counter. 'You never know what that sly ol' fox has got up his sleeve.' She briefly looked up over the top of her metal-rimmed spectacles, to find Granddad winking at her from the back of the queue. Knowing what an old flirt he was, she smiled to herself and handed the postal orders over to the young woman. 'One and eightpence please, dear,' she said.

The woman sorted through her purse, handed over the coins, then shoved the baby's dummy back into his mouth. 'Thank you, Mrs Raglan,' she said, leaving the counter to make room for the still indignant Ethel.

It took several minutes to clear the queue, and by the time Tilly had got to Granddad, it was time to lock up for the one-hour lunch break. However, whilst Tilly was attending to her last customer, Mr Braithwaite, Ethel and Harold were still arguing with each other outside about when the war was going to end, about who was right, who was wrong; the usual heated discussion in which no one would ever admit they were wrong.

'I must say, Tilly,' said Granddad, 'you're lookin' just as glamorous as ever terday. Rita Hayworth ain't got nothin' on you!'

Tilly went all coy. She loved playing up to Granddad's mischievous advances. 'Oh, I bet you say that to all the girls, Mr Trimble,' she said, taking his Post Office savings book, which had two pounds inside.

'Not with *you* around,' he said. 'Yer know what? I reckon it's about time you came an' had a drink with me round the Parrot.'

Tilly stamped his book and pushed it back to him beneath the counter grill. 'How're your family?' she asked, pretending to ignore his cheeky invitation.

'Far as I know, they're OK,' sniffed Granddad, determined to pursue her. 'Mary's comin' over to see me on Sunday mornin'. She only gets one day off a week. I just don't know 'ow she copes.'

Tilly nodded in agreement, then came out from behind the counter to lock up for the lunch hour, hotly pursued by Bessie the spaniel.

'So what about that drink?' asked Granddad, with another of his flirtatious winks.

Tilly went even more coy, and quite unconsciously tidied up a few strands of grey hair beneath a tortoiseshell comb on top of her head. 'Since my husband passed away, Mr Trimble,' she said, feeling more like Rita Hayworth every minute, 'I don't go into pubs on my own any more.'

'Yer won't *be* on yer own, you'll be wiv me!' he insisted, trying to fend off Bessie, who was once again up on her hind legs, her paws firmly planted on his chest. 'Come off it, Till. Yer don't 'ave any commitments, do yer?'

'You never know,' she replied, grandly, pulling Bessie off him.

'I can afford a good evenin' out,' he boasted. 'Yer *know* I can.' As if to prove his point, he held up his savings book.

Tilly gave him a nice, appreciative smile. 'I'll think about it, Mr Trimble,' she said sweetly, opening the door with one hand, and holding on to Bessie's collar with the other.

'Albert,' he said, trying hard to stare her straight in the eyes. 'That's me name – Albert. OK, Tilly?'

They were interrupted by the group who a few minutes earlier had been in the queue inside the post office, and were still hotly arguing on the street corner outside.

'Hey!' Granddad yelled. ''Aint you got no 'omes ter go to?'

They all turned to look at him and Tilly, who were both standing on the doorstep outside the post office.

As they did so, they heard a sudden, loud whooshing sound, which seemed to come out of nowhere. All eyes automatically turned to look up at the sky, but before they had a chance to see the monster and its vapour trail spinning down towards them, everything went black.

Mary loved the mornings. Apart from her one day off a week, with Thelma at work and Dodo and Billy at school, they were the only times that she and Lennie could have alone together. However, with Lennie now threatening to get a job, she was beginning to get a little anxious about what would happen in the future. He was right, of course, about doing something that would make him less reliant on *her*, but she was worried that he might be doing it for all the wrong reasons. Now that poor Winnie had gone, there was no doubt that he would be able to sell the farmhouse sooner or later, but if he *had* to find something to do, until that time came, she wanted him to find the type of job that he would be interested in even if it was just something temporary. That was one of the reasons why she was counting out the coins in her money box. They were not just for her holiday, but for a rainy day when times might be bad for the family, and that included Lennie.

'So,' asked Lennie, watching her pile up the different coins on the back parlour table, 'how much *do* you think it would cost to pay for this beanfeast down in Devon?'

'I've no idea,' she said. 'At the outside, it would be somewhere around fifty pounds. That's including all our meals and expenses, of course, depending on whether or not we take full board at our lodgings, or eat out in cafés. And then there's spending money, especially for the kids.'

Lennie sighed. He knew that this holiday was an obsession with her, but he could see no way that she would ever find that kind of money. It didn't help that his mum had died destitute, mainly because whatever little money she had was spent on medicines and looking after her during her final two years. It made him more determined than ever to find a job.

'Six pounds, eleven shillings, and ninepence exactly,' Mary said, returning the coins back into her money box. 'I've just put in another tanner which I found on the floor of the circle last night. Mr Bickley insisted I keep it.' She looked up and saw Lennie watching her. 'Dearest Len,' she said, stroking his hair with her hand. 'I'm sorry I behaved so badly this morning. It was selfish, and I'm ashamed of myself. Sometimes I think I'm like my mum, always dreaming, always trying to reach out for things that I can't have. Yes, of course you must get a job, and I *do* understand why. But as far as selling the house is concerned, you mustn't let that prey on your mind. There's absolutely no rush. In fact, I've got an idea that might help to solve the problem.' She got up from the table and added some more coke to the range oven fire. 'Suppose I gave up my job at the Marlborough?'

Lennie looked up with a start. 'What d'you mean?' he asked. 'I thought you liked your job there?'

'Of course I do!' she replied, emphatically. 'And I'll always be grateful to you for helping me to get it, but' – she turned, took his hand, and drew him across so that they could both squat on the floor in front of the fire – 'until the war's over, we could always go back to Epping and live in the farmhouse.'

Lennie was astonished by what she was suggesting. 'Are you mad or something, Mary?' he replied.

'Why not?' she continued. 'I mean, there'd be no rent, only gas and electricity . . .'

'Are you talking about the whole family?'

She shrugged. 'Well – yes,' she replied. 'I'm sure both me and Thelma could find jobs out there, and I'm sure the headmistress at Pakeman Street could help me to get Dodo and Billy transferred to a new school. We could even take poor old Granddad along with us. He does so hate living out there with Harry Watts.'

'Mary!' he growled, immediately getting up. 'You're out of your mind!'

She got up too. 'But *why*?'

'Because it's impractical, that's why! You can't just pull up all your roots, and start all over again.'

'*Everyone* has to do that at some time in their life, Lennie,' she said, trying to calm him down. 'Being practical is finding alternatives. The war's coming to an end. We can all muck in together until you find a buyer for the house.'

'No, Mary, no!' Lennie barked, thumping his fist down on the table. 'Absolutely not!'

'But why, Lennie? Why not give it a try?'

'Because I don't *want* to!' he snapped, turning on her. 'Can't you get that into your thick head? I don't *want* to go back to that house. I hate it! I never want to see it again as long as I live!'

This truly shocked Mary, who stood back and stared in astonishment at him. 'But . . . it's your home. It's where you were a kid, where you were brought up.'

'Well it's *not* my home any more!' he replied, turning aside from her. 'It's the past, it's history, it doesn't exist any more! If you and your family want to live there, then fine. But don't expect me to come with you!' He looked at her pained expression and wanted desperately to say something to her, to explain, to tell her that it had nothing to do with her, and that he loved her. The words simply wouldn't come, so he quickly left the room.

Completely dazed, Mary watched him go in silence. Then she flopped down on to the chair, before realising that it was time for her to go to work.

'You look like yer've been slapped in the face with a wet kipper!' That was how Alice Thompson greeted Mary when she arrived at the cinema just before the start of the continuous matinée performance.

'I wish I had,' replied Mary, as she rushed in to change into her uniform. She only had a few minutes before the queue outside started to file in, so she told Alice as much as she could of what had happened. 'There are times when I don't know what's going on in my life.'

Whilst she was changing, the telephone started ringing in Alf Bickley's office.

Alice yelled out at the top of her voice: 'Mavis! Can yer take that bleedin' phone? The old man's not in yet!'

The telephone kept ringing until Mavis, wrapped up in her woollies and fur hat, rushed into the office to take the call. 'Mary!' she yelled. 'It's for you!'

'Me?' Mary swung a startled look at her. 'A phone call – for *me*?'

'P'raps yer've won the sweepstake!' joked Alice, going out to deal with the queue of people who were being let in by the commissionaire at the entrance doors.

Mary rushed into Alf's office, and picked up the receiver. 'Hello?' she yelled, totally unused to using such a machine. 'Yes. This is Mary Trimble. Who's that, please? Oh yes, Mr Watts. Is anything wrong?'

What she heard totally shocked her. 'Oh God!' she gasped. 'Not Granddad! Please say . . . it isn't . . . it can't be!'

When Mary reached the demolished site in Edmonton which had once been the little post office, there was no sign that it had once been situated on a street corner. In fact, all that remained of the terrace of Edwardian houses was a pile of rubble. Mary was in a state of total shock. Accompanied by a grave-faced Harry Watts and a special constable, she looked on the scene of carnage with incredulity.

'Of course, they wouldn't have known much about it,' said the constable. 'That's the trouble with these things, there's no warning – they just come down at you, and whoosh! That's it.'

For several minutes they stood on the sidelines, watching the frenzied activity, the emergency services racing against time just in case any more victims were still alive and buried beneath the mounds of scattered debris. Alsatian tracker dogs were scrambling over the bricks and mortar and plaster, tails wagging, stopping every so often to investigate a particular smell that had suddenly excited them. The sounds were incredible; clanging fire, ambulance and police-car bells, rescue workers shouting out to each other, women crying in despair, dogs in the nearby streets barking. It was organised pandemonium.

Mary was still too stunned to take it all in. Although she felt as though the blood had been drained out of her entire body, she couldn't cry. All she could do was to hope. 'What time did this happen?' she asked.

'Soon after the post office opened this morning,' said Harry, whose overcoat and cap were covered in dust. 'I knew yer Granddad was going to the post office, but I didn't know when till I heard the front door close.'

Whilst they were standing there, a St John's ambulance driver strug-

260

gled past over the rubble carrying a blanket which contained the remains of a black-and-white dog, whose tail was hanging down limply.

'Are you sure Granddad's not in there?' asked Mary, tentatively. 'Are you *absolutely* sure?'

'I'm afraid I've already seen him,' said Harry, his voice cracking with emotion. 'He was one of the first they reached. I knew it was him by this.' He crouched down, and picked up Granddad's walking stick.

Mary looked at it. The moment she saw the stick, she knew. The pain in her face showed immediately.

'As soon as we get him out,' said the Special, 'I'm afraid we shall have to get you to identify him, over at the church hall. I take it you *are* his closest relative?'

'He has a sister in Mile End,' replied Mary, hoarsely, 'but he hasn't seen her for years. They didn't get on.'

The Special shook his head in despair. 'From what we've been told, there was a whole lot of 'em talkin' in the road outside the post office. I'm afraid poor old Tilly Raglan was the first one we found. She was such a lovely woman.'

Harry Watts agreed.

'They're still lookin' for a young girl and her baby,' continued the Special. 'She'd only just left the place.'

Two of the firemen at the scene came by carrying a large blanket which contained all kinds of personal possessions. Amongst them was a bright yellow woollen scarf, a pair of broken metal-framed spectacles, a checked cap, a pair of men's brown patent-leather shoes, and a baby's dummy. After that followed a succession of other articles, which were all being laid out on the back of an army truck parked nearby.

Whilst the Special moved away for a few minutes, Harry took the opportunity to take something out of his overcoat pocket. 'Before I forget,' he said to Mary, his voice low, 'I'd better give you *this*.'

Amongst the few personal possessions found in her granddad's trouser pockets was his Post Office savings book. She finally erupted into tears.

The moment this happened, she felt an arm gently sliding around her waist. She looked up, and with tears streaming down her cheeks, she recognised who was standing by her side. It was Lennie.

'But I thought the war was over?' she asked.

Chapter 20

The last V-2 rocket came down in Kent on 27 March. Although just one person was killed and twenty or so injured, it was, like all the other V2s, V1s, and aerial attacks, a tragedy for all those concerned. The death of Granddad Trimble in the rocket explosion in Edmonton had broken the hearts of all his family and friends, especially those in Roden Street. Even Nutty Nora turned up at his funeral in the Emmanuel Church just around the corner in Hornsey Road, and wept openly as his coffin was taken off in a slow motor-hearse procession to Finchley cemetery. But with the end of the war now truly in sight, Mary was determined to pull the family together, and prepare for the peace.

On the day of Granddad's funeral, Harry Watts handed Mary a letter which he said the old boy had given him just in case anything should happen to him. He had no idea what was in the sealed envelope, but suggested she read it as soon as possible. However, it was not until the evening that she managed to settle down to open the envelope. The only person with her at the time was Lennie, who, despite his tantrums about getting a job, had given her the support she needed so badly at such a time. Nonetheless, when she read the contents of the letter, she was in a state of shock. Although Granddad was no letter-writer, what he had to say was so poignant and extraordinary that she found tears welling up in her eyes once again:

Dear Mary,

By the time you reed this, God knows where Ill be — either pushing up daysies in finchley or stoking the fires for old bat face down below. But who cares, Ive had me time and that's all their is to it. Still, before I go I just wanted to tell you that Im sorry if I haven't been the best of granddads to you and the family. I blame meself for everything becos you Mary was always very good to me, speshully when we lost your mum and dad who always ment the world to me. Anyway I made up me mind to try and make it up to you by helping you to get that holladay youve always wanted — down in devon. Mind you I don't know why you think so much of a place like devon. I much prefer southend and the kursaal and the pubs and sossidge and mash. Remember the beano we all went on? so — let me get to the point. If you look in my savings book youll see that there shood be enuff to give you a good old bash down where you want to go. For the last few munffs now Ive been saving it up for you and I also had a bit left over from when your gran died (she had more money than I did. she hid it under the mattress). But remember — the money is for YOU. Dont you dair give any of it to my sister Gladys or her rotten husband becos if you do Ill come back and haunt you. So have a good time and do think of your old granddad who wasn't so bad — well not all the time.

God bless you, girl, and all the family and live well.

Granddad x

Mary gave the letter to Lennie to read, and sobbed profusely. For a moment or so she just perched on the edge of her bed, feeling the guilt rushing all through her veins. All she could think about was how terrible she had been to the old man during this last year or so, and how she wished she could turn back the clock and tell him how she and all the family loved him. But it was too late. In the last part of his life, Granddad had thought about her and the kids, but *they* had never

264

thought about *him*. After a moment, she dabbed her eyes with her handkerchief, then put the letter back inside the envelope.

When she went to her chest of drawers to leave the letter in the top drawer there, she suddenly remembered that that was where she had put Granddad's Post Office savings book. On the day Harry Watts had given it to her, she had been so upset, she merely put it into an envelope and sealed it, waiting for the time when she would deliver it to Aunty Gladys and Uncle Cyril over at Mile End. But now that it was Granddad's wish that whatever was in the book was for her and the family, she decided to take a look at it, hoping that there might be at least enough for her to buy Thelma, Dodo and Billy a new pair of shoes each. However, once she had ripped open the envelope and looked at the amount of money totalled inside the book, she started to tremble. 'Oh God!' she gasped. 'No! It can't be true! Granddad! Oh Granddad!' The savings book showed that over the past few years, the old man had deposited into his account the grand sum of one hundred and two pounds, twelve shillings, and sixpence. Once again she started to cry, but this time it was with tears of undiluted joy, of overwhelming disbelief, of gratitude to the old man for understanding, for giving her the chance to make her dream come true. 'Oh Lennie!' she cried. 'Just look at this!' She handed him the savings book then went to the window, drew back the curtains, peered up at the sky and, with tears streaming down her cheeks, yelled out: 'Thank you, Granddad! Oh, thank you *so* much, dear, dear Granddad! Don't worry, *I* know where you are, and it's where you *deserve* to be!'

Although the war was not yet over, as he expected, Lennie found it difficult to get a job. Despite being interviewed for work as an attendant at a petrol station, a trainee supervisor at the North London Drapery Stores, and a labourer on a building site in Holborn, he apparently did not attract enough interest from anyone. Furthermore, as each day drew closer to the ending of the war, there was the danger that men with far better skills than his own would soon be returning from active duty, which meant that he would be up against stiff competition.

After a time, Lennie realised that his personality must have something to do with his problems; he was, after all, not the easiest person to communicate with because, to prospective employers at least, he appeared to have a huge chip on his shoulder. It was therefore not long before he started to get a complex about his inability to sell himself, and this made him even more concerned about the way he was living off Mary. However, events took a strange turn one evening, when he turned up at the Marlborough, only to find the place in chaos, with the film on the screen frozen, and the audience whistling and booing and giving a slow handclap. 'What's going on?' he asked Mary, who had rushed down to the foyer to greet him.

'I don't know,' said Mary, in a panic. 'I've been banging on the projection-room door, but your dad always locks himself in.'

'We've got to do something quick!' added a very anxious Alice. 'If the old man *does* come in, there'll be hell to pay.'

Lennie rushed straight up the main staircase to the grand circle, where he went immediately to the projection room, and tried to open it.

'Dad!' he called, banging hard on the door. 'Dad, are you all right?'

In the auditorium, the customers were now getting more and more agitated.

'How long has it been like this?' Lennie asked, urgently.

'Nearly twenty minutes,' said Mary. 'Something must have happened. It's so unlike him.'

With that, Lennie started pushing against the door. At first, there was no sign that it was going to give, and it made it more difficult because the key was in the lock on the other side of the door. 'Stand back!' he said to Mary and Alice. With one almighty thrust, he practically threw himself against the door with his shoulder. The door flew open immediately, and he rushed straight in. 'Dad!'

To his horror, he found Ernie slumped in a chair against the wall.

Lennie hurried across to him, and Mary and Alice followed him in. 'Dad!' he said, trying to shake some life into him. It looked as though Ernie was fast asleep, for he was breathing quite deeply. However, when he drew closer, he could smell whisky. 'Christ!' exclaimed Lennie. 'He's bloody drunk!'

'What!' the two women gasped.

'Here!' Lennie called to them. 'Give me a hand!' With their help, they managed to sit him upright, and hold on to him.

Ernie groaned, and tried to open his eyes. Meanwhile, Lennie peered through the projection-room hole to where the picture from one of the two projectors had frozen on the screen. With some of the audience now on their feet, Lennie immediately launched into a frenzy of activity, turning to work on the film gate of the projector, where the film had stuck. 'Turn on the light!' he ordered. 'Hurry!'

Alice was nearest to the light switch, so she turned it on.

Lennie turned off the power at the projector, rolled up his shirt sleeves, and set to work on releasing the film. As he did so, sweat was rolling off his forehead.

The two women watched him in astonishment.

'Are you sure you know what you're doing, Len?' asked Alice, pessimistically.

'If I don't,' he called as he struggled with the film-gate mechanism, 'you'd better give them all their money back!'

The two women exchanged anxious looks.

There followed nearly five minutes of real tension, as Lennie worked frantically to pull out the damaged film before finally spooling it on. Then he quickly set about re-threading, and once he'd done that he quickly glanced back at Mary and Alice. 'Fingers crossed!' he said.

Mary and Alice closed their eyes tight and hunched up.

Lennie turned the power and the projector back on. In an instant, there was a whirring sound, followed by two crystal-clear voices, and the dramatic appearance of Fred MacMurray and Barbara Stanwyck in the tense thriller *Double Indemnity*.

The moment the film resumed, there were cheers, whistles and a loud ovation from the audience. Then the lights were dimmed again, and they settled down to watch the rest of the film.

Alice immediately rushed across and gave Lennie a big kiss on his forehead. 'You're a genius!' she proclaimed. As she rushed out of the room, Ernie groaned, and started to revive. 'I'll talk to *you* later!' she chided, wagging her finger at him menacingly.

Whilst Lennie used a cloth to wipe the projector oil from his hands, Mary turned off the light in the projection room and went straight across to hug him. 'How on earth did you know how to do that?' she asked in disbelief and admiration.

Lennie grinned. 'You're not the son of a projectionist without knowing what he gets up to,' he replied, wryly. 'When I was a kid, I spent an awful lot of my time in this den!'

On the far side of the room, Ernie groaned again.

Lennie went across to him. 'And what the hell d'you think *you're* playing at?' he snapped. 'D'you know you nearly had a revolution on your hands?'

Ernie struggled to open his eyes. 'I don't know what happened,' he replied, trying to smooth the pain in his head with one hand. 'I must have passed out or something.'

'You bet you passed out,' said Lennie, gradually easing Ernie up on to his feet. 'Since when have you started boozing at work?'

Ernie was struggling to relieve the pain by stretching his neck and head from side to side. 'It's a creeping habit,' he replied.

Lennie threw a worried look at Mary, who then quickly left the room.

'Since when?' asked Ernie.

'Does it matter?' asked Ernie, gradually coming back to life.

'Yes, it matters,' replied Lennie, tersely. 'If you want to keep your job.'

Ernie managed to open his eyes and stared straight at his son. 'Who said I *want* to keep it?' he asked.

Tanya Ling had just one more sketch to make before her forthcoming exhibition of her latest work in the church hall near the Archway. Of course she had already had one exhibition just a year or so before, but this one would be special. Apart from the fact that Sheila Nestor had been responsible for getting the event sponsored for her free of charge, there were sketches there that would mean a great deal to quite a lot of people, for this was to be an exhibition with just one theme.

In Roden Street, the residents gave her suspicious glances as they went back and forth. What was a Chinese woman doing in *their* street, they asked each other, and what was that she drawing in that big note-book? Should they call the bobbies? No. She had done nothing wrong – yet. But they should keep their eyes open. Tanya kept *her* eyes open too. After all, that was her job, that's what she was all about. Nobody had escaped her notice, not even Nutty Nora – *especially* Nutty Nora.

When Mary and Lennie had got home from the Marlborough the previous evening, they found the old girl sitting on the coping stone in front of the garden outside. It was still very cold, and the moon was darting very quickly in and out of dark, fast-moving clouds. When they drew closer they saw that the old girl was upset, constantly dabbing her eyes with her hanky. 'What are you doing out here in the cold, Mrs Kelly?' Mary asked. 'What's wrong?'

'E's gorn, ain't 'e?' said Nora, her eyes glistening in the moonlight, her cardigan not nearly enough to keep her warm, and her hairnet covering the curlers she put in every night before going to bed.

'Who's gone?' asked Lennie.

'My so-called bruvver,' replied the old girl. 'Not so much as a by your leave, just a bit of paper sayin' 'e was goin' off ter live wive some floozie. I always knew 'e was a bleedin' sex maniac!'

Mary sat down alongside her, and put a comforting arm around her waist. 'But I always thought you didn't get on with your brother,' she said. 'I remember you told me once you wished he'd never stopped behind to live with you.'

'That don't mean that I don't care about 'im, do it?' asked Nora, really quite agitated. 'After me mum and dad died, I got used ter livin' on me own – that is, until my bleedin' bruvver reckoned 'e was on to a good thing with me, takin' their place.'

This shocked Mary. 'But I thought – I was under the impression you had a husband. The family have always called you *Mrs* Kelly.'

269

'Well I 'aint, so there!' she snapped. 'I never 'ad a 'usband, an' I never wanted one. Men are all the same ter me. All they ever want is one thing.' She was doing her best not to be upset. 'But I liked lookin' after 'im. I didn't mind that he was lazy bugger, who'd sooner die than lift a finger to help. It's completely different when the person you're livin' with means a lot to yer, and then suddenly – whoosh – 'e's gone.'

'I'll go and put the kettle on,' said Lennie, eager to retreat from a situation that he knew Mary could better deal with alone.

'Yes,' said Mary. 'Come on, Mrs Kelly. Let's go inside and talk about it over a nice cup of cocoa.'

'D'you know 'ow long I've lived in this 'ouse?' continued Nora, ignoring Mary's efforts to cheer her up. 'Thirty-seven years. Thirty-seven years of goin' up those same bleedin' stairs, right up ter the top floor, day in an day out, wearin' meself out carrying me shoppin' bags, then 'urryin' ter get 'is tea ready before he come 'ome from work. When I think of all the times I cooked 'is favourite kippers for 'im, stinkin' the place out, waitin' on 'im 'and an' foot, with not so much as a nod ter say thank you before 'e pushed off ter bed ter read 'is bleedin comics. I ask yer – a grown man like that readin' comics!'

Mary held her arm around the poor old girl's waist, deciding that the best way to help her was to listen, something that not many people ever did for her. Whatever Nora's faults, she was something of an institution around the area. Ever since she was a child Mary could remember the old girl always leaning out of her window, her bosoms pressed on to the window sill. And if she wasn't doing that, her off-white curtains were nine times out of ten fluttering, letting everyone know that she was there – oh yes, she was there all right. Nothing and no one ever walked past the house or down the street without Nutty Nora seeing them. But this was a different old woman to the one she had known practically all her life. This was someone who had a heart, someone who should not just be considered a figure of fun, with jokes about her false teeth and her curlers, and her constantly runny nose. Nora Kelly and her ungrateful brother had been tenants in that house for thirty-seven years, and yet she still didn't know them – at least, not until now.

'Yet know *my* trouble, don't yer?' said Nora. 'I've lived fer too long. I'm eighty-one years old, and that's quite long enuff fer anyone.'

'Oh no, it isn't, Mrs Kelly,' replied Mary. 'You're only just starting. Despite all your aches and pains, you've got an awful lot of things to look forward to. And believe me, you don't need your brother to share them with you.'

Tanya Ling was thinking much the same thing as she watched the old girl coming back from getting a new haircut around the corner in Rita's hairdressing salon on Seven Sisters Road. She looked different to the last time she saw her. She had a bit of a smile on her face. That was nice, very nice. It would look very good in her picture.

Alf Bickley was looking decidedly glum. To lose someone who had given more than twenty-five years loyal service to the Marlborough cinema was something he hoped he would not have to think about for quite a time yet. But here he was, Ernie Backer, sitting there in Alf's office, looking older, pale and strained, and requesting to go into retirement. 'Well, I don't mind telling you, Ern,' he said, 'for the Marlborough, this is the end of an era. In fact, I can't even imagine the place without you. From now on, every time I look up at that screen I'll be thinking of you.'

'I hope not, Guv,' replied Ernie, who was not really comfortable with the cigar the Marlborough's manager had given him to smoke. 'Some of the folk you get up there are a good bit better lookin' than me!'

Alf chuckled, but it was tinged with sadness. 'Are you sure you're making the right decision, Ern?' he asked for the third time. 'I mean, if it's a question of more money . . .'

'Nothin' like that, Guv,' Ernie assured him. 'It's just that I've had enough of looking through that projection hole. Sometimes I think I'm getting square eyes, and it gets quite lonely up there. No. I've come to the stage when I need some time to myself. I want to be able to go out and watch some football up at the Arsenal on Saturday

271

afternoons, I want to be able to go and have a pint up the pub with a mate or two. I might even want to go to the pictures!'

Again Alf chuckled, but it soon gave way to a heavy sigh. 'But you're still only a young man, Ern,' he said. 'You're still only in your fifties.'

'Age has got nothing to do with it, Guv,' replied Ernie, flicking the ash from his cigar into the same ashtray that Alf was using for his pipe. 'It's how you feel that counts. I just feel worn out, that's all. It's time to move on, to give the younger generation a chance.'

Alf gave him a wry smile. 'Ah!' he said. 'Now we're getting to it.' He swivelled round in his chair, got up, and came round to perch on the edge of his desk facing Ernie. 'Are you sure your boy's up to doing this job?' he asked, point blank.

Ernie nodded, and leaned back in his chair. 'He's a bit of a muddle-head from time to time,' he replied, 'but his heart's in the right place. And as far as the work's concerned, I can't fault him. All those years when he was a kid, he used to sit up there in that projection room with me, watching every single thing I ever did. I tell you, Guv, if you think *I* know a thing or two, well – you won't regret what Lennie can do. He may not stick it out as long as me, but one thing I *do* know is that he'll never let you down.'

Alf sighed. 'Oh well,' he said, reluctantly. 'I suppose we'd better bring him in.'

He got up from the desk, went to the door, and called, 'Len! In you come, then.'

Lennie, waiting there with Mary, came forward.

'You too, Mary,' said Alf. 'Might as well have the whole family in on this!'

Lennie came in, closely followed by Mary, who was not yet in her uniform as it was still an hour away from the matinée show.

'Right you are,' said Alf, going back to his desk. 'Sit yourselves down, and let's have a talk about this.'

Mary sat down timidly on the small office sofa, and Lennie sat next to her.

'So you want to be in movies, do you, son?' asked Alf, mocking a Hollywood mogul.

They all chuckled except Lennie, who was more nervous than he showed. 'It's Dad's idea, Mr Bickley,' he replied.

'But the idea *appeals* to you?'

Lennie hesitated.

Mary exchanged a quick, anxious glance with Ernie.

'Yes, sir,' Lennie replied. 'I'd like to have a go.'

Mary sighed with relief.

Alf leaned back in his chair and took a deep puff of his pipe. 'You've got quite an act to follow,' he said, nodding towards Ernie. 'You know that, don't you, boy?'

Lennie looked briefly at his dad, and smiled weakly. 'Yes, sir.' He was suddenly aware of all the glossy, framed photographs around the walls, pictures of Alf's favourite film stars that he had admired over the years, people like Carole Lombard, Alice Faye, Clark Gable, Claudette Colbert, Spencer Tracy, and even the child poppet actress, Shirley Temple. It also occurred to him that over the years these same stars, and plenty more like them, were only on that screen thanks to his dad's long and tireless service.

'It's an arduous job, of course,' said Alf, 'stuck up in that pokey little room day after day, night after night, and while everyone else is out having a good time. How d'you feel about that?'

'I think I can cope, sir,' replied Lennie, with another shrug.

'It's not just a question of coping, son,' said Alf, introducing just a hint of authority. 'It's a question of dedication, skill and knowledge, and also a love of films. Think you've got the know-how for all that?'

'I've watched Dad quite a lot,' he replied.

'It's not just the technical know-how I'm talking about, son,' said Alf, wagging one finger at him. 'When I talk about dedication, I mean having to give up half your social life, just like Mary here, and Alice and Mavis outside, and everyone else who works in a picture house. One day off a week, plus your mornings, stuck in the place from early afternoon until the end of the last show at night, watching the same films over and over till you're nearly blind. I always tip my hat to the people who give up so much of their own lives to make other people happy.' He leaned forward in his chair. 'Think you can be one of them, Len?'

Lennie flicked a quick look at Mary. 'I don't see why not, sir,' he replied. 'At least I can have a go.'

Alf showed the first sign of wariness about the boy's reply. 'It would have to be more than that, son,' he said. 'If I'm going to take you on, I want to be sure that you know what you're doing.'

Alarmed that Lennie was not making the right impression, Mary leaned forward and added her support. 'Lennie's one of the most conscientious people I know, Mr Bickley,' she said. 'You should just see the way he helps out with my family.'

Lennie swung her a startled look.

'He's so caring,' continued Mary, unabashed. 'And the kids learn so much from him. Young Billy loves geography, learning about places all around the world that he'd love to go to one day. Lennie helps to bring it all alive for him.'

Alf nodded, then looked back at Lennie, showing a slight sign that he was impressed.

Mary didn't leave it there. 'Lennie and I often sit and talk about films,' she bubbled on nervously. 'He's always going on about how good his dad was at handling the projector, about coping with emergencies, about how he never lets down the audience. I know it's none of my business, but I'm sure Lennie is someone you can trust to do the same.' Suddenly realising she had been talking out of turn, she quickly slumped back on the sofa.

Lennie had a look of thunder on his face.

Alf grinned, first at Mary, then at Lennie. 'Well, looks like she has a point, son. This job is as much about personality as technical skill. After all, in the Marlborough, we're all part of a family too.' He got up from his desk. 'Right then, that's settled. But I don't mind telling you,' he looked across at Ernie, who had remained silent throughout,

'I don't like letting this man go. If I had *my* way, I'd chain him for life to that projector upstairs!'

With the exception of Lennie, they all laughed, and stood up.

'Oh, just one thing,' added Alf, just as they were about to file out of the office. 'How do you two feel about working together? I mean, I don't usually approve of married people working in the same place.'

Mary was taken aback. 'Sir?' she asked, flicking a puzzled glance first at Lennie, then back to Alf.

'Well,' continued Alf, 'you two are a couple, aren't you? You're not going to tell me that it's not for life?'

Mary froze. 'Bit early to say just yet, sir,' she spluttered with embarrassment.

Lennie said nothing, merely looked down at his feet.

'Well,' said Alf, 'you be sure to let me know when he makes an honest woman of you, Mary. I might even give you both the day off for that.'

Mary and Ernie laughed, but again, not Lennie, who remained dour.

'Good luck, son,' he said brightly to Lennie, offering his hand to shake. 'At least we'll be keeping part of your dad working for us.'

Mary watched anxiously, waiting to see if Lennie was going to shake hands with him. Despite the hesitation, he eventually did.

Alf closed the door, leaving Ernie inside with him to carry on their discussion. Once in the foyer outside, Alice and Mavis were waiting there impatiently to greet them.

'Well?' asked Alice, tensely, looking first to Lennie then to Mary.

Mary nodded to both her and Mavis.

'Hooray!'

Both women applauded, excitedly, and rushed to give Lennie a congratulatory kiss on the cheek.

'Welcome to the club, dear!' exclaimed Alice. 'Just keep away from the whisky!'

Both women left to get on with preparing for the arrival of the first customers, leaving Mary and Lennie alone in the foyer.

'I'm so pleased, Len,' Mary said. But when she tried to put her arms around him for a supportive kiss, he quickly moved away, and hurried outside.

'Lennie!' Mary called, as she rushed down the steps to catch up with him. But he didn't stop. 'Lennie!'

He only came to a halt when he was almost at the main road.

'Lennie!' Mary said, hurt and bewildered by his ungrateful behaviour. 'What is it? What the hell's the matter with you?'

'If you ever put me down like that again,' he snapped, 'I'll walk out on you!'

He tried to move on, but she quickly grabbed his arm and held on to it. 'What are you talking about?' she asked. 'What d'you mean "put you down"?'

'You know damned well what I mean!' he growled, turning on her. 'All that guff about how well I look after the kids, about how I help Billy to do his geography, about the family, the family, the bloody family. Getting a job is not *about* the family, Mary, it's about *me*, about me getting my own job, and not relying on you to get it for me!'

'You're wrong, Lennie!' Mary snapped back, thoroughly incensed. 'This is just as much about the family as anything else – not just *my* family, but about you and me and all the people we know and love. You can't separate what we do at work to what we do at home – they're all part of the same thing. Can't you understand that?'

Again Lennie tried to turn away, but again she held on to his arm.

'For God's sake, Lennie!' she said, raising her voice for the first time. 'What the hell's the matter with you? You and I are both old enough now to know that life isn't just about our own pride, it's about getting on with things, about making the best of a bad job – yes, and a *good* job too – just like the one you've just been offered. But if you don't want it, then it's fine by me!' She suddenly let go of his arm roughly. 'But let me tell you, Lennie Backer – as long as you go on behaving like a spoilt child, as long as you go on thinking about how hurt you are, you'll never get anywhere in this world. So if that's what you want – then get on with it!' She turned away from him and stormed off back to the foyer.

Lennie stood there in the cold watching her go. Outside the cinema, the first queue was beginning to form for the matinée performance, so after a minute or so he moved on, back towards the main road, out of sight, out of mind, away from everything he had had to endure during the past few hours. But then he came to a sudden dead halt, a solitary figure standing there motionless, with people pushing past him, hurrying to get on buses, a seething mass of humanity who were blind to anything in their path. After several moments of inner turmoil, he turned around slowly. Then, quite impulsively, he ran as fast as he could – all the way back to the cinema.

Chapter 21

In the early hours of the morning of Tuesday, 8 May, there was a thunderstorm so violent that it not only woke all the residents of Roden Street, but also sent most of them to their windows to peer out at the torrential rain, nervous that the war was not officially over as they had been told.

Mary, in her own bedroom, got up first, then Lennie downstairs, on his put-you-up in the front parlour. Not surprisingly, Thelma, Dodo and Billy were up too, despite the fact that the celebrations for the ending of the war would not be taking place until after the official announcement by Mr Churchill from Downing Street at three o'clock that afternoon. The previous evening had been a frenzy of excitement everywhere – in the streets, in the shops, in the cinemas, and, like everyone else, the Trimbles had been up most of the night joining in the premature festivities with all the neighbours. The war was finally over!

'It's all over, Lennie,' said Mary, as they later strolled together arm-in-arm down Holloway Road, where hundreds, probably thousands of people were already singing and dancing, holding up the traffic from the Archway to Highbury Corner. 'It's hard to believe that we'll never have to look up at that sky again and wonder if a buzz bomb or a rocket is going to come crashing down on us.' She took in a deep breath of fresh air. 'It really *is* over!'

As they went, Lenny tucked his arm around Mary's waist, and pulled her to him as close as he possibly could.

Thankfully, the early morning thunderstorm had not dampened

anyone's spirits, for the roads were already drying up in the hot morning sun, but it was odd to see the remains of those buildings that had been devastated during the years of conflict, with steam rising from the wet debris, a poignant reminder of the victims who had not lived to see this day.

It was the same in Seven Sisters Road. There had already been a run on everything from food to petrol, and what beer and other alcohol that had been available had very quickly emptied both pubs and off-licences. Every house, shop, store and building was adorned with red, white and blue bunting, the Union Jack, Stars and Stripes, and even the Russian hammer and sickle flags, and there were banners every-where proclaiming such things as: GOD SAVE THE KING!, GOOD OLD WINNIE!, VICTORY IN EUROPE!, and BYE-BYE ADOLF!

The air of excitement was contagious. It was as if all the human beings throughout the country had suddenly been released from a cage, a cage in which they had been tortured and locked up for nearly six years. However, VE Day did not mean the end of the war for everyone. On the other side of the world, America and her Allies were still locked in a deadly battle against the ruthless armies of the Japanese Empire.

'D'you think they'll do this all over again when the Japs surrender?' asked Mary, as she and Lennie dodged in and out of the partying crowds.

'I don't know,' he replied, having to shout above the din to make himself heard. 'If you ask me, it could be a good time yet. The Japs won't give up so easily.'

'I know,' replied Mary, gloomily. 'That poor Mrs Arden in Jackson Road. She lost both of her sons in Burma. Apparently they were taken prisoner and suffered a terrible death. I hope to God it's over soon.'

A short while later, after first making sure that Thelma was keeping an eye on Dodo and Billy, both Mary and Lennie turned up for work at the Marlborough. Although Alf Bickley had cancelled the evening performances so that customers and staff could join in the celebrations, he decided to continue with one matinée performance, mainly because, at three o'clock, Lennie, who had now taken over from his dad as projec-

279

tionist, was going to interrupt the film to relay Mr Churchill's speech to the nation on the radio, through the cinema's loudspeaker system. After the previous night's continuous performances, staff and voluntary workers had helped to deck out both the exterior of the cinema, and the auditorium with bunting, flags of every nation, and anything cele- bratory they could get their hands on. With Thelma's help, Mary had arranged with Jones Brothers to practically empty the store of every flag they had in stock, and at Woolworths, Mary and Alice queued for half an hour to buy streamers, confetti and paper party hats. Every balcony, window and terrace inside and outside the building was a blaze of colour.

As they waited impatiently for three o'clock, Lennie sat alone in the projection room spending part of the time keeping an eye on the return engagement of Charlie Chaplin's *The Great Dictator*, and the rest of the time listening to the VE Day celebrations being transmitted on the radio from towns and villages all over the country. As the time drew near to Mr Churchill's broadcast, Mary came in to join Lennie. Ever since he had taken over his dad's job, Lennie had done his best to make it up to Mary, who had been deeply offended by his outburst on the day he had been offered the job. After that difficult period, he had thought a great deal about Mary, and particularly about their future together, but so far he hadn't mentioned anything to her about his intentions. Until now.

'I haven't told you yet, Mary,' he said, standing close to her, 'but that letter I got the other day was from a property agent in Epping. He said one or two people are interested in looking at the farmhouse.'

Mary was overjoyed. 'Oh, Lennie!' she replied ecstatically. 'That's wonderful!'

'I told him I didn't want to be there when they came,' continued Lennie, 'so he said he'd take care of it, and let me know. I doubt whether it'll come to anything, but if it does, with the war over and all that – I think this is the time we should start thinking about – about well, you know – getting married. What d'you think?'

Mary was taken aback. 'Lennie! What d'you mean what do *I* think? Is that what *you'd* like to do?'

'Takes two to make a party,' he replied, flippantly. 'As the old man said when I got the job, we're a couple.' He hesitated a moment, looking closely at her. 'We *are*, aren't we? At least, I *hope* we are. I *do* love you, you know, Mary. Honest.'

For one long moment, Mary stared into his eyes, eyes that were full of love. Then she moved forward, embraced and kissed him.

They were suddenly distracted by the peels of Big Ben on the radio. 'Lennie!' cried Mary.

Lennie immediately broke away, turned off the film, and relayed the broadcast through the stage's sound system.

'This is London,' came the announcer's voice. 'Here is the Prime Minister, the Right Honourable Winston Churchill.'

Mary and Lennie rushed out of the projection room and stood at the back of the Grand Circle. The moment they got there, the auditorium echoed to the sound of the Prime Minister's majestic voice as he outlined details of the unconditional surrender of all German land, sea and air forces in Europe. His speech was received in solemn silence, so much so that you could hear a pin drop on the faded green carpet of the auditorium, and this held right through until the final, stirring words of Mr Churchill's broadcast, 'Advance, Britannia. Long live the cause of freedom. God save the King!'

By the time the Prime Minister had finished his speech proclaiming the official end of hostilities with the enemy from midnight that night, the entire cinema had erupted into yells of ecstatic applause, joyous and exuberant cheers, and shouts of 'Good ol' Winnie!' Although the cinema was not absolutely full, those who *were* there were overwhelmed with excitement; so much so that some of them even clambered up on to the seats, shouting and waving anything they could get their hands on. And then the dazzling sound of the Compton organ suddenly came to life with a rousing, deafening chorus of 'Land of Hope and Glory', played by Wilson Oliphant Chuckbutty, the renowned resident organist, now back at the Marlborough after his long break. The noise was deafening, infectious and good-humoured, tinged with the relief that everyone could start breathing again. The war was over!

At the back of the circle, Mary and Lennie kissed passionately in the dark, whilst down below, the audience were dancing in the aisles, climbing up on to the stage to do a 'knees up', with even Alf Bickley, the manager, partnering anyone who asked him, including his own staff, Alice and Mavis. Nobody even remembered the film show. The party was in full swing. They were free!

Having the evening to themselves, Mary and Lennie were able to join in the hectic street parties which had started in practically every street in Islington, and probably throughout London and the entire country. Thelma, Dodo and Billy had joined in the celebrations in the combined Roden Street/Pakeman Street, and Annette Road party the moment the Prime Minister's broadcast had come to an end. Long trestle tables borrowed from the nearby Emmanuel church hall were already covered with tablecloths and white bed sheets, the tables laid with everything from fish paste and sardine sandwiches, saveloys from Anderson's fish and chip shop in Hornsey Road, baked potatoes, oatmeal sausages, meat rolls, vegetable pasties, corned beef in bread rolls, cold spam fritters, Bakewell tarts, rock cakes, crumbed prunes, and more bowls of fruit jelly than any child or adult could ever possibly cope with. Smith's crisps from the pubs were, of course, out there in force, spread out in mountains of small packets all over the place, with their little bags of blue salt emptied and scattered all over the ground. It was a veritable feast, washed down with pots and pots of tea, and from the moment the parties began, a tidal wave of beer, brown ale and black-market gin and whisky were beginning to liven up the festivities no end! For one day at least, the years of food rationing had been totally forgotten.

For *her* contribution, Mary, helped by Thelma, had made a bread pudding, which was not an easy task because dried fruit was still difficult to get, but they had saved up as much stale bread as they could manage before Billy could polish it all off, gut that he was. Billy himself was, needless to say, completely out of control, making a general nuisance of himself by climbing up drainpipes to try and pull down flags that were draped out of shop windows, and making rude sounds

282

with the tops of empty Tizer bottles at any of the small girls who passed by. Fortunately, when there was a light shower of rain, he quickly abandoned his high spirits, and took to a more civilised game of hopscotch. Meanwhile, the men had got together to form darts teams, using a board with Hitler's face as their target, leaving various music-hall hopefuls to thump out all the popular tunes of the day on an old upright Joanna, compliments of Letty and Oliver Hobbs at number thirteen.

As night fell, and a huge bonfire was lit in the middle of the road on the corner of Roden Street and Annette Road, Mary and Lennie squirmed with horror as Dodo was lifted on to a table to do an impersonation of that junior screen idol, Shirley Temple. To witness Dodo attempting to sing, 'Animal Crackers in my soup', in the worst out-of-tune voice anyone had ever known, immediately turned the men back to take cover in their booze, leaving Mary the painfully embarrassing job of trying to lift her youngest sister off the table before she attempted to do any tap-dancing.

The one person who was clearly *not* enjoying herself, however, was Thelma. For most of the early part of the evening she had withdrawn to one of the few quiet corners of the area; the playground of adjoining Pakeman Street School. When Mary finally caught up with her, she was squatting on a bench in the seclusion of the school's open bicycle shed. 'What're you doing in here?' asked Mary, perching alongside her. 'Aren't you having a good time?'

'I would be,' answered Thelma, miserably, 'if only Chris was here. When he called in to see me at the store this morning, he told me he'd definitely be here before it got dark.'

Mary put a comforting arm around her sister's shoulders and gave her an affectionate peck on the cheek. 'I'm sure he'll get here sooner or later,' she said. 'If he's coming from the other side of London, he must be having a hell of a time getting through the crowds. I heard that most of the buses and the tube are not operating.'

'I don't think it's got anything to do with that,' replied Thelma, feeling thoroughly sorry for herself. 'Chris is a good-looking bloke. By now he's probably found someone he can really have a good time with.'

Mary smiled, and pulled her close towards her. 'D'you *really* think that's true, Thel?' she asked. 'It wasn't like that the last time I saw the two of you together.'

Thelma shook her head. 'The war's over now,' she replied. 'All the blokes are going to be different. They'll want to look around.'

'Look, Thel,' said Mary, who seemed to be becoming more like the girl's mum than her sister. 'You're only sixteen years old, but you're looking lovelier each day. Whether it's Chris or any other boy, they'd be lucky to hold on to a girl like you.'

It was true. Thelma *was* looking lovely. She had the most lovely clear complexion, and in recent weeks she had started to comb her hair into a beautiful, relaxed style that had only just started to drape over her shoulders. And the fact that she wasn't using any make-up other than a thin red lipstick, coupled with her slender waist and gradually maturing breasts, there was no doubt in anyone's mind that one of these days she was going to be quite a catch.

'It doesn't matter,' said Thelma, dismissively, trying to make light of how she was feeling. 'It doesn't really worry me if he comes or not.'

Mary stood up. 'Then come and join in the dance,' she said. 'Lennie's just waiting for someone to ask him.'

Thelma gave her a brief, embarrassed look.

'Don't worry,' Mary replied with a smile. 'He's asked me to marry him.'

The expression on Thelma's face changed in a flash. She was absolutely thrilled. 'Mary!' she gasped.

Mary rolled back her head and laughed. 'Come on!' she said, taking Thelma's hand and easing her off the bench. 'Didn't you know – the war's over!'

A few minutes later, Thelma was dancing a fox-trot with Lennie, both of them, like everyone else, wearing paper party hats. It seemed an odd experience to do such a thing out there in the middle of the street, beneath the stars, couples of all ages pressed against each other as they danced the night away to all the much-loved songs thumped out on an old Joanna by a woman named Bessie, who played for the customers each night at the Globe pub just a few streets away, a fag constantly dangling from her lips, the ash every so often dropping on to the faded white ivory keyboard, her left foot on one of the pedals, her other foot stamping heavily in time to the tune. And nearby, after a couple of gin and tonics, Nutty Nora seemed well away, her raucous laugh unheard until this evening, as she listened to some of the men's dirty jokes, and told one of them that it was about time he treated his betters, such as herself, with respect.

Watching with Letty and Oliver Hobbs from the coping stone of number thirteen, Mary was in contemplative mood. 'It's hard to believe, isn't it, Mrs Hobbs?' she said. 'When you think of what it was like that first time we heard the bombs falling, that terrible time during the Blitz. And here we are – still in one piece.'

'Yes,' replied Letty, who herself had suffered a great deal of heartache in both wars, with her husband losing a leg during the previous war, and a whole lot of her relatives being killed in one of the early V2 rockets to fall, close to the Archway. 'Unfortunately, it's not been the same for *everyone*.'

'I tell yer,' added her husband, Oliver, 'I never want ter see another war in *my* lifetime!'

Fortunately, the music changed to something more lively. To give Bessie the pianist a rest, someone had put on a gramophone record of a band playing 'The Jitterbug', and the antics that followed with mostly middle-aged men and women cavorting around like American teenagers in the films was, for everyone, a sight to behold. Mary laughed out loud with the rest of them as she saw how Thelma and Lennie were really getting into the spirit of the thing.

Whilst all this was going on, Mary decided that she needed a breather, so she left the Roden Street party and wandered around the corner, first into Mayton Street, where much the same thing was going on, and then into Hornsey Road. As she passed the Eaglet pub nearby, she could see and hear that the place was jammed to the rafters, with

285

men and women of all ages spilling out into the road, most of them pickled, and quite a lot of them enjoying a bit of lewd behaviour on the side. She strolled across to the other side of the road and, for a few moments, stood alone looking up at the old clock tower of Hornsey Road public baths, which had been so badly damaged alongside the police station during the early part of the war.

Although she could hear all the parties and merrymaking going on in the distance all around her, it was just a little quieter here, giving her time to think about what was going to happen once all this was over. Needless to say, the first thing that came to her mind was Lennie, and whether he meant what he had said in the projection room at the Marlborough that afternoon. For some reason or other, the idea of being a wife made her snigger, but only briefly, for when she thought about it more seriously, she started to wonder just how was she going to start arranging her life? More important however, was how she was going to be able to arrange her brother and sister's lives? Would it be fair to ask Lennie to let them all live together, and if she did, what if he should say no, and walk out on her? For whatever she thought of Lennie, no matter how much she loved him, he was a deep, complicated and unpredictable kind of bloke, someone who could never *ever* be taken for granted.

'It's a wonderful feeling, isn't it, Mary?'

Mary swung round with a start to find Tanya Ling behind her. Her face immediately lit up. She was so excited to see her friend again. 'Oh, Tanya!'

They threw their arms around each other and hugged.

'Dear, dear Tanya! I've missed you so much. Where've you been?'

Tanya chuckled. 'Well – there *has* been quite a lot going on, you know.' She indicated her sketch pad beneath her arm. 'I've had quite a busy day – *and* evening.'

'You weren't in Roden Street tonight?' asked Mary, utterly taken by surprise.

'Of course I was!' she replied. 'You didn't think I was going to miss out on all the fun, do you?'

'But why didn't you come and join us?' Mary asked. 'All the family are there, and I'd have loved to have introduced you to some of the neighbours.'

Tanya gave one of her knowing smiles. 'Oh, I've met quite a lot of your neighbours,' she replied. 'In a manner of speaking, that is. But I watched you for quite a long time – from the school playground. I can't tell you how much I loved seeing you enjoying yourself. You had such a smile on your face, especially when you were holding hands with that young man of yours.'

Mary beamed. 'Oh, Tanya,' she replied, breathlessly. 'He's asked me to marry him.'

Tanya's expression changed, not to concern, but to something far more questioning. 'Is it true?' she asked, directly. 'Is it really true?'

Mary was puzzled by her reaction. It was not what she had expected. 'Yes, Tanya,' she replied. 'It *is* true. At least – I *hope* it is. Why? Is there something wrong about that?'

Tanya shook her head. 'No, not at all,' she replied. 'As long as you are sure that this boy is – right for you.'

Mary was completely confounded by Tanya's strange tone.

'I love him, Tanya,' replied Mary. 'And I think he loves me.'

'Only *think*?'

Now Mary was really worried. 'Tanya,' she said earnestly, 'if there's something you want me to know about Lennie, *please* tell me. I know all about what happened to him in the army, I know about that girl and her baby, but is there's anything else?'

Tanya shook her head. 'There's nothing else, Mary, I promise you. But it *is* important for me to know if this really is the boy you want to share the rest of your life with. It's important to me, and it's important to your mother.'

Once Tanya had left, Mary felt a wave of mixed feelings about their strange conversation. As she made her way back to Roden Street, she found her pace quickening, as though hurrying to understand the odd questions Tanya had put to her. Time and time again she asked herself why her mother should have wanted to know if the boy she would one day marry would be the same boy she *really* wanted to share her life with? She sighed. If only her mum could have talked to her about this herself before she died. Passing on the responsibility to Tanya must have been a terrible burden on the poor woman.

By the time she got back to the party, it was in full swing. It now seemed as though everyone in the entire street was dancing, not least Nutty Nora, who, in spite of being tipsy, was being partnered in a slow waltz thumped out on the Joanna by old Bessie, who by now had had so many pink gins pumped into her that she missed more notes on the keyboard than she played. It was an extraordinary scene, with the reflection from the bonfire casting huge moving shadows of the dancers on to the window panes all around. It was nothing less than a Dante's *Inferno* of fun and games, with the excited laughs and shouts of the kids competing with that of their now totally boozed mums and dads. And why not, they all asked? Hadn't they earnt this after nearly six long years of war?

Mary, still wrestling in her mind with the effects of her meeting with Tanya, decided to get herself a shandy.

'A shandy!' gasped Fred Parfitt, who, for some unknown reason had been put in charge of the drinks table. 'The war's over, Mary. Surely you can now take somethin' a bit stronger than that?'

'If I did, Mr Parfitt,' she replied, 'you'd have to carry me straight off to bed. I've never touched the stuff in my life, and don't intend to start now.'

Fred felt as though he'd been torn off a strip, and quickly poured equal measures of beer and lemonade into a glass. 'Sorry about that,' he replied, sheepishly.

Mary suddenly felt as though her concern about Tanya had made her rather prickly. 'Sorry, Mr Parfitt,' she explained. 'All I mean is, good luck to anyone else who drinks. My dad loved the stuff, but it's just that it – well, I don't like it, that's all.'

'You don't have to explain to me, young lady,' replied Fred. 'Drink up and be 'appy, that's my motto!'

With Fred's motto firmly implanted in her mind, Mary moved on, her head swaying from side to side as she tried to see where Thelma and Lennie had gone, or whether they were still dancing together. She sipped her shandy, and wiped the sweat from her forehead with the back of her hand. It was now after midnight, but, for her, this monumental day of celebration was now becoming a bit of an ordeal. She was desperately in need of some sleep, and once she'd said goodnight to Lennie, she would head to bed. But, determined as she was to keep on the move, she suddenly bumped into one of her neighbours at the end of the street, a mean-faced little woman named Minnie Marker, whose husband had left her for someone else, years ago – and no wonder, according to most of her neighbours!

'Ah, there you are, Mary Trimble!' sniffed Minnie, whom Billy called Minnie Myna because she had a face like the myna bird he'd once seen in the zoo. 'So how d'you feel about the way your sister's makin' up to that man? I know it's the end of the war, but I 'ope that doesn't mean young girls are going to be allowed to carry on like that.'

Mary suddenly felt a cold chill go up her spine. '*What* man, Mrs Marker?' she asked angrily. 'What are you talking about?'

Undeterred, Minnie continued her criticism. '*Him* over there!' she cried, nodding her head towards the dancers. 'They've bin 'ead to 'ead ever since they got together twenty minutes ago. If you ask me, that kissin' and cuddlin' is nothing short of – well, unnecessary!'

Without addressing another word to the woman, Mary rushed off into the seething crowd of dancers. Her heart was racing fast as she pushed the couples aside to get a view of Thelma and Lennie, and when she did catch her first glimpse of them, over the heads of the other dancers, her heart sank. What the old bag had been saying was true. From behind, she could see the two of them together, locked in each other's arms, swaying to and fro to the music of a slow, smoochey waltz. And when she got up on tiptoe to try to get a clearer look over the dancers' heads, she convinced herself that Lennie's face was buried into Thelma's breast. Deeply upset, she quickly turned around, and pushed and fought her way out through the dancers again, until she reached a clear part of the street. Crying profusely, she came to an abrupt halt, and covered her face with her hands. All she could think about was what Tanya had asked, what Tanya was clearly trying to tell her. As she stood there, her face in floods of tears, she realised that someone was standing in front of her.

'Mary?' said the man's voice. 'What's up? What's the matter?'

She took her hands away, and opened her eyes. It was Lennie. She wanted to say something to him. The way she felt, she wanted to send him away and never set eyes on him ever again. And when he stretched out his arms to embrace her, she pulled back. But when she did so, Thelma came out from the crowd of dancers, and hurried across to her.

'Mary!' she called. 'What are you doing *here*? What's the matter?'

Mary was on the point of slapping her, when hurrying out from the crowd of dancers to catch up with Thelma was a young bloke in army uniform.

'You've met Chris already, haven't you, Mary?' asked Thelma, taking hold of her lance corporal's hand. 'Thank goodness he was able to get here after all!'

Mary looked at the two of them, then up at Lennie. The tears soon disappeared, and her face burst into a huge smile.

In the background, a series of loud explosions suddenly pierced the air. At first, there were screams from the deliriously happy crowds, but the sky gradually became lit up by the most beautiful, the most dazzling array of colours, all accompanied by the loud cheers of delight. But not from Mary. She hated fireworks. She would always hate them. They reminded her too much of the war.

Chapter 22

Throughout the war, Mary had never really believed that the day would come when she would actually be going to Victoria Coach Station to buy tickets for her dream holiday to Devonshire which was planned for the following month. But with the money Granddad had left her in his Post Office savings book, and with VE day now over two months behind, that dream was about to become a reality. With Lennie at her side, she got off the number 73 bus in the forecourt of Victoria train station, where a newsvendor soon directed the way, and started the few minutes' walk to the place she had only read about in advertisements in newspapers. Her heart was racing as they made their way along Buckingham Palace Road, and when Lennie finally pointed to the grand Art Deco building on the opposite side of the road, she thought her legs were going to collapse beneath her.

To Mary and Lennie, the coach station looked very new, even though it had been built about thirteen years earlier, in 1932. Mary, of course, knew every single thing there was to know about Victoria Coach Station, having looked up details about the place in library books, having found photographs in advertisements, and poured over London street maps to find its exact location. Nonetheless, by the time she finally made it, she was so excited that she had to leave Lennie to find the booking office. Needless to say, once they got there, they had to join a queue of people waiting to buy tickets to places all over the south of England, places Mary had only ever read about in newspapers and magazines; fascinating, exotic places like Brighton, Margate, Bognor Regis, Portsmouth, Exeter and Torquay.

The poster on the wall just alongside the booking counter sent Mary into such a quivering wreck that Lennie thought she was going to be sick at any moment: TORQUAY – GATEWAY TO THE BRITISH RIVIERA. The *British* Riviera! The very look of the words on a poster brought Mary's dreams to life so vividly, and even more so when they eventually made it to the booking counter, where, amongst the skimpy travel pamphlets, was one showing the pleasures and joys of Dawlish, the south Devon resort Mary had long ago chosen as the place she would most like to spend her 'holiday of a lifetime'.

'Next please!'

Mary was so goggle-eyed devouring the pamphlet, that she had failed to notice that she was now at the booking counter.

'Next please!' With dozens of people in the queue. The young female clerk was in no mood to be kept waiting. 'Haven't got all day, you know!'

The irritated voice immediately brought Mary back to reality. 'Dawlish, please!' she replied, trying to peer through the small, arch-shaped window. 'That *is* in Devonshire, isn't it?'

'Single, return, today, tomorrow, next week, next month?'

Mary was so completely flummoxed that Lennie took over. 'Saturday, 4 August,' he replied to the girl, curtly. 'To return Saturday, 11 August.'

'You'll be lucky,' sniffed the girl, haughtily, at the same time chewing gum. 'That's August Bank Holiday. Everything's full.'

Mary clutched her forehead in despair. 'It can't be!' she gasped.

'Are you quite sure?' asked Lennie, waving away the cigarette smoke that was seeping through the booking window from the girl's ashtray inside. 'Aren't there any cancellations?'

The girl sighed. 'How many?'

'Two adults, three half-fares.'

'How old are the half-fares?'

'Ten, eleven, and sixteen,' he replied.

'Full fare for the sixteen-year-old,' said the girl, who couldn't have been much older herself. 'That's three adults, two children.'

Whilst the girl consulted her vast coach-seat plans, Lennie turned to Mary and shrugged. 'Don't worry,' he said with a grin. 'Dreams sometimes have a few hitches.'

After a great deal of deliberation, the girl called through the counter window, 'You're lucky. They've put on an extra Blue.'

Once Mary had paid for the tickets, breathless with excitement, and with Lennie tagging on behind, she practically ran out into the main coach station. The place was full of vehicles of all shapes, sizes and colours. Some were fairly new, others had seen better days, but Mary's eyes were darting around from one part of the station to another, desperately searching for the one particular colour of vehicle that had been implanted in her mind ever since she had first seen it in an old magazine in the doctor's surgery a few years before. 'Oh God, Lennie!' she suddenly gasped. 'There it is!'

Lennie switched his gaze to the direction in which she was looking.

Parked amongst a maze of single-decker vehicles of the same colour and type, there it was – the Blue Coach, showing in bold letters its destination: TORQUAY via BASINGSTOKE, ANDOVER AND EXETER. Mary was shaking so much she hardly dared approach the vehicle, especially as it was so tightly crammed in with so many others, all going to different destinations around the south, south-east, and south-west of England. But as she and Lennie drew closer, she could see passengers boarding the coach, which was glistening with a bright blue-and silver-coloured livery. For a moment or so, all she could do was to stop and stare in awe and wonder, and when Lennie went to peer through the window to look at the interior of the vehicle, he stretched out his hand for her to join him. However, the windows were too high for her to look in through, so he put his hands around her waist, and with one quick heave, lifted her up. In the few seconds she was there she was overwhelmed by the luxury of it all, those beautiful blue upholstered seats trimmed with navy blue, ashtrays in the rear of the seats in front, and large windows through which she, Lennie and the family would all soon be able to watch the marvellous countryside drifting past.

'Are you travelling on this service, madam?'

Mary and Lennie turned with a start to see the coach driver standing right behind them.

'No,' said Mary, a little embarrassed to have been caught peering through the coach windows perched on Lennie's shoulders. 'But it won't be long now.'

Summer was turning out to be as hot as the winter was cold. The July nights were the worst, so much so that people everywhere were leaving their windows wide open, desperate to catch even the slightest suggestion of a breeze. In the streets, young women wore the flimsiest dresses they dared without offending public taste, leaving their older counterparts to sweat it out with more modest attire. The men came off best, with open-necked shirts and grey flannels the order of the day. The more affluent, of course, sported either straw boaters, or lightweight bowler hats, much to the amusement of the young blokes who had recently left the services with ill-fitting demob suits. However, as Lennie spent most of his time locked up in the artificial heat of the projection room, Alf permitted him to use a small fan, which gave him at least some relief from the soaring temperatures.

In both the auditorium downstairs and the grand circle upstairs, the patrons sweated it out by bringing bottles of soft drinks with them, and with the return of the ice-cream tubs, brought around during the continuous performances by the new girl, young Hilda Pendleton, Alf Bickley was glad to know that in this drab post-war period, things were gradually getting back to normal.

But for Mary, getting back to normal also meant having to endure a rather frightening encounter one evening with the 'Toff'. As usual, it happened whilst she was cleaning up after the audience had left, and not until after she had turned off the house lights in the grand circle. However, what made this particular visitation different was the fact that the ghostly figure seemed to know exactly the time he wanted to appear, for, although Lennie was still tidying up in the projection room at the time, Mary was alone. It was also strange that, the moment she saw the vision coming slowly towards her, her throat went so dry that she was completely unable to call out to Lennie. Frozen with fear, she watched from the front of the circle as the figure came down the stairs of the left-hand aisle from the back of the circle, his feet hardly touching the carpet as he came. It was as though he was walking on air without the slightest effort at all. And when he approached to within a few feet of where she was standing with her back to the edge of the handrail, he came to a stop, and stared at her. Mary felt all the hairs on her head tingling, so all she could do was to keep quite still. Finally, she could bear the strain no more, and after licking her lips, she croaked nervously: 'Wh – who are you?'

The figure remained motionless, exuding a bright white light glowing with just a tinge of blue.

For the first time, Mary could see the rather handsome face of a middle-aged man, with a slightly upturned nose, a long chin with a goatee beard, and deep-set eyes that, to her, looked sad but intense. His clothes, however, gave no clue as to who he was, or from what period he came from, for he was draped in some kind of cape that covered his head and shoulders.

'What do you want?' she ventured again.

The figure looked at her, and raised an outstretched hand towards her, which sent her into a panic, causing her to back away as far as she could without falling over the handrail and into the stalls below. He lowered his hand, and leaned his face slightly towards her. It was a pleading look, as though he wanted to say something, but just couldn't summon the energy to do so. But then he did something so extraordinary that she knew it would haunt her dreams for the rest of her life. He smiled at her. It was a sweet, loving smile, not at all menacing, not at all threatening, but beautiful and gentle. With that, he was gone, leaving Mary alone in the dark, as though he had never been there at all. Nonetheless, what he had left behind was something quite real. He had left her with a feeling of peace, a feeling of comfort, a feeling that he would not let any harm come to her.

'Mary?' Lennie was standing in the dark at the back of the circle. 'What are you doing down there?'

For just a few moments, Mary stood there in silence. There was nothing she could say, nothing she *wanted* to say. All she knew was that she wasn't scared. She wasn't scared at all.

A couple of days later, Mary and Lennie went to see Alf Bickley in his office, to tell him that they planned to get married a few weeks after they returned from their holiday with the family in August. This, of course, meant that they would need some extra time off, and, quite obviously, would be away at the same time.

'Wonderful!' said Alf, who immediately offered Lennie a cigar. 'I told you you were a couple a long time ago. What the heck's kept you?'

Mary and Lennie laughed.

'Basically – money,' replied Lennie. 'I've been trying to sell the farmhouse out in Epping, but every time it looks hopeful, the thing falls through. Then there are the kids to consider.'

'That's all *my* fault,' said Mary. 'If I wasn't committed to looking after them until they're old enough to look after themselves, we could have got married when we wanted.'

'Well, Mary,' said Alf, 'you've been a good worker here, there's no mistake about that, so if there's any way I can help, just say the word. I could lend you a bit of cash if that would help?'

'No – thanks all the same, Mr Bickley,' said Lennie, emphatically. 'The one thing Mary and I are in agreement about is that we won't start our married life in debt. I'm pretty sure someone will take on the house sooner or later. It's just a case of when.'

'Mmm,' Alf mumbled, taking a deep puff of his pipe. 'Will you continue living in Roden Street after you're hitched?'

'Yes,' replied Mary, after giving Lennie a quick glance for his approval. 'At least, until Lennie's sold the house.'

'What I really mean is,' said Alf leaning forward in his chair, 'will you both still want to go on working for the Marlborough?'

Mary and Lennie exchanged a sudden, startled look.

'Why, of course, Mr Bickley,' said Mary. 'Is that a problem for you?'

'Not really,' replied Alf. 'But by the law of averages, I shan't be here for ever myself. A couple of years at the most, I'd say. I've got a bit of a ticker problem — not much, but in the near future I'd like to be winding down my time here. There're plenty of youngsters just waiting to take over *this* chair.'

'None of them could do the job the way *you've* done it all these years,' Mary assured him.

Alf chuckled. 'That's nice of you to say so, Mary,' he replied, 'but time has to move on. I've seen more films than I can count since I've been here, and thank goodness I've always had the best of staff around me. I shall kick like hell when I go, but needs must. Anyway, as far as your having an extra week to get married is concerned, you don't even have to ask. You don't have to worry about this place. I'll get some cover in for both of you.'

'Thank you so much, Mr Bickley,' said Mary. 'I can't tell you what a relief that is.'

Lennie shook hands with Alf. 'Thank you, sir,' he said, heartily. 'Much appreciated.'

'Oh, by the way, Mary,' said Alf, holding the door open for them. 'I hear you had a brush with our old friend, the Toff again the other night. Is that true?'

Mary exchanged an awkward glance with Lennie. 'Yes, sir,' she replied.

'You're about the only one who's seen him since you came here. Did he have anything to say to you this time?'

'Not really, sir,' replied Mary. 'It was all over in a few seconds.'

'Well,' said Alf, 'I've been reading up a bit about him lately. Sounds like he was an actor in one of the theatre companies soon after the place opened in the early part of the century. The Edwardians used to do a lot of classical stuff in those days. It's just a rumour that one of them died of consumption in the middle of a performance. Anyway, congratulations to you both, and keep up the good work!'

They both thanked him and left his office. Once they had got outside into the street, Lennie turned on her. 'Why didn't you tell me about seeing the Toff?' he asked, with some irritation.

'I didn't think you'd want to know,' she replied. 'If you remember, the last time I told you, you said I was only seeing him because I *wanted* to see him.'

'And *did* you?'

'Did I what?'

'*Want* to see him?'

Now Mary was getting irritated, so she walked on. 'I don't get a kick out of seeing a dead man walking, if that's what you're saying!'

'I've told you before, Mary,' he growled, without raising his voice. 'I don't believe in ghosts.'

Mary brought them to a halt again. 'And neither do I, Lennie,' she replied firmly. 'But if you can't explain what you've seen, then you can't just dismiss it. Yes, it's probably all just imagination, but the mind has a funny way of trying to tell you something. At least, mine does.'

'All I'm asking,' pleaded Lennie, 'is that when these things happen to you, you tell *me* first – right?'

'Why?' asked Mary, confused.

'Because in a couple of months' time, I'm going to be your husband.'

Mary looked at him in absolute astonishment. 'Welcome to married life!' she spluttered, before moving off.

Tanya Ling was looking forward to receiving visitors. Ever since Mary had told her about Lennie proposing to her, Tanya had made up her mind that the time for telling Mary about what her mother had discussed with her before she died was now getting closer. But first, Tanya herself had to know more. She had met Lennie just once before, but that was not enough. Now she must try to get into the mind of Mary's mother, Jenny Trimble. And also to get into the mind of Lenny Backer to find out whether he *was* the person Tanya could trust to take care of Mary, whether he *was* the person Jenny Trimble had in mind when she knew she was dying and wrote that letter. This was going to be a day of candour and observation, a day Tanya had waited for for so long.

At exactly ten o'clock in the morning, the doorbell rang. Tanya knew they wouldn't be late because both of them had to be at work at the

Marlborough by 12.30 in the afternoon, and they would have to allow plenty of time to get back for the matinée performance. Wearing one of her favourite traditional three-quarter-length pink brocade dresses, relieved only by the slits down the lower part of both legs, Tanya rushed excitedly down the stairs as fast as her dress would allow. 'My dear Mary!' she enthused, the moment she opened the door. 'How wonderful to see you! Come in! Come in!' She and Mary hugged each other. 'And Lennie! Thank you so much for coming. I'm honoured!' She greeted him more formally, shaking both his hands at the same time.

A few minutes later, all three were seated around the kitchen table, laid specially with small porcelain cups and saucers, together with sweet Chinese delicacies such as ginger balls, small honey cakes and different dried fruits. Even though he had been warned by Mary in advance, Lennie eyed everything on the table with deep suspicion.

'We must take this as a celebration,' said Tanya, her voice as rhythmic as ever, as she poured boiling water into a medium-sized teapot decorated with Chinese emblems. 'It's not every day that two lovely friends decide to get married.'

Before she had set out on this visit, Mary had great misgivings. After all, Tanya had said during their meeting outside Hornsey Road public baths on VE night that she was wary of what she might say to Lennie. Why was it so important to Tanya to know if Lennie was the boy with whom she wanted to share the rest of her life? And why would it have been so important to Mary's mother, when *she* had died long before Mary had even met Lennie?

'You know,' Tanya said, as she poured three cups of primrose tea, '*I* was born in the year of the goat. In Chinese Astrology, it's said that we are elegant, charming, artistic, gifted and fond of nature.' She chuckled to herself. 'It's all nonsense, of course, although as a Chinese woman I shouldn't really question the stars! But we are creative too. That's why I want to tell you about the exhibition.'

'Oh, Tanya!' exclaimed Mary. 'Is it really happening – at last?'

'Oh yes,' replied Tanya, sitting at the table with them. 'It's going to be on the first weekend in September.'

'That's only a couple of weeks before we get married!' cried Mary. 'Lennie, we've got so much to look forward to!'

Lennie smiled bravely as he tried to drink the hot primrose tea.

'I just hope the war with the Japs will be over by then,' said Mary. 'It would be horrible to think we're all enjoying ourselves whilst so many of our boys are fighting for their lives out there.'

'The war *will* be over, Mary,' said Tanya, with a smile that hid so much.

Mary was puzzled. 'How can you be so sure?' asked Mary.

Tanya continued to smile, but was doing so looking at Lennie. 'Oh, we Chinese know quite a lot of things,' she said, lightly. 'It's all in the stars.' She held out a plate of ginger balls first to Mary, then to Lennie. 'For instance,' she continued, 'I knew that you two were going to get married long before you told me. Not the exact date, of course, but near enough. I suppose you could call it a kind of – intuition.' She turned to Lennie. 'What about you, young man? Do you follow any kind of philosophy?'

Lennie was a bit taken aback. 'I'm sorry,' he replied. 'I'm not quite sure what you mean?'

'I'm sorry, that sounds a bit grand,' she said. 'What I mean is do you believe in fate?'

'Well – yes,' he replied. 'I suppose I do really. What's to be, will be.'

'Precisely,' said Tanya, who was treating the whole thing as lightly as possible. 'Did you always imagine you would spend the rest of your life with someone like Mary?'

'I'd always hoped I would – yes,' he replied, warily.

Tanya was now in the position of trying to probe, without making it seem too obvious. 'So when you met, you knew straight away *she* was the one you wanted more than anyone else in the whole world?'

'I love Mary,' he answered, edgily. 'I can't say more than that.'

'No, of course you can't.' She turned to Mary. 'I know I don't have to ask *you*, Mary. From what you've told me, Lennie is the most important person in your life?'

300

'Well, of course he is, Tanya,' said Mary, who was getting just a little irritated by her questioning. 'Why should you think otherwise?'

'I only ask,' continued Tanya, cautiously, 'because when I first met my Robert, it was a long time before I knew whether I loved him. It was something to do with — oh, I don't know — a meeting of minds. It wasn't just that we liked the same kind of things, but that we understood each other, even when one of us knew we were in the wrong.'

Mary and Lennie flicked a puzzled glance at each other.

Tanya smiled. 'Oh, don't take me *too* seriously,' she joked. 'Robert always told me that I am far too inquisitive. But I don't think there is anything wrong with that — do *you*, Lennie?'

All Lennie could do was to shrug. Unaware that she was trying to look inside him, he was baffled by what she was saying.

Tanya got up, and lit an incense stick on the mantelpiece above the fireplace. 'You see,' she continued, 'it's part of my work to be inquisitive. When I see someone who interests me, I want to know more about them than what's on the surface. A face is only a clue.' She turned around to look at them with a reassuring smile. 'Come upstairs, and let me tell you what I mean.'

Feeling decidedly uneasy, Mary and Lennie followed her upstairs to the studio, where Lennie was suddenly astonished by her amazing collection of sketches.

'Are all these for the exhibition?' asked Mary, overwhelmed by the sheer intensity of some of her drawings.

'Most of them,' said Tanya, sorting through a pile of sketches piled up against the wall. 'There are some I want to keep. Of course, all of them first have to go off to be framed.'

Lennie wandered around, his eyes moving from one sketch to another, admiring the way in which Tanya had captured a look, an expression, a smile, a scowl, grief, joy, someone listening, another person in animated conversation.

'But Tanya, this is so strange,' said Mary, who was looking in awed fascination at a sketch of her neighbour, Fred Parfitt. 'I *know* all these people.'

Tanya smiled. 'Yes,' she said. 'That's the intention. My exhibition is about all the strange and wonderful people who live in not just your neighbourhood, but also in your own consciousness – in other words, the men, women and children you probably see every day of your life, but only with your eyes. Take this one.' She put a sketch on to her easel and stood back for Mary and Lennie to take a look.

'Good God!' exclaimed Mary. 'That's Sheila Nestor.'

'Yes,' said Tanya, arms crossed, looking at the picture with them. 'It's an extraordinary face, isn't it? But can you tell what lies behind it? At first I thought I knew, but I was quite wrong.'

Mary was truly impressed. 'You make her look almost human.'

'She *is* human, Mary,' replied Tanya, her bright red lips hardly moving as she spoke. 'But you would never know until you looked inside her mind.'

'I didn't know drawing pictures was about looking into people's minds,' said a somewhat confused Lennie.

'Oh yes,' Tanya assured him. 'Let me show you someone else.' She removed the sketch of Sheila Nestor, returned it to where she had taken it from, and once again sorted through the pile leaning against the wall.

Whilst this was going on, Mary clutched Lennie's arm, as though seeking protection from him.

Tanya returned, and placed another, larger sketch on the easel. 'I wonder if you know *this* chap?' She stood back to let them take a look.

Both of them were aghast when they saw whose face was the subject of the picture. It was Lennie.

'That's me!' he cried, immediately moving in for a closer look.

'Oh, thank God!' laughed Tanya.

Mary looked as closely as she possibly could at the huge sketch of Lennie's face. It had every nuance, every spot, every feature of his personality right there in that black-pencilled drawing. But most of all it carried the kind of expression that he rarely allowed anyone to see. He was smiling.

'Lennie!' cried Mary. 'I've – never seen you like that before. Only once – that was on VE night – round the bonfire.' She turned briefly back to Tanya. 'Am I right?' she asked.

Tanya merely nodded.

'Do I *really* look like that?' asked Lennie, turning his head from one side to another to get different views of his mirror image.

'That's what you look like to *us*,' said Tanya. 'But what does it tell you about *yourself*?'

'It tells *me* what a good-looking bloke I've got,' said Mary. 'That's such a lovely smile.'

'Oh, it *is* a lovely smile,' agreed Tanya. 'But what *I* try to do is to capture what is *behind* the smile. When I am sketching a picture, I try to work out what is going on in the mind of the person I am drawing. Now with *this* young man . . .' she turned her look to Lennie's sketch, 'I wonder if he is as inquisitive as me, how reliable he is, how he arrives – at decisions.'

Suddenly disturbed by staring at his own face in the drawing, Lennie turned away. 'I'm just an ordinary bloke, Tanya,' he said uneasily. 'What you see is what you get.'

For Tanya it was a lame explanation, one that, in *her* mind, concealed quite a lot.

'There's nothing ordinary about *you*, darling,' Mary said, defending him. She had the uncomfortable feeling that Tanya was getting at him. 'I'm the luckiest woman in the world to have you.'

Tanya smiled at her. 'You know, Mary,' she said brightly, 'I think you are. That's why I'm dedicating my exhibition to your mother and father, to you and the family, and, of course' – she turned to look at Lennie – 'to your future husband.'

Chapter 23

After the Labour landslide in the General Election in July, people now started to focus on the important fact that although the war in Europe was over, the struggle against the Japanese in the Far East was still costing thousands of lives amongst both Allied and enemy forces. In Mary's little corner of Holloway alone, there was enormous anxiety amongst some of the neighbours about the safety and well-being of men folk who were still fighting in Burma, Malaya, and other parts of south-east Asia. It was a bloody war, and unless something happened soon to break the almost fanatical will of the Japanese forces and their ruthless government, after nearly six years of war on their own doorstep, the people of Holloway and everywhere else throughout the world would not be able to live in the peace they had so long craved for.

However, life had to go on, and with the approach of the August Bank Holiday, Mary spent most mornings piling up all the clothes and other personal things that she and the family would need to take on her 'dream holiday'. If there was one thing she had learned when her mum was alive, it was that everything should be prepared in advance, and, as she was taking no chances, by the time they were ready to leave soon after the crack of dawn on the Saturday before Bank Holiday Monday, the cases and bags were packed the night before, ready for the cumbersome journey by tube to Victoria Coach Station. The only snag was that, because he had to be in Epping on the Friday in order to meet up with the latest people who were interested in buying the farmhouse, Lennie was unable to travel with Mary and the family to the coach station, but arranged to meet them on the coach before departure.

'Where you travelling to, little lady?' asked the coach driver, as Mary waited with Thelma, Dodo and Billy at the front of the queue piling on to the Blue Coach.

'Dawlish,' she replied. 'That's in Devonshire.'

'Yer don't say,' replied the driver with a harmless grin. He checked her tickets then stood back to help the family on board. 'Leave your baggage. I'll take care of it for you. Your seats are all in the back row. Have a good journey.'

'Thank you,' said Mary, trembling with a mixture of excitement and anxiety, concerned that Lennie had not yet turned up. 'There's still one of us to come!' she said to the driver when he boarded the coach. 'When he comes, his name's Lennie Backer.'

'I'll keep a look out for him,' the driver assured her.

The moment they were on board, Dodo and Billy rushed straight to the back seat, immediately arguing about who was going to sit by the window. However, Thelma soon shut them up, telling them that they'd both be left behind if they didn't keep quiet.

Mary was determined to savour the moment she had waited for for so long. Moving slowly down the aisle towards the back seat, she relished the luxurious look of it all, feeling the quality of the upholstery with her fingertips as she went. It was so different to those day trips to Southend on the Orange Luxury Coaches, where the seats were uncomfortable and there was so little room that you practically had to travel with your knees under your chin.

Once Mary had reached the back seat, the first thing she did was to keep Dodo and Billy quiet by unpacking some jam sandwiches, which they devoured as though they hadn't eaten for months, and a flask of tea. Thelma just sipped the tea from one of the old cups that were kept for rainy days in the sideboard back home. She was at the stage where she wanted to keep an eye on her figure, especially as Chris, her now demobbed lance corporal, had become her 'steady'. But for Mary, her mind was on other things. The coach was due to depart at nine o'clock, and when she looked at the station clock, there were only ten minutes to go. Her heart was racing. Had Lennie managed to catch the early Green Line Bus to Victoria from Epping?

Lennie stood at the Green Line bus stop just a few minutes' walk from the farmhouse. He had already watched two buses stop and depart, but, even though there was plenty of room on both of them, at the last minute he had changed his mind about getting on board. The reason was that his mind was in turmoil. Like so many men *and* women before they got married, he had misgivings about whether he was doing the right thing. He knew only too well that the moment he stepped on that Blue Coach with Mary and the family, his entire future would be sealed for ever.

His mind had been troubled ever since that strange visit to Tanya Ling just a couple of weeks before. It was as though she had got him there to look him over, to see if he was someone who was suitable for Mary. The whole episode had given him an inferiority complex, and it had shaken his confidence. Even so, whatever that Chinese woman had thought, he *did* love Mary and wanted to marry her; he wanted to marry her very much. But the question still remained: was he good enough for Mary? After the third Green Line bus had arrived and departed, he decided to turn around and go back home – to the farmhouse.

The sun was now gaining momentum, flooding the rooftops around Victoria Coach Station, the gold turning to a dazzling summer light, which was forcing its way through every gap between the buildings, until it finally reached the window of the Blue Coach where Mary was peering out frantically. Where was he? What could have happened to him? He had promised. He had promised her faithfully. Lennie wasn't someone who wouldn't keep his word. There must be a reason. Maybe he had finally sold the house and had been delayed? Yes, that's what it was. She could trust Lennie. There *must* be a reason. He would never let her down – never. She trusted him. In a few weeks' time they were supposed to be getting married. They would be husband and wife. Oh yes, she could trust Lennie all right. She could trust him more than anyone else in the whole wide world.

The hand of the station clock moved to the hour. It was nine o'clock. The Blue Coach left on time.

Lennie stood in the back courtyard of the farmhouse, his eyes focused on the beautiful array of meadowsweet, white daisies and yellow butter-cups, all swaying gently to and fro in a friendly breeze. The previous afternoon, the estate agent had introduced him to the people who wanted to buy the house. They were a nice couple – a farmer from somewhere in Durham and his wife, who clearly loved the old farm-house with its many period features and cosy atmosphere. Yes, they would look after the place. They would make something of it. It was a wise decision to sell to someone like them. In any case, a house was only a house, the land was only the land. No matter how much you love something, you can't expect to hold on to it for ever. Even so, he had an ache inside that just would not go away.

With endless queues of traffic it seemed to take for ever for the Blue Coach to reach the outskirts of London. By then its citizens were up and about, housewives scrubbing their front doorsteps, husbands at work in their small front gardens, the getaway crowds rushing for trains and buses and, despite the fact that it was the August Bank Holiday weekend, navvies, brickies and plasterers were getting on with the urgent task of restoring the capital's bomb-damaged buildings whilst every-where newsvendors were shouting out the headlines: 'War trials start today! War trials start today!' It seemed such a short time since the days when everyone had been so aware of what was up in the sky, and what horrors might be raining down on them, for the silver barrage balloons had now gone, and so had the tin hats, air-raid posts, and Anderson shelters. London was once again at peace.

Thelma was already fast asleep, but Dodo and Billy, their stomachs now bloated with jam sandwiches, were desperately trying to keep

307

awake just in case they missed something unusual as the coach purred effortlessly towards the suburbs.

Mary was wide awake. Despite getting up at the crack of dawn, having got all the family organised for the great adventure, there was no sleep in her, only a sinking feeling. Lennie had promised, was all she could think about. He had promised he'd be on the coach, he had promised he'd be at her side at the start of her magical dream. Her joy was now mixed with sadness, with regret and disappointment. All she could do now was to sit back and not only look forward to her luxurious journey of a lifetime, but also to the wonders of a small town in Devonshire, with the promise of sandy beaches, red cliffs and rolling hills. The dream was gradually becoming clearer.

Lennie stood at the river's edge in the woods. He was deep in thought, reflecting on what he had done, and the effect it would have on Mary. But in his mind, he was still churning over the things Tanya Ling had said to him, especially about that sketch she had done of him: '*Now with this young man . . . I wonder if he is as inquisitive as me, how reliable he is, how he arrives – at decisions.*' Since then it had been a question he had asked himself over and over again. Was he inquisitive? Was he reliable? Could he really make his own decisions?

He moved on, strolling aimlessly towards the old forge, where a couple of years earlier two children had been drowned in the fast flowing waters, something that had shocked Mary when he had told her about it. It gave him a strange feeling to relive those moments when he had leapt in to try to save them, but without success. And yet, *that* was a decision he had had to make very quickly, a challenge he had taken up in an instant. So what did Tanya mean about 'making decisions?' Gradually, the thought dawned on him that he wasn't strong enough to make the decisions, and left everything to Mary whilst he just went along with everything she said. Inquisitive he wasn't, and he readily accepted that that was something he should be aware of, such as understanding the reasons why Mary did things, why she was hurt by something he had said. But reliable? That was the real problem –

he just didn't know. All he could say was that he loved Mary, and would do anything in his power to protect her, but when it came to taking the initiative, he had no idea if he would pass the test. Reliability meant being there when she needed him, and at this very moment, as Mary embarked on the dream holiday she had talked over with him so many times, he knew only too well how much she must be needing him right now. Nonetheless if the two of them were going to have a lasting relationship, it would be up to him to take the initiative, up to him to be the stronger partner of the two, the man of the family, the father figure who knew how to steer his family through thick and thin. But could he *do* that? And *if* he could, would he *want* to?

Hands in pockets, he slowly turned around and looked back at the house, that grand, crumbling old barn of a place that had seen him grow up from child to adult. Soon, it would belong to someone else. Soon it would only be a memory for him to remember with a mixture of sadness and affection – the funny-shaped red-bricked chimney pots that were leaning over at an angle, looking as though they would topple at any moment. And the small, lead-framed windows, covered over with frost in the winter, stifling hot when closed during the summer. It was a paradise, a curiosity, a totally unmanageable lump of brick and mortar and flaking plaster. But it was *home*. Nonetheless, as he stood there staring with mixed emotions at the place, it spelt out only one word to him – money. There and then he *made* that vital decision, and knew exactly what he must do.

The Blue Coach glistened in the morning sun. As it sped along the main trunk road towards Basingstoke, the green fields of Hampshire competed with the gold corn of the wheat fields, shimmering majestically in the cool breeze from the east, waiting patiently for the day when the great threshing machines would leave them with no more than their stalks.

Inside the coach, Mary took in every inch of the passing countryside, lulled into a state of tranquillity by the haunting sound of one of the passengers playing 'Greensleeves' on a mouth organ, which was such a contrast to the endless 'Knees Up, Mother Brown' excitement on VE night. It was so beautiful that, what with the luxury and comfort of the seat on her beloved Blue Coach, and the constant hope that there would be a message from Lennie waiting for her at the digs on their arrival, her eyelids slowly flickered and closed. However, Thelma was now awake, staring drowsily out across Dodo through the windows, admiring the cosiness of the tiny old country villages that nestled so beautifully in the middle of nowhere, and yearning for the company of her lance corporal, who was now beginning to figure quite prominently in her life.

At the old market town of Basingstoke, the driver brought the coach to what he called 'a ten-minute convenience break'. For Dodo, and especially Billy, it came just in time, and they both dashed off into their respective public lavatories in the stopover café in the main thoroughfare known as London Street. Mary and Thelma took the opportunity to stretch their legs, and take a quick look at the town, which seemed to be pretty intact in spite of some bombing during the war, which included the destruction of St Michael's church. However, Thelma, who was now showing herself to be more grown up and lovable towards her elder sister, was only too aware that Lennie's not showing up for the trip was still on Mary's mind. 'Don't worry,' she said, trying to sound positive. 'He'll either be waiting for you when you get there, or you'll have some crazy message to say he's sold the house and will come down and join you as soon as he can.'

'I doubt that,' replied Mary. 'Even if he came down by train, he probably wouldn't get there until tomorrow. And if he's sold the house, he'd have to stay behind to get the papers sorted out with the agent.'

Of course, it wasn't only the fact that Lennie hadn't turned up in time for the coach that was worrying Mary, but a sneaking feeling that he was getting cold feet about their relationship. With the date of their wedding now only a month away, she was beginning to wonder if what Tanya had been trying to tell her was true. Was Lennie reliable after all?

The rest of the journey went smoothly enough, the only distraction being a husband and wife from the north of England speaking to each other so loudly that from that moment on, no one could get any sleep. And there was the overpowering smell of an orange being peeled by an elderly woman halfway down the coach, who was feeding each segment separately to what appeared to be her small grandson. But what impressed Mary the most was watching the sun get lower and lower in the sky the further the coach progressed. By the time they had made another 'convenience break' in Exeter and reached their destination, the afternoon sun had only a few more hours before dipping down into the sea for the night. Stepping off the coach so close to the Devonshire seaside was the fulfilment of Mary's dream. She was here. This was it. This was what she had scrimped and scraped for since she had first seen that advertisement in a colour magazine so long ago. The little town of Dawlish was exactly as she had always envisioned it, promenade front, railway line running right the way along the coast, and the sea – the beautiful sea, blue and calm and still, hardly a ripple on the surface. And to their right, through the railway tunnel and jutting out of the sea just offshore, was the famous red sandstone rock that looked like a spinning top, just like the picture Mary had cut out of that same magazine, and stuck up on the wall of her bedroom in Roden Street. Everything was pure magic. How her mum and dad would have loved this place. And Granddad too. Despite his grumpiness, Granddad loved the sea, and would have been in his element sitting for hours on a bench along the promenade.

After helping the driver to collect the family's baggage, the first thing Mary did was to ask the way to their board-and-lodgings place at Marine Parade. Fortunately, the person she asked at the little sweet stall close to the railway bridge knew the place immediately, and, struggling with the luggage as best they could, the family started the long trek through the covered walkway alongside the seafront. As they went, the tide seemed to be coming in, and as it did so, it seemed to be getting just a little more restless by the minute. A little later they climbed up the stairs of the old railway bridge and crossed over to the long terrace of houses that were facing the shore on the other side. Now out of breath, Mary and Thelma allowed Dodo and Billy to rush ahead and find the house they were looking for.

Number 12 Marine Parade had recently been painted and freshened up, probably for the first time since decorating materials had become available again after the war years. It was an elegant Edwardian house set on four floors, with a bow window on the ground floor, red-and-white geraniums hanging in a basket in the porch, and a large notice in the window which proclaimed: SORRY, NO VACANCIES.

'Hello, my dears.' The middle-aged lady who greeted them at the front door was just what Mary had hoped for. She was not very tall, but not very small either, plump, had a lovely open face with a small black mole on her chin, and she was wearing a well-chosen floral-patterned cotton summer dress. 'My name's Mrs Bunny,' she said. To Thelma, Dodo and Billy her Devon burr was a bit of a curiosity, but to Mary it was a pure delight. 'You must be the Trimbles, and I bet you're worn out after that long trip. Come you in now.' She stood aside to let them into the narrow hall. 'Have a nice cup of tea first, then I'll take you up to your rooms.' As they went, the one thing they all noticed was the strong sweet smell of furniture polish, never more prevalent than in the sitting room which had a lovely comfortable settee and armchairs, a mahogany wireless set, and the most magnificent sea views which stretched for as far as the eye could see.

'So, my dears,' said Mrs Bunny as she returned very quickly with a tray of teapot, cups and saucers, and ginger biscuits. 'Welcome to Sea View.'

'Sea View?' asked Billy, in his usual cheeky way.

'That's what me and my husband call the house,' replied their friendly landlady. 'Don't have to have *too* much imagination to know why!' As she laughed her rather ample bosoms wobbled up and down, much to the amusement of the two terrible youngsters. 'Breakfast is at eight,' she said, starting to list the B & B services. 'We've got most things: eggs – fried, scrambled, boiled or poached – bacon, mushrooms, a grilled tomato, toast or fried bread, tea or coffee. If you want half-board, you'll have to let me know in good time, but we do a very nice evening meal – seven p.m. sharp. Now, as soon as you've had your tea, I shall have to ask one of you to sign in, and then I'll take you upstairs to show you the rooms.'

After she had left, Dodo and Billy burst into laughter, grabbed all the ginger biscuits, and golloped them all down before either Mary or Thelma could get their hands on them. Then they started bouncing up and down excitedly on the two armchairs. Thelma got angry with them. 'If you two don't calm down,' she said, 'I'll fill your beds with crabs!'

'You behave now – hear me?' Mary's finger pointing threateningly at them was enough for Dodo and Billy to shut up, and sit together on the window bench to look out at the seafront.

'I see you're only four persons,' said Mrs Bunny, after Mary had completed the signing in, and they were climbing the stairs. 'I have you down for five – one double, one double with a put-you-up.'

Embarrassed by Lennie not showing up, Mary asked, 'I'm afraid . . . er, my husband can't make it just yet. There wasn't a message for me, by any chance?'

'No, dear,' replied Mrs Bunny, sorting out the bedroom keys as she reached the first-floor landing. 'Does that mean it's a cancellation?'

'No – not yet,' replied Mary, hastily. 'Hopefully, he'll be here by tomorrow at the latest.'

'Mmm,' came the reply. 'I'm not sure I can hold the room for that long, my dear. This is a Bank Holiday. I've had to turn people away. Anyway, if your party does come, you can always double up.'

Mary raised her eyebrows at that, and continued to follow Mrs Bunny up to the second-floor landing, breathless and struggling with her suitcase.

'Here we are, then!' said the landlady. 'Home from home!'

After showing Mary the double bedroom, she then gave her another key. 'I'm afraid the room with three beds is upstairs in the attic. But it's very comfy, and very quiet – except when the stupid gulls sit on the chimney pot!' She started to move back downstairs. 'If there's anything you need, just call either me or Mr Bunny. We share the work.

313

He's a great help around the place. Oh, and by the way, we have four other guests, a very nice select couple from Glasgow in Scotland, and a young lady and her mother from Cambridge.' She lowered her voice. 'They quarrel a bit over breakfast, but don't let it worry you. They're really quite harmless.'

Despite their high spirits on arrival, that night Dodo and Billy slept like logs. Thelma did too, but she wasn't too keen on being confined to the attic with her monster young brother and sister, who kept her awake for a long time while they played some terrible card game on Dodo's bed. Mary slept only intermittently. Although her double bed was far more comfortable than her own bed at home, she was weighed down with the unbearable thought that it might all be over between her and Lennie. Before she left home on Saturday morning, she hadn't told the others about the tiff she had had with Lennie the night before, about her relationship with Tanya, and the strange influence the Chinese woman appeared to have over her. It wasn't really a bad tiff, but it was enough to leave a bad impression on Lennie, who went off back to Epping in one of his moods, declaring that the trip to Devon was Mary's dream, not his, and that he would be glad when it was over and done with. In her heart of hearts, Mary was deeply upset about the argument, but distraught that it could have happened so close to what was supposed to be their wedding day. As she lay tossing and turning in the middle of the night, listening to the sea gathering force on the shore outside, she prayed Lennie would forgive her, and somehow join her the following day.

When the family met up for breakfast in the dining room downstairs, they were absolutely astonished by the transformation in the sea conditions. Huge waves were crashing against the sea wall on the other side of the railway track, which sent sea spray spiralling across the road to splatter the front windows of the house. The noise was almost deafening, and as the waves pounded the sea wall and shore, the vibrations shook Marine Parade so much that all the best china and brass figures in Mrs Bunny's glass cabinet rattled and jumped about without mercy. However, Dodo and Billy loved the excitement, and when they took their seats at the table reserved for them with Mary and Thelma, they spent most of their time trying to get better glimpses through the window behind them.

'Is it always like this?' Thelma asked Mrs Bunny, when she brought in the four cooked breakfasts.

'Goodness no, dear,' replied the dear lady, who was taking turns with her husband to serve each table. 'Most days it's as quiet as a lamb down here. You can hear a pin drop.' She turned to the elderly Scottish couple at the next table. 'Isn't that so, Mr and Mrs McFarland?'

The Scottish couple, their mouths full of fried egg and mushrooms, merely nodded with an 'Aye. That it is.'

The other guests, the young woman and her mother, were clearly not on speaking terms, for when they turned up ten minutes late for breakfast, much to the irritation of Mrs Bunny, they merely took their seats, and avoided contact with each other every minute they were there.

'Any message for me yet?' Mary whispered to Mr Bunny when he brought her a boiled egg.

'Not yet, Miss,' he replied softly. In any case, he was a quiet little man, who moved around so silently that some his friends called him 'The Undertaker'. 'Mind you, the phone's been down a couple of times during the power cut. But it's back now, so me or the missus will let you know the moment we hear anything.'

As soon as breakfast was over, the family collected their raincoats, mainly because, much to Mary and Thelma's dismay, Dodo and Billy wanted to play the game of dodging the spray by going into town via the sea wall. And what a rough game it turned out to be! The result was that all of them got thoroughly drenched, and if it hadn't been for the fact that it was turning into a really hot day, they would have had to go back to Marine Parade to change their clothes.

Dawlish town turned out to be everything Mary had read about.

Although the place was pretty packed with Bank Holiday day trippers, the family loved wandering around the shops, and sitting on a bench at the Brook, a beautiful small river running right through the heart of the town before flowing under the railway line and out into the sea. The great attraction of the day for Dodo and Billy were the two wild black swans which were so tame that they came right up to them, but for Mary and Thelma, it was the coastline, with the majestic red sandstone cliffs which rose right up from the water's edge.

With still no word from Lennie, Mary decided that it was now obvious that he would not be coming down to join her and the family, so the following day, concerned that her low spirits were going to prevent the others from having a good time, she sent them off on a day trip to the zoo in Torquay. After they had gone, she wandered off on her own, making her way to Smuggler's Lane, which she followed until she reached the sea wall where she could walk all the way to the nearby town of Teignmouth. The sea had now calmed down immensely, and as she strolled she could see the light shimmering on the surface of the water, and the deserted concrete bunkers that, up to only a short time before, had been used as observation posts in the event of an attempted enemy invasion.

When she had walked about halfway to Teignmouth, she paused a while, perching on the edge of the wall, thinking, and watching the outgoing tide. What had started out as a dream holiday, was now turning into a week that, for different reasons, she would never forget. If Lennie had decided to drop out of her life, she asked herself, where would she go from here? Her worries were deep rooted, caused by an isolated incident some weeks before when Lennie had quite inadvertently mentioned the fact that he had accidentally met his former girlfriend, Carole Pickard, when he had gone into Epping for a meeting with the estate agent. But was it *really* an accident, or was it a yearning to patch up their differences? Unlike what Lennie had told her previously, Carole Pickard was *not* married, and now with a child to bring up, she had no doubt that this girl had nothing to lose but to try to get together with Lennie again. Had Lennie fallen for what she was after? Mary had no way of telling. For all she knew, the two of them were together at the farmhouse this very minute.

The more she thought about things, the longer she sat there on the wall and the more depressed she became, so she got up and continued her stroll. After a moment or so, she was interrupted by the shriek of seagulls circling overhead, waiting for the chance to swoop down on to the surface of the water to make their strike at any poor unsuspecting fish that happened to be visible to them. Under normal circumstances, she would have been fascinated to just stand there and watch them, but it reminded her too much of the times she and Lennie had watched the swallows doing the same thing in the field at the back of the house in Epping. She moved on.

The sun was beginning to bite into her fair skin, and as she had no protection, she quickened her pace. But as she drew closer to Teignmouth town at the end of the sea wall, she could hear someone calling out in the distance. The breeze had now turned into a wind, and as it was blowing against her, there was no way she could determine in which direction the sound was coming from, so she carried on walking. But then she heard it again, and this time it was a little closer. She looked into the distance ahead, wondering if it was one of the fishermen calling to his mates on the beach to help him haul in his catch. But as she looked and listened, she realised that the fishermen were definately not calling to one another. Still she carried on, but when the sound grew louder and louder, she stopped, swung around, and saw someone running towards her, shouting her name, waving at her. At first the figure was too distant to identify, but gradually, as he came into focus, she knew who it was, and without a moment's pause she started to run back to greet him.

'Lennie!'

'Mary!'

They practically threw themselves into each other's arms. Lennie looked as though he hadn't shaved for a week, but Mary didn't care. He was there. She was in his arms.

'For God's sake, Len!' she cried. 'What the hell d'you think you're doing to me?'

'I'm sorry,' he said over and over again, hugging her to him, pressing his lips hard against hers. 'I had to work it out for myself,' he said. 'I held back, because I *had* to make the decision Mary, *my* decision. Can you understand what I'm saying?'

Mary, utterly confused and bewildered, stared at him, and shook her head. 'I don't know what you're talking about,' she said.

'I turned down the offer on the house,' he said. 'I've taken it off the market.'

Mary was taken aback. 'Lennie!' she gasped. 'But I thought . . . I thought . . .'

'I don't care about the money,' he explained. 'Yes, we need it, we need it badly, but if I have to rely on selling the house to support you and the kids, then I don't want to know. I have a job, Mary – a *good* job. As soon as we're married I want us to have kids of our own, kids we can *call* our own.'

Mary didn't know what had hit her. 'But – what about Thelma, and Dodo, and Billy? We have to live somewhere.'

'We *have* somewhere to live, Mary. The house in Epping is *our* house. We'll keep it on until we can do it up, make it a decent place again, where we can all live together, you, me, Thelma, Dodo, Billy – and our *own* kids! Until she goes off and gets married herself, Thelma can get a job out there, and the kids can be transferred to a local school. You said yourself the headmistress at Pakeman Street would help us with all that.'

'This is crazy, Lennie,' spluttered Mary, at the same time trying to contain a growing sense of excitement. 'How can we live in two places at the same time? It'll never work. It will mean too much of a change in our lives.'

'It *will* work, Mary!' he insisted. 'And d'you know why? Because I've made the decision that it's *got* to work! Isn't that what you want? Isn't that what your Chinese friend wants? Isn't that what your mother would have wanted?'

For several moments, Mary stared at him in utter amazement. Then she flung her arms around his neck and kissed him.

It was some time before the seagulls returned. After all, they were not swallows. Unlike them, they had no safe place to fly off to.

Chapter 24

With Lennie back at her side, the remainder of Mary's 'dream holiday' week was all that she had ever dared hope for, marred only by the news on the wireless that on Bank Holiday Monday, the Americans had dropped one of the most powerful bombs ever known on a Japanese port and army base called Hiroshima. It was not that anyone regretted that the Japanese regime had been dealt a devastating blow, but that such a bomb had been made at all, a sinister pointer to any future wars. Mary and Lennie were horrified when, together with Mrs Bunny and other guests at the boarding house, they listened on the wireless to accounts of the way thousands of people had just disappeared from the face of the earth, and the way the entire area had been blotted out by smoke and dust, followed by a mushroom-shaped cloud which stretched up for several miles into the air. Mary prayed that this terrible attack on the last existing enemy would mean that this was finally the end of the two wars.

Soon after the Saturday Mary had got back from Devonshire, the first person she wanted to see was Tanya, but as her Chinese friend was very busy preparing for her forthcoming exhibition, they couldn't meet until Mary's day off on the following Monday week. As the weather was now stifling hot, they decided to meet in the cafeteria at Finsbury Park, close to the boating lake. It was a lovely morning, so after buying tea, they took their cups to one of the tables outside.

'You were wrong about, Lennie,' Mary said, her flaxen-coloured hair now just long enough to hang over her shoulders. 'If you talk about initiative, then he's proved that he has it just as much as anyone else.'

Tanya smiled. She looked so cool in one of her silk three-quarter-length dresses, which always attracted admiring glances from passers-by. 'Oh, I wasn't wrong, my dear one,' she replied. 'It's just that I wanted him to be aware of his own potential. Ever since I first met Lennie, ever since I first *knew* about him, I felt that there was something inside just waiting to get out. When you used to talk to me about him, you mentioned how worried you were that he was not being entirely open with you, that he was afraid to tell you about the things that had happened in his life. I knew that, if you were going to have a life together with him, that had to change. But that change had to come from Lennie himself. It would be wrong for you to force him to do it.'

'Well, he's certainly taken the initiative about the house,' Mary said. 'I could hardly believe it when he told me he'd decided not to sell. Though God knows how we're going to cope living out there when we both have jobs here in London.'

Tanya leaned forward and gave her the reassuring look of an older woman. 'That is what married life is all about, Mary,' she said. 'You will have many an evening talking over how you can sort out problems like that.'

Mary sipped her tea, then dabbed a thin trickle of perspiration running down her neck with her handkerchief. 'But what I still don't understand is why you changed your mind about him?'

'His smile,' replied Tanya, quite simply. 'The smile I captured in that drawing I showed you.'

Mary was puzzled. 'You changed your mind about him – just because of the way he smiled?'

'No,' said Tanya. 'It was what was *behind* the smile that I found so fascinating. What I saw was someone who was far stronger than he was prepared to show. This was someone who has known pain, known unhappiness, known danger – but he has always been unprepared to talk about it, or, more importantly, to share it with *you*. I can see that he's done that now. I can see that he *is* capable of making decisions, that he does have the strength to give you the love you need, and what you deserve. That's what I promised your mother.'

Mary looked up at her with a start. 'What d'you mean?'

Tanya decided not to answer that question until they had left the table and wandered off to the end of the boating lake, where the resident muscovy ducks were getting very angry with three young boys who were making a lot of noise laughing and playing around in one of the rowing boats.

'Soon after we met,' Tanya continued, 'I told you that when the time was right, I would tell you what it was your mother wanted me to say to you. Well, I think that time has come.'

They sat down on a bench overlooking the lake, and not far from where a young mother was kneeling on the grass whilst her little girl was having a lovely time throwing bread into the water for a posse of ravenous ducks and swans.

'During those last weeks when your mother was so ill, before she and your father were killed in the tube station at Bethnal Green, we came here to the park, to this very bench. Of course, it was colder then, in the winter, *very* cold, but she had a lot to say, and in this place out here, she felt free enough to tell me.'

'Tell you what?' asked Mary, who was turned towards her in tense anticipation.

Tanya hesitated before answering. 'That you were *not* your father's child.'

Despite the intense heat, Mary went quite cold.

'According to your mother,' continued Tanya, her soft-spoken accent suddenly more pronounced, 'you were born before she met your father. She wasn't in love with the man involved, but she said he was kind to her, and it all happened when they least expected it. But the man drowned in a swimming accident while he was on holiday with friends down in – Devonshire.'

Mary clasped her hand to her mouth in deep shock.

Tanya took her hand, and covered it with her own. 'By the time she had met your father, you were six months old. They fell in love, *real* love, so much so that your father told her that if she would marry him, he would make sure you were brought up as his own child.'

Mary slumped back. She found it hard to believe what she was being told.

'I know this is a shock for you,' continued Tanya, 'but you have to know that your mother didn't have the heart to tell you herself whilst she was alive. Apparently her husband, your stepfather, wanted to wait until you were twenty-one, until you were old enough to understand. That's why your mother asked me to take on the responsibility of telling you. I know it was a cowardly thing to do, but in her dreadful state of ill-health at the time, I had no alternative but to agree. As it so happens, fate took a hand, and, as you know, both of those dear souls died together.'

Mary was so emotionally disturbed that she got up, crossed her arms, and stared down into the pond.

Tanya got up and joined her. 'I want you to know, Mary,' she said, 'that I've been dreading this moment.' She slipped her arm around Mary's waist.

The small boys out in the rowing boat were rocking it back and forth so hard that there was a danger it would capsize at any moment. But they settled down the moment one of the park attendants yelled at them.

Mary and Tanya started to stroll off slowly along the path around the lake.

'What your mother was desperate for me to do,' continued Tanya, 'was to make sure you didn't make the same mistake. She was desperate that when you found someone you loved, that he was the right person for you. I told her that it would be wrong for me to try and interfere in your life, and she agreed, but after what happened to her, she just didn't want you to get hurt.' She smiled wryly to herself. 'I asked her what things I should look for in the "right" man, and I can remember what she replied to this day: "If anyone can see inside a person's character, it's you Tanya."'

Once again, they came to a halt. The ducks and swans and wild-fowl were taking a bit of a break on their island in the middle of the lake, a great deal of flapping of wings as they settled themselves.

'I know she wanted to write all this down, so that I could give it to you in a letter from her.' Tanya was now in a reflective mood. 'But she just couldn't do it. She was far too ill. However, she did leave something for you, just a little something, she said, that she hoped would help you to remember and forgive her. I want to pass that on to you when you come to my exhibition.' She looked at Mary, clearly upset for her. 'I'm so sorry, my dear Mary.'

Contrary to what Tanya had been expecting, Mary wasn't upset. In fact, she was smiling. 'You don't have to be sorry, Tanya,' she replied, with affection. '*I'm* the one who should feel sorry – for *you* – for this great burden you've had to bear all this time. I suppose it's something that happens all over the world. But I have to tell you, after what you've told me, I don't feel any different. I still love my mum, I still love the dad who brought me up. But now I've got Lennie, now I know what you and my mother think about him, I feel stronger than I've ever felt in my entire life.'

That evening, Mary did something that she had wanted to do ever since her last encounter with the Toff. Once she had cleared up after the last performance, she turned off the house lights and went to sit in one of the seats in the grand circle. And there she waited. This time she *wanted* to be there, ready to meet him, to find out why he was destined to roam the old theatre, what it was he was trying to say to her. But, patient though she was, there was no sign of him.

'You're wasting your time, young Mary,' came Alf's voice, as he turned the circle house lights back on, and came down to meet her from the entrance doors. 'When I first heard about the Toff, I did exactly the same as you're trying to do. But it won't work. If you or anyone else *wants* to see him, he'll just keep away.'

'But why is that, d'you think?' Mary asked. 'That last night I saw him, I was convinced he wanted to say something to me, to ask me something. I even thought it might have something to do with my parents, and that perhaps they're trying to get a message through to me.'

Alf shook his head. 'If you're psychic enough, I suppose you *would* think that, but I doubt it. If he exists at all, in whatever form, I'd say it's something to do with being an actor, with wanting to continue being part of the theatre and the plays he was in.'

Mary moved her attention to the stage down below, to the green velour curtains, and wondered what it must have looked like in those far-off days, before pictures on a screen or a man playing an organ, when the curtains drew back and a play was performed. For a few split seconds, she thought she could almost *see* the Toff down there, dressed in a fine period costume, treading the boards in a highly digni-fied way, to be awarded by the high-class theatre audience with prolonged bursts of applause. No wonder they called him 'The Toff'.

'Why don't you and your bloke make your way home now,' said Alf, climbing back up the circle stairs. 'Don't worry. I'll lock up after you've gone. I've got a bit of work to do in the office before I go.'

Mary did as he said, and made her way up to see Lennie in the projection room. 'Mr Bickley,' she called, before she left. 'I just want to thank you for helping me and Lennie to have that week off. I can't tell you what it meant to me.'

Alf beamed, and shook his head. 'No need for thanks, young Mary,' he said.

'I also want to thank you for everything you've done for me,' she continued. 'You gave me this job at a time when I was at my wit's end. I don't know what I'd have done without your help. There aren't many employers like you around. That's why we all like working for you.'

A touch embarrassed, Alf grinned. 'I think I told you once before,' he replied, 'a pitture house is a very special place. The flicks we show help us to forget all our troubles – well, for the time being at least. The dear old Marlborough is a special place too. If *we* treat it well, it'll do the same for us. Goodnight, Mary. God bless you, gel.'

'Goodnight, Mr Bickley,' replied Mary, going round the back of the circle, which used to be the gallery.

When she got into the projection room, Lennie was just finishing off re-spooling and tidying up the place. 'Shan't be long,' he said. 'I've just tinned the news before the changeover tomorrow.'

'I watched it for the first time tonight,' said Mary, uneasily. 'I couldn't bring myself to do it before now. Those shots of the bomb, all those dead people with burns, and that horrible, frightening cloud – it was just dreadful!'

'Well, at least it ended the war with Japan,' said Lennie. 'But the way things are going, those two atom bombs they dropped are going to change the world.'

Mary squirmed.

'Hey,' he said, gently grabbing both her arms. 'Cheer up! We've got a wedding to look forward to – remember?'

He put his fingers gently under her chin, stroked it, raised it, and kissed her. 'Listen,' he said, softly. 'What would you say if we changed shop?'

Mary was puzzled. 'Change shop?' she asked. 'What d'you mean?'

'I hear they're advertising for a new projectionist at the cinema out in Epping,' he said. 'It's not for a couple of months, but I thought I might apply for it. What d'you think?'

Mary was taken aback. 'Lennie!' she gasped. 'Isn't that a bit early? I mean, you haven't been here very long. Is it fair on Mr Bickley when he's been so good to us?'

'Oh, he thinks it's a good idea.'

'What!' Now Mary was really shocked.

'He said, once he knew we were going to hang on to the house in Epping, it'd be stupid not to get a job closer to home. And since the farmhouse *is* going to be our home . . .'

'Well, *I* think it's not the right time!' said Mary, tetchily, pulling away from him.

'Too bad,' retorted Lennie, casually. 'I've already applied for the job.'

Mary's mouth fell wide open. 'And you haven't even asked me!' she snapped.

'No,' he replied. 'Why should I? It's *my* decision – not yours!'

Mary was so shocked, she could think of nothing more to say to him. All she could do was watch him piling up cans of news film, ready for collection by the British Movietone News people first thing in the morning. But he was right. Of course he was right. In a few weeks' time, Lennie was going to be her husband, and that was the time when, as the man of the house, he would have to bear the responsibility of looking after her and her family.

'In any case,' he continued, opening the projection room door for them to leave, 'if you want, I'm pretty sure they'll have a job for you at the cinema too – that is, if I want you to go on working.'

'Of course I want to go on working!' she protested.

'We'll see about that,' he replied, with a mischievous grin. 'I haven't made up my mind about that yet.'

Although Mary knew he was only teasing her, she had no time to protest before being shuffled out of the projection room and down the stairs.

As they went, there was a movement in the grand circle, which was now plunged into darkness. Whatever it was didn't show itself, but it was definitely there. Oh yes, it was there all right . . .

'I don't care *what* you say,' snapped the now very aerated Mary. 'I'm used to working. I've been doing it ever since I left school. In any case, I'd miss this place. I mean, just look at it.'

They stopped briefly in the foyer, their eyes quickly flashing around the glamorous film-star photographs that adorned the walls there and right up the stairs. Robert Taylor, Loretta Young, Lana Turner, James Cagney, Deanna Durbin, John Mills, Greta Garbo – they were all there, all of them part of an era, an era that had given so many people who went to the flicks the chance to enjoy themselves. And the foyer itself, with tiled steps and brass handrails, Mavis's cashier box showing the ticket prices and times of showing, and the colourful posters of forthcoming attractions, feature films such as the wartime RAF drama *Journey's End*, with Richard Attenborough and Edward G. Robinson, the Technicolor musical, *Can't Help Singing*, with Deanna Durbin, and the classical drama *Jane Eyre*, with Orson Welles and Joan Fontaine.

'How d'you expect me to leave all this?' she asked.

Lennie grinned, grabbed hold of her hand, and dragged her outside. Once they had almost reached the main road, he brought them to a stop, and turned them both around. 'Just look,' he said. 'One day, there might come a time when that won't be with us any more.'

Mary turned to see what he was looking at. It was the Marlborough cinema, now with all lights illuminating the place after years of the blackout during the war, once the pride of the Holloway Road, now, like a great grandfather, retaining its dignity again, defying the challenge of the modern age.

'But that doesn't mean we shall ever forget it, Mary,' he said. 'Does it?'

Mary looked up at what was once a building of great beauty and grandeur, until her face gradually broke into a faint smile. 'No,' she replied, with deep affection. '*I'll* never forget it.'

As they made their way from the cinema and crossed the now silent Holloway Road, Ernie Backer watched them from the doorway of the Nag's Head pub, where he had just spent a couple of hours with his drinking mates. It gave him a warm feeling to see his boy and Mary going off together, arms around each other's waists, starting out on their new lives together. For Ernie, it was so different to his days with Winnie. Why oh why, he asked himself, couldn't they have loved each other like Lennie and Mary did? Why did he let Winnie go when they had so much to offer each other? But although he had lost her, he hadn't lost his boy. At least they had put their differences to one side and come together like they should have done a long time ago. For that he would always be grateful.

It was pouring with rain in Essex. In the first hours of the day the skies had quite literally opened up, the clouds had become darker and darker, followed by a massive rumble of thunder, followed by some nasty forks of lightning which threatened to interrupt the power supplies if the storm went on too long.

Mary and Lennie watched it all from the safety of the farmhouse, where they had been toiling ever since arriving on the early morning

Green Line bus, doing their best to make some sense of the sitting room at the front of the house, which hadn't had a coat of paint on it for years, mainly due to the shortage of white distemper which was used to paint the low ceiling, and in between the old oak beams around the walls. As they were unable to open the windows, the place smelt a bit, so from time to time they took time off and went into the scullery to make themselves a cup of tea, and listen to 'Music While You Work' on the wireless set. However, once the storm started, the transmission crackled so mercilessly that they had to abandon that in favour of some old gramophone records such as Bing Crosby and the Andrews Sisters singing, 'Don't Fence Me In', and the Irish tenor, Cavan O'Connor, singing, 'I'm Only a Strolling Vagabond'. Although it was a slow, laborious job, they enjoyed themselves immensely, mainly because Dodo and Billy were at home in Roden Street being looked after by Thelma, who would be ruling them with a rod of iron if they didn't get on with their homework before going out to play games with their pals in the streets. The reason for all the activity was because Lennie had now been offered the projectionist's job at the cinema in Epping, but as he would not be taking up his position until 1 January next year, he and Mary had plenty of time to work on the house in order to get it into shape before they and the family moved in. Mary was still unhappy about having to leave her job at the Marlborough, and Thelma was a bit iffy about having to abandon her position at Jones Brothers in favour of something new in a smaller department store in the country. However, the future of Dodo's and Billy's education had posed no problem, for, as expected, Miss Neville, the Headmistress of Pakeman Street School, had been very co-operative in helping the two young thugs to transfer to a school in Epping.

As soon as the rain stopped, Lennie took Mary for a stroll outside. Both of them had to wear Wellington boots because there was plenty of mud around, but the views over the fields were, for Mary, quite mind boggling, especially when she saw a massive rainbow arched over a vast distance of the flat landscape ahead of them. As they stood there at the old stile gate, they stopped to listen to the meadow lark, which had launched into a favourite song from its repertoire, whilst fluttering those tiny wings non-stop, high in the sky above them.

'You know,' said Lennie, 'it'll take you a time to get used to living in the countryside. The people are very different to that lot in Roden Street. They're more friendly.'

Mary took a jokey exception to that remark. 'Don't you talk about my friends like that,' she snapped, haughtily. 'They're the salt of the earth.'

'*Friends?*' gulped Lennie, teasing her. 'I thought you've always said your neighbours are a real pain – always poking their noses into things that don't concern them?'

'Yes, that's true,' replied Mary. 'But I'd imagine they're no different to any other street in any other town across the country. I shall miss them when I leave – especially poor old Nutty Nora upstairs. I'll miss all that moaning and groaning and complaining. She's been a fixture at the top of that house for the best part of a lifetime.' She turned to Lennie with a grin. 'Perhaps I should bring her along with me. I'm sure you'd love to have her sharing the house with us?'

Lennie pulled a face. 'The moment she moves in,' he joked, 'I move out!'

Mary laughed out loud. 'Oh, she's not so bad,' she replied. 'They're *all* not so bad. I can't wait to see what they think of their pictures in Tanya's exhibition.' She suddenly changed her mood. 'Did you know she drew one of both my mum and dad? But she won't let me see it until the day.'

'Will that upset you?'

'Why should it?' asked Mary. 'It'll be interesting to see what Tanya's view of them is really like. Tanya is such an extraordinary woman. She seems to have the ability to look right inside one's very soul.'

'It doesn't worry you that the picture isn't of your real dad?'

Lennie's remark sank deep. 'As far as *I'm* concerned,' she replied, 'I only ever had *one* real dad. And I miss him very much. I miss them *both* very much.'

Lennie put his arm around her waist, and let her rest her head against his shoulder. 'I miss my mum too,' he said. 'It'll take me a time to forget her.'

'Why should you *ever* forget her, Lennie?' she asked. 'She's here, in every brick and stone.'

'I mean – after the way I let her die.'

Mary looked up at him. 'Don't ever look back, Lennie,' she said. 'Don't ever feel guilty, don't ever feel that you could have done more, because you couldn't have. The best thing you can do for her, the best thing I can do for my parents, is for you and me to have a good life together.'

They kissed, hard and long.

'But you know something,' Mary said, 'I think Tanya should have done a bit of homework on Thelma as well. The way she's going, she'll be following you and me to the altar. She's really got a thing about this Chris. He's invited her home to meet his parents. They live where the money is – in Kensington.'

'She's a bit young to get tied to one particular bloke, isn't she?' said Lennie. 'I mean, isn't it against the law or something?'

'When two people are in love – I mean *truly* in love,' said Mary, 'I don't see that age has anything to do with it. At least she's given up that urge to go out on the prowl up in the West End. I had real worries that something nasty could have happened to her. Thank God the bloke she tagged on to turned out to be different to what she expected.'

'Have *I* turned out to be what *you* expected?'

Mary turned to look at him. His eyes were bright and smiling, and she could see what Tanya meant about that smile, because it was there again, strong and positive.

This surely was what her mum would have wanted for her. 'Lenny Backer,' she said. 'You've turned out to be more than I ever *dared* to expect.'

He fondled her neck with his fingertips, and they kissed again.

'Then the sooner we get married, the better,' he said. 'I want us to start having kids – our *own* kids.'

'I'm afraid you're too late for that,' she replied, tantalising him.

His face crumpled. 'Oh God, Mary!' he gasped, fearing the worst. 'Are you telling me — you can't have them?'

She smiled at his anxious face. 'No, darling,' she replied. 'I'm telling you it's too late, because we already have one on the way. So the sooner we get to that church, the better!'

Lennie's face lit up. 'Bloody hell!' he gasped. 'Bloody, bleedin' hell! Oh, Mary! Mary!' He held her at arm's length, then picked her up, and swirled her round and round.

Mary laughed out loud, calling, 'Stop it, Lennie! You're making us both giddy!'

He immediately put her down, gently, then kissed her again and again. 'I'll take care of you, Mary,' he gushed. 'I promise I'll always take care of you, and when we have more . . .'

'Hey!' she cried. 'Give me a chance! One at a time, if you don't mind!'

It started to rain again, but they didn't move. They just stood there, staring, smiling, loving each other.

'Shall I tell you something?' she asked, staring deep into his eyes. 'I've been thinking a lot about the Toff. Despite what Mr Bickley says, *I* think he did want to say something to me. And d'you know what? I think he had a message from both our mums, a message to tell us that everything's all right now, that now — it's up to us.'

They embraced, the rain pounding down on them. But it made no difference. The swallows may have gone, but they'd be coming back again next year . . .

Epilogue

The old church hall in Archway Road was looking somewhat different to the days when it had played host to the British Restaurant. The makeshift kitchen was still there, but the area which had once been occupied by pews and the church altar had been cleared to provide an enormous space for the exhibition of Tanya Ling's sketches and drawings. Activity had been brisk the moment the doors were opened at ten o'clock in the morning, and each visitor who entered gasped in astonishment at the amazing and prolific collection. Tanya, of course, was there to greet the Mayor of Islington, who opened the exhibition with the words: 'A remarkable event by a remarkable lady.' And remarkable she was, wearing one of her special long, traditional brocade dresses, decorated with the most fine art motifs of Chinese wild mountain flowers.

Two of the first to arrive, of course, were Mary and Lennie who, before touring the hall, had a cup of Chinese green tea with Tanya. Mary was bubbling with excitement, and the moment she caught her first glimpse of some of the faces she knew so well, she waxed lyrical about them. 'Wait till Nutty Nora sees herself,' she cried. 'She'll be so proud, she'll probably want an invitation to Buckingham Palace!'

Both she and Tanya laughed, leaving Lennie to go off in search of his own portrait.

'Are all these pictures going on sale?' asked Mary.

'Most of them – yes,' Tanya replied, 'but not all. Some are too special to let go – as you'll see later.'

The young girl, who had helped her to catalogue the pictures, sat at a small table near the door, waiting to take the names and addresses of prospective buyers, the average price of the pictures being in the range of between one and six pounds.

'You'll have to guess which is the most expensive,' Tanya said to Mary, who hadn't really heard what she had said because she was so overwhelmed to see the title of the exhibition on the exhibition flyer, which read: THE FACES OF RODEN STREET

'Tanya!' gasped Mary. 'You didn't tell me about *this*!'

'Oh, it was a last-minute thought,' replied Tanya. 'It kept me awake at night trying to decide what to call it. Not every face comes from Roden Street, but most of them do. Go and have a look at the expensive picture. The one Lennie's looking at.'

Lennie was completely taken aback by the sight of his own portrait taking pride of place on the end wall. When Mary arrived and slipped her arm around his waist, he was first of all looking as close as he could at the beautiful lines of the picture, admiring the way she had caught his smile – *that* smile – and then standing back to see what he looked like from a distance.

'So what do you think of yourself?' Mary asked.

'Scares the life out of me!' replied Lennie. 'It's like looking at myself in the mirror when I shave in the mornings.'

'Well, you're honoured,' said Mary. 'It's the most expensive picture in the exhibition.'

'*Why?*' he asked, utterly baffled.

'Because you're so handsome,' she teased.

Over at the entrance door, Tanya was greeting more guests, who turned out to be the contingent of residents she had invited, through Mary, from Roden Street.

Fred Parfitt was first in, and he immediately looked a bit out of his depth. 'Don't know what this is all about,' he said. 'I take pictures with me box Brownie, but I don't know about *this* kind of fing. What're we s'pposed ter be doin' here, then?'

'Why don't you go to the wall over there, Mr Parfitt,' said Tanya. 'Look on the left-hand side.'

Fred wandered off in a daze, stopping every time he recognised the face of one of his neighbours in the pictures hanging on the walls. All he could say when he saw the portrait of himself was 'Blimey!'

'Boris Karloff's got nuffin' on you, mate!' said his drinking partner from the Eaglet, Sid Battersby, who burst out laughing until he suddenly caught sight of his own portrait. His response was exactly the same: 'Blimey!'

'Mrs Hobbs!' said Tanya, as she greeted Mary's great friend from number thirteen, who looked absolutely sweet in a cotton floral-patterned dress, her hair done in a tight perm specially for the occasion. 'How nice to see you. And you too, Mr Hobbs. Thank you both for coming!' Letty's husband Oliver, a mild-mannered man, looked decidedly uncomfortable, togged out in his best navy-blue suit, waistcoat, collar and tie.

The moment Mary saw Letty and Oliver arrive, she rushed across to greet them. 'Ooh, Mr and Mrs Hobbs,' she cried excitedly. 'Come and look at yourselves. You look wonderful,'

Letty's face beamed when she saw Tanya's drawing of herself and Oliver, but Oliver was so embarrassed, he immediately went hot under the collar.

At that moment, Mary caught a glimpse of Nutty Nora, who was coming in surrounded by scores of other people from the neighbourhood, entering the place as though she were Queen Mary, regal, superior, wearing an ankle-length dress, her hair washed and neatly cut, and her walking stick very firmly clutched in her right hand.

'Mrs Kelly!' Mary called as she rushed across to greet the old girl. 'You look wonderful!'

'I don't know why,' croaked Nora. 'Don't look as though this is the sort of place fer a knees-up!'

'Tanya!' called Mary.

Tanya, on seeing Nora, hurried across. 'Mrs Kelly,' she said, warmly. 'It's a great honour to have you here. Come! I want to show you something.'

The old girl looked very suspicious, but took the Chinese woman's hand and allowed herself to be taken off through the milling crowd.

Mary was having a wonderful time. Not only had several people told her how lovely she looked in her white frilly blouse and navy-blue knee-length skirt, but she was also mixing with all the people she had known since she was a small girl. She was thrilled, too, to see Lennie taking such an interest in the pictures, going from one to the other, and studying each one from every angle. However, the one picture Mary was waiting to see was not of herself, but of her mum and dad. She was interrupted by a loud wail from Nutty Nora on the other side of the hall, which sent visitors rushing across to see what was wrong.

Nora was looking at the portrait of herself in horror. 'Nobody told me I looked so old!' she cried. 'I should never've come! I don't want to look as old as that!'

Tanya was there, really quite concerned, trying to pacify her. 'But you *don't* look old, Mrs Kelly,' she said, trying to reassure the old girl. 'It's only an impression of you.'

'Mrs Kelly, you look wonderful!' added Mary, who had quickly joined the group around the old girl.

'I don't! I don't!' insisted Nora, not believing a word anyone was saying. 'I look like the wicked witch in Snow White.'

'Get off, Ma!' called Ken Barrington, the governor of the Eaglet pub. 'Nearest thing I've ever seen to Rita Hayworth!'

'Rita *who*?' groaned the old girl.

'Beautiful *young* film star, Ma,' said Sid Battersby, in an attempt to bolster up the old girl.

Nora's whole attitude changed. '*Really?*' she said, practically purring, as she patted her neatly cut hair into place.

'Living image!' called Ken Barrington.

Over at the refreshment table, Mary helped two other women to pour cups of tea. Whilst this was going on, eager hands from Roden Street stretched out to help themselves to the plates of plain Marie tea biscuits. But while she was handing out cups of tea to visitors, someone caught her eye over near the front door. She immediately rushed over.

'Mrs Nestor,' she said. 'It's *so* good to see you.' She stretched out her hand to the woman who had been her superintendent when this very hall was a restaurant.

After an initial nervous reaction, Sheila shook hands with her. 'Hello, Mary,' she said, falteringly.

Mary gave her a warm smile. 'I want to say how wonderful you've been in doing all this,' she said. 'Tanya told me about the support you've given her.'

Sheila shrugged. 'All I did was to speak to someone on the Council about it,' she replied. 'But I'm glad it's worked out.' She looked around. 'Well – it all looks a bit different to the restaurant.'

'It's strange how things happen, isn't it?' said Mary. 'When you think what this place was a few months ago. You ran the restaurant so beautifully.'

'You can't run a restaurant single-handed,' replied Sheila. 'I was lucky to have the people who worked with me. *All* of them.' She gave Mary a special, appreciative look.

Mary hesitated a moment, then gave Sheila a hug.

'Ah – there you are, Sheila!' said Tanya, as she freed herself from the crowd. 'So – what do you think?'

'I think – I *hope*,' she said, 'that you will make a lot of money. You really do have a wonderful collection here, Tanya. You're a very talented woman.'

'Any kind of talent,' replied Tanya, 'needs someone to appreciate it.'

A few minutes later, Tanya was helped up on to the makeshift stage, where she would say a few words to everyone there.

'Ladies and gentlemen,' she began, and, after a great deal of shushing from one or two of the visitors, continued, 'I just want to thank you all for coming here today. Although we are open over the weekend for the general public, this morning is for *you*, the residents of that illustrious street you live in – well, where most of you live!'

There were a few light-hearted chuckles amongst the guests.

'As you know,' continued Tanya, 'I am, to coin a better phrase, an artiste, and my job is to seek out what most of us don't see – the face.

We all have one, of course, but thanks to the miracle of nature, no two of us are alike, unless we happen to be twins.'

More chuckles from the guests.

'When I first embarked on this project,' continued Tanya, 'I hadn't really thought about who and what I wanted to draw, but after a great deal of thought I made up my mind to group together one small community. That's why, over the past year or so, some of you may have seen me cluttering up your pavements with my presence, with my sketchbook, pencils and charcoals. Roden Street seemed to me to epitomise what English people are all about, going about their daily business without fuss, taking each day as it comes, having respect for each other while not necessarily liking everyone you come into contact with. But the real reason I wanted to preserve as many of you on paper as possible was because, behind those smiles and tears and worries and anxieties, there beat many hearts of gold; hearts that have courage and determination, hearts that are willing to help in times of your neighbour's needs, hearts that had the strength to survive the worst of a terrible war. As I stood there, or sat on your coping stones whilst I drew pictures of you, my own heart was full of admiration for you all. As I look around you now, it's still full of admiration, because to me, Roden Street represents all that is good in British life, the life that I embraced a long time ago with the man I loved so much.'

Tanya's words were moving Mary very much, and she only held back her tears by slipping her arm around Lennie's waist.

'Therefore,' continued Tanya, 'I tried to think of a way to thank you, to thank you for allowing me to peer into your own private world, to see what makes you what you are, and how and why you have influenced someone like me. And so, my dear friends, I would like to dedicate this exhibition to you all, to *you*, to Roden Street, and to all those faces that disguise the many good things that lurk behind them. Thank you all *so* much.'

There was a fraction of stunned silence, before one person started to handclap, which was immediately picked up by the entire crowd, who burst into wild applause.

Tanya went across to Mary, who hugged her tight.

Whilst the applause continued, Tanya took Mary's hand and led her off into the former kitchen. 'I know you have to go soon,' said Tanya, 'but there's something I have to say to you first.' She went across to collect some drawings, which were leaning up against the wall there. 'These are for you,' she said. 'They come with my love and devotion.'

Bewildered, Mary looked at the first picture, which was of herself when she was a child. 'Oh Tanya,' she gasped, 'how could you . . . all those years ago.'

'Look at this one,' said Tanya, holding up the second picture in front of her. This time it was the picture Mary knew had existed, and which she was longing to see. It was of her mum and dad, arm in arm; a portrait drawn by Tanya which she had taken from an old photograph.

Mary started to crumple up. She wanted to cry, but was only prevented from doing so by Tanya, placing the third picture in front of her.

'And finally,' said Tanya, '*this*.'

Mary looked at the picture, which was a family portrait: her mum and dad, Thelma, Dodo and Billy, Granddad – and Mary herself. She was choked, and for several moments couldn't say a thing.

'Keep them safe, Mary,' said Tanya. 'It took me a long time to bring your parents back to life. Put them on the walls of your house, and always remember what they mean to you.'

Mary was about to say something, when Tanya put the tip of her fingers to Mary's lips. 'Just one thing more,' she said. 'But this time, it comes from your mother – not me.' She went to her handbag, and took out a small package wrapped in brown paper. 'Before she died, your mother asked me to give this to you. She said, even if it doesn't fit, keep it safely for the day when you join with the man you love.'

Mary stood there, staring at the packet.

'Go ahead,' said Tanya. 'Open it.'

Her hands trembling, Mary struggled to untie the string, and finally managed to open the small packet. Inside was her mother's gold wedding ring.

'It was *her* way of asking you to forgive her.'

Slowly, methodically, Mary took the ring from the box, and kissed it. Then Tanya held on to her whilst she broke down.

'Let it bring you good luck, dearest Mary,' Tanya said, holding on to her. 'You deserve it so much.'

A short while later, clutching her mother's ring box firmly in her hand, inside her dress pocket, Mary walked arm in arm with Lennie down Holloway Road, back to work at the Marlborough. There were people everywhere, all shapes and sizes, different-coloured hair and eyes, but faces that told their own individual stories. However, as she passed them by, Mary didn't even glance at them. She didn't have to, because she knew they were there.

The walk with Lennie in the late-August sun was just as they had done together so many times before. But, for Mary, *this* time it was very different. For as long as she lived, she would never forget it.